C000261186

SUMMER IN ANDALUCÍA

LUCY COLEMAN

Boldwood

First published in Great Britain in 2021 by Boldwood Books Ltd.

Copyright © Lucy Coleman, 2021

Cover Design by Alice Moore Design

Cover Photography: Shutterstock

The moral right of Lucy Coleman to be identified as the author of this work has been asserted in accordance with the Copyright, Designs and Patents Act 1988.

All rights reserved. No part of this book may be reproduced in any form or by any electronic or mechanical means, including information storage and retrieval systems, without written permission from the author, except for the use of brief quotations in a book review.

This book is a work of fiction and, except in the case of historical fact, any resemblance to actual persons, living or dead, is purely coincidental.

Every effort has been made to obtain the necessary permissions with reference to copyright material, both illustrative and quoted. We apologise for any omissions in this respect and will be pleased to make the appropriate acknowledgements in any future edition.

A CIP catalogue record for this book is available from the British Library.

Paperback ISBN 978-1-83889-066-7

Large Print ISBN 978-1-80162-711-5

Hardback ISBN 978-1-80162-710-8

Ebook ISBN 978-1-83889-068-1

Kindle ISBN 978-1-83889-067-4

Audio CD ISBN 978-1-83889-064-3

MP3 CD ISBN 978-1-80162-707-8

Digital audio download ISBN 978-1-83889-065-0

Boldwood Books Ltd
23 Bowerdean Street
London SW6 3TN
www.boldwoodbooks.com

In loving memory of my great-aunt Else.
Days spent wandering around your beautiful and fragrant garden are
among my favourite childhood memories.

PREFACE

The setting often inspires the story and in 2019 I undertook a research trip with only a draft title in my head and the names of the two main characters, Lainey and Rick. I was excited not only to be visiting Andalucía for the first time, but also to be staying in a monastery. It was a trip I will never forget, and I knew that when it was time to sit down and begin writing the story the words would flow with ease.

Staying at the Hotel Monasterio de San Francisco, in Palma del Río, I was totally captivated by my surroundings. My sincere thanks go to the owner, Alonso Moreno De La Cova, who took time out to give me and my husband a tour of the private areas not on view to the public. The monastery passed into the secular hands of his family in the nineteenth-century and a programme of restoration work began. It is an amazing place to stay and the wonderful food served in the monastery's renowned restaurant gave me the theme around which the story would unfold.

While I'm limited to the amount of history I can include in a fictional novel, I believe that the past leaves its mark in many ways. The sense of peace and tranquillity that surrounded me while I was there was both energising and renewing. It was then that I knew it would have a life-changing effect on my characters, even before I'd written the first word.

I would also like to express my gratitude to acclaimed artist, Cristina Ybarra, for showing my husband and me around her beautiful home. Since 1868, the palace has been passed down through six generations of the same family. The Palacio de Portocarrero is a living project, and her vision has succeeded in bringing it back to life. The palace and gardens are captivating and transported me to another time and place.

Marlyse B. Marin came to my rescue not only in her capacity as an interpreter, but also due to her close links with the monastery. The time that Marlyse and I spent together was both fascinating and informative. It allowed me to include some authentic, descriptive detail of the monastery to satisfy those readers who might never have a chance to visit and experience it for themselves.

The day my husband and I took a trip to the Castle of Almodóvar del Río, we arrived around noon and for about an hour and a half we were among a mere handful of visitors. It was a wonderful experience and, ironically, turned out to be perfectly timed. We left just as two coach parties were arriving and a steady stream of tourists filtered in. I guess only mad dogs and authors go out in the midday sun.

2018

JANUARY

1

GASTRO HEAVEN

As I push open the door to what is *the* number one restaurant on everyone's radar at the moment, *Aleatory*, I can't believe how lucky I am. Opportunities like this are rare and, for some reason, fate picked me. I was in the right place, at the right time. Having recently become a feature writer for the popular *Upscale Dining* magazine, all eyes are now on me to show everyone I have what it takes to get the story behind the headlines.

It's been nine months to the day since Aleatory opened in Piccadilly, where the restaurant faces onto the magnificent Green Park, and there is a five-month wait to get a reservation. Virtually overnight, being able to say you've dined here has become a status symbol, and #Aleatory has been trending on Twitter at least once a week for months – it's crazy.

So the pressure is really on for me to deliver. Our readers will expect an article that won't just make their mouths water over the culinary delights on offer, but also shed some light on a new rising star who has hasn't just stepped but *leapt* into the limelight. Jaws dropped when word got out that chef Rick Oliver, and pop icon Cathy Clarkson were joining forces to set up a stylish new restaurant. And now I'm here, nervously excited about what is the biggest interview of my career so far.

Inside, although the lights are on, there is no one in sight, but before we reach the smart glass reception desk, a waiter comes striding towards us.

'Good morning. How can I help? I'm afraid the restaurant doesn't open until noon if you have a reservation.' The tall, smiley-faced young man is welcoming, but apologetic.

'I'm Elaine Summers and this is my colleague, Anthony Preston. We're here to interview Rick Oliver?' I have no idea why this comes out sounding like a question, as if he'll check the diary and send us away like two imposters.

'Oh, of course. I'm so sorry, but Cathy and Chef are in a meeting right now. I will, however, let them know that you have arrived.'

There's a loud crash in the background and both Ant and I wince, but the waiter's face remains immobile as if the noise didn't register at all. The sound of escalating voices indicates that all is not well in the kitchen and we find ourselves following our guide as he leads us off in the opposite direction. The waiter seems totally unfazed by what sounds like a full-blown argument taking a turn for the worse, as the volume increases.

'If you'd like to make yourself comfortable in the lounge area,' he continues, indicating with his hand. 'Can I bring you a cup of tea, or coffee?'

'Coffee would be nice, thank you,' Ant replies, and I nod my head.

'Two it is, then,' the young man smiles politely before hurrying away, seemingly still oblivious to the commotion going on in the background.

We stroll past an impressive floor-to-ceiling wine rack which serves as a screen, partially obscuring the main body of the restaurant.

'I wonder what that's all about? Clearly someone isn't having the best start to their day,' Ant whispers as soon as we're alone.

'Indeed, it seems we might have arrived at an inopportune moment. I hope it doesn't affect the interview.'

'Maybe the rumours are true, after all,' he replies, raising his eyebrows.

Rick Oliver became a name to watch, working as the sous-chef to the revered chef de cuisine, Martine Alvarez, at the Food Haven. During his four years working at the infamous restaurant, it went from one Michelin star to three, which was a phenomenal achievement. But then, one day, there was an almighty row and Rick walked out. The rumours spread like wildfire in the industry and a scandal like that could kill someone's career overnight. The big question was whether Rick was, in fact, sacked. Martine sat back, seeming to gloat over the speculation but, naturally, Rick was keen to limit the damage in any way he could. All eyes were on him, wondering what he would do next. Finding himself a backer and setting up his own restaurant was a bold and daring move to say the least, but he has turned into a trailblazer.

'They've done a brilliant job of designing the restaurant, and this refit must have cost a small fortune.'

Ant is right, everything is sleek and uncluttered, and the bar itself is glossy white marble, accented with mirrors and soft lighting. The lounge has a contemporary feel with a variety of designer armchairs in electrifying colours. It reminds me of a tropical rainforest in bloom. There are vibrant shades of green and little pops of vivid colour that jump out like exotic flowers.

Ant deposits his black holdall discreetly behind one of the chairs, before settling himself down, and I suppress a grin. It's the sort of environment where anything out of place immediately looks like clutter.

'It's very artsy,' Ant continues, as I sink down into a lime green chair shaped like a huge leaf. I tuck my work bag in neatly along-side me and then pull out my compact, tidying a few stray hairs that have escaped my ponytail. Wearing a new, pale grey trouser suit at least I look and feel the part, even though my nerves are jangling. However, being here with Ant, who is the magazine's number one photographer, I know we make a great team and this article is going to really grab the reader's attention. So, it's time to take a deep breath and compose myself.

'I'm sure that's Cathy's influence,' I reply. 'Her videos are always eye-popping, colourful and different. Actually, this chair is more comfortable than it looks.' Sinking back, my fingers instinc-tively run over the basket-weave fabric.

I've done my homework and read everything I can get my hands on about Cathy and Rick, but what interests me most is how their paths crossed and what inspired their partnership. Whether that will come out in the interview though, I have no idea.

Scanning around, I notice that in the restaurant there are an increasing number of staff toing and froing. I can't help wondering whether they are all desperate to distance themselves from whatever is happening in the kitchen, or merely getting ready for opening. It's no longer possible to hear raised voices, but then again, we're a fair distance away.

Ant leans forward. 'Do you think they've forgotten about the interview?'

I shrug my shoulders, glancing across to see our waiter heading in our direction. He's sporting a big smile, which seems genuine enough, as he places a loaded tray down on the table in front of us.

'Cathy apologises for the wait and will be with you as soon as possible. In the meantime, she would love for you to sample some new items that are on today's dessert menu. We have pink champagne cake with a candy floss cloud, butter cake with a pistachio and rose crumble topping and a chocolate truffle infused with citrus sherbet gin. Enjoy!'

It looks amazing, but it's Rick we're really here to interview, and if he's not available, then we're wasting our time. I wonder if the cake is a peace offering to soften us up with a quick sugar fix, but I'm not going to say *no*. Sampling a wide variety of amazing dishes is a part of my job, but the restaurants aren't always as upmarket and expensive as this one. It would have to be a special occasion indeed for me to come and eat here if I was paying for the meal.

'Wow,' Ant remarks, as we both scoot forward on our chairs to eagerly grab one of the small forks.

'They're so beautiful, it's almost a pity to tuck in and spoil them,' I remark, dithering over what to taste first.

'Stop!' Ant yells and I freeze.

The fork in my hand is just inches away from one of the three-inch square cakes sitting on the narrow slate platter. Ant jumps up to grab his camera and, seconds later, begins clicking away. He indicates for me to pose and I put on my photo face.

'That was meant for tasting, not photographing.'

I immediately look up to see the smiling face of Cathy Clarkson, this year's veritable Queen of Pop and a Grammy Award winner. She's every bit as glamorous up close as she is whenever I've seen photos of her. Every time I turn on the radio, I swear that within five minutes they air one of her tracks. Standing up to hold out my hand, we shake and her grasp is firm.

'It's lovely to meet you, Cathy. I'm Elaine, but everyone calls me Lainey, and this is Ant.'

'Thank you for coming, guys, it's much appreciated. We're thrilled to be appearing in the magazine,' she remarks, as she turns to look at Ant.

'As you can see,' I continue, 'Ant hasn't given me permission to get to the tasting yet, but the presentation alone is stunning.'

Cathy smiles appreciatively as her intriguing pale blue eyes sweep over me. Has she come to break the news that we're going to have to reschedule the interview, I wonder?

Our attentive waiter hurries across to pull up a chair for Cathy, while Ant settles himself back down. Having gotten his shots he will be eager to tuck in.

'Rick is a perfectionist, of course,' Cathy replies, taking a seat. 'We had an accident with the candy floss cloud and all hell broke loose, so I apologise for the explosion just now. I'm afraid this business is still all rather new to me and I had no idea how fraught things can become in the kitchen.'

That's quite a statement to make in front of a journalist you've never met before. Cathy is obviously keen to make it clear that the ruckus is nothing to do with her, but I'm shocked by her candour.

'I don't think fraught is quite the right word,' Rick corrects her as he approaches, and Cathy half-turns to acknowledge him.

I'm looking at the back of her head now, so I can't see her expression, but I can tell by his grin he's teasing her. The first thing that comes to mind seeing them together is what a handsome couple they make. Cathy is stunning, of course, but up close Rick too has a charming, almost magnetic quality. He's handsome, with short, dark hair that is a little longer on the top but not overtly fashionable, just practical. Rick doesn't strike me as the sort of man who spends hours looking in the mirror, rather he comes across as genuine and instantly likeable. When he looks directly at me, there's an intensity and yet I also sense a little humour, and maybe a hint of reserve, which I hadn't expected. Unless he's feeling embarrassed and realises we haven't had the best start to an interview.

Rick reaches out to drag a chair across to join us and we briefly shake hands as we make our introductions. He has certainly recovered well after what sounded like quite an explosive episode as now he looks relaxed. But when Cathy turns back around, I notice she's frowning.

'Well, let's say how *hot* it gets in the kitchen, at times,' she corrects herself, labouring the point as she stares at him. Then she turns to look at me. 'The proof is in the eating, of course.'

Is there a frosty edge to her voice, or am I imagining it?

They are now both looking at me in fervent anticipation, but I hesitate for a second to marvel over the attention to detail. The dessert is perfection on a plate. I tentatively dig my fork into the delicate pink nest sitting on top of an even paler pink sponge base. The cake stands just over three-inches high and, miraculously, I manage to extract a thin sliver without totally wrecking it. Nervous tension makes my hand waver a little as I guide the fork back to my mouth. They are all watching me intently and Ant looks decidedly nervous, making no attempt to follow my lead.

Then the taste explosion hits me.

'You paused for a moment there before you took a bite, which for me means we did a good job. How the dish is presented is the first part of the culinary experience. And now, what are you picking up? Tell me!' Rick Oliver's voice is demanding, as his eyes search my face. His mood has changed and his brow furrows into a deep frown.

'Strawberry. Bubblegum? And... crystallised pear?' My voice rises with incredulity and he laughs.

'Spot on. I told you, Cathy. Discerning diners will be able to differentiate each of the flavours and that's why we need to sneak in the little surprises.'

One glance in Cathy's direction and I know I've said the wrong thing. When her smile slips for a moment or two, what I see on the face of the music industry's sweetheart is annoyance. It's clear that she is a very hands-on partner and not just an investor, even though her background is far removed from the food industry.

The restaurant has gained a following in record time, not least, I'm sure, because some of the diners come in the hope of catching sight of her, but the memories diners leave with are all about the food. And, surely, that's down to Rick and his team, including sous-chef, Pierre Verbier. But the relationship between Cathy and Rick seems more complicated. Perhaps the rumours of a romance are true, because she's sporting a huge engagement ring.

'Yes, well, let's agree to disagree about the bubblegum flavour, shall we? Right, I have some urgent calls to make, but once you are all set up for the formal photographs, please send someone to find me. I'll leave you in Rick's hands until then.' Her tone is curt and there's a residual moment of awkwardness as she disappears out of earshot. Clearly, while Cathy might not want to answer any questions, her business head is telling her the smart thing is to make sure her face appears in the spread.

I forage around in my bag, pulling out a notepad, pen and phone, placing them on the coffee table in front of me.

'Rick, is it okay with you if I make a few notes as we talk? And would you be comfortable if I also use a recording app?' The important thing now is that I make him feel at ease. Our email exchanges leading up to today have been extremely encouraging and chatty, so I'm not anticipating any problems.

'As long as you don't ask any questions I don't want to answer, it's fine by me. But first, your tasting session isn't over,' he replies. It's obvious from the way he flashes his eyes at me, that it's food first, always.

I glance at Ant, who immediately begins tucking in. He'll eat anything, but as for appreciating the finer details, he's no gastronome.

'I'm interested to see what you think of the butter cake,' Rick says.

I stoop forward to rescue a forkful, after Ant has succeeded in decimating the perfect little tower. Popping it into my mouth, I close my eyes for a moment and when I open them, Rick is, again, watching with interest. Both Ant's bio and mine were in the pre-interview pack. In my case, after freelancing for several newspapers around the country, writing independent reviews for local restaurants, I gained a following. Now I have my dream job. I'm here today because I have a reputation for picking up on even the subtlest of flavours. There is a bit of a frustrated chef inside of me but, sadly, my talents lie elsewhere. I might not be able to conjure up a truly memorable plate of food, but my taste buds don't lie, and my skill is in sharing the experience with my readers. If I'm not mistaken, Rick looks like he's actually holding his breath.

'Smooth, buttery and the crunch of the pistachios is a wonderful contrast, but – oh – that hint of rose... it lingers on the tongue. Wonderful.'

Rick sits back in his chair beaming, and I look at him, a tad embarrassed. We turn to stare down at the platter at the chocolate truffle which is now merely crumbs. I look at Ant.

'Best truffle I've ever had,' he replies, and both Rick and I begin to laugh.

While I might not have made the best first impression with Cathy, Rick Oliver is turning out to be a pleasant surprise. He is, without a doubt, a daunting presence in the kitchen, but with

great skill and talent comes great passion, and you can tell immediately that he has plenty of that. I don't think I can recall ever
meeting a man where two words instantly jumped into my head
like they did with Rick – enthralling and dynamic. With him, you
simply know you are in the presence of someone remarkable.

* * *

'Hey, Dad, how are you doing?'

'I'm good, Lainey. What's happening with you? Problems?'

There's no fooling Dad. Having spent most of his career
working as an investigative journalist, even when he can't read my
body language, he immediately picks up on the tone of my voice.
And my tone tonight is, sadly, a tad deflated. I settle back against
the cushions and draw my legs up onto the sofa.

'I have a dilemma. I've been asked to cut a few things from an
article I wrote last week about a smart new restaurant that is *the*
place to go right now. If you can succeed in getting a reservation,
that is.'

There's an ominous silence before he clears his throat. 'Asked,
or told?'

'Yes, well, it was presented as a suggestion, but I did a little
nosing around and my boss's assistant confirmed my suspicions.
There was a closed-door telephone conversation with the agent
of one of the two people I interviewed.'

'Ah, bit of a delicate situation, is it?'

Dad knows all about that. Being labelled a whistle-blower
shut a lot of doors for him. Now he writes fiction for a living
and his days are spent creating and solving crimes; how close
they come to mirroring reality, I dread to think. However, he's at
a point in his life now where he can be prosaic about the price
he paid and grateful to have moved on. Dad has a growing fan

base who appreciate the realism in his stories and that has done wonders to lift him out of the depression that claimed him for a while. But he'll never get over the way people he considered to be staunch friends, and long-term colleagues, rushed to distance themselves from him when he wrote his exposé of a scandalous cover-up. The fallout was ugly at the time, but he refused to be a part of a scam and that took courage.

'It's not exactly contentious,' I explain. 'I simply aired a few truths. It's a fabulous restaurant with amazing food, but the two partners have an unusual, and somewhat volatile, relationship. There were a couple of explosive conversations going on in the kitchen when Ant and I first arrived. I hung around outside the next day and managed to bump into one of the waiters. It was obvious he had something he wanted to say, as he accepted my offer of grabbing a quick coffee together. He was naturally a little guarded, but apparently a pan was thrown across the kitchen and it wasn't the first time.'

'Who did the throwing?'

'I can't say for sure, but he did tell me that the chef's business partner had a meltdown and the kitchen staff couldn't get out of there quickly enough. All of this was going on in the background as Ant and I were waiting to begin the interview. I didn't put any of that in the article, of course, but our readers are interested in the dynamics between this power couple, as she's a big name in the music industry.'

'Ah, and you gave a little insight into that?'

'I was only repeating the words that came out of her mouth. This is a couple who don't see eye-to-eye on everything and she's no silent partner, I can tell you that for a fact as I saw her in action. I was diplomatic, naturally, but if I cut out all references to her, then it's just an ad for the restaurant and the readers are going to wonder why I've skipped over the obvious question on everyone's lips.'

Dad sighs. 'Compromise is never easy, Lainey. Especially when you sniff out a story, like a subplot going on behind the scenes. But my advice is to stick to the remit, bearing in mind that it's a food magazine and the fact that you're still very new there.'

I guess he's right. Having started my career as a freelance reporter for several local newspapers, I'm probably too used to everything being about getting a lead and jumping on it to see what I can dig up. Old habits are hard to shift. 'You know me, Dad. I try to see things through the eyes of my readers and answer the questions I think will be in the forefront of their minds. It's a good article and Ant did an amazing job of the photo spread, but it rankles with me to gloss over the human element of the story. I mean, they are a dynamic duo, but sparks are flying and that might be the reason why the restaurant is so successful. I could be the first one to put that into print.'

Dad let's out a loud *hmm*, as he mulls it over. 'Whether it's a favour being asked of someone at the top or concerns about being sued if a complaint is filed, you've obviously touched a raw nerve somewhere, my darling. I'm not saying there aren't times when it's worth sticking your neck out, as that would make me a hypocrite, wouldn't it? But, as tempting as it might be to say it as it is, my advice is that you choose your battles. And is this one really worth it? You aren't writing for a celebrity gossip magazine, are you, and perhaps that's the point your editor is trying to make.'

'But I was shocked at the difference between the sweet, public persona of a well-known icon and the sharp businesswoman I glimpsed that day. It's not unheard of for a chef to throw a wobbly, as they're all perfectionists, but she's even opinionated about the food. And the truth is that the chef was noticeably different when she joined us for the photographic session at the end of the interview.'

A little laugh echoes down the phone line.

'The apple doesn't fall far from the tree, Lainey, does it? No one is going to tell you what to write, but, look, have you considered that you might have caught her on a bad day? If she's popular, then I seriously doubt that she spends much of her time there, anyway. Just grab a coffee, sit down quietly and go through your article line by line. Switch off and focus on the words. Your instincts will tell you what to do now that you know there might be one or two things that come across as a little contentious, or superfluous – dare I say. Does a row, or two, in the kitchen spoil the gastronomic experience for the diners? Who knows what goes on behind the scenes in any restaurant and if the food is good, surely that's your story in a nutshell.'

Dad is right, of course, and I have the distinct feeling that he was being diplomatic when he used the word *superfluous*, because I think what he wanted to say was *judgemental*. 'I hear what you're saying, but won't people wonder why I didn't see the obvious power dynamics if I totally ignore what is a huge and potentially destabilising factor in this unusual partnership?'

'Read it through again and if you still feel the same way, then resubmit it and see what happens. The decision may well be made for you anyway, you know how it is, and if that's the case, then take it on the chin. It's not worth making waves so early on when this job is perfect for you. You're a foodie at heart and your reviews inspire people who appreciate the way you are able to deconstruct flavours and verbalise taste sensations. If readers can't visit the restaurant in person, it might encourage them to experiment with a new combination of flavours at home. That's where your focus lies now, so don't forget that.'

'Oh, Dad. Why do I have this need to always tell the truth,

warts and all, as Mum would say. To me, leaving something out feels as bad as telling a lie.'

'Because that's the way we brought you up, Lainey. But the world is changing, and it doesn't hurt to stand back at times and consider what's best for you and your situation. I ploughed forward to fight for something I believed in and it ended up turning our lives upside down, and that's something I will always regret.'

'Ah, Dad, please don't feel bad. I'm proud of you and we got through it. And I think being an author suits you! Right, I'll make myself a strong coffee and then look at the bigger picture.'

Dad gives a throaty little laugh. He knows this decision could go either way. 'Talking of your mother, have you checked on her lately?'

'No. We talk probably once a month, but getting to grips with the new job means that life's been hectic.'

His silence feels like an accusation.

'I know,' I blurt out, 'that's just an excuse. But I still struggle to accept Mum's decision, after the divorce, to run off to France so she could follow her dream. I want her to be happy, of course I do, but I know you still love her.'

Clearing his throat, Dad's tone is firm. 'Let's not go there now, Lainey. Besides, she didn't *run off*, she's free to do exactly as she pleases. It was all my fault. Just don't forget that your mum's been through hell and she deserves a quiet, happy life. Don't make her feel guilty about that.'

What I admire most about Dad is that even though life will never be quite the same again for him, he can still stand back and apply that logical common sense of his. His heart might be broken, but he doesn't blame Mum for that, he blames himself. And in a way, he's right, but how was he to know things would go the way they did?

'Point taken. I'll try harder, I promise. We'll speak soon, Dad. Love ya.'

As the phone line disconnects, a sense of emptiness washes over me. Or is it a niggling resentment for what happened to my parents? When two people are right for each other, it's tantamount to a crime to let other people cause so much havoc that it tears them apart. And I still can't let that thought go.

2

NO ONE IS PERFECT

'Is that, uh, Lainey?'

The voice on the other end of the line is faint and I put a finger in my left ear to block out the background noise in the office. 'Yes, Lainey Summers. How can I help?'

'It's Rick Oliver. I was, uh, wondering if you'd written up the interview yet? I mean, um... do we get to see it before it's published? It's in next month's issue, isn't it?'

'Oh, hi Rick. It's due for publication on the twenty-eighth of next month. Is there a problem?' I skip over his question, hoping he'll get straight to the point.

'No. Not really. I was just wondering if you could spare me half an hour? I'm in a coffee shop around the corner from your offices as we speak. Butler's, do you know it?'

Intriguing. 'Yes, I do. Okay, give me five minutes and I'll join you.'

'Thank you, appreciated. See you soon.'

Clearly, he's on his way to the restaurant, but he's taken a detour for a reason. Grabbing my coat and bag, I shovel in my phone, iPad and a notebook before I head out.

'I have an unscheduled appointment with Rick Oliver,' I inform Sally on reception. 'It shouldn't take long and I'll be back in time for the staff meeting.'

'Lucky you,' she replies, grinning at me. 'I hear he's a bit of a charmer. I can't wait to read your article.'

'It seems he can't wait either,' I mutter under my breath as I walk briskly across the foyer and head out into the fresh air.

Having taken the decision to make a few little tweaks to the article, I resubmitted it and have heard nothing further. I'm hoping the reservations had been about an overzealous use of a couple of forthright adjectives, which, when softened, made the references less contentious. One of them being the word *powerful* and the other *controlling*. After two strong cups of coffee, I decided that Dad was right, and I was being a little harsh. On reflection, the words *proactive* and *enthusiastic* put a more positive spin on Cathy's behaviour.

As I scurry away from the office deep in thought, I almost collide with someone as they step directly in front of me, bringing me to a sudden halt.

'It was crowded in the coffee shop so I thought we could stroll over to the square and enjoy a takeaway.' I make an effort to hide my surprise as Rick Oliver looks at me with a half-grin on his face, holding up two reusable coffee cups. 'I try to avoid plastic and cardboard if possible, so you can choose your colour.'

He's clearly hoping I'll choose the purple one as he's holding the blue one closer to his chest. I take it, giving him a brief smile and wondering what on earth he's after.

'Thanks. That's kind of you, Rick.' It occurs to me that I could invite him back to the office, but it's open-plan and we hot-desk. Today also happens to be the monthly meet-up, where ideas for future features get kicked around and the gathering beforehand can get a little noisy. 'The square it is, then. What a coincidence you called me on a day I happen to be in the office,' I muse suspiciously.

He turns to look at me, his face reflecting unease. 'The truth is, I had a tip-off. Look, let's grab a quiet seat somewhere and I'll tell you exactly why I'm here.'

Dodging in between the stream of pedestrians heading in both directions, we cross the road and make our way to what the locals affectionately call 'the garden'. It's a small, gated area with a dozen towering trees, a swathe of grass and a couple of borders dotted with rose bushes. It's a place where office workers come to sit and while away their lunch break on sunny days, but at ten o'clock in the morning, there are only a handful of people strolling around.

'Let's sit here,' I suggest, as I settle myself down on the nearest empty bench. 'I can only spare half an hour before I have to head back for a meeting, I'm afraid. You were lucky to catch me.'

His visit has rather caught me off-guard and he doesn't seem to be in a hurry. I don't really know how to react, as his behaviour is bizarre.

Rick sits down, places his coffee on the bench next to him and immediately jumps back up again to forage around in his pocket. He produces a handful of little packets of brown sugar.

'No stirrer?' I enquire.

He looks at me apologetically, shrugging his shoulders. 'Sorry.'

'It's fine. I'm trying to cut out my measly one spoonful, anyway. Right, what's on your mind?'

He lowers himself back down onto the seat, and I watch as he takes the lid off his coffee and empties in four packets of sugar. He places the lid back on, giving it a cautious swirl and then sets it back down in the space between us. In the meantime, I'm happily sipping away and thinking that the jump from one sugar to none isn't quite as awful as I'd thought.

Staring at him pointedly, I raise my eyebrows, implying that he'd better get on with it because the clock is ticking.

'I can't even begin to imagine what impression you walked away with that day you came to the restaurant, and I hope I'm in time to explain before you go to print.'

He glances at me, awaiting my response, but I continue sipping my coffee for a moment, considering how honest I should be with him.

'Someone has already been in touch with my boss, no doubt calling in a favour,' I inform him, and I'm hoping he can see from my expression that this hasn't gone down well with me.

'Please believe me when I say I didn't know that. It was probably Cathy's agent. He wasn't aware that she was going to be a part of the interview and now he's getting anxious about it. She's in Los Angeles at the moment, but he quizzed me about it and, given what happened, he suggested I come to see you to set the record straight. I agreed to do that, even though I told him straight that Cathy wasn't supposed to be there anyway. She was the one who insisted on talking to you after the photo session. Cathy isn't, um, she isn't...'

The pause goes on for several seconds and I look at him, questioningly.

'The truth is that she'd been up all night at the studios filming her latest music video and came straight to the restaurant afterwards. In hindsight, she admits that was a huge mistake. Cathy has learnt the hard way that what gets into print isn't always accurate. Not that I'm implying what you write wouldn't be fair,' he hurries to reassure me.

I stop him there. 'My article is based on the time I spent at the restaurant and our conversations, it's as simple as that.' I try my best to sound neutral and ignore his implication that I might have another agenda, because I don't.

'Please let me explain,' he continues. 'You arrived at the precise moment that we were in the kitchen rowing and the timing was obviously very unfortunate. It took a while for us both to cool off, so we were edgy. What I'm here to ask is that you recognise it had nothing at all to do with the restaurant. It's a huge investment for us both and I know all eyes are on us.' He sounds, and looks, pretty convincing, as if he's speaking from the heart. 'I'm well aware that it's risky utilising Cathy's fame to gain exposure for the business, whilst trying to keep our relationship out of the public eye.'

'Naturally, I spotted the engagement ring that Cathy was wearing,' I confirm. 'I can assure you, though, that has nothing at all to do with my article.'

He rolls his eyes. 'I wasn't even aware that she was wearing it that day, I'm sure she meant to take it off. We argued over the stupidest of things because Cathy was dog-tired and I was stressed. It was one of those days, that's all.' He lapses into silence.

'Ah, the bubblegum flavour,' I reply and he shrugs his shoulders, a hint of amusement lighting up his eyes.

'Yeah. She was so tired it tipped her over the edge. Look, I want to be straight with you here. Everything with the restaurant is going brilliantly at the moment, it's almost too good to be true. When Cathy commits to something, she does it whole-heartedly, not just financially. She likes to be hands-on. And everything I have is on the line, too,' he admits, with a grimace. 'Cathy is probably the only woman I've met who understands that, with me, work comes first, every time, because it mirrors her own life. We're keeping the engagement secret because she doesn't want it overshadowing what she sees as my success. But it's *our* success, really, because I couldn't have done it without her. Aside from what the public see, behind the scenes she is a strong, determined woman with enormous drive, but there is also a softer side to her that goes unseen.'

He stops to pick up his coffee, taking a sip and making a face before swirling it around yet again.

'I have a sweet tooth,' he admits, grimacing as the second mouthful doesn't appear to taste much better. 'I know it's a big ask, but if the interview had been scheduled for another day, we wouldn't even be having this conversation, I promise you.'

Scanning his face, he looks tired and concerned.

'So, what are you asking of me?'

He swallows hard, taking a deep breath in through his nose as if to bolster his confidence.

'It would be better if the article didn't feature Cathy, other than to loosely mention that we are in partnership together. And, obviously, any photographs you use featuring her will benefit both the magazine and the restaurant because she's hot news right now. I'm not trying to gloss over anything, but, in terms of running the restaurant, Cathy is rarely around and after a few hours' sleep she was mortified about the impression you must have left with.'

Was she? I wonder. But the look on his face seems sincere as I mull over his words.

'After all, it's all about the food and that was good, wasn't it?' he asks, as if he isn't sure what my answer will be.

'It wasn't just good, it was amazing, Rick. Okay, I'll take out any reference to Cathy in the article but will credit her as your business partner in the photo spread.'

It can't be easy, living one's life in the limelight, I suppose. That's the problem with publicity, it isn't always positive, and it isn't always within a person's control. However, it would be unfair of me to make assumptions based on catching someone on a bad day, because we all have them. The fact that Rick came here of his own accord and Cathy didn't send him makes me even more inclined to agree.

The look of relief on his face is genuine and his shoulders sag a little, as he leans back against the paint-blistered wood behind us. 'Thank you, I really appreciate it. That, of course, leaves me in your debt, Lainey. If you ever need anything and I can help, just call me. I mean it. Sometimes it's the little things that get blown up out of proportion and reputations can be damaged. Cathy doesn't deserve that. But I owe you big time and I'll make it up to you when an opportunity presents itself.' He offers me his hand and we shake on it.

As a journalist, it's useful to make friends and not enemies, and you never know when it might come in handy to be able to call in a favour.

'You're a lifesaver, thank you!' he adds.

As our eyes meet, something deep inside of me stirs. Oh no. Not this, not now. Why is it that the best ones are always taken?

* * *

'Hey, Mum. How are you doing?'

'I'm fine, Lainey. How are you?'

It is good to hear her voice and I feel bad that I've left it so long to call. Mum has always said that I know where she is if I need anything but that she won't interfere in my life. I was twenty-one when my parents' divorce was finalised and I guess I did take my dad's side. I felt it was a travesty the way he was treated and I was shocked when Mum said she'd had enough. It was as if she was abandoning him when he needed her the most. Now, five years on, I'm older and a little wiser. I can at least understand why she did what she did. Whether I agree with that, well, I'm still not sure, but it doesn't mean I love her any less, only that I'm sad that it all went wrong because they were so good together.

'Busy, as usual, but happy enough,' I reply.

'And how has it been, settling into the new job and a new flat?'

I ease myself back into the corner of the sofa and idly gaze around. 'The job is great. The flat not so great. Unfortunately, I soon discovered that I have a noisy neighbour upstairs. I like the place, though. It's small but immaculate as it's not long been refurbished.'

There's an awkward silence, as we both cast around for something to say. I owe her an apology and it might help to break the ice.

'I've been meaning to ring you for a while now, but it's been hard juggling everything. I am sorry, as I think of you often. How are things with Le Cuisinier de Campagne?'

She gives a little laugh and I can hear the contentment in her voice. 'It's fun. The country cooking courses are really beginning to take off and I need to think long and hard about next year. If I offer more places and more dates, I'll have to consider employing someone to help on a permanent basis. For now, I manage with a few helpers who come in as and when I need them. I'm finding that quite a few of my guests are rebooking for next year already, which is great. The main thing is that everything is ticking over quite nicely, and life is sweet.'

That sums up my mum. Who uses the word *sweet* these days unless it's connected to something full of sugar? Grandma was a hippie in her teens and she always had a laid-back, bohemian mindset. And, of course, that rubbed off on Mum. Gran was unconventional, it's true, but she always impressed upon me that it was important to question things in life, rather than live by other people's rules. Ironically, that turned out to be the deal-breaker in my parents' marriage. Dad had ambitions, but Mum simply wanted a quiet life. Well, I guess they both ended up getting what they wanted, in a strange sort of way.

'That's wonderful to hear. I do miss your cooking,' I reply, feeling wistful.

For ten years Mum ran a little café attached to our local garden centre. In the school holidays I'd go along and help out. Every morning we'd bake huge trays of cupcakes, scones and savoury tarts. She was happy there until they decided not to renew her lease. She was a victim of her own success, having turned it into a very profitable little business. They didn't bake on site after Mum left and everything was delivered by van each morning. After that Mum decided to turn a part of our large back garden into a little allotment and it wasn't long before she added a greenhouse. Fresh fruit and veg was always on hand and something that I took for granted in those days.

'I'm still keeping it simple,' she says and I imagine the smile she has on her face right now. 'It works for me. And are you looking after yourself?'

'Hand on heart, I can't say I always get my five-a-day, but I do look for the organic options whenever I can.'

'In between the takeaways, you mean?'

I try not to laugh out loud.

'It's hard cooking for one.' The moment I stop speaking, I could kick myself. I know what's coming next.

'No, it's not, it's just a case of bothering, Lainey. It matters what you put into your body and you're worth the effort.'

I cooked all the time when my childhood sweetheart, Warren, and I eventually moved in together. We called it quits after two disastrous years and our split coincided with Dad's troubles, which made for a terrible time. No wonder Mum fled to France, just to save her sanity. She begged me to go with her, but we both knew it wasn't the right decision for me. It was rural and much too quiet.

'I know, but what I really need is to find myself a man who can cook me interesting little meals, while I slave over the keyboard writing up articles extolling the flavours of the exciting food I get to taste when I'm working.'

Mum sighs and it's a reminder that even though we are miles apart, she still worries about me. 'You don't need a man for that when God gave you two perfectly good hands and a brain. The internet is littered with healthy recipes that take less than half an hour to prepare and cook, so there's no excuse. Now, I've said my piece, you can relax. Except that I'm going to ask how your dad is doing.'

'Still writing. He's on book number six now!' I reply, not sure if Mum is aware of that fact.

'Hmm, that's impressive. It's been what, four years since he first sat down to write? Gosh, that time has flown by, hasn't it?'

'He seems happy enough, these days. I often wonder whether he gets lonely, though. Working from home isn't as sociable as going to the office, is it?' Was that a tactless thing to say? But Mum is probably way past caring what he gets up to.

'Your dad will find it hard to forgive those who shied away when he needed support. It's time he moved on, though, and made new friends.'

That's easy for Mum to say, but I won't point out the obvious, that being self-employed and working from home has turned him from a social animal into a bit of a hermit. He's not hiding, as he did in the early days, but he enjoys his solitude and that's a personal choice only he can make.

'Maybe. He's busy, though. Have you read any of his books?'

'No. But let me know if he changes genre, as I only read happy, uplifting stories. I'd watch the news if I wanted to read about murder, mystery and conspiracy. There are more good people on this earth than bad ones, but if all people spread is the negative stuff, this world is never going to heal itself.'

Mum's solution to avoiding anything negative is to go back to basics and lead by example. Growing your own and cooking with fresh ingredients, rather than buying ready-made meals, is a healthier option. She believes that teaching the kids to get hands-on is important, and she does just that on her little plot in France.

'And how are the *petits jardiniers* doing?' I ask.

'Oh, it's no longer the little gardeners' club. Many of the homes around here grow their own produce anyway and so things have moved on. A group of local children and parents come along once a month on a Saturday morning and they bring something that is home-grown. Sometimes it's fresh produce, even fish, as one of the families have a lake, and in winter it's often fruit from the orchards that has been stored in trays covered with straw. The sessions have turned into a community get-together and it's so much fun.'

'You sound really happy, Mum.' The truth is that since she left, Mum has never shared her problems with me. I wish she would let down her guard and talk openly as we did in the old days. The longer we go between contact, though, the harder it is to talk about anything really meaningful.

'I am, Lainey. This is where I was meant to be, but that's not to say I don't have regrets. It's not quite how I thought my life would turn out. And I miss you, lovely.'

'I know, Mum. I miss you, too. And I will take time out to finally come and visit this summer, I promise.'

'That would be marvellous, Lainey. I think you'll love it here.'

I end the call, as always, with mixed feelings. Uplifted because we've talked, and sad because our lives are so far apart in so many ways.

NOVEMBER

3

FRIENDS IN NEED

'You were right, Lainey.' Thomas, the managing editor of *Upscale Dining* magazine, scans around to take in the buzzing atmosphere at Aleatory. 'It is impressive and my wife is extremely cross with me because we couldn't get a reservation until the second week in May.'

We chink champagne flutes and I give him a sympathetic nod.

'Well, considering they'll be celebrating their second anniversary around that time, I'm sure the menu will be extra special.'

Even I'm surprised to have been on the exclusive invite list for tonight's Christmas Taster party. When I opened the innocuous-looking envelope and pulled out the elegant invitation card, a little thrill coursed through my veins. It was addressed to me personally, and a plus-one, as if it were an invite for a wedding. There was no way of knowing whether Rick was behind the invitation, or whether I was on the invite list given that I'd interviewed him back in January. But looking at the other attendees here tonight, there are a lot of famous names. It's great PR and the exclusivity of the party helps to keep the hype going.

Thomas was delighted when I flashed the invitation under his nose. I didn't ask him just because he's the boss; the truth is, I would have struggled to find a suitable escort anyway. My second option was Ant but given that he and his wife are struggling to cope with a five-month-old baby who prefers to sleep all day and stay awake at night, he may well have turned me down.

Suddenly, a smiley face appears in front of me and I see it's Neil, the waiter I took for coffee and a confidential chat the day after I interviewed Rick. Ever the professional, only the tiniest lift of his left eyebrow as we look directly at each other serves as an acknowledgement. He extends the platter he's balancing on his upturned hand towards me, turning to include Thomas as he talks us through the selection of canapés.

'Here we have Chef's hot picks – winter sausage with sage mash in a berry and port jus, then a seared scallop in a rock samphire and cream sauce and a winter root vegetable stack.'

Thomas and I lean forward, inspecting the ceramic tasting spoons, and my stomach immediately begins to grumble. Thomas indicates for me to dive in first and I go for the scallop, while he chooses the sausage and mash.

I'm in gastro heaven as the velvety creaminess of the sauce, the saltiness of the samphire and the tenderness of the scallop combine into one as I swallow.

Neil looks on, patiently waiting until we've finished. Another waiter appears behind him, holding out a stainless-steel basket for the empty spoons. Neil swoops in with the platter once again. I'm sure he's supposed to be circulating, but Thomas is eagerly looking on and isn't about to say no, and neither am I.

This time, I go for the vegetable stack. The presentation is unbelievable as the little dishes hold no more than a single bite of food. This stack must have at least four very finely sliced vegetables, interlaced with puff pastry. As I pop it into my mouth and bite, there's a hint of sauce between each layer. My mouth tingles with the flavour of a tart balsamic vinegar and then a sweet lift of honey.

Thomas is already placing his second empty spoon into the basket, looking extremely impressed by the scallop. 'Wonderful. The samphire gives it a salty kick and the scallop is cooked to perfection.'

'That is precisely the response we love to hear.' Rick's voice filters over my right shoulder and I turn to see him standing behind me.

As he joins us and I turn back around, I notice that Neil has already discreetly moved on, much to Thomas's disappointment.

'Hi, Rick. What a great party! Let me introduce you to Thomas Morrison-Wyn, *Upscale Dining*'s managing editor. He was just saying how envious his wife is that he's here tonight as they couldn't get a reservation until May.'

Thomas offers his hand and they shake. 'Yes, I'm in deep trouble now as her birthday is in January, so it will have to be a belated celebratory meal,' Thomas says, with a broad smile. 'Anyway, may I congratulate you on what has been a phenomenal success story.'

'Thank you, Thomas. And I'm sorry about the long wait, but it's been crazily busy, virtually since day one. I can't believe we'll soon begin making plans for a party to mark our second anniversary. I'll make sure you are both on the list and that way you can bring your wife with you to the party to hopefully make up for her disappointment.'

'A happy wife means a happy life, as they say,' Thomas retorts with a grin. 'Much appreciated, Rick. And what a wonderful way to introduce your Christmas menu, with a tasting party.'

Rick and I exchange a conspiratorial look and I can see Thomas notices, although he says nothing.

'I'd dearly love to stay and chat, but I've been ordered to speak to everyone at least once. I'll give you a call around eleven tomorrow morning, Lainey. It's good to finally meet you in person, Thomas. Cathy and I are most grateful to *Upscale Dining* for its ongoing support. We had some great feedback from Lainey's feature – she has quite a following.'

As Rick heads off to continue mingling, Thomas glances at me, unable to contain his curiosity. 'Ongoing support?'

'You didn't think I was going to waste an opportunity, did you?'

Thomas stares at me, narrowing his eyes for a second or two, before breaking out into a broad smile.

'Naturally, when the invitation arrived, I immediately called Rick to thank him and asked if there was any chance of a few pre-party photographs of the food. Ant popped in for an hour earlier on, but left shortly before we arrived.'

Thomas raises an eyebrow and I shrug my shoulders.

'I thought I'd put something together for the website under the Food in the News feature. And Rick suggested a quick video call, so clearly he has something coming up he thinks might be of particular interest to us.'

'Ah, marvellous idea, thanks for jumping on it, Lainey. While Rick's in the spotlight it would be great if we could get another exclusive at some point.'

Suddenly, behind us, there's a massive influx of people spilling in through the door and all heads turn. Cathy has just arrived with a group of friends in tow and they're in party mode. Immediately the vibe in the restaurant changes and it's like an electric charge surging through the room. Most of the faces are instantly recognisable by the majority of us, as we all look on in amazement.

I turn my head to see where Rick is and he's already weaving his way through the crowd, as he makes a beeline for the bar.

Cathy and her group are being fussed over by two cocktail waiters and it's starting to get raucous.

It might be my imagination, but Rick seemed surprised to see Cathy at first, yet as she throws her arms around his neck and he looks down at her, smiling, he's clearly taking it in his stride.

'Well, that's livened things up a little,' Thomas says, keeping his voice low as he leans in. 'And by the look of it they've already had a drink or two on their way here. Anyway, while everyone else is momentarily distracted, let's head over to one of the tasting tables. In the line of duty, of course.'

There are times when I think Thomas would happily turn back the clock and come out from behind his desk. He's great at what he does, but I can tell he misses the good old days, as he refers to them, when he was a feature writer and experiencing everything first-hand. I wonder if someday that will be me, having climbed further up the ladder, only to find that I'm missing the action.

As I'm pondering my future, Cathy walks past, her arm linked in Rick's. She's in full flow, but I can't catch what she's saying. One thing I do spot is that she isn't wearing her huge engagement ring.

* * *

Hugh is our IT guy and I'm in the office today so he can transfer my files over to a new laptop and load up a few apps for me. It's my least favourite job and he can do it so much quicker than I can. Sitting here with him as he patiently explains what he's doing, my eyes are glazing over. In fact, when my phone starts to buzz, I snatch it up, grateful for a pause in Hugh's running commentary.

'Lainey, it's Rick.'

'Ah, Rick. Um, you're a little earlier than I expected. Can I video call you in about half an hour?'

'Apologies for the interruption, but I'll be quick. I was wondering if we could meet up in person today instead, to discuss this idea of mine? But you'll have to come to me as I've had a bit of an accident and my ankle is all strapped up.'

His voice is unusually quiet. Fortunately, the line is perfectly clear, but I'm straining my ears to hear what he's saying. 'Oh, I'm sorry to hear that, Rick. Text me the address and a time. I'm free from about ten-thirty onwards.'

'Thanks, I really appreciate that. So, I know this sounds a little weird, but humour me, will you? When you arrive, just go along with whatever I say. You'll understand why when you get here, but it would really help me out big time. I must go, see you later.'

Well, that was odd. And why was he whispering? I hope I'm not walking into an awkward situation.

'I'll just be a couple of minutes, Hugh, I promise. I need to talk to Dario, urgently.' Everything Hugh is telling me is going straight over my head anyway and I'm glad of an excuse to leave the IT room. It always feels a little too hot and stuffy in here for my liking.

'It's going to be another twenty minutes, at least, so take your time,' he calls over his shoulder.

I smile back at him, looking suitably ashamed of myself. It's hard to look and sound enthusiastic, when watching paint dry would be far more interesting. I'm going to forget everything he's telling me, anyway, because my head is somewhere else entirely.

Aside from the awesome Hugh, my other go-to man in the office is Dario Labruto, who is a good friend, as well as being our social media coordinator. He's the sort of person you turn to when you need to offload your problems. His partner, Ian, is an accountant and they have a very eclectic mix of friends, so their parties are always great fun.

'Dario, are you busy?' I ask as I approach his desk. It's quiet in the open plan area today, I notice.

His head pops up above the two large monitors in front of him. 'Never too busy for you, Lainey. Why?'

'This is off the record.'

'Ooh, that sounds interesting. What's up?'

'I wondered if you'd seen anything online this morning about Rick Oliver, or Aleatory? Thomas and I attended a party there last night. There wasn't an official photographer, but I wondered if any of the guests were hashtagging photos on social media.'

He looks at me blankly, but I can see he's thinking about it. 'I haven't spotted anything, so it's not trending. Do you want me to have a scout around and see what I can find? What am I looking for, exactly?'

'That I don't know, call it a hunch. When we left, the party was getting lively as Cathy Clarkson had just arrived with a small group of A-list music people. It looked like it might turn into quite a raucous party once the other guests left. I'm meeting with Rick in about an hour's time and I just want to be up to date with whatever might be out there.'

'No problem. I'll text you links if I find anything out of the ordinary. Bet it was a great party once Cathy arrived though,' he remarks.

'What do you know that I don't?' I ask, peering at him.

'Oh, nothing really. I just heard a rumour. I'll dig that out, too.'

As I'm walking back to the IT suite, my phone pings and Dario has sent me a link. It's a selfie from Cathy's Instagram page. Her head is tilted, as she's cheek to cheek with someone I don't recognise and they look very cosy together.

Who's the guy?

Zane, the lead singer from Outer Zone.

Whatever they were doing, they were clearly having a lot of fun doing it.

It's a screenshot a mate of mine captured last Thursday. It disappeared from Cathy's page about an hour after she posted it. I'll be in touch if I find anything illuminating.

You're a star!

I know.

Instead of heading straight back to see Hugh, I take a short detour. The idea is that he will have finished the job by the time I get back. The door to Thomas's prestigious corner office is ajar and I ease it open a couple of inches to peer inside.

'Morning, boss. Slight change of plan as I'm going to meet up with Rick at his place. I'm not sure how long it will take. As soon as Hugh has finished with my laptop, I'll proofread that piece I wrote up about last night and get it on the system.'

'Good. Am I allowed to ask what Rick wants to talk to you about?'

'He just said it's an idea he's been mulling over for a while and he thinks it might be of interest to us. As soon as I know more, I'll call in and brief you.'

Thomas looks directly at me, suddenly all ears. 'Well, we could do with a big splash, something a bit different. I'm in the mood to shake things up a little.'

I roll my eyes as he leans back in his chair, doing that

annoying thing where he presses down on the arms and begins to rotate from left to right. As I watch him, it makes me feel the floor is shifting beneath my own feet, but this is his thinking mode and I fear we're in trouble. 'How?' I ask.

'What we need is a feature to catch the eye of our readers next summer. Something like *A Foodie Abroad*?'

This is so typical of Thomas. He comes up with a one-liner and we spend a whole day brainstorming it. Sometimes it works and sometimes it doesn't.

'Hmm. Interesting. Food for thought,' I chuckle, wondering if I could swing a little jaunt to France. A road trip to discover those little tucked-away places to dine that don't always get featured in the guidebooks and, in the process, tack on a couple of days' leave to visit Mum. I keep promising her I'll make the trip, but my plans always change last minute. I'm beginning to think I'm simply not ready to rake over the past. But we'll only be able to move forward if Mum is prepared to talk through the issues we've both skirted around for a long time.

As I retrace my steps, he calls out, 'Let it *simmer* for a bit, Lainey. You'll come up with something with a twist, I know it.'

I groan, but I can't resist. 'It's a half-baked idea, Thomas, but I'm not dismissing it out of hand.'

He's chuckling away to himself, but having thrown out a challenge I need to rise to it if I'm serious about impressing upon Thomas that I'm ambitious.

* * *

Grainger Court in Dover Street is a brisk, three-minute walk from Green Park station and an equally short walk to work for Rick. The building itself was formerly office accommodation that has been converted into smart flats, in the last year or two. Looking up, I can just see the edge of the roofline. Set back are what I assume to be either one, or possibly two, penthouse apartments, and a balcony runs the entire width of the building. The views from there must be amazing. Rick's text says to head to flat 3.02.

The reception is accessed via a glass-fronted unit next to a boutique designer outlet, the other side of which is a remote-control up-and-over door, which I assume is the entrance to a private underground car park. As I step inside the foyer, there is a small desk, but no one's around, so I head straight for the lift. The décor is smart, but not lavish. I can't really see Cathy strolling in here with her posse for a nightcap.

The lift is a good size and stepping out into a long, narrow corridor, there is a sign indicating that flats 3.01 to 3.03 are to the right. It's deserted up here, too, and when I find myself standing in front of Rick's door, a moment of apprehension hits me. I don't quite know what I'm walking into given his warning. Will Cathy be here?

I ring the bell and take a little step back, loosening my scarf as I begin to warm up a little. There's an icy blast out there today and I'm conscious that my face is probably glowing from my brisk walk.

'Ah, you must be Lainey,' the middle-aged woman who swings open the door greets me cordially. 'Lovely to meet you. Do come in and let me take your coat.'

The woman's warm welcome is as much of as a surprise as the fact that she knows my name. Remembering Rick's request to humour him, I step over the threshold, wondering what's in store for me.

The inner hallway is square, with three doors off to the right, and it leads into a narrow corridor. There's another door at the very end.

'Do come this way. The patient is resting,' she informs me as I follow her straight ahead. 'But only because I won't take *no* for an answer.'

I don't say anything as she opens the door in front of us and we step into an open-plan living/dining area and kitchen. It's light and bright, being a corner flat with three large, floor-to-ceiling windows on the long wall and two on the return wall. It looks out onto a similar building on the other side of the street. The two windows either side of a shiny, white island in the back right-hand corner look out onto a stone wall. The room is probably only seven metres by five, but it's a lovely space and a great little find when you are looking for something a stone's throw from where you work.

I'd like to take in the detail, but my eyes are now drawn to the L-shaped sofa and Rick, who is propped up by a couple of pillows, his right leg extended along an oblong footstool. He shifts a little as we exchange a brief glance.

'Now don't you go moving around, Rick. You know what the doctor said. If you can keep it still for the first twenty-four hours with minimal movement, you'll heal much quicker.' The woman turns to look at me, shaking her head sadly. 'He thought he was going into work today, imagine that! Still, I'm so glad you're here.'

'That means you can get off now, Mum,' Rick interrupts, as he can see I don't quite know how to react. This is his mum? Is she under the impression that I'm a nurse?

'I'd rather not leave you like this, my dear boy. I know what you're like and, mark my words, you'll be in a sorry state if you aren't sensible.' She turns to face me. 'You agree with that, don't you, Lainey?' she asks and I feel obliged to play along.

'Of course. Rest, ice, compression and elevation.'

'Precisely,' she replies, giving me a grateful smile. 'He has a special boot to wear if he needs to go to the bathroom, but he's not supposed to put any weight on that ankle until tomorrow morning at the earliest. So, he'll need reminding to use the crutches and keep his foot off the floor.' I can tell she's concerned and worried that he won't rest up.

'Mum, you've been through this with me several times already. Now off you go. You can't expect Dad to do the packing all on his own, can you?'

She pauses, clearly torn. 'I suppose not. Anyway, thank you, Lainey. You know how Rick hates to be fussed over and it's a relief to know there's someone here he can count on.'

I'm speechless, as I have no idea what Rick has said to her. I decide I have no choice but to plaster on a warm smile, because she's such a lovely lady and if I don't reassure her, she's not going anywhere. 'You can absolutely count on me to take over. My father sprained his ankle at a football match once and it wasn't easy making him do as he was told. But he thanked my mum and me for it, later.'

'That's such a relief,' she replies, letting out a deep sigh. 'There are spare ice packs in the freezer, and I stocked up the fridge.'

'Okay, Mum. That's enough. Seriously, Dad will be getting anxious if you don't leave now.'

I avoid looking at Rick while his mum gathers her things together, placing them on a chair. She walks over to him, stooping to give him a hug, and then plants a kiss on his temple.

I try to melt discreetly into the background as they say their goodbyes.

'If the swelling has gone down by the morning that boot goes on and you take regular breaks to elevate your leg. Do you hear me?'

'Yes, Mum. And thank you. Have a wonderful holiday and we'll catch up properly when you get back.'

'Right, I'm off then and I'll leave you in Lainey's capable

hands. You really are a star and a true friend, coming to Rick's rescue like this,' she says, as I follow her out into the hallway.

I wait while she pops her handbag and a large hessian shopping carrier on the floor so she can pull on her coat.

'It's really cold out there. It looks bright and sunny, but the temperature has plummeted in the last hour,' I warn her.

I pick up her bags while she buttons her coat to the top and then pulls out a pair of fine leather gloves.

She leans into me, her voice low. 'If you weren't here, I'd have cancelled the trip to Scotland. It's our thirtieth wedding anniversary tomorrow and we have family there we haven't seen in a while, but I don't think Cathy is very sympathetic and so it's wonderful to know he has a good friend to be here with him overnight. Fingers crossed his ankle will be a lot better in the morning, as my son isn't one for sitting at the best of times, is he? I'm Shari, by the way.'

Overnight? She puts her arms around my shoulders to give me a quick hug and the look of relief reflected on her face when she pulls away means I simply nod my head. 'Well, have a lovely time, Shari, and I'll be applying those ice packs religiously, I promise. And watching him like a hawk.'

She gives me a beaming smile. I can only hope that after a few hours Rick will be moving around on his crutches with confidence. If that isn't the case... well, I'll cross that bridge when we get there. 'Thank goodness he's got at least one sensible friend and I'm very grateful to you for stepping in at such short notice. Take care, Lainey. It's lovely to meet you, even if it's briefly, and I do hope our paths cross again before too long.'

As I shut the door behind her, I slump back against it, wondering what on earth I was thinking. For a moment there, I forgot myself.

Forcing myself to stand up straight, I walk back into the open-plan area and Rick stares back at me, mortified.

'I am sooo sorry about that. But my mother would literally have cancelled their holiday to stay if I hadn't—'

'Lied to her?' I offer, shaking my head at him. 'You can't blame her for worrying about you.'

'It looks worse than it is. I simply missed my footing and twisted it, that's all.'

In fairness, he does look a tad ashamed of himself and my remark has obviously pricked his conscience. And now he's a little embarrassed.

'How long has that ice pack been on?' I ask.

'About twenty minutes.'

'Right. That needs to go back in the freezer then, and I'll set my phone for a reminder in three hours' time. Are you seriously thinking of going back to work tomorrow?'

I sink down onto the single chair alongside Rick, as he nods his head.

'Yes. And I'm not expecting you to stay, naturally. I couldn't cope with the pain and with pacifying my mother, so I panicked. As I was going to phone you anyway, it just seemed like a quick fix. Cathy isn't around, as she was due to fly off to Paris early this morning for a charity event she's involved in this weekend. Besides, I'm perfectly capable of coping on my own.'

'The plan is that we have a chat about this idea of yours and then I leave you to it? Even though your mum thinks she's left you in safe hands?'

Rick shrugs his shoulders. 'I had to do something. I think I'm capable of applying a little ice and keeping my leg elevated for a while.'

Hmm. It's a long way from the sofa to the freezer, that's for sure. Is this a male thing, I wonder, not wanting to admit that he needs help? And why didn't he call a friend, unless there's more to it and he didn't relish the thought of having to explain what happened.

'Good for you. Are you thirsty? Hungry?' I ask.

'I would love a coffee, and I'm starving. It's been a stressful day so far.'

'Me, too. Go ahead.'

Rick stares across at the island and his eyes search around for his crutches. They're hooked onto the back of the sofa and I hand them to him. He accepts them with a wicked glint in his eye.

I lift the now squidgy ice pack off his strapped ankle and watch as he tries to manoeuvre himself forward into a sitting position. With his good leg anchoring him to the floor, he winces as he tries to move his right leg. It's obvious there is no way he's going to be able to lever himself up on one leg, let alone get the crutches in place once he's standing.

'As I suspected... Mums usually know what they're talking about,' I point out.

He looks totally helpless and, dare I say it, a little sorry for himself. 'Okay. I give up. The sofa is too low and my legs are too long. That's not my fault.'

'What a shame. I was looking forward to whatever ingenuous idea you came up with for carrying a coffee mug while propping yourself up with two metal sticks.'

'All right, you've made your point. If I can avoid putting any weight on it for a few hours, then I'm sure I'll be fine.'

'So, it's best I stay for a while, then?' I ask, trying not to gloat.

'Is this really how you want to spend the rest of your day?' Ricks enquires, sounding dubious.

I shake my head at him as he sags back against the pillows, looking weary. 'It's just one of those things. I've already sorted the two most urgent tasks on today's to do list, then I'd pencilled out a block of time for our meeting. After that I was going to head home. But, as payback, if you could arrange for Thomas's table reservation to be brought forward, he'd owe me a favour.'

Rick looks at me, a grin gradually creeping over his face. 'Do you make a habit of that?'

'Of what?'

'Collecting favours,' he jokes. 'It's the second time you've come to my rescue.'

'So much for knights in shining armour and damsels in distress. The classic fairy tales could do with a bit of a rewrite,' I reply, laughing at him.

Rick at least has the good grace to give me an acknowledging nod. 'Well, I'm hoping I can repay all these favours before too long.' He looks at me with a gleam in his eyes and I turn, heading over to familiarise myself with his pristine, and by the look of it seldom-used, kitchen.

4

THE GOOD SAMARITAN

Two cups of coffee and one sandwich later, we finally get down to business. As I take the empty plate from Rick, he smiles up at me.

'Not bad, not bad at all,' he remarks, as if surprised I could think beyond the same old lunch deal specials.

Well, I wasn't about to let myself down when I was preparing something for a superstar chef! Lightly toasted ciabatta, a drizzle of virgin olive oil and a hint of balsamic vinegar, with thinly sliced avocado, ribbons of Parma ham and my cheat's version of aioli. Because the kitchen is open-plan, Rick no doubt spotted the jar of mayonnaise and the squeezing of the tube of garlic, but it's the thought that counts. I did suppress a grin, though, as I doubt either of those two items would have been on Rick's shopping list. The contents of his fridge do look little his mum did a quick supermarket sweep. There's a little bit of everything, bless her.

My phone begins to ping and I dig into my bag to mute it.

'Sorry about that. Right,' I flop down into the chair and look at Rick expectantly. 'Do I need to take notes?'

'Not at this stage. Let me bounce the idea off you first and see what your gut reaction is before we put anything down on paper.'

'Fire away.'

'I've been approached by an independent production company who are planning a four-part TV series entitled *New and Inspired: The Next Generation of Master Chefs*. A list of commis chefs who have recently completed their culinary training were whittled down and the top seven candidates have been invited to take part in the competition. I've been asked to hold four master-classes, each demonstrating a three-course meal. The contestants will do their own take on each of the dishes spread out over a period of three days and, as the judge, I will be awarding marks for each course. There is a significant prize at stake for the overall winner and I'm excited about it.'

Rick stares at me intently, studying my reaction, but I'm at a loss to see how this might involve *Upscale Dining*.

'Oh, I thought this was going to be a chat about some publicity for the anniversary celebration.'

'No. Cathy is keeping tight control on that. She has a thing about the value of exclusivity and the right sort of social media presence. It's going to be a star-studded night to create some spec-ulation and chatter apparently. She'll make sure that a few exclu-sive photos are released the following day, of course, but there won't be any official coverage.'

Hmm. I can see that route might be perfect PR, but surely the food created by the chef and the Aleatory team should be the main focus, not the celebrities who are invited to dine there.

'Oh, I see,' I reply, thinking it best not to voice my opinion. 'The show sounds like a wonderful opportunity. I'm assuming you jumped at it.'

'Well, it's not quite that simple, unfortunately.'

'That's a pity. The exposure you'd get would be priceless in terms of getting your face out there.'

Rick is beginning to grow fidgety and he tries to ease himself forward. 'Argh,' he groans, wincing a little as he pushes down onto the sofa with his arms to lever himself forward. 'I need to take a trip to the bathroom.' He is muscular and he obviously works out, but the sofa is squidgy and it's low to the ground.

I jump up to grab his crutches and offer an arm to pull him upright. 'Hang on a second, let's get organised first,' I say, firmly. 'Right, shuffle forward a little closer to the edge of the seat, then slide your leg off the stool. That's it. Now, place your right hand on my shoulder and lever yourself up.'

This would be so much easier if the sofa was firmer, or he wasn't quite so tall. But between us, we get him standing on his good leg and he grins at me, gratefully, as he grabs onto the crutches.

'Do you need me to walk with you?' I ask.

Rick takes a tentative step forward, keeping his right leg bent, his foot hovering above the floor. I can see from the grimace on his face as he takes his next step that it's not as easy as he thought it was going to be.

'I'll get the doors for you. Just take your time.' The last thing he needs is someone anxiously watching him, and it's painful to witness. It's a minute or two before he shuffles along the hallway and as he comes closer, Rick's forehead is glistening with beads of sweat. He looks pale but manages to raise a half-hearted smile.

'I think I'm good now,' he replies. 'I've got this.'

Thank goodness for that. To be honest, this meeting is beginning to feel a little bit too personal for me and it can't be easy for Rick, either.

'Brilliant. I'll uh... just disappear to make a phone call, then,' I say, making a quick exit and heading back into the sitting room.

Grabbing my phone from my bag, I walk over to the kitchen area. Dario has messaged three times asking where I am and why I haven't responded. That means he's found something.

'Hi, Dario. Sorry, I had my phone on mute. What's happening?'

'Well, there were a few foodie photos with the restaurant's hashtag, just people bragging and making it known they were at the party. However, a source I cannot reveal told me in confidence that Cathy was whisked off in a taxi after an unfortunate incident occurred at the tail end of the evening.'

'An incident?' I repeat, keeping my voice low.

'It seems Cathy wasn't happy about something and a row developed. One of Cathy's friends joined in and there was a bit of a scuffle. Hence the quick exit. You never know if someone might catch an unfortunate photo and they wouldn't want something like that going viral.'

Was Rick involved? I wonder.

'Thanks, Dario. I have to go, but I owe you a drink for this one. Have a great weekend, my friend.'

'You, too. Speak soon.'

By the time Rick has made his way back to the sofa, his pallor is a little worrying. I take the crutches from him and as he gingerly lowers himself back down, his discomfort evident. To distract him, I ask Rick what inspired him to become a chef. Maybe there's an element of curiosity involved, too, but he smiles back at me, amiably. As I take a seat, Rick tells me a little bit about his childhood. He was the odd one out at school and several of his peers made fun of him for spending time in the kitchen *cooking*. It didn't deter him, though, and it's heart-warming to hear how he turned his dream into a reality. It simply feels like we're two old friends catching up and while a part of me wonders if this is wise, I'm enjoying myself.

* * *

'I think it's almost time to ice that ankle again. How's it feeling?' I'm conscious that the afternoon has slipped by without either of us really noticing and I head over to the freezer.

'Thanks, Lainey, my ankle is beginning to throb again, but it's not as swollen as it was earlier on. While you're getting that ice pack, would you mind opening a bottle of wine? I don't know about you, but I could do with a little fortification. It might help take the edge off the pain.'

Turning my head to look back at him, his smile is disarming, and I can see how grateful he is for the company. 'Sounds good to me. Um, you haven't taken any painkillers, or medication, have you?' I check, trying to sound compassionate and not bossy.

'I'm not a total wimp, except for when it comes to my mum, who is a force to be reckoned with at times. I just feel bad that you're still here and please, don't feel you have to stay and spoil your Friday evening.'

'If I were at home I'd be sitting in front of the TV with a glass in my hand and unwinding after what has been an exhausting week. But at least mine didn't end as badly as yours,' I commiserate.

'Well, it teaches me to be more careful next time,' he informs me.

My back is towards Rick as I grab a fresh ice pack from the freezer and I turn to look at him, making an effort not to register surprise at his admission. 'Where will I find a bottle of wine?'

'There's white in the fridge and red in the wine rack under the island. The choice is yours, I'm easy. Glasses are in the wall unit next to the window in the far corner.'

'Ah, I've got it,' I reply, grabbing a bottle of red and noting from the label that it's from a very selective vineyard I've heard people talking about. 'So, you did this to yourself, then?' I busy myself searching around for the glasses and then de-cork the wine bottle, studiously avoiding looking in Rick's direction.

'Someone annoyed me last night, and he didn't like it when I advised him to leave before I threw him out. It wasn't one of my most eloquent of moments, I'll be honest. When he didn't heed my warning, my fist swung his way, but he dodged it and I fell over, making a complete fool of myself. Fortunately, there were only a handful of people around to witness it. There are times when I'm vocal in the kitchen, but not much outside of that lights my fuse.'

'But this incident did?'

A drawn-out sigh escapes his lips. 'How much can I trust you, given that you're a journalist?'

I'm walking towards him, a glass in each hand, and I stop momentarily. 'How many journalists have you met who would promise your mother they would stay to keep you out of trouble?'

He hangs his head in mock shame. 'This is all off the record, then?'

'Absolutely.'

I hand him the glass of wine, placing mine on the coffee table and going back for the ice pack.

'I don't make friends easily. I've learnt the hard way in the past and it taught me to be cautious. I like to keep my private life private.'

I can only guess that he's referring to his time working with Martine Alvarez, at the Food Haven. He must view Cathy as a life-line, as the minute she popped into his life that news eclipsed any future speculation about what happened.

I return, placing the ice pack on a towel over his ankle. 'Here you go and don't forget to keep wiggling your toes.'

'I hate feeling vulnerable. Believe it or not, I don't make a habit of lying to my mum, either. But my parents have been planning this trip for nearly a year and there was no way I was going to rob them of it just because I made an ass of myself.'

Maybe Rick did make a bit of a fool of himself and Dario mentioned that there was a row before the scuffle took place.

Picking up my wine glass, Rick pats the seat next to him on the sofa. 'If we're going to talk openly, let's get comfortable.'

I gingerly lower myself down next to him, not wanting to disturb his extended leg.

'What would make you trust me? Sharing some of my own dark secrets?' I ask.

Rick seems to find that funny. '*You* have dark secrets? Sorry, but I don't believe it.'

I shoot him a withering glance. 'More than you can imagine, actually.'

He holds up his glass and we chink. 'To the demons we try our hardest to keep at bay and to the angels who rescue us.'

My heart starts to beat wildly in my chest. My head is telling me very firmly that this isn't personal, but why is my pulse racing as those deep brown eyes of his search my face? His guard is lowered and we're just two people, admitting that life hasn't been easy.

'Come on then, are you going to share?' he asks, as I settle back against the cushions.

'Where do I start? My father is Mike Summers. Have you heard of him?'

Rick immediately turns his head to face me. 'Really? Of course I have. I followed the case in the newspapers.' He sounds shocked.

'Yep. And I took his side when everyone turned on him, which sent my mother hurrying off to France because she couldn't bear to see the way he was being ostracised.'

Rick takes a big gulp of his wine. 'That must have been tough to get through. What does he do now?'

'He's an author, but he uses a pen name. He's still on a quest, but his conspiracy theories are now channelled into fiction.'

I can see that was the last thing that Rick was expecting to hear.

'And a relationship I'd been in for two years fell apart at roughly the same time. It seems that my former childhood sweetheart had changed in the intervening years. He wasn't so sweet when it came to surviving the tough times.'

Rick shakes his head, sadly. 'I'm sorry to hear that, Lainey. You deserve better.'

'I know. But we don't always get what we deserve, we get what life determines we need to make us stronger.'

'You really believe that?' he asks, sounding incredulous.

'Well, my dad taught me that you can't always believe what you see. And my mum, well, she thinks people have simply forgotten what really matters in life. That's why she now runs cookery workshops in Le Crotoy and teaches people about growing your own produce. It was interesting, being brought up by parents who didn't always see eye-to-eye on the possible solutions to some of life's stumbling blocks. But it taught me a valuable lesson.'

'Which is?' Rick looks at me, frowning.

'Everyone has a right to their own opinion. And who am I to judge someone else when I'm still getting things wrong.' The little smile that tweaks at my lips is full of irony.

'Now I feel guilty for ignoring my instincts and suddenly doubting you. You've already bailed me out once, and twice should tell me something, shouldn't it? I owe you an apology, Lainey.'

'It's fine. I understand. It's why I decided to change the focus of my career. I simply love food, but as a journalist, I discovered that bad news sells more papers than the happy stuff. My job didn't always make me feel good about myself and what I do now is a step up in my opinion.'

'It's hard to have a conscience. Many people don't these days, it seems.'

We lapse into silence for a brief moment before Rick turns to look at me, his gaze intense.

'Cathy has two completely different sides to her. The façade she shows to the world when she's putting herself out there is her armour. And then there's the private person lurking in the shadows and fighting the battle that rages on inside of her.' He sounds distant, preoccupied.

'A battle?' I enquire, gently.

'Child stars rarely choose their own path in life. There's always someone in the background, pushing them forward and using them. How can anyone believe it's normal, or healthy, for a child to be thrust into the limelight? It's hard to comprehend in today's world. Since about the age of five, normality isn't a word that has factored in Cathy's life at all.'

How terribly sad his words sound.

'None of us realise how lucky we are if we've had the luxury of being allowed a childhood and I'm grateful my parents weren't pushy. Neither of them ever thought I'd become a chef, but if I'd wanted to become an astronaut, they'd have been equally as supportive. Their dream for me was simply to find my passion in life. And that's what I did.'

As the light begins to fade and we continue chatting about all sorts of things, I can't help thinking how surreal this is, being here in Rick Oliver's flat and talking about the love of his life, as if we've known each other forever. The more he opens up, the more I know it's wrong of me to be here. He isn't trying to connect with me, he's simply offloading the stuff he feels he can't say to anyone else. I'm just a listening ear, but every word is drawing me closer to him in a way he doesn't intend.

'Shall I turn the sidelights on?' I ask as a diversionary tactic.

'Yes, it's getting dark out there, but I can do it from the remote.' Rick's hand dives beneath one of the cushions and, moments later, the background lights give a cheerful glow. Then he turns on some music and, surprisingly, it isn't one of Cathy's records, but something by Sam Smith. 'I feel guilty lounging around on a Friday evening,' he comments. I realise that normally he'd be at work, but Rick has no choice but to be sensible, whether he likes it, or not.

'I think it's time for that ice pack to come off.'

Rick leans forward, gingerly lifting it up and passing it to me, before pulling back the towel. Wriggling his toes back and forth as I stand watching him, he nods his head. 'It's working.' He gingerly runs his hand over the thick, crepe bandage and a look of relief passes over his face. 'At least I can touch it now without wincing.'

'It bodes well for tomorrow, as long as you don't do anything silly overnight.'

'I'll be fine. Really. It's time you headed off.' He sounds upbeat, but I can't leave him like this. There's no way he can cater for himself. He can hardly get around, let alone fetch himself a drink.

'How about I cook you something before I go?' I offer.

'That's very kind of you, Lainey, but I could order a takeaway.'

'And hobble to the door when it arrives? I can throw something together,' I reply, confidently.

'Well, only if you'll join me. Mum made a butternut squash lasagne earlier on if you don't mind putting that in the oven. I'm sure we can stretch it to feed two if you pull a garlic bread out of the freezer. And a top-up would be nice,' he adds, holding up his empty glass.

As I busy myself in the kitchen, Rick chatters away.

'Plates are in the second drawer beneath the island. Knives and forks are in a tray in the top one. I feel bad sitting here watching you wait on me. Anyway, I suppose I'd better get back to the real reason why you're here.'

Time to focus, Lainey. This isn't just a cosy little evening in with a friend. Thomas will be disappointed if my meeting with Rick doesn't produce something positive. 'You were saying there was a problem with accepting the offer to take part in the TV show?'

'Yes. It means being away from the restaurant for a whole month. I have no doubt at all that my sous chef, Pierre, is more than capable of running things and we'd draft in extra help. But Cathy, wearing her investor's hat, is nervous about the timing. The focus for the restaurant is on winning Michelin-star status and an inspector could visit at any time. The award ceremony is in October and making myself absent from the restaurant for the whole of June is a risk.'

'One Cathy would prefer you not to take?'

'Let's say she's anxious to ensure that standards don't slip. Cathy invested in *me* and I can understand her concerns. It would be easier to get her on board if I could guarantee similar exposure in the UK, as then the publicity and PR would link back and hopefully benefit Aleatory. That's what I want to talk to you about.'

'The show's not being filmed in the UK, then? Now you've really grabbed my attention.'

'That's just the sort of reaction I'd hoped for,' Rick replies as I glance at him, raising my index finger to halt him before he goes any further.

'Give me a moment to pop this in the oven. Then you can tell me more about this masterplan of yours and what exactly it involves.'

My mind is racing as I get the meal under way. It's obvious that Rick isn't the sort of man to walk away from a golden opportunity, but I can't really see what's in it for the magazine. Sure, we'd run a short piece in the news section on the website when Rick formally announces his involvement in the show, but unless a feature is unique to us, we're talking paid advertising.

'Here you go.' Walking back to the sofa, I top up Rick's glass and he gives me an appreciative nod.

'Thank you, Lainey. Now take a seat, relax and humour me. First of all, I want to paint you a picture. Forget about the gloomy darkness outside the window and imagine standing among groves of oranges and lemons which stretch out as far as the eye can see as you soak up the wonderful Andalucían sunshine...'

He begins what is quite an impressive sales pitch, his light-hearted delivery engaging. However, when he gets down to the nitty-gritty detail, his eyes rarely stray from my face. This is important to him and yet he's trying to mask that fact.

When the food is finally ready, the conversation draws to a halt as I head over to the kitchen to make up two trays. Glancing across, I notice Rick gingerly adjusting his position and he uses his arms to lever himself upright. It jolts his leg and he screws up his face, the pain momentarily taking his breath away.

'Are you all right?' I ask, unable to mask my concern, and he nods.

'Yes, it's just awkward. My leg is getting stiff.'

As I carry a tray over to him, I can see that he still isn't comfortable and he's rubbing his thigh as if it keeps cramping.

'Look, why don't I put a couple of cushions on the floor so you can rest your foot on them just while you're eating?'

'That's a great idea, thanks. I don't think I've ever sat in one position for so long and I feel like everything is locking up.'

It takes a couple of minutes to get him set up, but in between mouthfuls of food our little chat continues. Rick's attitude about circumventing Cathy's concerns is surprisingly cavalier. He's determined to make it work and that's obvious as he outlines a proposition he's well aware I'd be mad to reject. And Cathy won't turn down the chance of free promotion for the restaurant.

'So, are you up for it?' he asks as I take the tray from him, surprised at how quickly he demolished a very generous helping. 'It's a win-win situation and you... I mean, *Upscale Dining* will get exclusive coverage.'

'It is an area of Spain that I've never visited,' I reply casually. My head is screaming *hell yes*, but the final decision isn't mine.

'But do you think you can sell the idea to Thomas?' Rick asks, mirroring my own thoughts.

'Maybe.' As I load the dishwasher I'm trying to evaluate potential stumbling blocks and it all comes down to budget really. Thomas is desperate for fresh new ideas, though, so the timing might swing it in our favour. Especially given that Thomas himself was thinking along the lines of a feature entitled *A Foodie Abroad*. 'It's certainly an interesting proposition.'

'Well, that had a positive ring to it. I'll pull up an aerial shot of the monastery on the iPad to give you a general idea of the surrounding area. Your glass is empty, by the way,' Rick flashes me an engaging smile. 'Perhaps you should bring another bottle back with you.'

* * *

When eventually I check my watch, I'm shocked. 'It's gone eleven. My goodness, I didn't realise it was that late.'

'Sorry, Lainey. You've been here for hours and that's my fault entirely, but I've really appreciated your help and the company. I'm more than happy to pay for a taxi to take you home.'

How can I possibly leave him like this? While it seemed like a good idea to relax him, after three glasses of wine, Rick's next attempt to get to the bathroom on crutches is so unsuccessful he has no other option than to lean heavily on my shoulder as I lead him out into the hallway. I'm pretty sure it's as much down to the sense of exhaustion that has suddenly overcome him, as it is the effects of the alcohol on his system. After a little wait, he reappears looking flushed and apologetic.

'What if you fall over on your way to the bathroom, or something? Your mum left because she was labouring under the impression that I'd be here if a problem arose.'

'Despite what my mum said, I didn't actually tell her you were going to stay overnight, she just made the assumption. So please don't feel obliged in any way. The problem is mine, not yours. Barring any overnight incidents, I hope to be able to put that boot on tomorrow and get a ride to work.'

Oh, this is so awkward. If Rick was a friend, there's no way I'd leave him alone with no one to call on in an emergency.

'Although I do have a perfectly good guest bedroom,' he continues. 'It's the last door at the other end of hallway, if you want to check it out. I'm conscious that it has been a long and tiring day for you, too. The en suite next to it only has a shower, I'm afraid. And, um, in the bottom drawer of the dresser you'll find some new T-shirts. The sizes are on the packets. They're left over from the launch of the restaurant. We were giving them away to customers on the first night. That's if you don't mind looking like a walking advertisement.' It's great to see Rick's amusement and, if I'm not mistaken, relief. I don't think he wants to be alone and we both know he's going to need a hand to get him into the bedroom. But first I think a strong coffee might be a good idea.

Besides, I need to keep him sweet because I think Thomas is going to be well impressed when I sit down and run Rick's proposal past him. So, this is the least I can do in return. Isn't it?

5

A DONE DEAL

'This is a surprise. Nine o'clock on a Monday morning when you're supposed to be at home drawing up plans for your spring feature. Should I be worried?'

Thomas gives me a fixed look of his, the one that implies he doesn't like surprises. Particularly if it's going to upset his plans.

I drop down onto the chair in front of his desk and watch as he scans my face. I've thought of little else since leaving Rick's flat early on Saturday morning and I'm convinced this is going to be perfect for the magazine. And, I will admit, I am flattered that Rick reached out to me, when he could so easily have approached someone elsewhere. When I asked that very question, he said that we had a natural rapport and that's something I can't dispute.

'I come bearing good news and I wanted to deliver it in person,' I reply.

Thomas purses his lips as he settles back, a wary look on his face. 'This is going to blow the budget then, is it?'

'You get what you pay for, and please don't start spinning in that chair of yours,' I warn him. 'It'll interrupt my flow and I might end up missing something out.'

He has already begun to shuffle his feet to the side and he immediately sits upright, planting both feet firmly on the floor. 'I'm listening.'

'You wanted something different. Something we can link into the holiday season and Rick Oliver has made us an interesting offer.'

'I thought your meeting on Friday was just an informal chat to bounce around a few ideas about Aleatory's anniversary?' Thomas remarks and I keep a deadpan face. He wouldn't believe me if I told him what actually happened.

'It was very informal, but there was only one idea on the table. A Spanish film company have approached Rick to hold a series of masterclasses with a group of newly trained chefs. Each will then cook their own version of the dishes he demonstrates, reflecting elements of their own country's flavours, styles and traditions.'

Thomas shrugs his shoulders. 'That's wonderful for him, but where do we come into it?'

'The filming will take place in a well-known monastery in Andalucía which dates back to the fifteen-hundreds, but it will only be televised in Spain. Rick will agree to do it if he can get some publicity for it at the same time over here.'

'We don't run ads, Lainey. Well, not for free.'

I look Thomas in the eye with a determined stare. 'He'll sign the contract if, and I say *if*, *Upscale Dining* are given exclusive permission to cover the entire event, which is spread out over four weeks. We take some still shots of the contestants and publish the recipes, with photos, for each of the masterclass dishes Rick creates. We also get to feature the winner and share a little of their own culinary journey.' It's hard to contain my excitement, but as a professional I can't let my personal feelings show.

Thomas frowns as he begins to mull over the idea. 'We?'

'Myself and a photographer from the magazine, naturally.'

'That's a big ask, Lainey, and you know it.'

'Imagine the Andalucían sunshine,' I say, softly. 'Fabulous food, wonderful location, a UK chef who is making his mark, and seven rising stars hand-picked from among Europe's most promising, newly qualified chefs. If you are looking for something to boost sales this has to be it!' Maybe I said that with a little too much gusto and I'm a little cross with myself. But it's obvious I want to do this, and Thomas is no fool.

His left eyebrow shoots up. 'And you get to spend the best part of a month eating and sunbathing.'

I give him my best impression of a hurt look. 'It's going to be hard work. But what a coup for the magazine.' You nailed that, Lainey, it sounded cool and professional.

'And what about Ant?'

'I wanted to gauge your reaction first before I run it past him.'

'This might not be right for him.'

'I know and I've already thought about that. If he feels it's too big an ask to be away from the family, we could employ a local photographer? That would help to keep costs down and Rick says there will be an interpreter on hand, so the language barrier shouldn't be a problem.'

Thomas leans forward, drumming his fingers on the desk while he thinks about what I've said. 'And we get it in writing from the production company. The permission, and the exclusivity I mean?'

'Yes. And Rick will also get the UK angle written into the contract.' Or rather, Cathy will insist it's written in.

'Okay,' he replies, finally allowing a hint of a smile to grace his face. 'Go for it, and well done you. That'll be a strong feature to run this summer, and exclusives are always great for sales. When does filming begin?'

'At the start of June. The competition is being televised in July.' He'd be a fool to turn this down and we both know that, but as the reality begins to dawn on me that this is really going to happen, I'm so happy I could hug him.

'Okay. We split it over two months, August and September editions. Let's aim for two six-page spreads. Do you think that's achievable? It would be a tight deadline to meet the cut-off point for the August edition. If it was anyone else but you, I probably wouldn't take the risk and do one spread in September. But we need to get what we can out of it.'

'I know and I appreciate that, but I have everything mapped out. The first article will be taken up with the intros to Rick and the contestants, which I can write up in advance, and the first week of the competition. I can get the copy, together with the photos of all those wonderful dishes, loaded as a priority as soon as filming finishes. For the September feature, I will focus on the setting, with photos of the monastery itself, and filming over the following three weeks. I'll finish with a short piece about the winner. Trust me, I can make it work.'

Thomas raises his eyebrows heavenwards. 'It's not a project for the faint-hearted, but if you say you can do it, then I guess you can.'

'Oh, and I want Rick to feature on the cover of the August edition.'

'You're a tough negotiator, Lainey. That's a big ask considering what could go wrong. What if you don't make the deadline and we have to use a back-up piece? It's not so easy to change a cover last-minute.'

'But you'll have a reserve lined-up. I know how you work.'

'Done. Don't disappoint me. And go easy on the expense account.'

'I will, boss. Oh, and if you ring Aleatory, Rick assures me they will be delighted to rearrange your booking so you can wine and dine your wife on her actual birthday.'

Thomas's smile stretches from ear to ear. 'You've just rescued me, big time. I'm already in trouble with Viv for forgetting the anniversary of the day we met. I mean, who remembers these things? It's bad enough remembering the birthdays and actual wedding anniversaries.'

I shake my head at him, sadly. 'It's the day fate smiled on you, Thomas, and gave you the woman of your dreams. Surely, that a big one to celebrate!'

He puts his head back and laughs. 'When you put it like that, I can't argue, can I! But then, I'm good at choosing the right people. I think I made the right decision hiring you, even though you weren't the most experienced candidate who came forward.'

I squint at him, slightly confused. 'Because I'm not afraid to disagree with you?'

'Well, that too, but that's not what I meant. I've been impressed with your creativity and instincts. In fact, I've had approval to create a new post as a trial for twelve months. It would mean you would go up a pay grade and also have a new title: special features correspondent. If it works out and the post is made permanent, we'd have to advertise it internally, of course, and there is no guarantee you'd get to stay in the role, but ideas like this one you're bringing to me are going to set up your CV nicely. There's no one else on the team at present who could step into this role and hit the ground running, so you're the natural choice. What do you think? Are you up for the challenge?'

This opportunity has come out of nowhere and for the briefest of moments I'm speechless. As it sinks in, it's a fight not to jump up and punch the air with excitement. 'It sounds good. I'd love to give it a go,' I reply, ever so coolly.

Thomas has a satisfied look on his face, knowing full well he's made my day. 'Now, get back to thinking about the spring feature. I don't want you daydreaming about summer sunshine just yet. I'll tell HR you've accepted and announce it at our next team meeting. Until then, keep it under your hat. You've worked hard, Lainey, and you deserve this step-up.'

It would be a lie to say there isn't a bit of a swagger in my walk as I leave Thomas's office. Rick's proposition is too good to turn down and I had realised that the moment he laid it all out to me, but, deep down inside, my heart is warning me to get my feelings firmly under control. This is just business, but it doesn't hurt to expand my horizons and, who knows, the man of my dreams may be waiting for me in Andalucía.

* * *

'Four weeks?' Ant's smile fades as I tell him about the new project. I can see the disappointment etched on his face.

'I know it's a long time to be away from home, Ant.'

He groans. 'Why does something like this come up now? This parenthood lark isn't easy, and I promised Hayley at the start I'd be hands-on. It's not just the fact that neither of us are getting much rest, but every day I see little changes in Ellie. This is going to be a tough decision and I can't make it on my own.'

'I understand you don't want to miss those precious moments you'll never get again and I'm sorry to spring this on you.'

After miscarrying their first baby at six months, it took Ant's wife another two years to get pregnant again. An experience like that changes everything and, emotionally, it's been tough for them. I can see his inner turmoil, as this is an assignment he would normally have jumped at.

'I could fly back each weekend, I suppose. Hayley's mum could come and stay to help out during the week.'

It would be wrong of me to try to influence him either way, even though the thought of working with a photographer I don't know is daunting. There won't be time for mistakes, or retakes, and with Ant I can leave him to do his thing. I've come to realise that Thomas hand-picks his staff and, once you've proved yourself, he's happy to give you free rein, but it's always on the understanding that you deliver what you promise. 'I don't need an answer right now. Take some time to talk it through with Hayley and then let me know.'

'Will do, and thanks, Lainey. Normally it would be a resounding yes from me, you know that. I'm glad for you, though, as this will strengthen your position here.'

'You've heard the rumours, too? I've been privy to a few comments from the usual people who like to stand around gossiping, but I never join in.'

'At the moment it's merely speculation, but whenever there are changes at the top of the tree there's always a bright spark who decides the old structure can be improved upon. In the last restructuring some departments were pared down and others expanded. They use the term "in line with the company's future operating requirements" but we didn't lose any posts. Has Thomas said anything to you?'

I shake my head. 'Not directly, but he told me that he wants to shake things up a bit. If there is a storm brewing, I wonder if he's trying to get ahead of the game.'

Ant nods, in agreement. 'He's a good boss. Guess our next monthly meeting is going to be a heavy one, then.'

I don't have the heart to share my other good news, given Ant's sombre mood. And if changes are coming, then why is Thomas so keen to force through this temporary promotion for me? Unless it's to show that he's being proactive and he sees this golden opportunity with Rick as a springboard. Enhancing my role sends out a message that this is only the beginning. On the other hand, this could be a move on Thomas's part to get me out of the firing line. I'm the one with the least amount of time served and, therefore, vulnerable if they start cutting posts. Either way, the pressure is really on, given how heavily Thomas has come to rely on me. It's frustrating not knowing what's really going on and it's going to be a case of waiting to see what happens. It's unsettling, though, for sure.

* * *

'Dad, your office needs a good tidy.'

There are piles of stuff everywhere. Neat piles, admittedly.

'It's my filing system,' he retorts, shrugging off my comment.

'Then you need a bigger space in which to work.'

'Funny you should say that, but I was thinking about turning the sitting room into my study.'

I shake my head, sadly. 'Seriously? You're supposed to work to live, not live to work. When was the last time you invited someone back here?' It breaks my heart to think of Dad hiding away as if he did something wrong when that wasn't the case. He did the honourable thing, the right thing, and was ostracised for it.

He peers at me across the desk. 'I could level the same question at you.'

'That's different. I get out and about talking to people all the time and I'm in the office at least once, or often twice, a week.'

'I'm always interacting with people. You know how much research I do.'

'Video calls are different. I mean when did you last go out for a pint, or a leisurely meal. Or to the cinema. The things you used to do all the time. You were such a social animal, Dad, always meeting up with your friends.' My heart sinks. I've unwittingly said the wrong thing.

'Well, those are friends I no longer want in my life. Even the ones who didn't turn their backs on me kept very quiet. I'm surviving and I don't want you worrying about me, Lainey. Mrs Mullins fills me in on what's happening out there in the big, wide world, when she comes in to clean.'

That makes me laugh. Dad's housekeeper is like a whirlwind and never stops chatting. If there's gossip going around, Mrs Mullins will know the full story, from start to finish. 'You need something, someone... to make you step away from your desk. Don't pretend you don't know what I'm talking about. Get your coat and let's go out for a bite to eat.'

Dad sucks in a deep breath. 'You aren't going to give up, are you? Okay. Give me five minutes to spruce myself up. But don't touch a single thing. It might look random, but it's all in a set order. And Mrs Mullins carefully dusts around everything, so stop nagging me.'

There is a bit of a spring in his step as he exits the room and although he won't acknowledge it, I didn't have to badger him into saying yes. We both know he's ready to stretch his wings again, but the problem is that he doesn't know how.

Wandering around what was formerly the dining room, it now has the feel of an old library. The main wall is covered in shelves heaving with books, and there are boxes on one side of the room full of research documents going way back to a time when the paper trail was all important. But what Dad needs in his life now is people, not boxes he'll probably never dip into again.

My phone pings and it's a text from Ant.

Count me in. Hayley says it's too good an opportunity to pass up.
That's love for you! 😊

I feel like punching the air.

Turning around, I glance down at Dad's desk and reach out to
pick up a framed photograph I haven't noticed before. It's a family
photo of Dad, Mum and me, taken over twenty years ago. I
wonder where he found it because it wasn't here the last time I
visited. I must have been about four, or five, at the time. The
image brings a lump to my throat as I place it back down. Next to
it is a stack of A4 sheets and I assume it's the current work-in-
progress.

Slipping into Dad's seat, I begin reading.

Into the Darkness
by D. I. Chamberlain
Chapter One
When everything you have is based on a lie, there is only
one way forward. Amassing a fortune changed everything
for Philip Hargreaves and, in the process, he ended up
selling his soul to the devil. One man's greed, his thirst for
power and total lack of conscience was now threatening to
take the world into a very dark place indeed. A place
where your thoughts would no longer be your own—

'I'm just putting on my shoes, Lainey. Are you ready?' Dad
calls out from the hallway.

I try to shake off the chill that has hit my stomach like a physical blow as I read the words. Is this just fiction, I wonder, or is
Dad continuing his crusade? Is this the real reason he still shuns
people? Is his obsession with getting people to open their eyes
beginning to suck all the joy out of his life?

'I'm coming,' I reply.

Seeing him with his hair gelled and smelling a squirt of after-shave as I walk past him to grab my coat makes me smile. This is more like the dad I had before our lives were turned upside down. The one who saw a sunny day as a bonus and dragged us outside for a family barbecue. These days, I doubt he even notices what goes on outside his study window.

'Are you in the mood for pizza?' I ask.

'Why not? Do you have somewhere in mind?'

I stare at him, wide-eyed. 'Dad, how long is it since you ventured out?'

'Oh, places come and go all the time. There used to be a good wood-fired pizza place on Howard Street.'

'Yeah, how many years ago?'

'Cheeky. Right, come on then. So, what's new at *Upscale Dining* these days?'

It's wonderful to step outside and link arms as we walk, something we haven't done in a long time. It's freezing but invigorating, and I feel sure that this was so the right thing to do.

'Well, there are rumours about a restructuring.'

'That sounds like trouble. Will your job be safe?'

'I think so. I'm moving into a temporary post which runs for a year,' I explain.

'Is that wise when things are shifting?'

'Yes, I think it's the right thing to do. It's also a promotion and the bit of extra money couldn't have come at a better time. My lease is up next month and the landlord is pressing me for a decision. You have no idea how good it will be to say bye-bye to my neighbour from hell.'

'The noise is still bad, then?'

I nod. 'There's little soundproofing between the floors and, aside from the parties, she has her TV on until late, with the surround sound blasting out. I wear earplugs when I go to bed.'

'Sorry to hear that, but I'm happy the job is working out for you, Lainey. This was definitely a step in the right direction for you.'

'Oh, and I'm off to Andalucía in June to cover a cookery competition that's being televised in Spain.'

'My goodness, well done you! How long will you be away?'

'Four weeks. The timing is unfortunate as I had two weeks' break booked bang slap in the middle of it.' Conscious that my holiday plans always change last-minute and then I end up taking odd days here and there, which is a waste, I finally made a firm commitment. Well, that was the original intention before Rick put forward his proposal and threw me off track. That seems to be the story of my life.

'What a shame. But at least you'll be able to enjoy the wonderful sunshine.'

'It wasn't a holiday I was planning, though, I promised to lend someone a hand. I haven't broken the news to them yet and I feel horrible, as they are counting on me and I don't know what to do about it.' If I say straight out that it's Mum, Dad will just switch off.

'That's unfortunate but given the circumstances I'm sure they will understand.'

As we turn into Howard Street, Dad turns to look at me, smiling.

'There you go, it's still in business! Best pizza ever, I promise. So, when will you break the bad news?'

'I'm going to phone Mum tonight and tell her.'

Dad's face falls. 'Oh. Right. She's still running the cookery classes, then?'

'Yes. After a bit of a quiet period, bookings came flooding in for the two, week-long courses Mum is running in June. Normally, she has a helper – a semi-retired languages teacher who moved there from Surrey a few years ago – but he'll be away on a walking holiday. When Mum asked if I could lend a hand, I knew she was desperate. She's all out of options apparently, as the other people she relies upon to help out speak little, if any, English. That's fine when it comes to changing beds and weeding the garden, but she needs a second in command who isn't going to struggle to understand her mainly British guests. But that was before this opportunity came up at work for me.'

Dad looks at me, raising his eyebrows as he swings open the door to the pizzeria. 'Rotten timing, for sure.'

I have about an hour to try to work a miracle and I know the best place to start is with a good meal. Doesn't everything look and feel better on a full stomach? It might be wishful thinking, but Dad already looks a bit perkier. It could be the chill in the air and the walk, of course, but it's cosy and warm in here, and the smell is great. Reminding him there is life outside of his own four walls might be just the thing to put some balance back into his life and to get him to do me a favour. It would mean helping Mum, and me, out, which isn't asking too much, is it?

2019

APRIL

'How are you feeling today?'

It's Thomas and he sounds a tad subdued.

'Better. Not quite so achy, and the cracking headache has finally lifted. I'm over the worst of it and hope to get back to work online tomorrow.'

After having to fight to extend my old lease one month at a time, finally being able to move into the new place and coming down with flu the day after was a total nightmare. I think my body is sending a clear message that I've been overdoing it.

'Did Viv enjoy Aleatory's second birthday party? I'm livid I couldn't be there, but running a raging temperature isn't the prettiest of sights and I didn't want to spread my germs around.'

'It was... ah, great. The food was brilliant, and you wouldn't believe how many big names were there from the music and film business. Dario tells me that it's trending on Twitter this morning, but the photos popping up are focusing on a few familiar faces. The usual: who was there and with whom. I passed on your apologies and Rick said to get well soon and take it easy. With five weeks to go until you fly out to Spain, it's better you get this bug now rather than later. Your first week in Andalucía is going to be full-on.'

'You paused for a second there, Thomas.'

'Did I?' Now he sounds guilty.

'You did. What aren't you telling me?'

He clears his throat, another sign that he's uneasy. 'An argument broke out between Rick and Cathy. The restaurant was crowded, fortunately, and it was quite noisy, anyway.'

'Seriously?'

'I was at the buffet table when it kicked off, so right next to the action. As I turned around, I briefly caught sight of Rick's face as someone grabbed his arm and he looked furious. I've seen chefs kick off before, but never like that. Fortunately, two people came over and bundled them both off out of sight. I think one of them was Cathy's agent, the other was a waiter. If it had all played out in front of everyone it could have been a total PR disaster. And, um, I owe you an apology. You did say it was a fiery relationship and that their personal lives might affect the way the business is being run.'

Is Thomas regretting letting me strip everything out of the original article I wrote, aside from the briefest mention of Rick and Cathy's partnership? On reflection, it was Rick who talked me into that though, Thomas only wanted me to ease back when describing Cathy's hands-on approach.

'Your gut instincts are good, Lainey. But it's probably best you know what happened, given that you're going to be spending a fair bit of time in Rick's company.'

'Appreciated, Thomas. I'll tread warily. I hope things aren't deteriorating between them as that wouldn't bode well for the restaurant. The timing of this trip for Rick might be spot on if they need a little time apart. I know he's hoping to get a visit from one of the Michelin inspectors and Cathy was worried about

Rick's absence, but Pierre Verbier is a good sous chef and he knows Rick's standards by now.'

'You might be right, there. But if you discover what's behind this tension, let me know, just out of curiosity of course.'

Hmm, that's interesting. Is Thomas sensing there's a story here? I hope it isn't the demise of a promising business if Cathy suddenly pulls out and leaves Rick with no financial backing.

Immediately after he rings off, I search for Neil's number. Admittedly, he gave it to me in case there was anything he could help with when I was writing the article, but if there's one person who really knows what's going on, it's him.

'Hi, Neil, it's Lainey.'

'You sound full of cold. Ah, that's why you missed the party. I did wonder. Oh, and what a night that turned out to be,' he groans. 'I can't talk right now as I'm working both shifts today and it's hectic. I'll phone you tomorrow if that's all right? There are a couple of things I want to share with you, things I couldn't mention the first time we spoke. Anyway, speak later.'

Suddenly my feverish head is as clear as a bell. What happens if I unwittingly discover the real story behind Rick and Cathy's troubled romance? A story like that wouldn't be right for *Upscale Dining*, but as a part of a group we have close links to a lifestyle magazine which would do anything to uncover a scandal at the heart of their celebrity love affair. A tip like that would put Thomas in a very strong position with the people at the top. My heart sinks a little at the thought. I wouldn't relish getting caught in the middle of it, but for my own sake, it would be worth knowing if things are going to fall apart. What on earth would I conjure up at short notice if the trip to Spain doesn't go ahead?

Calm down, Lainey, I tell myself. *Arming yourself with information as you are about to spend a lot of time in Rick Oliver's company is one thing, investigative journalism is another. No one can force you to share anything told to you in confidence.* As Dad says, stick to the remit – stick to the food.

* * *

'Lainey, my lovely, I didn't know you were poorly.'

Mum's face stares back at me from the screen and I realise my red nose is giving me away, although at least I no longer have a pink hue about me. And I'm dressed for the first time in four days.

'Thanks, but I'm much better now.'

'And counting down to your big adventure no doubt. The sunshine will do you the world of good.'

When Dad said he was prepared to step in for me and help Mum out, I decided that wasn't a piece of news I could deliver unless it was face to face. And yes, maybe I could have found a friend who would have been willing to cover for me in exchange for two weeks' free food and accommodation in a picturesque farmhouse in France – after all, it sounds like great fun – but my instincts were telling me that my parents weren't in touch because it was hard to reconnect. They still asked about each other from time to time and that left me wondering. I felt it was worth at least giving them the opportunity and Dad's generous offer was a starting point. Since then, Mum and I have been video-chatting once a week. She was hesitant about Dad's offer at first, as they hadn't spoken in a long time, and I didn't push it. But, having exhausted all other options, Mum had little choice in the end. It took me a couple of weeks of gentle encouragement to get them talking, but now they at least have a semi-regular dialogue going.

'At least I'll be back to normal by the time I fly out and I can't wait!' I enthuse.

'I'm thrilled for you, lovely. You work really hard and I'm so proud of you.'

'Thanks, Mum. If I can't cook like you, at least you taught me that flavour is everything. Not many kids grow up able to run out into the garden to pick a handful of fresh herbs and then get to savour them in a meal an hour later. You were the one who turned me into a foodie, you know that.'

'I guess I did,' she replies. I can see the pride reflected in her eyes and with each call we're gradually slipping back into a more comfortable relationship again.

'And Dad is still keeping in touch?'

Her smile is merely a twitch around the edges of her lips. 'Surprisingly, yes. You were right to be worried about him, but he's beginning to open up and relax a little. I reassured him that all I need is a second person to be in the room while I'm demonstrating. Just to make sure the attendees have everything they need, to allow me to focus without having to worry about our guests. I told him to think of it as a holiday and the perk is that he'll get to taste some wonderful dishes. Maybe not restaurant quality, but hearty food. I've found that there's a lot of laughter and general camaraderie when people attend these courses. It will do him good to lighten up a little.' I look at Mum, trying not to make a face as she continues. 'Yes, I've read one of his books and he's still trying to save the world.'

'That's what worries me, but I suppose someone has to speak up, Mum.'

'I understand that, Lainey, and I admire his strength and courage. I'm sure you do, too. But if the world ended tomorrow, my last day would leave me with a smile on my face. I've talked to my lovely daughter and I've just spent an hour teaching three teenagers how to prepare a healthy meal. My trainees didn't spend that time worrying about the multitude of things they can't influence. And if the world doesn't end tomorrow, then at least I've shared something that will benefit other people. Can your dad say the same, I wonder, or is he butting his head up against a brick wall, time and time again?'

I feel disloyal agreeing with her. Shouldn't we all constantly battle against what is wrong and stand up for what is right? But how do you achieve that and still manage to live a normal and happy life? 'Maybe some people are born to be warriors, Mum.'

'Well, if he does turn up at my door, as he's promised, then I'll be doing my best to encourage him to relax, have some fun and enjoy the simple things in life. I don't see that as wrong or selfish, Lainey. I see that as the gift that life gives us. Even when times are hard, nature is there to remind us that beauty is all around if we choose to see it. And so is goodness.'

Mum always seems to make sense of things in a way that's easy to understand and hard to dispute.

'Grandma Rose always quoted the Serenity Prayer. *Give us grace to accept the things that cannot be changed and the courage to change the things which should be changed.* It's not always that easy to know which is which, though, is it?' I reply.

Mum reaches out to touch the screen, placing her hand flat against it and I do the same. 'But the important bit came next, my lovely. *Living one day at a time, enjoying one moment at a time, accepting hardship as a pathway to peace.* Your dad deserves happiness and peace, too.'

A weary frown begins to settle on my brow. Will he ever be able to look at it that way?

'At least Dad will be around to help out, Mum, so I don't feel quite so bad. And I'll be thinking of you and wishing I were there.'

'I know. I think it's his peace offering. I just hope he gains something in return. Other than a few companionable meals, with produce fresh from the garden. I won't pressure him in any way, I promise. He's his own man and I have accepted that now. And so must you. Stop worrying about us and get yourself well so that you can enjoy your own adventure.'

'I will. I'm sure it's going to be a wonderful experience.'

As I peel my hand away from the screen, Mum blows me a kiss and I pretend to catch it. She hasn't done that since I was six years old.

'And I will make it over for a visit before the autumn, I promise.' I don't care what crops up, next time nothing is going to stop me from heading to France. It's time to heal the rift between us and I'm more than ready.

* * *

'Lainey, it's Neil.'

'Oh, thanks for getting back to me, Neil. How are you doing?'

'Good, thanks.'

'You're still working all the shifts you can get at the restaurant then.'

'Yes. My brother and I are probably only six months away from having enough in the bank to start up our little business. We're finally getting there, and our parents have said they want to invest in us, too. It means a lot, but it's scary. We don't intend letting them down and whenever we have any spare time we're working out of a small unit, producing some display items.'

Neil and his brother have a passion for working with wood and dream of making bespoke furniture. It sounds unlikely, given that Neil's a waiter and his brother drives a London taxi, but when we went for a drink together, he showed me photos of some of their pieces. They certainly know what they're doing and I was impressed by what I saw.

'You're hanging in there, then?'

'Just.'

I let out the loudest, explosive sneeze and start laughing. 'Sorry about that, it came out of nowhere. This cold sounds worse than it is though now, I'm much better tonight. Anyway, things aren't good at Aleatory?'

'Things are certainly up and down,' he reveals.

'Oh, I'm sorry to hear that.'

'Seriously, I don't know why someone as talented as Rick Oliver would put up with the constant bullying. Cathy won't listen to anyone and meanwhile her agent trails around behind her, trying to smooth the waters after she stirs everything up.'

Neil doesn't sound jaded, he sounds angry.

'It's that bad?'

'Well, it is when she's around. Fortunately, she's not there all the time. But she arrives unannounced and chaos ensues. She not only criticises the menu, but the way the food is presented. I've been on the end of a tongue-lashing from her and it's not pleasant.'

'What did you do that was so bad?' I find it hard to believe he could put a foot wrong, as Neil always has such a welcoming persona, and nothing is too much trouble.

'One of the diners complained that I took someone's order ahead of theirs. I did because the policy is that we attend to people in strict rotation. First come, first served.'

'It's not right to pander to someone just because they don't want to wait their turn,' I observe.

He grunts. 'No, but when it's one of her friends, the rules don't count apparently. She says high-profile people are good for business. Admittedly, the customer in question was a big name in the music business, but, quite frankly, he's obnoxious. The staff are sick of people turning up without a reservation, thinking they'll get a table if they drop Cathy's name. It puts Rick on the spot, because we're working flat out and, suddenly, we have to conjure up another table. It's crazy when she knows how far in advance people have to book to get a reservation.'

It seems that Cathy is causing problems even when she isn't on the premises.

'What happened at the party?'

'Oh, that was a total nightmare. Seriously, it was diva time and three-quarters of the people there were her personal invitees. At one point, she was talking to Rick and, from what I can gather, her phone rang. I had my back to them at the time, but I span around when I heard the commotion. Rick looked seriously angry and I saw Cathy lash out at him and she literally pushed him over. I bent down to help him up as it looked like his ankle had given out again. By then Cathy's agent was dragging her off in the direction of the kitchen, physically restraining her. Two of us managed to get Rick back up onto his feet, but he needed help walking as he was limping. The kerfuffle was over in seconds and only a couple of people closest to them saw Rick on the floor. Luckily the restaurant was packed solid, so they probably thought he'd tripped over. But it was a close call.'

'What caused the fight?'

'This is strictly in confidence, Lainey. Cathy would sack me on the spot if she knew I was repeating this, but I guess I have the least to lose of anyone who works there. The row continued out back and seems to be about her friendship with Zane. He's not a good influence on her and Rick knows that. It's not just jealousy I don't think, but sometimes when Cathy and her little group pile into the restaurant at the end of the evening, they're high on something, that's for sure. Rick doesn't know how to handle it. Cathy's always sorry afterwards, but if her friends need to let off steam, she shouldn't be bringing them to Aleatory.'

Poor Rick.

'Six months and I'm out of there. But it's hard to watch, Lainey. And if something doesn't change, one of these days it'll be headline fodder. Pierre can't stand her. Fortunately, she's doing a few gigs in North America, so we're hoping she won't be around much when Rick's away. To be honest, if that weren't the case, I think Rick would have found himself without a sous chef. Pierre could get a job anywhere and he has no intention of putting himself in the firing line for four whole weeks.'

I'm shocked. It's even worse than I thought and yet Thomas came away from the party thinking it was Rick's fault. 'What an awful situation for everyone involved. It can't make working there easy.'

'Everything is fine when she's not around, but when she breezes in, we're all on edge. The reason I'm taking a huge risk and telling you this is that you're on this shoot with Rick. It's hard to stand by and see what's happening and I'm not just a lone voice, we all feel the same. It's not our place to speak out, although Pierre has tried. You seem to get on well with Rick and... maybe if he starts talking about it, then at least you know the truth about what's going on behind the scenes. It's a disaster waiting to happen, Lainey.'

I do believe those were the exact words I said to Thomas after the first interview I did at Aleatory. 'It's a delicate situation, there's no doubt about that. Thanks, Neil, and what you've told me will go no further. I'm not sure the working relationship I have with Rick would ever mean that our conversation would stray in that direction, but if it does, then from the little I've witnessed and from what you've just told me, it's enough for me to maybe pose a few questions. It might help to make him stop and think, I suppose, and perhaps see it from a different perspective.'

'And I didn't say this, either. Several of us believe the Michelin inspector has already been and, thankfully, it was a day when Cathy wasn't around. We could be wrong. They might even send in a decoy ahead of an inspector's visit, who knows? But I wasn't the only one who had a strong feeling that we had a man who was sitting back and observing the smallest of details. His eyes were everywhere and at one point his napkin dropped to the floor. I wondered whether it was a test. I was surreptitiously watching his every move, and I was right there.'

'What did you do?'

'I stepped forward, plucked it from the floor and immediately raised my hand in the air. Another waiter came hurrying across with a freshly laundered one, which I handed over with due reverence and my signature smile.'

I start laughing. 'You'll be missed when you move on, Neil. But you must follow your dream. And thank you, not just for alerting me in case I can help, but for having Rick's back. I'm sure he'd be touched by that.'

'It's the best I can do. Rick's been good to me, giving me extra shifts whenever he can. Especially when he's aware that I'll be heading off at some point. Anyway, I hope I get to see you at the restaurant before I leave. I expect to be long gone before the next Christmas Tasting party, though. Have a wonderful time in Spain. I hear it's being filmed in a monastery.'

'Yes. My bedroom is a former monk's cell.'

Now it's Neil's turn to laugh. 'Maybe that's just what Rick needs. A little solitude to break the hold Cathy has over him. He might come back a different person.'

The financial hold Cathy has over Rick doesn't help matters, I reflect. However, by the sound of it, the romance might be waning, and I wonder what sort of impact that will have on the business as times goes on.

JUNE

GOODBYE CLOUDS, HELLO SUNSHINE

It's Friday morning and I collapse down into the middle seat in the centre section of the plane heading for Seville airport, feeling that if life throws me one more curveball, then I'm going to turn into a tearful mess.

Come on, Lainey, woman up, I tell myself in no uncertain terms. *You've got this.*

But the truth is, I haven't got this at all. I was in the process of putting the last-minute items into my suitcase late yesterday when I received the bad news. Flying off to Spain this morning, I no longer have a photographer and filming begins on Monday.

It's not Ant's fault. Poor little Ellie broke out in spots a little over three weeks ago and the doctor confirmed it was chickenpox. What began as a few random eruptions turned into a severe case and she ended up plastered in them. They were on her scalp, the inside of her mouth and on the soles of her feet – it sounded horrendous. When Ant quizzed the doctor, he told him he'd be fine to travel at the beginning of June. Ant had it himself as a child, anyway. In the meantime, Ant's been working from home helping Hayley cope with a very poorly little patient. In between, he's been digging into the photo archives for *Upscale Dining's* autumn readers' bonus. We're giving away a free recipe booklet featuring the best-of-the-best winter-warming dishes the magazine has featured over the past couple of years. I've been wading through past recipes, choosing which ones to feature and everything seemed to be slotting into place quite nicely. That is, until my phone rang at 6 p.m. last night.

'You aren't going to believe this, Lainey. The doc has just confirmed that I've got shingles. The blisters are breaking out like corn popping in a microwave.'

'Oh Ant, that's awful! Shingles? Is that linked to Ellie's chickenpox?'

'Sort of, but being in contact with Ellie isn't why I've come down with it. Apparently, it doesn't work like that. Once you've already had chickenpox the virus stays in your body and can get activated at any time but presents as shingles. He thinks it's been triggered by stress in my case.'

'I can tell by your voice that you're suffering.'

'It's like having a bad case of the flu, accompanied by blisters that itch so much they are driving me crazy. But the pain is awful as it travels along the nerves. The rash is in my armpit, but the pain is radiating down my side.' He sounded totally miserable. 'I can't begin to explain how sorry I am to make this call at the eleventh hour. Especially after reassuring you I'd be fine for this trip. I've dropped you in it, Lainey, and I know it.'

I could hear in his voice how ill he was feeling and how guilty, and my heart went out to him. 'These things happen, Ant, it's no one's fault. Send Hayley and Ellie my love. By the time I get back, you'll all be fighting fit and we'll get together for a barbecue at my place. Please, just rest up and get well.'

The moment I put the phone down, I crumpled. The copy and the photos for the August edition need to be sent off in nine days' time. In my panic, I did the only thing I could think of and I reached out to Rick, but so far I've had no response to my email. All I need is a telephone number of a local contact in Palma del Río who speaks both English and Spanish. Rick told me there would be an interpreter on site, so I'm keeping my fingers crossed that he can put me in touch with him as soon as possible to help track down a photographer. Until I land, there is absolutely nothing else I can do. I promised Thomas I'd deliver, and I can't go back on that.

* * *

The driver pulls up in front of two enormous, dark wooden gates set in an impressive stone archway. The stonework above it is shaped like a bell, with a scroll carved into either side, supported by two solid pillars. Both gates are covered in metal studs, each set within a flat collar, and the overall impression is one of impenetrability. Curiously, a large, rusting metal chain hangs like a swag between the scrollwork at the top.

As the driver waits patiently for the gates to open, I look to my left and gaze out at the high, whitewashed stone walls. They are gracefully curved and, in places, covered in a dark-pink bougainvillea that drips down almost to the pavement. To the right, a long line of orange and lemon trees is visible above the wall, the pavement covered with a scattering of overly ripened fruit.

The car pulls into a shady parking space beneath the tall trees and, impatiently, I swing open the door and step out into the sunshine. As I do so, a falling lemon from one of the branches above my head drops with a bounce on the floor next to me, making me jump.

'Welcome to Hotel Monasterio de Córdoba,' Rick says, as he hurries towards me. 'That was a near-miss,' he laughs.

There is a fluttering sensation within my chest and I take a deep breath, shaking it off. 'It most certainly was,' I reply as he leans in to kiss my cheek. It takes me by surprise and, as I step back, I see that the driver has already taken my bags out of the boot.

'Lainey is in room number six, Alejandro, *muchas gracias*,' Rick informs him.

'*Si, número seis. Buenos tardes*, señorita Summers.'

'*Gracias*, Alejandro,' I reply. 'That was a very comfortable ride,' I add, hoping he understands my words. We barely spoke in the car, but when he flashes me a fleeting smile, he shrugs his shoulders apologetically. It's obvious he has no idea what I said, so I simply return his smile.

'Come on, let's head off to reception and get you signed in,' Rick says, turning on his heels. 'And I'll organise some coffee. How was the flight?'

'Good. I'm just a bit stressed right now, but this sunshine is like a soothing balm.'

'Well, one thing you get an awful lot of here is sunshine. And don't stress, we have a potential solution to your problem.' He glances at me, a smug look on his face and I can tell he's pleased to see me. It's been a while.

* * *

It's as if I've been transported into another world, and sitting here on a tiled patio in the shade of a covered walkway with Rick Oliver feels surreal.

'When did you arrive?' I ask, as we wait for someone to bring our coffees.

'Yesterday morning. I spent the afternoon with the producer and the team in their offices in Seville going through the filming schedule. I have a copy and I'll email it to you when I get back to my room. I've been tied up today with the crew assembling the kitchens ready for filming.'

It sounds like he hasn't stopped since he arrived, so I don't like to jump straight in and ask him outright about the photographer as that seems rude. 'I bet you can't wait to get started.'

Rick rubs his chin with his left hand, as if he's mulling it over, which surprises me. 'I'm a little anxious actually,' he replies. 'Mainly due to the heat, but on the days we're filming we'll begin quite early when it's cooler and the sessions will be finished by lunchtime. It's only twenty-five degrees Celsius today, but it could climb higher, into the thirties. Not a lot happens in the afternoons, here.'

A young woman approaches the table with a tray in her hands. She's wearing a smart black dress with a pristine white apron.

'Ah, Rosalia – this is Lainey Summers. Lainey, Rosalia is one of the few waiting staff here who speaks a little English. Fortunately, the menus are in several languages.'

'It helps, no? *Bienvenida*… ah, welcome, Lainey.'

'*Gracias*, Rosalia.'

She places the coffee cups in front of us and Rick gives her one of his dazzling smiles before she walks off. It's great to see him so relaxed, as whenever we've met up in the past it seems to have been at a time when things are going wrong. Maybe this break away from the restaurant is exactly what he needed.

'Our interpreter, Miguel Tejero, is going to be busy. The staff here are very accommodating, but without him it would be difficult, as only one of the film crew speaks English – well he is English, but he's fluent in Spanish as he lives here.'

'Can I get by on just a handful of words? *Please, thank you, good morning...* or am I in trouble?' I ask.

'I'm not much better off, but I'm sure we'll manage. Miguel was able to locate a local photographer based on a friend's recommendation. I have his card here for you, it's in Spanish of course. His website is on the back, so you can check him out. Miguel has arranged for him to come to the monastery at 8 p.m. tonight to talk to you. I hope that's okay?'

'Perfect, thank you, Rick.' Actually, it's a huge relief and I can finally sit back and begin to relax.

'Miguel is very knowledgeable about the monastery, too, so it might be worth picking his brains. I think you'll find him very obliging.'

Sounds like I'm in for a real treat and I can't wait to meet him.

'That's useful to know and I'm very grateful for the pointer. When do the contestants arrive?'

'Tomorrow. The restaurant is putting on a special buffet for us tomorrow night. You'll also get to meet the producer and the director of production.'

I've already had the contestants' bios and written up the introductions, waiting to slot in the headshots. Having made a start on the first article, everything now hinges on filming this week. There is a lot of space to fill and aside from my write-up, its success is reliant upon getting those perfect shots of exciting dishes that will send our readers scurrying off to recreate them at home. And, photos of our celebrity chef, of course, looking calm, enthused and handsome.

Handsome? I smile to myself. I meant, professional, of course.

'Thanks for sending everything across. I'm really excited to see what recipes you have in store for us and how the new chefs are going to interpret them. You're going to be a hard act to follow, Rick.'

His eyes sparkle as he looks across at me, before placing the empty coffee cup back down on the table. 'I'm hoping to walk away with a few fresh and innovative ideas inspired by the contestants. And maybe the name of someone I can entice over to the UK.'

'Really?' I wonder if Neil was right and Rick is aware that Pierre isn't happy.

'Cathy is talking about the possibility of setting up a second restaurant, outside of London. Assuming we get into the Michelin guide, of course.'

'Fingers crossed, then. How is Cathy?' It seems impolite not to enquire after her, I tell myself. It isn't that I'm... what? Looking for signs that the cracks are beginning to show, because that would be unfair of me.

'Good. She's touring and hasn't been around much. It's a hectic time for her.'

Whenever Rick talks about Cathy, there's no sense of... I don't know – closeness – or do I mean fondness? He always sounds so business-like. And I know for a fact that there's been no official announcement yet about their engagement, as Dario is keeping me up to date on the social media front for both Rick and Cathy. All in the line of work, naturally.

'Would you like me to show you around?' he asks.

'Appreciated, thanks. I hope there's a floorplan because the hotel is much bigger than I was expecting. Do the owners live here?'

'Yes. Our hosts, Víctor and Isabel Corberó, will put in a brief appearance at our little gathering tomorrow night, but they are flying off the day after tomorrow. They won't be around while we're filming but will be leaving us in the hands of their manager, Felipe Pascual. Let's head back to the car park, as it might help you to get your bearings.'

The building is a labyrinth of corridors and courtyards, but as we stand with our backs to those impressively tall gates, Rick gives me a quick overview.

'Through that arch in front of us is one of the inner courtyards. To the right, this building is separate to the hotel and is the owners' accommodation.'

We saunter over to the far end of the rectangular car park, which only has about a dozen spaces, nestled under the burgeoning fruit trees. It's such a delight to see full-size oranges and lemons weighing down the branches. Behind us a member of staff is sweeping the sandy floor, making little piles of general garden debris and fallen fruit.

Rick draws to a halt, pointing at a gated area. 'This leads to the private gardens, which are walled off.'

We peer through into a secluded square surrounded by bushes and a few fruit trees. Most of the trunks, I notice, have been painted white.

'Curious, isn't it?' Rick says, following my gaze. 'Apparently it's a form of protection against insects and sunscald. I didn't even know that was a thing.' Beyond the square, I can only catch a glimpse of a wall and a variety of trees towering above it. 'Okay, if we head back across the car park, I'll show you where tomorrow night's gathering will be held.'

As we walk past the private accommodation my eyes glance up and I spot a charming, Juliet balcony in front of a pair of French doors with a rustic wooden canopy sheltering it. I'm still adjusting to the heady smells around me, but the balcony itself is almost totally obscured by a glorious, pale pink bougainvillea snaking up from ground level. I stop, leaning in to smell a cluster of blossoms and their surprisingly subtle perfume. I'm curious because what I'm smelling, in amongst the citrussy notes from the orange and lemon trees, is a strong, heady scent.

'Wonderful, isn't it?' Rick turns to look at me. 'The scent is coming from the dark pink flowers over here.'

Trying my best to avoid an army of very insistent bees who are moving diligently from blossom to blossom, I tentatively poke my nose as close as I dare into the profusion of delicate flower heads and, my goodness, the smell is stronger than some of the perfumes I use.

Rick is laughing at me. 'Come on. The formal restaurant is down here, on the right, just past the archway opposite the gates, which takes you into another of the three inner courtyards.'

My head is buzzing as I try to take it all in. We walk on and the space narrows a little as we step between two stout palm trees whose fronds create a wonderful screen and a grand entrance to a glorious patioed garden beyond. The curved whitewashed wall continues to our left, but the line of fruit trees in front of it is intermittent here. However, the bougainvillea that has consumed much of the wall is running rampant through two of the trees in a riot of colour. There are some metal-framed couches with plump cushions and an array of smaller bistro tables and chairs, giving the garden an intimate feel, although it could accommodate sixty-plus people comfortably. The floor throughout has a sandy, almost gritty covering, which lends it that distinctive Mediterranean feel. In front of us is a bar with a dark wooden counter and tall chairs. Overhead, strings of lights weave back and forth between the trees on either side.

'The main restaurant is in there,' Rick says, pointing to some steps off to the right, flanked by a range of potted plants.

I see four tinted, glass-panelled doors, in front of which two staunch wooden doors with metal studs are pinned back. Everything about the monastery is solid and while it doesn't present as a fortress, it was clearly built to deter intruders.

'If we take the shortcut over there in the far corner, you'll recognise where you are as the reception is on the left. Before I show you up to your room, I thought you might like to check out the grounds, though.'

'Absolutely, thanks, Rick. This place is amazing. It's so atmospheric and much bigger than I was expecting.'

As we enter a wide corridor, it looks familiar, but there's no time to glance around as Rick is already striding off in the opposite direction. The vaulted ceilings of the covered walkways make them feel spacious and a series of arches and columns border the central patio on three sides. We continue straight ahead and in front of us a pair of ornate ironwork gates stand ajar. Beyond that is a vista of green.

Rick nudges the gates open wide and stands back as I step through. The backdrop is a mass of trees, a long line of firs on the far side marking the boundary. Directly in front of us is a flat area, edged with a low wall into which a small flight of stone steps leading up to a raised garden is set. It's a riot of a vibrant pinky-red colour, with potted geraniums sitting evenly spaced along the top of the whitewashed walls.

We climb the steps and walk along the narrow, gritty path that borders a formally laid-out cottage garden. The sections are bounded by low hedging to delineate each area. The beds are either square or rectangular in shape and are planted with cabbages, onions, lettuces and a whole host of different vegetables. The individual areas each have their own watering system, with pipes running between the straight rows of plants and leading back to an ornamental pool in the corner. It's the sort of kitchen garden that wouldn't look out of place in an English stately home.

'Now I understand why the competition is being held here,' I remark. 'My goodness, this must take some tending, but how wonderful to have so much fresh produce to hand.'

'Yes. It's incredible to think that the land once worked by monks is still being used to grow fresh food for the table.'

Rick leads us across a grassy area next to an impressively sized, elongated pool, which is partially hidden by a mass of towering trees.

'What are these?' I ask, as we walk between the boughs which hang down low over the grass.

I watch as Rick reaches out to pull the end of a small branch down to show me. Unfortunately, I find myself studying him more so than the mass of greenery in his hands. He's dressed casually in an open-necked, white linen shirt and a pair of navy cargo trousers. We're both equally as pale-skinned, I muse, as I move closer to inspect the greenery.

'These are carob trees. The pods are dried, roasted and then ground into a powder. The flavour is similar to cocoa but is a healthy alternative to chocolate, with the added advantage of having a pleasing, nutty flavour. Have you ever seen the pods before?' Rick pushes back a large cluster of leaves to show me what I can only describe as something akin to a blackening broad bean pod. 'The clusters of pods don't look very attractive as they take a year to ripen. But the trees are interesting, and the gnarled boughs extending out, some dipping almost to the floor, give a lot of shade.' He turns to me. 'You approve of the location?'

'I do. Ant would have loved this,' I reflect, turning around to gaze back at the monastery. The pristine white walls offset by muted, salmon-pink roof tiles are stark against the vibrant, and cloudless, blue sky. It's breathtakingly beautiful. 'Just thinking about the history of this place adds a sense of awe and mystery to the charm of it.'

Rick gives me one of his engaging smiles and as we head back, he points to the row of windows at first-floor level. 'Your room is... that one, I believe.'

'What a great view of the garden I'm going to have. I had no idea what to expect, but this is amazing.'

'And relaxing, isn't it?' As we're about to descend the steps, Rick stops for a moment and I turn to look at him.

I was just thinking the exact same thing. Suddenly, I feel that everything is going to be fine and yet I don't know that for a fact until I meet with the photographer. Normally, I'd be on edge with this much uncertainty, so I hope my sense of calm is an omen.

Rick's eyes don't move from my face, as if he's in a trance for a couple of seconds before he clears his throat, and the moment passes. Is he wishing that he was standing here with Cathy? 'Right, we have to head this way and when I get back to my room, I'll send the schedule across to you.'

I can sympathise with his attempts to focus. The monastery is totally captivating and it's hard to think about work when at every turn there's something beautiful to catch your eye. It's a place to visit with someone special by your side and yet here we are, two colleagues sharing an experience of a lifetime. I'm sure the novelty will wear off once I stop thinking like a tourist and get into work mode. Well, I hope so, because if not, I'm in serious trouble.

FEELING THE BUZZ

'Hi, Mum, how's it going?'

'Good. I've had some help here on site today to do a deep clean of the workstations in the kitchen block. With no last-minute cancellations still, it's looking promising for a full house.'

'When does Dad arrive?'

'Not until next Thursday. But that's fine. It's enough time for him to get settled in before it all kicks off a week on Saturday.'

I am a little disappointed as I had hoped he might want to lend a hand in the run-up to what is going to be two very intensive, back-to-back weeks. If he's doing this simply to please me, then that would be a shame in my opinion. The thought that it might be too late to rekindle the love that they had for each other breaks my heart. But at least they'll know for sure.

'Anyway, never mind us – how was the flight?'

'A little stressful. Ant has shingles, so I'm a photographer down.'

'Oh, poor Ant, and poor you! The panic is on then?' I can feel her disappointment on my behalf.

'It was a blow, I will admit, but I'm meeting with a local

photographer this evening. Keep everything crossed for me!' I laugh.

'You don't sound stressed,' Mum replies, questioningly.

'Oh, Mum, you simply can't imagine what it's like here. I thought a monastery would be austere and even a little formidable. It's anything but that. And my room, well, it was a monk's cell originally. It would have been spartan, with just a single bed and a desk back in the day. The monks spent hours in isolation, studying and praying in their rooms, but stark as it was back then, I guess it was home. Now, here I am, looking out over a swimming pool and with a king-sized bed, marvelling at how things have changed over the years. You'd love it because the garden is full of orchards – orange, lemon, lime and carob trees. The produce goes straight into the restaurant kitchen; it couldn't be fresher.'

'The sunshine will pick you up after that flu, too. Let me know how your meeting goes tonight. A text will do, but if this photographer turns out to be a suitable replacement for Ant, then I can relax. I can't believe he has shingles, I hear it's very painful.'

'I know. He felt so guilty, but he sounded awful, Mum. And he is in a lot of pain, apparently.'

'That little family has had a tough time of it lately. And the celebrated chef is there and raring to go?'

'Rick Oliver? Yes, he showed me around earlier on and tomorrow night there's a buffet where I'll get to meet the contestants and the people involved with the filming.'

'I can hear the excitement in your voice, lovely. I can't remember the last time you sounded so carefree.'

That stops me in my tracks. Mum is right and if my little bubble of happiness is that obvious, then I need to tone it down a bit. I'd be mortified if she realised that being around Rick is the reason for the lift in my spirits and not my surroundings.

'It's just work as usual, but the sunshine lifts everything doesn't it.'

'Perhaps we can video call once your dad is here? Just let us know when is best for you, as I know you'll be busy and rushed off your feet. But if you can text me before bedtime to let me know how it goes with that photographer, I'd be grateful.'

'Stop worrying, Mum. I brought a camera with me just in case. It's not the best solution, granted, as Ant makes it look easy and I know it isn't. But I have a good feeling it's all going to be fine.'

Mum starts laughing. 'You've been there, what, a couple of hours? Already you're into that ethos... what's the term Spanish people use?' A few seconds elapse and I'm at a total loss to fill in the blank. 'Got it! *Mañana!*'

'Tomorrow?' I query, thinking back and wondering whether Mum spent any time over here in her youth. I know she went backpacking for a while before she met Dad.

'Literally, yes, but the sentiment is that most things can wait a while. Spanish people can be as relaxed as they are passionate about a healthier, more fun style of living. I admire a people who have such a rich and varied cuisine. It's because of all that sunshine. Vitamin D boosts the immune system and helps to ward off depression, for starters.'

'Hmm. Well, I'm certainly glad that I brought an extra-large bottle of sunscreen with me,' I declare, pointedly.

Mum sighs. 'I'm not suggesting you should lay out on a sunbed for hours on end like a kipper under a grill, Lainey. But look at your dad. He's been stuck in that house, probably holed up in his study, for at least twelve hours a day working constantly. He'll arrive as pale as the milk I pour into my tea. All I'm saying is that life is about everything in moderation and a little sunshine on your skin will lift your spirits. Don't spend all your time there indoors. Get out and about a little. Cover your arms and wear a sun hat if you're out in the middle of the day, but life is for living and enjoying. Don't forget that, lovely!'

'I won't, Mum,' I reply cheerfully. A part of me agrees with what she's saying. And she's right about Dad. I'm concerned he'll develop a real fear of the outside world if he doesn't make an effort to step outside his front door now and again. He enjoyed our trip out to grab some pizza, but when I spoke to him shortly before I left, he admitted that he hadn't been out again since. 'Right, I'm off to run a nice cool bath and have a relaxing soak. Love ya, Mum.'

'Love you too, Lainey. And remember you are young, single and free so enjoy every moment, lovely.'

As I'm about to put the phone down and ease myself off the bed, there's a ping and it's Thomas.

How's it going?

My fingers hover for a moment or two.

Good. I've met up with Rick and I have a photographer all sorted, so you can relax.

His response is instant.

Thank goodness. With the cover all lined up and only half an article written, my blood pressure thanks you, Lainey. Let's just get the first article done and then the pressure won't be quite so great. Appreciated!

I didn't realise Thomas was so on edge about the project. His words are straight to the point and I might be mistaken, but I'm picking up a sense of panic. That's not the man I'm used to dealing with.

* * *

'Hi Emilio, I'm Elaine Summers from *Upscale Dining* magazine, please call me Lainey. Thank you for coming at such short notice. Take a seat.'

'Is most certainly my pleasure, Lainey,' he replies, his accent easy on the ear as we shake hands.

I'm relieved that his English is so good, and I return his smile. He's very personable and I settle myself down in the armchair opposite him. Felipe, the very attentive hotel manager, has been most accommodating, making this quiet little lounge area available for me to use this evening.

'Please, help yourself to coffee,' I indicate to the tray on the low table in front of us. 'I gather you live locally?'

Emilio places the portfolio he's carrying down next to his chair before picking up a cup and saucer, and settling himself back into the plush, velvet armchair. 'Thank you, and yes. Merely a five-minute drive.'

'I had a look at your website and it's very impressive.'

He looks pleased. 'I have been in the business for nearly twenty years now and I cover most things, from weddings to portrait photos and animals.'

'Photographing plates of food would be a first for you, I assume?'

'For a magazine, yes, but I'm one of a small team who cover the annual Festival of Three Cultures held in Frigiliana, Málaga. The sleepy streets of this beautiful village come alive with street performers, dancing, and food and drink stalls. So, I have a little experience.'

As we leaf through the folder he brought with him, Emilio is keen to show me examples from last year's festival and I'm happy – more than happy.

'And you are free for the next four weeks?' I ask.

A frown settles on his brow. 'Four weeks?

'Yes, four days each week – Monday to Thursday. The programme will only be shown in Spain, but the magazine I work for, *Upscale Dining,* has exclusive coverage for our readers in the UK. I've written a couple of articles featuring the chef, Rick Oliver, in connection with his London restaurant, Aleatory. We're very excited to be able to run two, six-page spreads covering the competition. You will, of course, be credited and links to your website will be included in both articles. I will also need a short bio and a headshot of you.'

I pause for a moment and it's obvious that I have Emilio's full attention. This is going to be a learning curve for him and it's essential he understands the level of commitment required. If he can follow my direction, we'll be fine, but I won't know that for sure until the first photoshoot is done, and I can see the results for myself.

'Chef Rick Oliver's masterclass will be filmed each Monday. He'll make sure the three dishes are set aside for photographing separately afterwards, too. Filming of the contestants' cook-offs will take place on Tuesday, Wednesday and Thursday mornings – one course each day. I'll need you here between the hours of 9 a.m. and noon, or just after. The idea is to get a series of photos of the various stages during the preparations, as much as filming allows. Obviously, we can't interact with the chefs while they are in session, but if the cameras stop for any reason, then it will be a chance to grab a few shots. Is that doable for you?' I suck in a deep breath as I await his response.

Emilio gives me what I can only describe as an apologetic look. 'Am very sorry, I thought it was only for one week.'

He can tell by my reaction this isn't the best news and it sends me into a momentary panic. It isn't Emilio's fault, of course, but now I have no idea what I'm going to do.

'Oh, I see,' I mutter, my stomach beginning to churn. 'I'm sorry that wasn't communicated to you.' Obviously, Rick's interpreter didn't go into detail and now I'm having to think on my feet. 'Emilio, this leaves me with a major problem as obviously I don't know anyone here. The photographer who was due to fly over with me had to pull out at the last minute due to illness, I'm afraid. That's why I'm in this position.' It's impossible to keep the disappointment out of my voice.

'I'm sorry to hear that. This is a wonderful opportunity for me, Lainey, I realise that. Rest assured, I will try my best to rearrange my diary. I will make myself available for the four days this week. I can promise you that now. I have a colleague who owes me a favour or two and will, I hope, cover for me. I'll go and see him immediately after I leave here. If I can't cover the whole four weeks myself, I will find you another person to take my place on the days I can't get here. Please relax and leave this in my hands. I will not let you down.'

'Oh, Emilio, you have no idea how grateful I am, that is most kind!'

It's not quite the cast-iron result I was hoping to achieve, but it's good of him to come up with a solution. *Have faith, Lainey*, I tell myself, pushing my shoulders back and assuming an air of positivity.

We sit and chat about the wonderful restaurant here at the monastery, as we finish our coffees, and Emilio tells me that he brings his wife here every year for her birthday.

'Nine o'clock on Monday, then?' he reiterates, as our conversation draws to a close.

'Perfect, thank you so much,' I reply, my voice hopefully reflecting how genuinely grateful I am to him.

'I will look forward to it and am most excited to be involved.' Judging by the smile on Emilio's face, I can see he means it. Although, I think it's still sinking in that this isn't a run-of-the mill job he's stepping into.

We walk down to the reception together and I can only hope Emilio can make himself available as continuity is key from my point of view. His English is perfect, and I think we'd work well together.

'*Adiós*, Emilio, and *muchas gracias.*'

With a parting smile, I turn around and saunter off in what I hope is the direction of the restaurant. I don't pass anyone to ask and end up walking through an archway, only to find myself facing the huge wooden gates in the car park. I'm sure I remember there is an entrance to the restaurant down here on the right and when I enter, I immediately spot Rick sitting alone at a table. He stands, pulling out the chair opposite for me.

'I was going to hang on another half an hour before texting you as I didn't want to interrupt your meeting. Please, take a seat. How did it go?'

He helps to manoeuvre my chair a little closer to the table. I wasn't anticipating that we'd eat together this evening, so this is a bit of a surprise.

'Good, although Emilio might not be available for the entire time. He has offered to find someone to step in for him if that's the case.'

Rick's eyes sweep over my face. 'Ah, not such a simple solution, after all. You're being remarkably calm about it. It must be a little daunting, as you and Ant work so well as a team.'

He settles back in his seat, then reaches out to pick up a bottle of white wine from a silver ice bucket, tilting his head in my direction.

'Oh, yes please. I think I've earnt this tonight. And thank you for waiting around for me, you didn't have to, you know. The chat with Emilio went well, so thanks for that and I think we can safely say that you and I are quits now.'

A playful smile tweaks his lips as he pours the wine into the glass in front of me. It sparkles in the flickering light from the candle in the centre of the table.

'Not according to my mother, who was appalled that I hadn't introduced you properly that day, when she found out the truth. I figure the very least I owe you is a pleasant dinner on your first night here.' He raises his glass, and we toast. 'Here's to a month of good food, stunning photographs and exciting copy to please Thomas. And, who knows, maybe we'll get to explore a few of the local sights. What do you think?'

Ours eyes meet and I feel my mood instantly picking up.

'I'm up for that.'

'I'll have a chat with Felipe and arrange something, then. Right, I think it's time we got around to looking at the menu. The first one is in Spanish, the one behind in English. Rosalia intends to take good care of us.'

Taking a moment to scan both menus, I can't suppress a tiny smile. 'It loses a little of the mystery in the translation, doesn't it?'

'Hmm. Cheek stew doesn't sound quite as enticing as it does in Spanish. What are you going for?'

Rick has already closed his menu. 'Pork loin cooked in Pedro Ximénez, which is a sweet sherry. It's very good.'

'Well, make that two, then.'

He raises his hand and a waitress who has been hovering immediately comes to the table. I'm impressed when Rick orders the dish by its Spanish name, but when the young woman goes on to ask him a question, he looks lost for a moment before nodding his head.

As she walks away, he stares at me. 'I have no idea what she said, but let's hope it was a side dish or something.'

Raising the wine glass to my lips, I take a quick sip.

'This is going to be a novel experience in more ways than one,' I reply, shaking my head at him and laughing.

'Well, I sincerely hope you are laughing with me and not at me.' Rick's eyes search out mine and what I see looking back at me is a sincerity that is touchingly honest. He cares about what I think of him. The truth is that I could drown myself in those dark brown eyes of his, but I'm not the sort of woman who would try to steal someone else's man. '*Salud*, Lainey,' Rick says, raising his glass to take a sip. He has no idea what effect he has on me when he catches me off guard like that and I swallow down a lump that has risen in my throat.

Fortunately, there's a buzzing sound and we both stare down at his phone as it starts to vibrate.

'Sorry, I should take this. I'll be back in a moment.'

He walks out through the doors and up the steps out onto the sandy, gravelly area between the palm trees. And suddenly it's like the warm glow around me has been extinguished and I feel truly alone, even though I'm not. The light is beginning to fade quickly now and the outdoor space is lit up with what must be hundreds of nightlights. Inside, the ambience in the restaurant is restful, with only the flickering candlelight and the soft glow from the uplighters highlighting the beams overhead. There are four other groups of diners, including a very loved-up couple who even held hands while tackling what looked like bowls of gazpacho. The Spanish do tend to eat later and it's only just coming up to 9 p.m. so they will be serving for at least another hour.

I turn my attention to the décor of this grand, rectangular room. The ceiling is magnificent, the exposed boards above are made up of sturdy, dark pine wood, sitting on solid beams and each one is finished off with a carved, scrollwork corbel. It reminds me of the hull of an old ship, functional and yet with the odd touch that speaks of the pride of the artisan. The floor is a chequerboard style, with muted grey and off-white marble tiles adding a formal elegance to the setting. A further sense of grandeur is created by the beautiful arched alcoves which house the leaded windows. An old tapestry covers two-thirds of the end wall and even though it's so old that it's threadbare in places, amongst the faded colours there are still pops of a vibrant red and a rich blue on the bodices of the women's dresses. I can just make out that it depicts a market scene outside the walls of the monastery, with baskets of citrus fruits and vendors selling live-stock as the crowds wander around. Then there are various paint-ings hung beneath downlighters to pick up on what remains of the contrasting colours, which, again, have faded over time. I can sense there's a pride in rescuing and displaying these items and revealing the monastery's importance in the community. I'm sure I've read somewhere that, historically, monasteries never turned away a traveller in need. I wonder if that is true, making it a refuge as well as a community of its own?

'Sorry about that. Cathy is on a high after her performance this afternoon. She was appearing at a festival and Cathy thrives in that sort of environment. Being in different time zones is diffi-cult at times.'

Rick looks happy and I try to be glad for him.

'It must be tough for her, being in the limelight all the time.'

'It's certainly not easy. Her meltdowns are usually linked to overwork and not enough sleep. It's a constant pressure.'

Rick is very forgiving when it comes to Cathy and her behaviour. It might be my jaded view of things, but it seems that whenever he talks about her, he ends up making excuses for her, but he obviously doesn't see it like that. Most people work hard in what they do and get tired, but they don't take it out on those around them. Goodness, Rick himself is a workaholic and under constant pressure every time he's in the kitchen. Striving for perfection comes at a price, but I've never seen Rick in a bad mood, or disrespect anyone.

'Ah, here's our food.'

As the plates are laid down in front of us, the smell wafting up is incredible. My mouth instantly begins to water.

'Great choice, Rick,' I say as we both stare down at the beautifully presented dishes. The pork loin has been sliced and sits in a stack on a rich, dark jus. 'Is that puréed potato?' I ask, dipping the tip of my fork into the creamy little swirl that has been piped around one side of the plate.

'No, it's apple purée, the perfect accompaniment, trust me.'

And he's right. This evening couldn't be more perfect in terms of food, company and surroundings. I feel like I'm in a dream and my worries have all melted away.

9

NEW DAY, NEW EXPERIENCES

I've been awake since 5 a.m. because I didn't close the internal wooden shutters, affixed to the large window, but left them slightly ajar. Before I fell asleep, I laid here for a while thinking about the monks who have slept in this room in the past and the lives they led. And now as the light filters in, I'm content to listen to the birds and surf the net to catch up on social media. As I do, I notice that Ant is online.

Hey, you're up early!

His response is instant.

The pain kept me awake most of the night and I've given up trying to sleep. Just lying here distracting myself to take my mind off it. Why are you awake? Is everything okay?

Ah, poor Ant.

It's all fine. You know what it's like sleeping in a strange bed.

That would be the hair mattress, then?

The bed is huge and very comfortable, actually. Can I call you, or will it wake anyone?

Please do. I'm relegated to the box room, so I don't keep anyone else awake.

I hop out of bed and pull on my new cotton dressing gown, then ruffle my hair, even though Ant has seen me looking a lot worse than this. We were caught in a thunderstorm once, and soaked to the skin, my mascara slid down my face like a rain of black tears. It was Halloween stuff as, with tendrils of dripping wet hair, and being freezing cold, I looked more like a zombie than a ghost.

'Oh, you do look fragile,' I empathise as his pale face looms up on the screen in front of me.

'Maybe a little, if I'm being honest with you. So, come on, tell me all about it. That's a bigger room than I was expecting considering it was a monk's cell.'

I hold up my phone so he can get a better view. 'Aside from completing their daily manual tasks as the monastery was self-sufficient, they each spent hours in isolation, praying. Apparently, most monks were highly educated and could read and write in Latin. There are a couple of framed prayers around the monastery that are stunning examples of their mastery of calligraphy. Some of the individual lettering is a little work of art in itself. It must have taken hours, especially considering they only had candlelight. Hang on, I'll give you the tour. Let me start at the entrance to the room. Look at the door, sturdy isn't it?' I turn around, showing Ant the long run through to the double window, where the shutters allow a narrow stream of daylight to peek through.

'Goodness, it looks like the intention was to keep them locked in,' he exclaims.

'There's a window seat and double glass doors opening inwards, so the metal bars are there to stop anyone falling out. There are internal shutters to cover the glass. I'll move closer and swing them open wide so you can get a glimpse of the grounds. It's amazing here, Ant, truly amazing.'

Walking slowly across the polished wooden floor, I pan around so he can catch the bathroom on my right. I ease the door open, snaking my hand inside to switch on the light.

'Jazzy tiles,' he comments. He's right that the tiles in the bathroom are colourful, with vibrant blues and soft green, interspersed with tiny little flowers in rich reds and oranges.

I carry on panning around the main bedroom area so that he can glimpse the huge bed and the beautiful, wooden cupboards which serve as wardrobes. The rest of the furniture is simple, comprising two bedside tables and a desk and chair on the far wall. The table lamps have pretty, etched-glass shades, with what looks like clusters of lemons surrounded by leaves.

'There's something about the simplicity and lack of clutter that is so restful. The ceilings are high, and the building feels remarkably airy. How I wish you were here to experience this with me.'

Ant sighs. 'Me, too. I'm bored to tears already.'

I push open the shuttered glass doors and kneel on the window seat to give Ant a close-up view of the gardens, even in the early-morning light it's captivating.

'Is that a swimming pool?' he groans, making me feel a bit mean.

'Ah, sorry. Chances are that I won't have much free time to

hang around and enjoy it, though. There's so much to do and the language barrier isn't going to make my life easy.'

'But you have a photographer lined up?'

'Yes, sort of. He wasn't aware I needed him for four weeks in total, so he's trying to sort out his schedule. Fortunately, Emilio's English is good, but if he has to get someone else to step in that's yet another unknown. I'll feel happier once I've seen the first batch of photos.'

'You sound nervous about it.'

'I'm not as stressed as I thought I'd be due to the amazing setting. I'm sure it's going to hit me like a proverbial hammer once I start work. My first task is to begin the write-up on the monastery itself and get my head around the terminology for the architectural features here. Rick put me in touch with the interpreter who will be here during filming and I've booked him for a session this morning. And as for working with a new photographer, well, we both know that styles vary. You instinctively know what I'm looking for and I don't even have to think about it. I hope Emilio is open to suggestions.'

Ant chuckles. 'Hmm... it's not easy interpreting the image inside someone else's head when you think you know what you're doing. It took me a while, but I got there in the end, didn't I?' He sounds amused.

'You certainly did.'

'How about the contestants. Have you met them yet?'

'No. They're arriving today and there's a meet-up tonight. I've already written up a short piece about each of them, so I feel like I know them a little, but they don't know me, of course.'

'And how is Rick?'

'He looks at home here, already, but then he's well-travelled.'

'I expect he's enjoying a break away from Cathy,' Ant says, rather pointedly.

'She's on tour, apparently.'

'Peace reigns, then.' He pauses. 'You have no idea how disappointed I am not to be there. Not just for the experience, Lainey, but Thomas is sticking his neck out on this one, too, and that's added pressure for you.'

'I know. Visually, everything about the setting and the food is going to be stunning. Let's hope, with a little teamwork, I can do it justice and Emilio will grab those perfect shots for me.'

'I'll be thinking of you. And when you have a little downtime in between, enjoy the sunshine, Lainey. You've forgotten how to switch off and you deserve a break.'

As we say goodbye, I know Ant means well. I've neglected both friends and family, recently, in my quest to propel my career forward in the direction I want it to go. Food is my passion and writing about it excites me. A simple recipe can encourage someone used to grabbing a ready-made meal off the shelf, to have a go. That's why I love what I do, and the added attraction is that no two days are ever the same. Along the way I get to meet some interesting people, too. That thought immediately brings a smile to my face. Some are definitely a little more interesting than others.

* * *

As I shake hands with Miguel Tejero, this tall, handsome young man standing before me casts his eyes over me appreciatively. It's a little disconcerting.

'Hi Miguel. I'm Lainey. Thank you so much for making yourself available this morning.'

'It is my absolute pleasure. Rick Oliver said that you were interested in some information about the monastery itself ahead of filming?'

His voice is low, warm and that accent of his is almost hypnotic. In comparison, my English accent sounds stiff, even to my ears and I try to relax a little.

'Yes, I'll be doing a little write-up about it as part of the feature. I have a whole list of questions, I'm afraid, which I've printed off. It's mainly terminology so I can describe this wonderful setting accurately.'

He takes the folded sheet of paper from my hand, opening it, and I watch as his eyes skim down the various items.

'I see. Some things I know, but some I will enquire about on your behalf.'

'Wonderful. And you have time to walk around with me and point out a few of the most prominent features?'

'Of course. I would be delighted to pass on what I know. I am lucky enough to enjoy a special relationship with the Corberó family, who restored the monastery and now run it as a hotel. I often come here to talk to parties of tourists. The Americans, in particular, are very interested in the history of the place as it was the monks who went from here to California who founded numerous cities such as San Francisco and Los Angeles.'

'I didn't know that. Do you mind if I record bits of our conversation? It saves me taking notes.'

Miguel smiles at me, nodding his head. 'Please do. Shall we begin with the courtyards and then head back to the restaurant, which was originally the Chapter Hall? It has a lot of history.'

'Yes, thank you, or I should say, *muchas gracias*. I feel embarrassed only knowing a handful of Spanish words and saying them with an English accent probably totally ruins the gesture,' I reply, returning his smile.

'No. It's good to try. There aren't many English-speaking people in this area and we have the same problem. Our ears are not attuned. Possibly because most of the foreign films we watch are dubbed into Spanish, so we do not get to hear the various accents. Unless, of course, it is a necessary part of our business. Spanish people are very proud and, like you, feel awkward trying new languages. I spent two years working in the UK on an exchange programme and was able to hone my skills.'

'Somehow you manage to make English words sound much softer than we do. Our natural accent is a little stiff and that's why it's not easy to get that warm intonation of your beautiful language. I really must relax a little and practise while I'm here.'

'I am a phone call away if you need my services at any time.' The glance he gives me is a hopeful one.

Is Miguel flirting with me? Gosh, I hope I'm not beginning to blush and this heat in my cheeks is simply the exertion of keeping up with him as he strides across the courtyard.

'Spanish people are not hard to figure out. We are by nature very family-orientated. We love good, fresh food and we have the best wines in the world. And we are not biased, of course.'

We begin laughing in unison. He's easy to like, that's for sure.

'You will no doubt notice that Spanish people also have a tendency to be loud because we are passionate people. It is especially noticeable whenever we are watching *fútbol* – you say football, of course. We start our day a little later than most Europeans, eat late and go to bed even later.'

Rick waves as I spot him exiting the breakfast room, but he doesn't make his way over to us, and I notice he has a file under his arm.

'I'm looking forward to seeing chef Rick Oliver in action. I read your article in *Upscale Dining* about his new restaurant and his partnership with Cathy Clarkson. I saw her in concert in London, at The O2, a couple of years ago. It was a great performance.'

I'm impressed. He's done his homework and despite that laid-back appearance, Miguel is on the ball. I've never seen Cathy perform live, or even on TV, although I often catch her songs on the radio and I have watched a few of her videos.

'It's a fabulous restaurant, and the food is amazing. Their success is a credit to the whole team,' I respond enthusiastically.

A white cat with pale green eyes appears from behind one of the pillars and begins meowing, but as we walk forward, it runs off across the quadrant.

'There are seven or eight cats who live here. Some are a little timid, but there is a black and white cat who is very friendly.'

I press record on my phone and stand a little closer to Miguel. I don't want to miss a single thing. I'm sure that my readers are going to be fascinated by all of these little details, as it's a part of the overall charm of the setting.

'There are three patios, as they are referred to, around which the monastery is organised. The fifteenth-century Claustro del Noviciado – the area used by the novice monks – is at the entrance to the monastery. I'm sure you will have noticed the beautiful frescos on the arched ceiling of the entrance which is adjacent to the car park. This here is the Patio Reglar, which dates back to the sixteenth century. It has the portico on three of its sides and the round arches that are supported by brick pilasters.'

Strolling along the whitewashed walkways, I'm already beginning to notice things that I missed yesterday, and I want to soak everything up.

'Finally,' Miguel indicates as we step through into the next courtyard, 'we have the third cloister, with the open upper gallery above. It's from the eighteenth century and leads us to the gardens and the orchard.'

'Ah, yes. My room is above here,' I remark as I stop recording. 'If we head back inside, maybe I can order us some coffee and we can sit for a while on the sofas at the far end of the restaurant area and talk.'

'That would be nice. Let's backtrack.'

'While I think of it, what is this floor made of? I love the herringbone pattern and the muted colours.'

'They are mud bricks, made in the old style. You will also notice the gravel paths and areas around the gardens, car parking area and the outside bar. This is purposeful, as the heat builds during the day. It is easy to hose down these areas and the material helps to retain the water. That can lower the temperature by two or three degrees to make sitting out pleasanter. Particularly in the evenings, which is why we eat so late.'

'I had no idea, but what a simple solution. Clever. Can I ask about the short lengths of chain that hang above the wooden gates and also there's a smaller one hanging on the wall by the bar.'

'Whenever a monk saw the symbolic chains, they knew they could get asylum and protection within, which would have been bestowed at some point in the past by a king. In years gone by, travellers would have presented their chains to the head of the monastery while they were there. The fleur-de-lis is a popular icon, too, it represents the Holy Trinity.'

'Why would monks travel between monasteries? I had this notion that when they went into a monastery it was for life.'

'Monks often travelled as a part of their work to spread the word and this included tours abroad. Some never returned, so many lives were lost as they fought for their beliefs. Others would eventually return to what they considered to be their home. But, sadly, wars and kings saw many monasteries plundered, destroyed by fire, or simply having their land seized. I am no historian, so my knowledge is sketchy, but the way this place is built shows how important it was to protect themselves from intruders.'

'I think you're going to more than earn your coffee,' I reply, grateful to Miguel for sharing his knowledge with me. This is exactly what I was hoping for and more.

10

THE CAST AND CREW HAVE ARRIVED

The excitement is tangible as soon as I step outside. Apart from a brief glimpse of Rick earlier this morning, our paths haven't crossed today. I spent most of the morning with Miguel and the afternoon in my room typing up some notes.

I feel a little awkward as it looks like I'm one of the last to arrive and people are already clustered into small groups, chatting. Clearly from the sound of their conversation, the people standing to the left of me are Spanish and I assume they are members of the film crew. Gazing around, I can't see Rick, so I make a beeline for the bar to kill some time. I'm not comfortable aimlessly standing on my own.

There are two people serving, but there are also three trays of drinks ready and waiting and I indicate with my hand to ask if it's okay to take one. I understand the first word, *sí*, but the rest of it is lost on me. Plucking a glass of a deep ruby-coloured wine, I nod my head and smile gratefully. As I turn to walk away, Rick is standing there looking at me and I'm really pleased to see him.

'Great choice, that's an Evodia Old Vine Grenache. It's fruity, smooth and goes well with both white and red meats.'

I make way for him to grab a glass off the tray.

'How do you know that off the top of your head?'

He indicates for us to walk over to a quiet area in front of one of the two palm trees. 'It's my business to know that. I've toured the wine cellar here and familiarised myself with the local wines. It's been a productive day.'

'Of course,' I kick myself for asking such a lame question. Rick is thirty-six hours away from cooking his first three-course meal and he won't have left a single thing to chance. 'You're just counting down now. Is everyone here?'

'Yes. We'll do a general introduction to kick off before the buffet is served. How did you get on with Miguel?'

'Great. I left a list of questions with him but I'm confident I will get more or less everything I need to do justice to this amazing location. I just need the photos to go with my descriptions now.'

Someone raises their hand to attract Rick's attention and encourage people to step closer. There are about twenty of us in total.

Rick leans into me as we walk forward. 'That's the owner, Víctor Corberó and his wife, Isabel. The man standing next to him is from Tauro Recreativas S. L. He's the producer for the show and standing next to him is the director of production, Javier Torres.'

Miguel appears next to us, tilting his head in acknowledgement and I nod back.

After a short welcoming speech from Víctor, which goes completely over my head as it's all in Spanish, Rick is called upon to introduce himself while Miguel translates. Rick then calls each of the contestants forward as Miguel reads a short bio from a printed sheet. Suddenly, Rick points to me and Miguel continues reading. As soon as he mentions *Upscale*

Dining magazine, all heads turn in my direction. When he finishes, it's clear that the introductions are over and there's a huge round of applause. Whether that's because everyone is delighted to be here, or because the waiters and waitresses are now laying out the buffet table, I'm not sure, but the atmosphere is festive.

Rick invites the contestants to come over and shake hands and most speak at least a little English. Miguel is fluent in several languages and manages to keep the conversation going, jumping in to help out when necessary.

I was studying our little group while Víctor was speaking. India Serrano, the Spanish contestant, is strikingly pretty, with long, jet-black hair. Erick Baer hails from Germany, but from what I've already heard, his English is excellent. Ben Andrews lives in Surrey and he seems very friendly. From France, there is Louis Reno, a quiet man I notice, but he's a good listener with a ready smile. I think he'll be popular amongst the group. Mirra Cegani is Italian and says as much with her hands as she does with her words. Alexis Di Angelis looks like a Greek god, tall, dark-eyed and charming. Joana Barradas is the Portuguese contestant, and I can tell how nervous she's feeling just by her body language. I do hope she begins to relax once things get started.

I keep it simple and thank them for the information they submitted for inclusion in the magazine, wishing them luck in the competition.

Rick is keen for us to move on as there are more introductions to be made and we excuse ourselves.

'Javier, this is Elaine Summers from *Upscale Dining* magazine.'

Javier extends his hand and, as we shake, he holds onto mine for a moment or two, as his eyes scan my face.

'Please call me, Lainey, Javier. It's great to meet you. What a fantastic project this is; the magazine is delighted to be covering the competition.'

'It is a pilot, so let's hope we do well. Any publicity outside of our own country is most welcome as this is a celebration of international cuisine. Maybe next year we will be back and the competition will be even bigger.' He certainly looks optimistic.

'I know our readers will be fascinated to see how chefs from seven different countries take Rick's demonstration dishes and put their own spin on them. It's an interesting approach for a competition and quite unique. And, of course, with an array of fresh, local produce on hand with such a wide variety of flavours, I'm sure we're going to be amazed by the results.'

'I certainly hope so. The idea is that the contestants are required to pick at least one element from each of my recipes around which to create their own, unique dish, Lainey,' Rick explains. 'But whichever item they choose must be the hero of the flavours they present. And talking of dishes, I think it's about time we sampled this wonderful buffet.'

The sense I'm getting from Javier is that he's quite a serious man, but then it's very clear that there is a lot riding on the successful outcome of this project. He might even be hoping to sell foreign rights, if not for the pilot, for the next series if this takes off. And I had the distinct impression that he sees *Upscale Dining* as a vehicle to help publicise the competition, so hopefully I will have his full cooperation. I'm hoping we can get some photos of the chefs in action to add that sense of tension that is bound to grow as the days pass.

Javier heads off to catch up with one of the other crew members, leaving us to stand in line for the buffet. 'There are a variety of tapas dishes. Is anything familiar to you?' Rick enquires, and I nod my head.

'I recognise the salsa verde dish, which looks like it could be pork, and the *patatas bravas*, fried potato with what looks like a spicy sauce. Is there anything I should definitely try?'

He points to some little ramekin dishes filled with a salmon-pink dip. '*Salmorejo Cordobés*, it's a cold soup made with tomatoes, onions, bread and a small glug of sherry, so it's quite thick. The garnish is Iberian ham and a little chopped egg. It's delicious. The *bacalao rebozado* is extremely good, too – battered cod to us,' he smiles genially. 'Come on, there's a small table over there under the lemon tree in the corner.'

I'm surprised Rick hasn't made his way over to the large, central table where most of the other chefs are sitting, as they would have made room for us, I'm sure. But he seems content and I realise that as he's also the judge of the competition, I'm a neutral option when it comes to company.

'It's beautiful at night, isn't it?' I ponder, thinking aloud. 'With the lights overhead and the magnificent palms as a backdrop, along with the perfume in the air, it's heavenly. There's obviously jasmine close by, but the scent of those geraniums is really coming through. They're one of my mum's favourites, so it reminds me of her. She has a large patio with pots everywhere.'

'She lives in Le Crotoy, you said, is that right?'

'Yes. As it's a little smallholding, much of the garden is culti-vated, and there are orchards too, but she loves her flowers. In fact, if this trip hadn't come up, I'd be packing my bag ready to head over there next Thursday. I'm sad to say that so far I haven't made it over, but she's been sending me photos.'

'You cancelled your holiday to come here? Now I feel bad.' Rick sits back, his eyes scanning my face.

'Don't be. It's a bit complicated, anyway. I was going to help her run two back-to-back courses, but my dad offered to step in when Mum couldn't find another English-speaking person to assist her.'

He looks apologetic. 'I'm really sorry the timing of this was awkward for you, personally.'

'Some opportunities are too good to miss and this was one of them,' I reply as my eyes linger on him while he's eating. If I admit that the last time I saw my mum in person was four years ago, he'd probably ask why and it's not something I'm willing to discuss.

Rick makes an 'hmm' sound and I wait for him to finish his mouthful of food. 'This is really good,' he confirms, pointing his fork in the direction of his plate. 'Anyway, I'm glad it worked out well in the end and I hope you get to visit with your mum really soon. I spent two nights in Le Crotoy on a long road trip back from Nice. That was a few months before the restaurant opened. It's a beautiful area and the beach is wonderful. We stayed in a hotel looking out across the bay. The building was an interesting place actually, it even had those iconic turrets, like a fairy tale castle. It also had a great chef at the time, and we were impressed, but he told us he was moving on. Good people get poached and they're hard to replace.'

The cold soup is absolutely delicious and as I scrape out the dish to scoop up the last dregs, I notice Rick is watching me, amused.

'You enjoyed that, then?'

'I did. Now to try the cod.'

We each pick up one of the battered chunks and take a bite. Rick looks at me, raising his eyebrow and inviting me to comment.

'Light, crisp and the fish is cooked to perfection.'

As he pops the remainder into his mouth, I wait to see what he has to say.

'It's good but I think I can beat this with my extra-special batter.'

Dipping the remaining half of the little ball of fish into the spicy chilli sauce, I savour it for a moment. 'Cod is on the menu for at least one of the meals, then?' I enquire.

He runs his fingers across his lips as if zipping them shut. 'All of my recipes are top secret for now, but I think it's safe to say that's one ingredient they will all be anticipating.'

I love the way Rick is such easy company, even though this is work. On the two occasions I met up with him at the restaurant he was more formal and less at ease. I tend to forget that he's in the lime-light and it won't be too long, I should imagine, before he becomes a recognised face on TV. Then surely it will be a foray into publishing and the obligatory cookbooks. His future is exciting, that's for sure.

'You're going to enjoy this competition, aren't you?' I reflect.

'I think I will. It's certainly a welcome change from the restaurant right now. And absence makes the heart grow fonder, so my mother tells me.'

I'm not sure what to make of that, but it doesn't sound good. Before I can comment, Rick continues.

'And how is the timing for you? I mean, four weeks away from home takes some organising.' Rick wipes his mouth with the napkin as he pushes his plate away. It didn't take him long to demolish the food in front of him, but I notice he took one of everything. For him this is a tasting session, even when he isn't working, he's still taking note of every little thing.

'I love my job, but I'm hoping a break really is as good as a rest. I still have a lot to prove to get to where I want to be and it's important that I don't ease up. But simply being in a different environment for a little while will hopefully allow me to step back and appreciate how far I've come.'

He nods in agreement. 'Same here, really. When things take off in your career, it can be non-stop, can't it? It helps to have a partner who understands. I've fallen foul of that in the past. Cathy takes it all in her stride and I admire her for that.'

'It must be tough at times, though.'

Rick looks at me, narrowing his eyes a little as if he's deep in thought. 'You're easy to talk to, Lainey, maybe too easy.' It doesn't sound like an accusation but as if he's wondering where to draw the line.

'I'm here to write about the competition, Rick. Besides, I've already shared a few of my secrets with you, while we were at your flat. Let's agree that any personal stuff that comes up remains off the record. I don't usually talk about my family to anyone other than people I trust.'

'I'm flattered, and absolutely, it's a real drag having to be careful what you say every single minute of the day. I'm passionate about what I do and sometimes my focus is a little too... narrow. Cathy is the one who makes me step back occasionally to consider the bigger picture. It's one of her key strengths. Besides being an award-winning singer, Cathy is an astute businesswoman and that's not a side of her the public are used to seeing. And in private she's completely different yet again, so she has three personas.'

I almost blurt out *thank goodness for that*, but manage to stop myself just in time. 'That must be difficult to juggle. It's like wearing three entirely different hats and becoming a different character depending on who you are with.'

'Most people don't understand that side of her life. Cathy's journey to stardom came at a price. What money she did make in those early years was frittered away by a series of managers out for their own ends. Those experiences toughened her up, she told me, but it must have hurt being used like that. Her parents didn't really have a clue about the business and the pitfalls. Cathy wanted to sing, she wasn't forced, but it's an industry rife with exploitation.'

I've often thought the same thing whenever I see kids being thrust into the limelight. 'It's hard enough for adults to cope with fame, isn't it?' I reflect sadly.

'Yes, and it's a poor reflection of a world where there are unscrupulous individuals out there ready to exploit innocent people and constantly getting away with it. I regard myself as lucky, as Cathy came along at just the right time for me. It helps having someone in your life who understands the pressure of a life under the spotlight. And how about you – is there a significant other in your life?' Rick looks at me questioningly, and it's my turn to open up a little, I suppose.

'The truth is that I'm not looking to get into anything right now. I did the dating thing for a while after I split up with my ex, Warren, but it was difficult given the bad press my dad was getting at the time. I had to be very careful about what I said and to whom, so anyone I barely knew who started asking questions about him made me immediately head for the door.'

'That must have been tough,' he empathises.

'Friends and family mean well and if you don't make an effort to get back in the game, they assume you're feeling lonely and miserable. I wasn't when we broke up and that's still true now. This is my time to grab what opportunities come my way, like this one. I'm guilt-free and available to go where I please and if I want to work myself into the ground, it's no one's business but mine.'

Rick starts laughing. 'You role with the punches, Lainey. I can identify with that.'

Clearly, there's more to his story but it's obvious it's not something he's willing to share. At least, not with me, anyway.

'I want to be judged on what I achieve in my professional life, not my personal life. I figure everyone has a right to separate the two and I sympathise with people whose private lives are splashed all over the tabloids. Unless they break the law, of course. I was brought up having that distinction explained to me very clearly by my dad, so I think it's wrong to sell someone out simply to get on. Joining the team at *Upscale Dining* has got my career on track at last, and one day I want to be an editor. I can learn a lot from Thomas and I'm grateful for the chance to do just that.'

'Make friends, not enemies, right?' Rick replies. 'I think that's worthy of a toast. Red, or white?'

'Surprise me. I'm here to experience everything Andalucía has to offer and I'm going to make our readers fall in love with this magical place right along with me.'

11

A LEISURELY STROLL

I'm up early as I figure that's the best time to wander around, when most people are still fast asleep. It's blissfully cool at this time of the day and I decide to spend an hour snapping as many photos as I can of the monastery as a back-up. *Just in case.*

I'm not a photog, as they say in the business, by any stretch of the imagination. But I've learnt a fair bit by watching Ant as he works. I know exactly what I want to see in the frame and how a tiny adjustment to the angle of the plate can make all the difference.

When it comes to photographing plates of food, my byword is *interact*. Place a spoon, or fork, to gently lift one of the elements on the plate as if someone has already begun to dig in, or lift an item off, like a sprig of mint, and place it on the tabletop along-side it. Perfect is fine, but it needs a *softener*, that human element that reminds the reader that they're not seeing a computer-gener-ated graphic but a delicious plate of food they could recreate for themselves.

Walking around and zooming in on some of the finer details I see around me, like a few of the stout pieces of Gothic-style furniture and some of the religious artefacts, I do feel a little like a tourist on holiday. The tranquillity is broken only by the sounds of a group of birds squabbling in the fruit trees nearby, and the occasional footsteps as a member of staff arrives to begin their working day. It's blissful.

I walk through to the next patio, which Miguel referred to as the third cloister. It's different from the other two areas, having an open upper gallery which looks down onto a formal garden. One of the covered walkways leads directly through to the main gardens and orchard, but this is like an inner sanctum. It's rich in colour, the plastered walls and pillars are a warm, pink terracotta, interspersed with panels in a sandy-coloured hue. The ambience is warm and inviting, like a hug, and with the beautifully mani-cured, low box hedging surrounding a wide variety of aromatic plants, the smell is heavenly. The arched walkways feature vaulted ceilings, painted white, and the brick pilasters supporting them have uplighters which, last night, added a warm glow to the scene. This is already becoming one of my favourite spots.

Taking a moment to stand in the middle of the four rectangular beds, I breathe in the sweet, fragrant air. Bay, rose-mary, and thyme are easy to identify visually and by their distinct smells, but there are other plants I don't recognise. Gazing up beyond the covered walkways around the square, I stare at the bell tower high overhead. The church itself isn't a part of the monastery but abuts one corner of the building. One of its walls backs onto the market garden area to the rear.

The arch at the top houses not one, but two bells. The arch is tall and narrow, like a chimney. Many of the bricks are chipped and damaged, but it still looks sturdy. I can't begin to imagine the size of the main bell up close, as even from here it looks impress-sive. Set on a brick plinth, at least a dozen birds walk along the little platformed edge surveying the views.

Each time I've heard the booming toll, it has made me pause for a brief second. It rings on the hour now, but in the past, presumably, it would also have been used to call the congregation to worship, or even as a warning to the inhabitants of the monastery and the town of the imminent arrival of invaders. Almost on cue and taking both myself and the birds a little by surprise, the bells begin to move. As I count the chimes, I realise it's 8 a.m. and people will soon begin to filter down for breakfast.

Instead of taking the quickest route back to my room, which is to head for the small lift tucked away in a little corridor off the far corner, I decide to take the stairs and head back to the Patio Reglar. The dark wood of the bannisters, spindles and steps is broken only by a splash of colour from the tiled risers. The oblong Spanish tiles are in muted blues and yellows, enclosed in white circles, giving the impression of flowers. On closer inspection, though, as I zoom in to take a photo, I see that the petal shapes are set within an interlocking chain and I realise that the circles must be symbolic.

I'm so glad I spent time gleaning as much information as I could from Miguel and that I asked about the relevance of the rusty old chains. There is an air of austerity to the monastery, as one would expect, but that's created more by the simplicity, given the scale of it and the lack of unnecessary clutter. And yet, when you take the time to look at the smaller details, they reflect the pride of those involved in the building processes way back in the fourteen-hundreds, and their beliefs. The restoration has been sensitively executed and I feel lucky to be experiencing it. If it wasn't for this assignment, I doubt I would have found my way here and that would have been a shame.

As I insert the heavy, cast-iron key to unlock the door to room number six, my phone kicks into life and I grope around in my shoulder bag to retrieve it.

'Morning, Lainey. How's that tan coming along?' Thomas asks jovially, as I swing the door open and step inside.

I'm surprised to get a call from him on a Sunday morning.

'I haven't had chance to break out the tanning lotion yet, you'll be glad to hear,' I reply, returning his banter.

'I'm disappointed. I thought you'd be all set to go and waiting impatiently for things to kick off tomorrow. How's Rick doing?'

'Fine. It's all good here, but the language is a bigger barrier than I'd anticipated. I spent some time with the official interpreter yesterday, and it was well worth it, as I've now pretty much finished drafting the piece about the monastery to slot into the second article.'

'That's good news. And you said the meeting with the photographer went well. No surprises?'

'No surprises. It's all sorted,' I reply, sounding as cool and confident as I can, given the situation.

'Great, that's a relief.'

Thomas's voice drops a little and I find myself biting my lip. Does he have a problem? Before I can say anything, he begins talking again.

'And our celebrity chef is all geared up for tomorrow's masterclass?'

'It seems so. Whenever our paths cross, he sounds happy enough with how it's all been set up.'

'Please continue to keep me in the loop as the week goes on, Lainey. This is going to be an important feature for us, and we need to make the most of it.'

I can't help wondering why Thomas feels the need to talk to me again today, when I texted him last night with an update. I told him that I'd be in touch tomorrow.

'I know what I'm doing, Thomas. Just relax. There's nothing wrong, is there?'

I hear a sharp intake of breath, as he realises I feel he's doubting my abilities. 'No. Not at all. I'm not checking up on you, Lainey, honestly. I wanted to make sure you're happy with the way things are going, that's all. Have you spoken to Ant?'

'Yes. He sounds rough. And disappointed he isn't here.'

'That's understandable. Anyway, give me a call at any time if anything untoward crops up,' Thomas concludes. He leaves me with a puzzled frown on my face. It's obvious he's uneasy for some reason, but about what exactly?

Placing the phone down on the bed and walking towards the window to push open the shutters, a flock of birds land on the roof above my room. Their noisy chatter is more of an intense squabble and I suspect they've discovered a few juicy insects hidden among the tiles. My phone lights up again and I hurry back to retrieve it, surprised to see that it's Rick.

'Good morning, Lainey. I didn't wake you, did I? I doubt anyone can sleep through the tolling of the bells, though,' he laughs.

'I've been awake since about 5 a.m. and I just took a call from Thomas, actually.'

'On a Sunday? Doesn't that man ever switch off?'

'No, clearly he doesn't. I think he was doing his due diligence, you know, making doubly sure I have everything I need.'

'I'm tied up with a practice run of tomorrow's dishes, this morning. Mainly with a view to testing out the temporary kitchen facilities and check that everything is working properly. However, I wondered if you fancied a little excursion this afternoon? Or were you planning on working?'

I gaze across at the paperback book lying unopened on the bedside table. The one I envisioned myself reading as I lazed on one of the sunbeds, under the shade of the trees next to the pool. 'I'm up for that. There's only so much preparation I can do, and I've pretty much hit that point now. What did you have in mind?'

'It's a surprise. But we wouldn't be going far, an easy walking distance Felipe assures me and he's given me a map. We'd need to leave about 2 p.m. Unfortunately, I'll be skipping lunch as I will be doing the tastings myself to make sure I get it spot on. It'll be good to walk that off.'

'Sounds good to me, I'll look forward to it. See you later then, Rick.'

My spirits rise at the prospect of exploring the local area with Rick alongside me for company. I'm not used to simply lazing around and that book is going to have to wait, because I've had a much better offer – one I simply can't refuse.

* * *

'Nice hat,' Rick levels at me, cocking an eyebrow.

Instinctively, I put up my hand to press it firmly down on my head, wondering how flat it's going to make my hair when I take it off. But it shades my face and neck, even though it's not exactly a fashion item. 'Don't laugh. I'm not used to this heat and I'm beginning to think we're mad going for a walk at this time of day.'

He looks at me, squinting his eyes and tilting his head to one side playfully. 'It suits you! Anyway, I think you'll end up thanking me. We're about to take a tour of the Palacio de Portocarrero. Víctor Corberó very kindly arranged this for us as a surprise before he and his wife left. It's by appointment only, so we are extremely lucky that he called in a favour. He said he thought we'd be impressed by it, as we have both shown an interest in the history of the monastery itself.'

'Ah, no doubt he's been talking to Miguel. The history is intriguing, though, isn't it?' I comment, unable to hide my enthusiasm. 'I don't know what your room is like, but I haven't slept this soundly for years. Admittedly, I'm waking up early, but I feel refreshed.'

We walk across the reception area and I look to see if the woman who checked me in is around, but there's no one behind the desk. Rick steps in front of me to hold open the heavy wooden door and I walk out into the blazing sunshine. The sky is such a deep blue it almost doesn't look real and there isn't a single cloud in sight.

'It's thirty-two degrees,' Rick informs me. 'The palace will be wonderfully cool inside, though, and it will only take us about twenty minutes to get there. Right,' he stares down at the map, adjusting his sunglasses. Turning it at right angles, he glances around to find out exactly where we are, and to establish which direction we're heading in. 'If we cross the road here and then head for those traffic lights over there, that's the turning we need.' He points to a narrow-looking street on the far side of the road and we set off.

'I can't believe you have a map. I'd use my phone, it's much easier.'

'Hey, don't spoil it. We're doing this old-school. I hope you aren't one of those annoying people who takes down copious notes as you tour around, scared you'll forget something instead of enjoying the moment. This is an experience and it's going to be fun.'

Rick is in a jovial mood, so I'm guessing his trial run this morning went well. It's clear he has no intention of talking about work and as we saunter along at a gentle pace, he chats about his experiences on family holidays when he was young. The snippets he shares are funny and he's good company. Having met his mum, it's obvious that while she adores her son, she didn't spoil him unnecessarily. Firm but fair, a bit like my parents, I suppose.

'You've gone quiet,' Rick remarks, drawing to a halt as he slips his backpack off his shoulder. He reaches inside and pulls out a bottle of water. 'Here you go. Can't have you getting dehydrated.'

'Thanks. I should have thought of that myself.' I break the seal and take a welcome slug of the still chilled water. 'I was just thinking how clean it all looks and how pretty. Even the leaves seem greener here and the bursts of colour are like clouds of happiness. All that sunshine makes everything thrive, and yet you'd think the heavy blossoms would wilt in this heat.'

'The landscape is certainly well-tended, but I agree. Some things get watered, but it's surprising how many shrubs and climbers survive on not a lot during the hottest season, which is yet to come.'

Everywhere you look there are little areas of neatly clipped hedges or shrubs to brighten the surroundings. Here, in the centre of town, it's like turning back the clock. Individual shops probably owned by generation after generation of the same family.

There are a lot of people strolling around, but considering that the labyrinth of limestone cobbled streets is quite narrow, the town has that lazy Sunday afternoon feeling. Most of the shops appear to be shut, but it's often hard to tell. I suspect they close at lunchtime for a couple of hours and early evening the doors will be propped open to welcome visitors, as the heat of the day begins to cool.

Virtually all of the buildings are rendered and painted white, with feature brickwork in either a sandy-colour or the popular pinkish-terracotta. The Roman, pan-tiled roofs are a variety of faded reds, through to a heather brown, and with the grey cobblestones, it's all very pleasing to the eye. As I tilt my head and look up, I suspect that the metal balconies above street level belong to apartments. When we turn a corner, into a smaller side street, some of them have washing suspended over the handrails.

Rick stops for a moment to check the map and I watch as he rubs the back of his hand across his brow. 'It's not far,' Rick confirms.

We take a right and then a left, which seems to leave him scratching his head as he checks the now crumpled sheet grasped tightly in his hand.

'I assumed we'd spot it from a way off. I mean, it is a palace,' he mutters, turning full circle, and I follow suit. But nothing stands out above the rooflines as we scan around what is a modest little alleyway, so we keep walking.

Just a couple of minutes' later, we spot a line of black bollards set in the pavement ahead where the alley ends and on the other side we discover a large, picturesque, square.

'This is it, Plaza Mayor de Andalucía,' Rick declares as if I should congratulate him on his map-reading skills.

It's a large public area and meeting place, with a stream of people milling around. There are families with small children, who are fascinated by a series of water jets set in the pavement in front of a high wall.

'And that, I presume, is one of the exterior walls of the palace,' Rick comments, pulling another sheet of paper from his back-pack. 'The entrance is through that archway and there are some gates on the right.'

We gaze around, laughing as a group of youngsters – two of them riding bicycles – run the gauntlet, traversing the wet pave-ment. Suddenly the jets begin to shoot up into the air, catching one of the girls and she screams out, running to the side as water drips from the hem of her skirt.

'Kids, eh?' I muse, thinking how much I took my childhood for granted. 'I remember being impatient to grow up and have more freedom. I didn't realise it was a time to enjoy life and a little innocent fun, before being an adult and having to follow endless rules and regulations.'

'It does feel like that, doesn't it? My dream was always to have my own restaurant, but I had no idea what I was letting myself in for. The paperwork, the legislation and the general running of a business is a headache. I was rather naïve, my head in the clouds just thinking of having a free hand to create the dishes I wanted to present to my diners. Fortunately, Cathy has all the right contacts, but I can see how easy it might be to get into trouble if you choose the wrong advisors, or take on too much debt.'

I turn to look at him, surprised by his admission. 'It's all a learning curve, isn't it? And it was a huge step for you, at the time.'

He glances back at me, wrinkling his brow. 'I didn't have a choice,' he sighs. Then his expression changes in an instant and he dismisses his thoughts with a mere shrug of his shoulders. 'Right, so shall we do this? It's time to explore.'

Rick turns to begin walking towards the entrance to the palace and I fall in alongside him.

'The palace certainly dominates the square,' I point out, more than happy to spend a few hours simply being a tourist. 'And look at those walls, they're amazing. You can just imagine the battles that took place between the Moors and the Christians.'

Leading off from the plaza are four roads and alleyways, but we're heading for an archway adjoining the massive palace wall in front of us. To our right, there are a series of towers and buildings set within the grounds. It's possible to glimpse the tops of trees and palms on the other side before the wall rises much higher, obliterating the view beyond. To the left of the archway is La Oficina Municipal de Turismo. It's attached to the stout, outer wall and is a grand-looking building. Three storeys high, both the ground and the second floors have tall columns supporting an arcade of double-width, arches. La Oficina Municipal de Turismo is all glass and beautiful brickwork, the tints of grey and the slightly pinkish hue mirror the paved square, which also features a long run of limestone cobbles.

While the centre of the plaza is a wide-open space, around the perimeter are benches and in one corner there are some bistro tables and chairs. With black, wrought-iron lamp posts with triple lanterns, clusters of tall palm trees and a couple of fruit trees to add a little greenery, it's a lovely place to sit and while away an hour or two.

The other buildings surrounding the square are two-storey, white-fronted properties with windows mirroring the arches. Many of them have black, wrought-iron balconies looking out over the plaza and together with their heather-coloured pan-tiled roofs, the scene is picturesque.

'You love all this, don't you?' Rick asks, sounding amused, as I take in the minute details.

'Yes. It takes vision, time and money to preserve buildings as old as these and, clearly, there's a sense of pride in keeping the history of the square alive for future generations to enjoy. It's very special.'

Walking through the arched tunnel, Rick points up ahead, 'Come on, I think the gate we're looking for is up here.'

The pavement has a strip of cobbles running down the centre and it leads to a church with a very ornately carved entrance and a bell tower above. But off to our right is a low wall with black railings and a pair of modern, black metal gates leading into a vast, cobbled courtyard. As we step through the gates, there is a separate building on the left with another set of gates in the far left-hand corner. The other two sides of the square are bounded by an L-shaped building. It's not quite the historic beauty we were expecting to see and Rick glances at me, raising his eyebrows. The walls are rendered and painted; the dozen or so windows and glass French doors all have either metal balconies or grilles. There are two sets of huge, double wooden doors that are built to withhold a siege by the looks of it. It's impressive but given the exterior to the palace walls adjoining the plaza, I was expecting ancient, crumbling walls.

We saunter up to the enormous pair of metal-studded doors, into which a smaller internal door is set.

'I feel like Daenerys, stepping into the unknown.'

Rick looks at me for a brief second, quizzically.

'Ignore me, I'm having a flashback to a TV moment, when all hell was about to break loose on screen.'

'I think you're safe,' he says, half-whispering.

There doesn't appear to be any means of attracting attention and I wait while Rick pulls out his phone and dials.

Either side of the entrance are two large, manicured shrubs, shaped into gently curving pyramids. It's all so pristine and well cared for and yet despite the fact that it's understated by its simplicity, I just know this is going to be an amazing experience.

12

TIME TO SOAK UP A LITTLE HISTORY

'*Buenas tardes*. Rick Oliver and Elaine Summers. We have an appointment?'

Seconds later, the small door swings open and an old lady dressed in black bids us to enter. She says something in Spanish as we step inside, but we're oblivious to her words as both of our jaws drop simultaneously.

The woman hurries off, leaving us standing there as if we've stepped through a black hole and reappeared in another place and another time. We're in what could be referred to as a little vestibule, except that this isn't a room with four walls because the fourth wall is a floor-to-ceiling, wrought-iron gateway. If someone breached the heavy wooden doors, this would certainly slow them down. The walls are the warm, mellow terracotta pink colour the Spanish favour. On the wall to our left are several plaques made out of sets of four ceramic tiles, examples of traditional Spanish designs. Beneath them is a carved consul table, which, I should imagine, dates back to medieval times. It's dark, almost black, and the carving is a simple geometric shape, repeated to form a square.

But it's what's beyond the metalwork that draws our eyes and it's like looking at a mirage. I feel I've been whisked away to Marrakesh.

There's a metallic scraping sound as a narrow door to our right opens and a young woman comes to greet us. 'Welcome, my name is Jazmín and it's my pleasure to be your tour guide for today.' I don't think she's Spanish by origin and I'm guessing she's maybe Iranian. Wearing a flowing and colourful kaftan, and a huge smile on her face, her welcome is very gracious.

I step forward to offer my hand. 'Hello, Jazmín, I'm Lainey and this is Rick.'

He reluctantly drags his eyes away from the scene awaiting us to shake hands.

'Please come this way,' she says, as we follow her through the gateway into the most unimaginable setting.

'This is a total surprise. What an oasis of calm,' I mutter, enthralled.

Jazmín smiles. 'I like to say that it soothes one's soul. The Palacio de Portocarrero is a historical landmark here in Palma del Río. Originally built as the residence for the Roman consul and governor, Aulio Cornelio Palma, it is now famous for its Mudejar gardens. That term references the Arabs, or Moors, living under Christian rule in mainland Spain during the Middle Ages. Is history of interest to you both?'

We nod in unison.

'In brief then, after the spread of Islam in the seventh century AD, the Moors, as the Arabs were called then, invaded Spain. They conquered much of the peninsular, bringing with them an alien civilisation and a high culture that included, among other things, ornamental gardens, pools and fountains. But also, more practically, a revolutionary system of agriculture, with innovations such as new food crops and waterwheels to provide irrigation. However, nothing lasts for ever; the ruling Moors were defeated and driven out of Spain in 1492. But although they had been defeated and subdued, the influence of the Moors, or *Mudejars*, remained.'

It's a lot to take in as we gaze around. An open, two-storey, porticoed patio surrounds the central courtyard, which has a traditional mud-brick floor laid in a herringbone pattern. The rendered walls are painted in a rich terracotta. But it's the beauty and majesty of the arches supported by the slim pillars that adds an easy elegance to the architecture. It's a grander version of the monastery, with an almost decadent, eastern feel. It's unlike anything I have ever seen up close. There's an opulence, a richness of design, which conjures up images of bazaars in exotic places, sacks of spices, flowing kaftans and colourful silks.

I've fallen in love with the towering palms and cypress trees, which rise up beyond the level of the roof and turn this beautiful setting into a virtual paradise. I can't even begin to imagine the age of these trees. Around the bases of several clusters of trees are squares of neatly clipped box hedging, which not only hint at a formally laid-out garden, as it does in the monastery, but succeeds in making the arches look even more graceful.

'Let's head over to the far corner, where I think you will be enchanted by what we sometimes refer to as the secret garden.'

I notice a headless Romanesque statue standing on a plinth, set back beneath one of the arches. The second floor above is a simple blank wall with no openings whatsoever.

'The renovations continue,' Jazmín explains. 'Much has been done, but there is still a lot of work to do.'

Rick points to a pyramid of wooden barrels next to the statuary. 'Notice that they are stamped *Alvear Wines* and one of them carries the word festival. Remember the dish you had with the sweet sherry, the amontillado Pedro Ximénez? It's produced by the Alvear winery,' he half-whispers, although our guide has already disappeared through a passageway ahead of us.

We hurry to catch up with her and find ourselves stepping out into a totally different environment.

'Surprised?' Jazmín is standing over to the right-hand side.

The doorway leading out of the covered walkway is a frame for another, headless Roman sculpture set on a plinth in front of us. It stands surrounded by knee-high, white flowers and setting it off in the background is a rough-rendered, terracotta painted wall. As I glance around, there is indeed the feel of a secret garden, long and narrow and enclosed by the high walls surrounding it.

'Please, follow the path,' Jazmín invites us to walk on.

Beneath our feet, the stones are old and well-worn, and the floor is patchy in places where it's been filled in with other materials. The wall to our right is roughly rendered and painted, but to the left are the original walls of the palace, which give a clue to how extensive the renovations have been. There are areas where chunks of the stonework have crumbled away, perhaps even damage from an attack on the palace in the dim and distant past.

'Carry straight on and then turn left at the end,' our guide informs us.

With a corridor-like feel, enhanced by the towering, slender fir trees, and a mass of what I presume are local wildflowers scattered among the borders and spilling over onto the path, it's delightfully informal. When we reach the end and step out into the main garden, Rick and I both draw to a halt.

Standing alongside a small, raised pool with spiky green plants, we stare at the sheer beauty of the vast gardens in front of us. The palace's boundary wall to our right rises up, reminding us that we are within a fortress, and I feel that I've been spirited away to yet another place. Even the air I'm breathing in is different here. I'm growing accustomed to the dry heat that leaves a slightly dusty taste in my mouth. But here there's a smokiness in the air, despite the fact that there is no sign of a fire anywhere, so it must be from a plant or a shrub.

Drawing in another deep breath, my nose is filled with a whole host of fragrances, from the sharp citrus smell that is never far away in Andalucía, to a variety of intense perfumes from the aromatic plants around us.

'The gardens are actually Hispano-Mudejar in style,' Jazmín informs us.

Rick walks forward into the middle of the square patio and turns to look at the boundary wall which towers above us. 'It's incredible that these fortress walls are still standing after all these years and countless battles.'

'It is, indeed,' Jazmín agrees. 'Even though they are aged and, as you can see, crumbling and patched in places with a variety of materials, they remain solid.'

'Are the small holes that appear at semi-regular points to do with the construction process?' Rick enquires.

'Yes. It is a mixture that comprises mainly of mud, soil, clay and small stones, together with straw and, often, lime, which makes it more resistant to weathering. Boards were erected, one level at a time, and the workers would pack in this mix. When it was solid, or cured, the shuttering would be taken down and another level begun. The multiple rows of small holes were a part of the scaffolding process. Originally, that would not have been seen, as the completed walls were covered with a lime stucco to further protect them. As you can see, in a few areas, even bricks have been used in the past to make repairs and this, too, is a part of the history.'

'It's truly fascinating,' Rick replies as I walk over to join him.

'Would you like to explore the gardens for a while? If you retrace your steps back when you are ready, someone will fetch me, and I will give you a tour of the inside.'

'That would be perfect, thank you.'

Jazmín turns to walk back as we set off. The brick-paved square leads into an even larger patio area, but instead we follow the path in line with the outer walls. We're in the furthest corner closest to the palace now and the grounds extend out way beyond our view. The formal layout doesn't look symmetrical from here, but instead it's geometrical and divided into sections. Each section has formal, waist-height, clipped box hedging, creating little gardens, each displaying individual collections of specimen plants. In between, the tall palms and cypress trees are dotted around everywhere as far as the eye can see and the whole effect is exotic and luxurious.

'The palms are amazing, but are those regular cypress trees? Or do you think they are a different species? I've never seen them grow as tall as that,' I ask Rick.

He shrugs his shoulders. 'I think they might well be, given they are so slender. There is a Spanish fir, of course, but they're bushier. Some of these others are juniper trees, I think. I find it astounding, though, given how hot and dry it is, that even with irrigation the trees can grow so tall. I can't even begin to imagine the age of some of them.'

Immediately in front of us are triangular sections with an assortment of both trees and manicured bushes shaped into balls, ovals, and pyramids. Then the path we're on meets another and we take a left turn, to make our way across into the centre section.

Some of the bordered areas are denser here, with burgeoning

fruit trees and there are sections with smaller palm-like bushes sporting wider fronds, and succulents, too.

'Those are aloe vera plants, I know that much,' I inform Rick, confidently, and he looks impressed.

'Now this is more my thing,' Rick points as we head toward a large, rectangular area which looks like a market garden. But even though we can see little subdivided plots with vegetables, they're interspersed with flower beds and manicured standard trees and shrubs. We step through one of the gaps in the hedging to take a closer look.

There is a wide variety of vegetables and herbs, everything from bay to thyme and rosemary and, in between, rows of lavender bushes, a castor oil plant and even a section with rose bushes. The irrigation here consists of a series of pipes which lay exposed on top of the soil. What I don't see are weeds, which is incredible given how easily things grow here, flourishing in the blazing sunshine.

I look directly at Rick. 'Well, I'm waning in this heat,' I admit. 'How are you doing?'

'I'm loving this climate, but if we can find somewhere shady to sit for a while to cool down, that would be perfect. Shall we head over to the citrus grove, as it looks like there's a grassy area on the far side.'

We make our way out of the maze of little beds and back onto one of the main pathways, as we head in the direction of the burgeoning fruit trees. I'm surprised to look over the hedging and see not simply a large expanse of lawn, but little clusters of cast-iron garden chairs and tables spread out in spots beneath some of the larger trees.

'Here we go,' Rick says as we find a way in and head over to the shadiest spot.

'At first glance I couldn't believe my eyes, as I was convinced this had to be an apple tree given the size of the fruit. But look, they're limes. I'm used to the small, dark-green ones you can buy in the supermarket that always look as tart as they taste. These are the size of small apples.' I collapse onto one of the chairs and, thankfully, it's more comfortable than it looks. Kicking off my flat shoes, I wiggle my toes appreciatively. 'That feels so good,' I half-groan, grabbing the water bottle from my backpack.

Rick, I notice, downs the remainder of his in one go. 'It's like an oasis, isn't it? It's hard to believe that the other side of this huge wall behind us is the plaza. All I can hear right now are the birds squabbling and the noise from the group of men assembling that rather large marquee over by the rear wall of the palace.'

We walked past them just now and it looks like they are preparing for a party. From where we are sitting, though, we can't see them. Over the tops of the citrus trees, I gaze at the brick arches of a whole wing of the palace that is undergoing renovation. There are at least fifty birds, maybe more, sitting on the ridge tiles enjoying the view. What I can't see from here are the two lower floors with gaping holes for windows as the basic structure is being virtually rebuilt. It must feel like a never-ending project, but it's amazing to see what has been achieved already.

'Did you know that some of the scenes from the film *Kingdom of Heaven* were shot here? It's about the Crusades in the twelfth century,' Rick says, settling back contentedly and stretching out his legs.

'Who was in it?'

'Liam Neeson and Orlando Bloom. And, uh... what's her name? She was in a Bond film—'

'Eva Green. Yes, I vaguely remember watching it. Amazing film work with the battles and the crowds. I'll have to watch it again and see if I can spot the palace.'

'I often watch films I like several times over. Cathy can't

understand that, but then her attention span is shorter than mine,' he grins at me, shaking his head as if he finds that amusing. 'She's used to watching music videos.'

'Oh I agree with you, it's like reading a good book over and over. Each time, you notice something new you didn't pick up on before.'

'That's another thing we have in common, then, besides a little bit of history.'

'It's funny, but when I was at school, history seemed to be about an endless succession of facts and figures, but the minute you relate the stories to something physical, like these old stone walls, it has more meaning. Even a film brings history to life in a more meaningful way than dry history books.'

We lapse into silence and are content to sit for a while resting and enjoying the shade, even though the air we breathe in is so warm I can taste the heat. Rick closes his eyes for a few minutes, and I find myself watching him, taking in little details I haven't noticed before. He has a small scar, just below his hairline, on his right temple. It's silvery-white and with a hint of a tan beginning to develop it's suddenly noticeable. Rick's hair is several inches long on top and almost totally shaved up the back, but the front bit is flopping today with the heat. Usually, it's perfectly gelled and he always looks well-groomed, but this look suits him, too. He shifts position and I look away in case he opens his eyes and catches me studying him.

As I glance around, I haven't felt as at one with myself as I do right now for a long time. I'm not worrying about work, family and friends, or whether I'll ever find someone and feel true love. I thought I had that with Warren, but love, it seems, can evaporate as quickly as it can come into your life. Perhaps it never was love in the first place, but how can you be sure at the start?

'You look serious there.' Rick's voice makes me instantly turn my head to look at him.

'Just thoughts running through my head,' I reply, trying to sound casual.

'Hmm... it's more than that, I think,' he informs me. 'I'm good at listening, you know, if you want to share,' Rick adds.

Is he right? I don't know. I'm not even clear in my own mind why I suddenly feel so maudlin.

'Perhaps it's the history you're feeling,' he continues. 'Imagine all the things that have occurred on this very spot. And now, here we are – you and me, a part of the palace's history too.'

I glance at him, unable to hide my surprise at his words. As I continue to stare at him, I'm seeing him in a different light. Am I kidding myself, or is he a man who needs rescuing?

'It's probably because it's been a while since I've been in such a peaceful and tranquil setting, or had any real time to just sit and unwind,' I respond.

This is getting too personal for me, and Rick, being a gentleman and sensing my unease, suggests we make our way back to find Jazmín. As we walk side by side, my head is full of a whole range of disparate thoughts and, without thinking, I go to reach for his hand. Instantly I remember who I'm with and, thankfully, Rick is totally unaware of my faux pas. I let my guard slip for a moment and that's something I can't let happen again.

It's loneliness, Lainey, I tell myself. *You're allowed to feel sad about the past, but when you truly can move on, life will be good again. Just hang in there. The right man for you is out there somewhere, you simply need to be patient.*

* * *

When I arrive back in my room and pull out my phone, I realise that it's been on mute all afternoon and there are three messages from Dario, two with screenshots from Twitter attached.

Hey, Lainey. Bit of a backlash after Cathy walked off stage early last night. Give me a call.

The next one was sent an hour later and is a video clip of what appears to be Cathy having a public rant after a fan called her out for a lacklustre performance.

Obviously, you are busy, but that thread just got worse and here's another screenshot. Do you want me to keep you up to do date? Hope you're the enjoying the sunshine! 😊

Now my conscience is pricking me. Should I tell Rick about this in case he doesn't know, or should I just leave it alone? Even if things blow up with Cathy wherever she is right now, it has nothing to do with the filming here. And Rick might not appreciate me keeping tabs on social media. It would be a nightmare being here together for four weeks if he suddenly felt he couldn't trust me. I don't really want to say too much to Dario, so I dash off a quick reply.

Thanks, appreciated, but things have moved on, so no need to keep an eye out. I hope that thread has already been taken down, though. Nightmare!

I head off to grab a quick shower and when I return, Dario has already replied.

It's like it never happened. The problem these days is that people take their own screenshots, so this sort of stuff never really disappears. Send photos of you at the monastery and I'll put them out on the *Upscale Dining* account. Our readers love that sort of stuff. It's raining here by the way. Thomas was in a bad mood on Friday and I'm dreading tomorrow's meeting. Anyway, have fun. We're about to order takeout!

I feel better getting Dario to stand down from the social media watch. I'm sure if Cathy has a problem, then she would talk it through with Rick, anyway. As for Thomas, he might just have had the week from hell, who knows?

As I'm sitting on the edge of the bed with the phone in my hand, it lights up.

'Hi, Dad, how are you?'

'More to the point, how are you doing?'

'I'm good. Really good, thank you. The weather is fabulous, the monastery couldn't be more perfect a setting and this afternoon Rick Oliver and I had a personal tour of the Palacio de Portocarrero. It was like stepping into one of the tales from the Arabian Nights.'

'Sounds like you're having fun.'

'What are you doing?' I reply, trying to sound blasé.

'Finishing off some admin stuff and then I'll start doing some packing. I want to get things ready so I can load up the car Wednesday afternoon, ready for an early start.'

That brings a smile to my face. The fact that he's planning is a good sign and means he's unlikely to change his mind last-minute.

'You're not going to be working while you're there, are you?' I ask, pointedly. 'I mean, it's not a jolly. Mum really does need help, or she wouldn't have asked me.'

It won't go down well if he's preoccupied and doesn't take the work seriously. The business is Mum's livelihood, after all. She's hoping to continue to grow it enough to be able to afford some permanent help.

'No. I wouldn't do that. But you know me, I like to cover all bases, and if I do get any time when I'm at a loose end, at least I'll have my stuff with me.'

'Dad, if you find yourself with time on your hands, why not take a stroll through the country lanes, or visit one of the local markets? Or you could hang around with the other guests in the evenings, rather than shutting yourself away. It's just a thought and the company will be a tonic.'

He gives a groan. 'I suppose. Anyway, it all kicks off tomorrow for you, then?'

'Yes. It's the first of Rick's demonstrations. He'll be cooking a three-course meal and it will be interesting working with the local photographer for the first time. The competition itself is over three days and the contestants focus on one course each day. It's too hot to film past noon, so the mornings are going to be quite intense.'

'This photographer is good, is he?'

'Looking at his website, he's fine and he covers a food festival each year. I'm looking forward to it, as there's an easy camaraderie amongst the group, even though the competition is going to be fierce.'

'This will be a real boost for your career, too. You arrived at just the right time, Lainey. Show them what you can do, my darling, they haven't seen anything yet. I'm glad you changed tack and followed your interests. I can't wait to read the articles and I bet your mum will be poring over those recipes for inspiration.'

For a second there, my heart skips a beat. It's been a long time since Dad casually mentioned Mum without me mentioning her first.

'Now there's a thought,' I laugh. Dad's downplaying this trip, but I think he might secretly be looking forward to it.

'Text me tomorrow to let me know how it goes and if we don't get a chance to speak in between, I'll let you know when I arrive on French soil.'

There's a definite lift in his voice, even if he doesn't realise it.

13

THE EXCITEMENT IS TANGIBLE AND WEEK ONE IS A WHIRLWIND

Rick isn't at dinner, in fact, he's nowhere to be seen. We didn't make plans to meet up, but he didn't mention he wasn't going to be around, either. After spending such a pleasant day together, I feel a little lost and I end up sitting at a table with four of the contestants. They're a lively bunch and knowing a little about them helps. And, of course, while I'm new to them, everyone is aware of *Upscale Dining* magazine. They are genuinely interested in what I do and ask a lot of questions. With no one around to interpret, we manage well enough between us all, and I tell them about the average day in the life of a food writer. It's nowhere near as glamorous as they believe it to be, imagining a constant round of invitations from wonderful restaurants wanting to be featured. Of course, the fact that I'm here in Spain to cover this event makes it sound like I'm playing the glamour down, but I'm not.

'Is still a wonderful job tasting food and then writing about it,' Louis Reno, who works in a small restaurant in a family-run chateau close to Rennes, remarks insistently. We're sitting in the courtyard clustered around one of the small tables alongside the bar, languishing over our after-dinner coffees. 'And you have been to Rick Oliver's restaurant many times?'

'Several times. And yes, that is a privilege. His food is incredible, as you will all find out tomorrow.'

'If you had to give us one tip, knowing the man himself, what would that be?' Louis asks.

They are all looking at me as if I know something they don't and my mouth goes dry for a moment or two, before I dismiss the feeling. They only know Rick from what they've read, I suppose, so it's a fair enough question and their nerves are beginning to show.

'When I first met Rick, he told me that even if the flavours leap off the plate, the visual appeal is the precursor to an amazing dining experience. Without that level of perfection, the dish is an imperfect marriage.'

Eyebrows rise and I can see they are taking this very seriously indeed.

'I'm not sure who said this, but I know he was one of the most celebrated chefs of his era. It was something along the lines of, "You experience the food with your eyes, before it even touches your taste buds", and there's a lot of truth in that,' I add.

'I have heard that said before. Now I'm nervous,' Louis replies, but he's smiling.

'Well, I wish everyone the best of luck in the competition! It's time to call it a night for me, but I will see you all tomorrow. Sleep well.'

* * *

The next morning, the breakfast room is busy and I grab a coffee and a croissant to take outside, settling myself down at one of the tables on the open patio area. People are coming and going, most of them I recognise as being connected to today's filming, and you can feel the excitement in the air.

I notice Rick and Javier approaching and they head straight towards me.

'Good morning, Lainey, we've been looking for you,' Rick says, giving me a warm smile. 'Do you mind if we join you?'

'Please do. Take a seat.'

'Your photographer will be here soon?' Javier asks.

'Yes, Emilio will be here for 9 a.m.'

'*Perfecto*,' he replies.

'I will plate up special dishes for the still photographs, Lainey, once we're done,' Rick confirms.

'Thank you. If there's a suitable pause in recording during the morning, would it be possible for Emilio to grab a few photos of Rick talking to the contestants if we promise not to get in the way?' I ask and Javier nods his head.

'Is fine by me, and you, Rick?'

'Yes, of course. Just get Emilio to grab me if there's a break and let me know what sort of shots you need as and when, Lainey.'

'Brilliant. Thank you.'

Javier is already checking his watch and I can see he's anxious to get people moving. 'Perhaps we can head over to the kitchen now and the others will follow.'

I finish the last of my coffee and stand, grabbing my things as Javier is already a few strides away. Rick hangs back for me.

'How are you feeling?' I ask.

'Good. I just want to get on and do it now.'

I give him a sympathetic look. 'That's understandable. The waiting around is the hardest part, isn't it?'

He nods in agreement. 'You'll be glad to see Emilio arrive, won't you? Has he been in touch?'

'He texted me first thing this morning.'

'Listen, once he's here and there's a pause in the proceedings make sure you get whatever shots you need. If I'm talking to someone just interrupt me, okay?'

We step through the double glass doors, which are pinned back, as everyone heads inside.

I lean into Rick. 'Break a leg,' I half-whisper, as we part company.

I head over to take a seat in the wide opening between the two rooms. Rick's temporary kitchen and prep area are on the far side, opposite the glass doors. This area is normally used as the hotel's breakfast room and it has the feel of a rustic chapel. The floor is the same, pale pink/terracotta hand-made mud bricks as in the cloisters and patio area outside. On this side of the room, the ceilings, which are the underneath of the galleried walkways on the first floor, are supported by a series of sweeping arches. As a striking contrast between the white walls and plastered arches, the ceilings are exposed. The floors above are made up of wide planks, with narrow tree trunks running the length of the room serving as the main supports. In between is a network of small crossbeams. In terms of a photo shoot, the space couldn't be more perfect, or charming.

A row of seven chairs is set out in front of the main stainless-steel workbench, beneath which is a display of fresh fruits and vegetables. To one side is another bench housing several pieces of standard kitchen equipment, an oven, a large gas hob and, next to it, a commercial fridge/freezer.

Rick is now standing in the centre facing us, as the contestants take their seats. He doesn't look at all nervous, he looks confident, and I realise there's an element of performance attached to being a chef. Even if you don't have an audience, every professional kitchen I've been lucky enough to visit is, in a way, a constant place of learning. Chef is always on alert, prompting here and there, whether it's in terms of presentation or checking the food is perfectly cooked before it goes out to the customer. It's a tough industry to be in and I suppose that constant level of scrutiny is something they learn to live with. The old saying that if you can't stand the heat, you should get out of the kitchen has never seemed truer than it does now. The kitchen is about to get very hot indeed.

While Javier is busy getting his small team into place and they adjust the lighting, I pull out my camera and take a few discreet shots. Then it's time to adjust the position of my chair so that I can see a little better and I pull out my notepad and pen. I half-turn in my seat to look over at the contestants' kitchens, which are set up in the second half of the room. The long line extends down the full length as it's narrower, but it works. Here, the arched ceilings are all plastered and frescoed with delicate drawings of luscious lemons in a soft yellow and branches of leaves in a vibrant green. There are dishes with various citrus fruits and pictures of springtime blossoms. It's charming and the lower section of the walls are painted in the same pale-yellow colour, adding a warmth to that side of the room. Sometimes, I'm told, it's used for small wedding parties and I can visualise a long table laid out with white tablecloths and chairs with elegant linen covers.

Javier and another man are now standing next to Rick, as they adjust his microphone and, after a thumbs-up, they leave Rick patiently waiting until the final countdown begins. To my horror, it looks like we're going to start fifteen minutes early. I told Emilio we wouldn't begin until 9 a.m. A movement out of the side of my eye makes me turn my head and there he is, hurrying over to me with the brightest of smiles on his face. My body almost sags with relief as I jump up and organise a chair for him. I give him a grateful smile, although I could cheerfully give him a hug just for making it here.

'It's going to be fine,' he whispers, 'everything is sorted. I can make myself available for the entire time.'

* * *

The crew and contestants have all headed off to grab lunch, leaving Rick, Emilio and me to fuss over the still photos.

The hero of today's starter was the zingy Spanish orange. Three gloriously seared but opaque scallops have been drizzled with nut-brown butter. On top of each is a nest of finely chopped, deep-fried crispy kale. A graceful swirl of an orange butter sauce sweeps around the side of each of the little rounds, as if an artist had painted it with a brush. My notes say little other than quick, simple and exquisite to look at and I can't wait to taste it even though it's cold.

Rick has spaced each of the dishes out on the table and Emilio is snapping away. Lifting one of the twigs of leaves from the large bowl of oranges beneath the bench, I lean in and Emilio stops while I place it next to the plate. Then he continues.

'Is that a criticism of my lack of decoration?' Rick's voice is playful.

'Not at all. I mean, that is perfection on a plate and the smell is divine. But look how that cluster of green picks up the kale.'

Rick shrugs his shoulders as Emilio stands back and we turn our attention to the main course.

Two small rounds of local, pan-fried beef tenderloin served medium rare, with tail of veal, make a simple yet elegant dish. Next to these are three small, *patatas risoladas*, the Spanish version of roast potatoes in miniature. The beef sits on a slick of a red wine and shallot reduction, with two spears of asparagus and a baked, honey-glazed carrot.

Emilio looks at me and I nod, inviting him to snap away. He does his close-ups first, then indicates for me to move the starter, as he zooms out. Rick offers me a small white jug of the rich, wine jus and he grins at me as I take it from him. Placing it on the over-sized white plate, to the side of the beautiful little island of food, he nods his approval and Emilio is on it.

'It doesn't need any additional sauce, of course,' Rick informs me, with a mock sense of gravity. 'But the beef is the hero of the dish and the flavours are emphasised in the jus, so it too is a star.'

Emilio seems oblivious to the banter going on between us.

Dessert is simply a vision to behold, but as it's a flambé, Rick recreates it for us while we wait. The small ramekin of Crema Catalana sits undecorated on a teardrop-shaped, white dish. Flavoured with lemon peel and cinnamon, it's similar to a crème brûlée and cooked in a bain-marie, but thinner in texture. Rick sprinkles a liberal amount of brown sugar on the top before grabbing his blowtorch and a tiny jug of a Spanish lemon liqueur. He clears the table and both Emilio and I stand back, but I see that Emilio has his camera ready to capture the perfect shot.

Rick is oblivious to us as he lights up the torch and caramelises the sugar, then quickly pouring over a small shot of liqueur, he allows it to flame for a few seconds. The result fills the air with a toasty, toffee flavour and a strong hint of citrussy zest. Then he turns to grab the small bowl of citrus jam he made earlier on, scooping a heaped pile next to the ramekin before adding the final touches. A small sprig of three mint leaves, an oval, cinnamon biscuit that looks like it will melt in the mouth and he's smiling.

'I'm done,' he says, stepping back and looking down at the plate with pride.

Emilio continues clicking away and I'm happy. More than happy.

'Well, we have some pretty amazing shots there. Can I be a little cheeky and ask if I could take a photo of you with Chef Rick for my website?' Emilio asks me tentatively. 'This is an exciting project for me and I'd love to mark the occasion.'

Rick holds out his hand, indicating for me to step around, into his kitchen.

'Do you mind if I rearrange the table a little?' Emilio has already put his camera down and has picked up one of the printed logos for the competition.

Rick and I shrug our shoulders, laughing.

Emilio lays it next to Rick's stunning dessert and we stand awkwardly, side by side waiting for the shot.

Then Rick turns to me. 'We don't look like we're having much fun,' he comments, and I agree. So, while Emilio concentrates on getting us into focus, I pick up some lemons, plucked from the trees outside first thing this morning and still attached to twigs bearing leaves. Rick picks up his blow torch. We look at each other, laughing as Emilio snaps away.

The first of the four masterclasses is done and it's a wrap. Rick can now relax, and so can I, because Emilio has stepped up and produced the goods.

* * *

Thursday is a little unsettling for me as I anxiously await Dad's call, wondering whether he'll change his mind and let me, and Mum, down. So, when my phone begins to ring, I snatch it up, smiling when I see that it's him.

'Only me, calling to let you know that my feet are on French soil.' It's hard to tell from Dad's tone how he really feels about that, but at least he's there safe and sound.

'What's the weather like?' I ask, to stop me from asking about Mum.

'Sunny, but it's quite windy today. Anyway, more importantly, how it's going your end?' His voice lifts and I know he realises what a wonderful opportunity this trip is for me. That's why Dad stepped in to help me out, so I could fly off with a clear conscience.

'Things just seem to have slotted into place quite nicely. Emilio was a little nervous to begin with, but now he knows exactly what I'm looking for, he's nailing it.'

'And you're enjoying yourself, too? It's not all work, I hope.'

'No, it's fun. When the crew are around, there's quite a large group of us, so the atmosphere is lively. They're a friendly bunch. And this place is amazing, it's just full of history and I actually feel like I've stepped off the treadmill for a while.'

'That's exactly what you needed, Lainey. You know what they say, a change is as good as a rest.'

That makes me smile. 'And this is just that.'

'Oh well,' he sighs, 'I'd best finish unpacking and make myself useful, I suppose.' He doesn't sound overly keen, but, at some point, the two of them will have to begin talking and agree some ground rules. Hopefully they will draw a line under the past and focus solely on getting through the next couple of weeks. I can only hope that it will be possible for them to establish an easy peace and focus on the task in hand.

'Try to relax and go with the flow, Dad, and thank you. I mean it. Love you!'

'Love you, too, Lainey. We'll speak soon.'

I am grateful to be here and Dad is right, I did need this. It's been an incredible week. If the contestants were nervous to begin with, they don't have time to dwell on that now because each cook-off represents a fresh challenge. They are all determined to give their very best.

It wasn't really until today, when they moved onto the final course, that it became apparent some are skilled across the board, while others have a leaning towards one specific area. The best dessert was undoubtedly delivered by Alexis Di Angelis, the Greek contestant, but his beef was overdone yesterday, which was a rookie mistake. The points awarded are a secret, but each day the top three dishes are announced in order. So far, the French candidate, Louis Reno, has taken two out of the three number one spots. However, the competition is still wide open, and everyone knows that.

My phone begins to ring once more, but this time it's Rick.

'Hey, what's up?' I enquire, stifling a yawn.

'I was just wondering if you have to work all weekend to meet your deadline?'

'Tomorrow and Saturday I'm going to be flat out, I'm afraid. Is there a problem?'

'No, not at all. You might have Sunday free, then?'

My spirits suddenly lift. 'I think that might be a possibility,' I reply, trying not to sound as enthusiastic as I feel.

'Good. Assuming I can hire a car, I thought we could head off for the day and do some sightseeing, what do you think?'

'Count me in. I work best when there's a deadline and I'm sure I can get it done in time. I'm a champion prevaricator, which is a really bad habit of mine if I'm not careful.'

'Ah, so I'd be rescuing you, in fact. Excellent. Right, goodnight then. Sleep well, Lainey.'

* * *

The following morning, Rick phones to apologise profusely, saying that he's flying out to meet up with Cathy for a long week-end. He sounds a little put out. Given that the first week has been exhausting, I can't help thinking he'd probably have appreciated the chance to simply kick back and enjoy his surroundings. But I guess being apart isn't easy and Cathy, too, will be missing him.

I end up working a solid twelve hours, trawling through the photos Emilio sent through and uploading them to the system. It was tough when I could hear the fun everyone else was having around the pool and Saturday isn't much better. With a minibus collecting the contestants to take them to a vineyard for lunch and a tasting session, it's a struggle spending the entire day proofing the remainder of the copy for the first article.

Miguel wasn't available to pop in, so I've sent him the draft piece about the monastery and he's going to fact-check it for me. He also offered to cast his eye over the Spanish words I've used in reference to the buildings and some of the classic Andalucían dishes I've mentioned.

Sunday is supposed to be some well-deserved downtime, my reward for the hard work I've put in as no one works on a Sunday, do they? But I don't have the energy, or the motivation, to sort out something to do, and I'm not in the mood to join everyone when they head off to savour some of the local food. Instead, I lie out on one of the sun loungers, intent on reading a self-help book entitled: *When to Call it Quits and Start All Over Again.*

It begins with a single question printed in the centre of page one. *What's your one biggest regret in life, so far?* The instruction printed below it is to not turn over the page until you have a definitive answer, because your future hopes and dreams rest upon it. Ten minutes later, I'm still sitting and contemplating my answer.

I decide to pop up to my room to grab a pen and paper and before too long I have a little list started. As I begin to rate each item to find out which one soars above the others, it hits me. I'm clearly in deep trouble. I pick the book back up and turn the page, and this is what I read:

> If you answered the question correctly, then congratulations, you can skip straight to Chapter Ten. If you didn't get it right, then you haven't yet learnt to listen to your inner voice. In which case read on, because if you can't trust yourself, then every decision you make could be influenced by someone who won't necessarily have your interests at heart.

Each word is painful to read and it is as if the author is talking to me, about me. Times in the past when I've done things just to please other people demonstrate a lack of self-esteem.

I read late into the night because now I'm hooked, but when I find out what the solution is to get back on track, it comes as a bit of a let-down. I flick through each of the endpapers, but all three pages are blank. The last printed page says:

> Take each thought and spin it around to see it from another angle. If it still makes sense, then fine, but if it doesn't, then your perception is skewed. Eventually the day will come when you finally let go of the baggage you carry from previous mistakes. You will have broken the circle of negativity and be truly free to manifest what you desire.

I'm so annoyed with myself for expecting this book to give me a definitive answer, that I know there's no way I can simply lie down and get to sleep. Instead, I finish off my covering email to Thomas and upload everything to the portal to complete the first article. It's 3 a.m. when my head finally touches the cool, cotton pillowcase and I feel myself relax. At least one part of my day wasn't a total waste of time.

14

TIME TO RELAX

'What time did you get back last night?' I ask Rick as he picks at the array of tapas dishes laid out on the low table in front of us. It's quiet here tonight as a whole group of the cast and crew have taken a trip into town to visit one of the local restaurants again. I said I was too tired to go, and Rick probably used the same excuse.

'Just after midnight. It was a crazy, last-minute decision and I don't intend on doing it again. Monday is gruelling enough, and I feel wiped out now.' He looks tired and is slumped back in his chair. 'I'm done,' he says, pushing his plate away. 'It's delicious, but I'm not that hungry. This chair's a bit hard and I need to stretch my legs. We could take the wine over to the pool and stretch out, what do you think?'

'Sounds good to me. I had a late one last night, too.'

Rick picks up the bottle and the ice bucket and I grab our half-empty glasses. Rosalia walks past and Rick holds the bottle up, pointing in the direction of the gardens. She waves her hand, smiling and nodding.

'Why did you have a late one?' Rick asks as he falls in alongside me.

'Oh, I had this book I wanted to read,' I reply, quite casually. I'm not in the mood to dwell on it right now. 'And then I was so wide awake that I decided to get everything sent off to *Upscale Dining*. At least the first article is now awaiting sign-off. The deadline is tight, but it will be a little more relaxed for the second one.'

We step out onto the gravel the other side of the covered walkway and climb the steps, listening to the sound of some windchimes hidden amongst the trees.

'That little breeze is lovely and refreshing isn't it,' Rick murmurs, staring at me for a moment so intently it makes me feel a little flustered.

I have no idea what he's thinking, but my pulse is racing. 'So, how was your trip?' I ask, because it's the first thing that pops into my head.

'Hard work,' he replies soberly.

We walk on in silence, past the carob trees, and Rick holds open the entry gate to the pool area for me. We walk past a couple with their two children, sitting on a blanket on the grassy area playing snap. The children wave as we wish them good evening.

Rick points to the far end of the garden, where a two-tiered fountain feeds a constant stream of water into the pool. The soft sound of the gentle flow grows the closer we get to the source.

'I thought it would be quieter down here,' Rick says, the tiredness in his voice very evident now. Is it simply weariness though, or is he feeling down?

'It's a lovely evening and it's nice to make the most of being here. Last week flew by and this week is going to be the same, I think.'

Rick places the wine bucket on the floor and I pass him his

glass. 'We should make a toast,' he reflects. As he reaches out his hand and I step closer, what I see reflected in his eyes it not so much tiredness as a lack of enthusiasm and I can feel that something isn't right. 'Here's to the rise of some promising new talent. May their respective journeys be pleasant ones.'

'Amen to that,' I reply as we briefly touch glasses and take a sip before settling ourselves down.

I assume Rick will kick off the conversation, but he doesn't. Instead he empties his glass in just a couple of gulps and then he leans over to pick up the bottle, offering to top up my glass first.

'No, I'm good, thanks.'

He pours himself another generous measure and then lies back, shifting his position until he's comfortable.

'Considering you didn't get that much sleep and you were up early prepping, today was a real triumph again. I loved that candy floss topping on the cake today. It reminded me of one of the tasting desserts I sampled that day when I first interviewed you.'

Rick turns his head to look at me, resting his wine glass on his chest. 'Ah, the bubble gum flavour that incensed Cathy. It's fun, but today it was more for the visual effect. I want to encourage the chefs to demonstrate some of the techniques they've learnt but perhaps don't use very often. This week I want to push them even harder to show me something different and not stick to what they're most comfortable with.'

'You like taking risks?' I ask, genuinely interested.

'As a general rule, no. But when I'm cooking I like to experiment and see where it leads. The smallest of touches can really elevate the presentation, for example, and visually delight the diner as they prepare to take that first bite. It's all about making it an experience they will remember from start to finish.' He pauses for a moment before continuing, taking yet another hefty gulp from his wine glass. 'You must forgive my moodiness tonight, and if I'm bad company, please don't feel you have to stay and put up with me. I won't be offended if you head back to your room.'

I manoeuvre myself into a better position, so that I can see his face more easily. 'I'm feeling a little tetchy myself, tonight. The book I was reading was all about self-help. It turns out I needed it more than I thought, but the message at the end was a bit of a conundrum, which wasn't exactly helpful.'

Rick looks directly at me, questioningly. 'Well, that's a bit of a surprise. Why do you need help? You look and sound perfectly fine to me.'

His tone is light and I can see that he's teasing me.

'Oh, it's all an illusion! I'm good at that, pretending I'm fine, pushing the hard stuff to the back of my mind to sort out at a later date, but, of course, that day never arrives. And I'm terrible at tackling difficult things head-on.'

Now I can see he's intrigued.

'Is it catching,' he laughs, 'because I'm in the same boat. Cathy has an investor friend lined up because she wants us to open a second restaurant as soon as possible. I think it's much too soon, but did I say that outright? No. I gave her the impression I would think about it.'

Ah, now I understand the bad mood. I don't feel it's my place to make a comment, so I turn to gaze out over the shimmering water of the pool and take a sip of my drink. The lights just below the waterline give the subtlest hint of blue and even this late in the evening it looks inviting.

'This book you read, what advice was it peddling?' There's amusement in his tone.

'Oh, just the idea that you should turn every question around to see it from another angle. The answer we tend to come up with, it said, is somehow influenced by the mistakes we've made in the past, so we end up going around in a never-ending circle. It didn't make any sense to me.'

Rick pushes his head back against the lounger, looking up at the darkening sky. 'I think it makes some sense to me. The question is "should we open another restaurant?" and whichever way I look at it, the answer is *no*. I just can't bring myself to say it to Cathy.'

'Ah, you might not be an entirely lost cause, then, unlike me. I'm not great at listening to my gut instincts.'

'Well, I might listen to mine, but I don't act on them. Martine Alvarez is a case in point.'

That instantly makes me turn my head to stare at him again and my eyes widen as I look at his face.

Rick shrugs his shoulders. 'I loved working at the Food Haven, but I knew Martine was trouble. I'm not absolving myself of all blame here, as it takes two, doesn't it? She's an attractive woman and we were working very closely together. Late one night, well, you know how it goes, we crossed the line and began a romantic relationship, as people often do in that type of situation. The awful thing was that almost immediately I realised it was a mistake. Did I listen to what my gut instincts were telling me? No. When I admitted to her that I couldn't see our relationship going anywhere, I was simply being honest with her. But Martine wasn't just upset, she wanted revenge as if I'd purposely hurt her. She told me she was going to ruin me and my career, and I saw a whole new side of her which few get to see. And now I wonder if I'm in danger of making a similar mistake, because I know Cathy isn't going to like hearing the truth that she's risking everything trying to move forward too quickly. I'm not sure I can find the energy, though, to psych myself up for yet another battle, given how rocky the last few months have been between us.'

Now I feel awkward.

'Oh, well, thinking things through is good, but don't make any hasty judgments, Rick. I wasn't suggesting you need help when I mentioned the book, I'm just trying to sort out my own life.'

'No, it was helpful. I need to be honest with Cathy. I can't raise any more money as I cashed everything in that I had. The apartment I'm renting belongs to a friend who is on secondment in Saudi Arabia. If the restaurant fails, then I will literally lose everything. Cathy, obviously, put in a lot more capital than me, so she is the major shareholder and calls the shots. This music guy she knows, well, he's into lots of things and I'm not at all comfortable getting pulled into a business deal with him.'

I'm shocked by Rick's admission as his financial situation is none of my business.

'So, back to you. What's the burning issue that you're grappling with right now?' Rick asks, and I let out a sigh.

'Compared to shouldering the responsibility of running a successful business and providing jobs for a whole team of people, it sounds silly, really,' I reply truthfully.

'No, come on. I shared, now it's your turn.'

It takes me a minute or two to collect my thoughts.

'At the time when my dad was going through his worst nightmare, I just added to the misery. I'd been coasting along with my ex Warren because I didn't want to face up to the fact that our relationship had changed. Looking back, I'm not sure we were ever really in love, we were just so young. When I moved back home, Warren appeared at the door one day. Mum invited him in, and Warren said a lot of things I'm sure he regrets in hindsight, but he seemed to suggest that the stress around Dad's work had made things impossible between us. It was shortly after that my mum walked out. She blamed Dad for ruining my relationship, but, of course, it wasn't that and it wasn't even Warren's fault, it was mine. I kept putting off having the conversation because I didn't relish the upheaval.'

Rick shakes his head, sadly. 'That sounds hard, Lainey, but you can't blame yourself in a situation like that. People believe what they want to believe.'

'If I'd just hung on a while until things had calmed down between Mum and Dad, then maybe she'd have stayed to see Dad through it all. After she left, Dad filed for a divorce and Mum didn't contest it. Warren was angry and said the scandal had changed me and it had, in a way, as it made me re-evaluate what I wanted out of life. Warren just didn't want to face up to the fact that we'd slipped out of a loving relationship into friendship and it wasn't enough for me. He said some shocking things and I found myself looking at him and thinking he never was the man I thought he was, we'd been living a lie virtually the whole time.'

'Relationships aren't easy at the best of times,' Rick replies, gently. 'So, now you carry around this guilt because you think you're responsible for pushing your parents apart?'

I nod miserably. 'I don't think it, I know it. Everything I am is because of them, they put my needs first when I was growing up. And I failed them when they needed my support.'

The look on Rick's face is one of shock and then dismay. 'And you agreed to come here because you saw it as a chance to bring them together again? That's dangerous, Lainey. If they wanted to get back together, then they would have realised their mistake and found a way by themselves, don't you think?'

My heart is heavy, and I know Rick is right. Thomas could easily have found someone else for this assignment and I'd be in France right now. But the truth is that I wanted to be here with Rick and everything seemed to fall into place when Dad offered to step in for me.

'That wasn't my intention, originally,' I explain. 'I promised

Mum in good faith that I'd be there for her because she's never asked me for anything ever before. It was going to be an opportunity for us to bond again. And then, when this trip came up, I...' My words tail off. How can I admit that being with Rick is exhilarating at times; the moments in which we connect on a personal level make my heart pound and my head buzz. I know it's wrong, but it's a fact that I can't deny and one I cannot share with him.

'It seemed like too good an opportunity to miss to get your parents together?'

'Yes.' It's hard to hold back the truth, which is that I'm here on false pretences. I've kidded myself up to this point, but I can't share that with Rick as what will he think of me? I'm very aware that he isn't available, but I can't seem to help myself.

He swings his legs over the side of the recliner, leaning forward as he cradles his glass in his hands. 'That book of yours might be more insightful than you thought, Lainey. If you look at the situation from a different angle, your father didn't have to agree to step in for you, you know. He could simply have refused.'

'But I knew he wouldn't because he feels he owes Mum for what he put her through.'

'I can understand that.' Rick nods in agreement. 'But the decision was his and it's time for you to step back and allow them to sort it out between themselves. Whatever happens, happens.'

I know he's right and that it's out of my hands now. I never meant to hurt anyone, but I'm feeling selfish because it was as much about me, as it was about giving my parents a chance to get together. Being here with Rick is a temptation that I simply couldn't resist and I had to make it happen.

'And tomorrow I'm going to phone Cathy and speak my truth, as they say.'

My heart sinks in my chest as I look at him and it's tough to plaster on a reassuring smile of encouragement.

'Anyway, we were robbed of our day out. Can we reschedule for this coming Sunday?'

I hesitate because I know the answer should be *no*. 'I'm not sure...'

'Oh, come on! Let's be tourists for the day and forget all about work, family and the vagaries of life.'

As we look at each other, I can see he's much happier. He looks lighter and brighter. I wish I felt the same way, but I don't.

'I don't know about you, but that water looks inviting. I'm tempted to take a dip just to cool off a little before bed. What do you think?' Rick asks with a mischievous grin.

Glancing around, I follow his gaze and notice that we're alone.

'Um, it's tempting, but I thought you were tired.'

'I was, but now I'm awake. Come on, let's go and change. Meet you back here in ten minutes.'

I like that nothing drags Rick down for long and he doesn't stew on things as I tend to do at times. I've been looking longingly at that pool for the last half an hour, but I would never have suggested getting in. Perhaps I need to let my guard down and trust myself more. Besides, what harm can it do to have a little innocent fun?

Except that it's never quite as simple as that, is it? After doing a few laps up and down trying to keep up, I swim over to one side, content to watch him for a while. He's a natural in the water, slicing through it effortlessly. The lighting around the edge of the pool makes the water glisten on his skin. As he raises each arm, his muscles tensed and his focus one of pure concentration, a sense of longing wells up inside of me.

I close my eyes for a moment, wondering if I will ever find a man as good as Rick. When I open them, I jump. Rick has stopped, only a couple of feet away, and the look on his face is one of concern.

'What's up?' he asks, softly.

'I'm tired, that's all.' I reply. But that's not the entire truth.

'You look sad.'

'Do I?'

Rick's eyes suddenly light up and before I know what's happening his hands are around my waist and he's lifting me up out of the water. As I drop back down into his arms, I can't help but smile.

'That's better.' He looks down into my eyes and something deep inside of me melts. If it's my resolve, then I'm in deep, deep trouble.

* * *

It's gone midnight when we eventually part company and Rick and I find ourselves at the point in the corridor where we go our separate ways.

'Thanks for cheering me up tonight,' he says, keeping his voice low as there isn't a soul around and everyone else appears to be in bed.

'Same here. And I enjoyed getting into the pool.'

And then it happens. I begin to turn away at the precise moment that he leans in to plant an affection kiss on my cheek and suddenly our lips are touching and we both freeze. But not before the softness of his mouth on mine sends a shockwave through my body. Pulling back sharply, we stare at each other for a moment. He doesn't apologise, he just lets out a loud sigh.

'Goodnight, Lainey. Sleep well,' he mutters as he turns and walks away from me.

It wasn't planned and yet I find myself standing here wishing that it had been a real kiss, one that meant something.

15

FANNING THE FLAMES

The competition is heating up. At yesterday's session, chef Joana Barradas, the Portuguese contestant, blew everyone away and was on the receiving end of a well-deserved round of applause. The hero of the starter was a cold soup and Joana made *Sopa de Ajo Blanco*, a white soup consisting of bread, olive oil, almonds and garlic. She teamed it with olive ice cream, local air-dried tuna known as *Mojama*, and a Parmesan crisp. The *Mojama* was salty and piquant, and complemented the dish to perfection, resulting in Rick awarding the first ten out of ten. Joana was moved to tears. He asked her to plate up the entire pot of soup so that everyone could taste it.

Today, the hero ingredient is Iberian pork. The contestants' dishes are inspired by Rick's grilled Iberian pork fillet, with a stunning citrus hummus, pickled carrot and a tiny trickle of a thick, pork jus reduction flavoured with a little of the sweet Pedro Ximénez sherry. Rick outdid himself and Emilio was all smiles. I just stood back and let him snap away.

We're forty-five minutes into the cook-off and the pressure is beginning to take a toll, as this also happens to be the hottest day we've had so far. Rick walks up and down, stopping to chat to each of the chefs so they get equal time on camera. Some chefs welcome the interruption and Louis Reno is usually one of them, but today things aren't going smoothly for him. He cut his finger early on and filming had to be halted for several minutes. Louis isn't the only one, two other chefs have nicked themselves while chopping, but Louis' finger took a while to stop bleeding. It threw him off course and when filming resumed, he was all over the place. Up until today his focus has been admirable; he's like a machine. Some of the others occasionally stop and you can see they're deep in thought, as if the recipe is etched in their brain and they're going through it, line by line. Louis isn't like that, his actions are instinctive and in this way he reminds me a little of Rick.

When the clock resumed counting down, Rick gave Louis some space. But eventually Rick had no choice but to head back to Louis' workstation.

'You've decided to go with a different cut, I see,' Rick remarks as the cameraman zooms in on Louis' chopping board. Four of the chefs stuck with the tenderloin, two went for chops and Louis has chosen quite a fatty-looking cut.

'Yes, fat equals flavour and I wanted to keep this dish simple and really let the flavour of the pork come through.'

'The marbling looks good. And you are grilling this?' Rick enquires, seemingly impressed.

'Yes. First, I will marinade it in the sauce I made earlier. I ground up whole peppercorns, then added garlic, ginger, chilli, fresh coriander and parsley to the mortar. I crushed the herbs until they turned into a smooth paste and then gradually added some extra virgin olive oil, a little lemon juice and salt. I'm about to cut off some of the fat before I apply the dressing and let it rest before grilling. I'm going to team it with a rosemary and thyme potato gratin and roasted shallots. It will be served with a ginger and apple compote.'

Rick peers into the bowl and Louis offers him a small teaspoon to taste it.

'Hmm. Great flavours, I like the idea of the bite of the ginger with the pork. I'm looking forward to tasting this, Louis. It's a good combination of simple flavours.'

Louis doesn't normally sweat, but he's sweating now and I catch him mopping his brow as soon as the cameraman moves away. He's glancing at the clock and I see a look come over his face. It's one of utter panic as I follow his gaze. He's forgotten to put his potato dish in the oven, it's still on the countertop. My stomach does a flip and I feel nauseous. The poor man. He rushes to finish cutting off the surplus fat from the meat and grabs an empty dish, bathing it in the marinade and popping into the fridge.

Louis stands for a moment and then turns on his heels, grabbing the dish of potatoes with one hand and a baking tray with the other. There isn't time now to cook it through and brown it, so he rushes off to find a couple of small ramekins. Louis disassembles the main dish, which he'd so carefully layered up, and butters the smaller dishes, spooning in the mixture and placing them on the baking tray in the oven. He has twenty-five minutes to go as he turns his attention to heating up the grill.

This is nail-biting stuff. No one, so far, has failed to get their dish plated up in time. There have been problems and panics, sauces separating and meat slightly overcooked, but it has always come together on the plate. But looking at Louis now, it's obviously going to be a close call.

Glancing at Rick, I can see that he's worried. He doesn't want anyone to fail and to have to give out a low mark would devastate him.

I turn away for a moment, following Rick as he talks to India Serrano, the Spanish chef. She's a bubbly personality and flings her hands in the air as she talks, which makes for good TV. Suddenly, there's a shout and I see that Louis' grill is on fire. The producer rushes over as Louis grabs a pouch from the side of his workstation, ripping it open and throwing the fire blanket over the top of the hob.

'Stop filming,' Javier shouts out in Spanish and Miguel is quick on his heels to make sure everyone understands.

Javier and several others rush to Louis' aid and my heart dips as I can see how dispirited he is, but he recovers quickly.

'It's all okay. You are sure?' Javier asks, his concern genuine.

Louis nods, gingerly lifting up the edge of the blanket to check. Javier helps him to fold it up and as he disposes of it, Louis has a quick clean up. This man is not about to give up and after a thumbs up from Louis, Javier indicates for the cameraman to recommence filming.

Rick is staying back, no doubt feeling Louis has enough to deal with. But Louis grabs a pan with one hand and the bottle of virgin olive oil with the other and he's back in business.

'Eighteen minutes, everyone,' Rick announces, more for Louis' benefit than anyone else's. He wants him to succeed.

I watch as Louis heats the oil in the pan, then throws in a knob of butter. The heat is on high because he knows time is running out. He disappears out of view and when he pops up, he has a meat thermometer in his hand.

The other chefs are already beginning to clear up in preparation for plating. Louis checks the oven and I crane my neck to see that the potatoes still look quite pale. Louis slides them back in and turns up the temperature. It's all or nothing now.

The minute the pork hits the pan, I take in a sharp breath, keeping my fingers crossed that it doesn't all go up in flames for a second time. The smell is wonderful and dominates this entire side of the room. If he pulls this off, he could be today's winner, but he's not safe yet.

As the seconds tick by, the tension is agonising. There's no other way to describe it and, for the first time since the show started, Rick is on edge. He'd be as gutted as Louis if his plate doesn't make it to the tasting table. I almost feel like covering my eyes as the stress is building. Louis is constantly mopping his brow and tucking the tea towel back into the apron string around his waist.

'Time to think about getting the food on the plate, guys,' Rick calls out, but the only one not already working on plating up is Louis. He's still turning the meat, knowing that because the heat is so high, he can't leave it for long on one side or it will burn.

Finally, he pulls the pan off the ring, grabs some tongs and puts the pork on a plate to rest. Immediately turning around to grab a glove, he retrieves the ramekins from the oven. Louis grabs a large spoon and eases the gratin out of one of the dishes, placing it carefully in a stack in the centre of the plate. He takes a clean tea towel and gently wipes around the edges to make it uniform. Seconds later, the pork is on the chopping board and he's slicing it into thin slivers. He lays them over the top, before drizzling the hot juices directly from the pan onto the plate using a small spoon.

'Three minutes and thirty seconds to go, guys,' Rick calls out.

And then Louis turns around to grab the chutney and disaster strikes yet again, his arm knocks the chutney dish and it slides agonisingly towards the edge of the countertop. I'm looking on in total disbelief as it disappears from view and there's a loud shattering sound as the ceramic dish comes into contact with the tiled floor.

Louis glances down, squares his shoulder and immediately

turns the heat up to full on one of the rings on the hob. He wipes
a red pepper with his tea towel and, grabbing a pair of tongs,
holds it close to the flame, constantly turning it until it blackens.
There's a huge difference between blackened and burnt. It's the
difference between a sweet, delicious pepper beneath and the
bitter taste of a disaster. I can see it's almost too hot to stand in
front of the flames, but he won't give up and keeps constantly
turning.

'Three minutes to go,' Rick calls and the atmosphere in the
room is electric.

Louis scrapes away the charred outer skin, his fingers
constantly moving because it's so hot as he cuts the pepper into
wide strips and then into diamond shapes. He scoops them up
into a little pile and deposits them on the plate, like a little heap
of glorious, sweet, red jewels and his body visibly sags as he driz-
zles a little oil over the top.

Rick begins the final countdown. '...Three, two, one and time
is up, ladies and gentlemen. Please step away from your dish.'

I feel like I'm going to faint, and I can't even begin to imagine
how Louis feels as the two contestants either side of him rush
over to give him a hug. I feel tearful and, looking at Rick, his relief
is evident. That fact that everyone was rooting for Louis even
though this is a competition says so much about the popularity of
the man himself. Friendships have been made here that will
continue on even after everyone returns home, because it's been a
bonding experience. One that none of us will ever forget.

* * *

'Sorry I missed you at lunch.' Rick's voice makes me instantly
glance up. I'm sitting at a little table in the shade, making notes.
'Am I disturbing you?'

'No. It's fine, please, take a seat. I'm about to pack up.'

I can see he wasn't entirely sure how I was going to respond and he looks relieved.

'It's been quite a day,' he mutters.

And last night was quite a night, but that was a simple mistake, wasn't it? I tell myself.

'You can say that again. Talk about edge-of-the-seat stuff. Cooking doesn't get much more fraught than that,' I acknowledge.

The only way to deal with that accidental kiss is to pretend it didn't happen and that suits me just fine. Glancing at my watch, I see that it's almost 5 p.m. and I'm pleased with today's write-up. 'I managed to get a few snaps of the kitchen drama and I'm hoping one of the photos will be good enough to use. It was a lesson in thinking on your feet and while Louis didn't come top today, he was a close second and that was an incredible achievement.' I'm babbling and we both know that we have to get past this.

'Wasn't it! Are you really packing up or just being polite?' Rick smiles across at me engagingly.

'Why?'

'I wondered if you fancied a walk through the park? We could grab an ice cream, or a drink.'

It's clear he wants to talk, and I'm done working. 'Give me ten minutes to take this upstairs and splash some cold water on my face and I'll meet you in reception. Does that work for you?'

'Great. See you in a bit.'

Rick lowers his sunglasses, settling back in the seat and tilting his head to feel the sun's rays on his face. His usually pale skin is picking up a golden tan, which matches the healthy glow I now see when I look in the mirror. A little sunshine does us all the world of good, and as I stride off, I'm feeling more at ease again.

I take the stairs two at a time, slowing when my phone kicks into life and I see it's Dario.

'This is a nice surprise. How are you doing, Dario, and how is Ian?'

'We're good. A few sunny days have cheered everyone up.'

'I was just thinking the same thing. Not that I'm getting much time to laze around and take advantage of the weather, of course,' I say emphatically and Dario chuckles.

'Don't give me that. I bet you're having a fabulous time. I'd swap places in an instant, although I doubt Ian would have been happy to let me fly off without him. He's up to his eyes in a big audit right now and being boring as hell. You know what he's like when he gets his teeth into something and the figures aren't stacking up.'

'Sorry to hear that. Is everything else okay with you?'

There's a short pause. 'I think so, but things are tense at work. Thomas is walking around with a face that looks like thunder and we're all avoiding him. Rumours are starting to circulate that there's some bad news coming, but he isn't giving anything away.'

'You mean, you're hoping I'll call him and see what I can find out,' I reply, laughing, but letting him know that he's been rumbled.

'No, honestly, that wasn't my intention at all,' he says, but I'm not convinced.

'I seriously doubt he'll let anything slip to me. You're really worried, aren't you?'

Another ominous pause. 'I'm thinking of jumping ship.'

I gasp, holding the phone even closer to my ear. 'Why?'

'I've been offered a job by a friend of a friend who works for an advertising company. If there's going to be a shake-up, I'd like to get out before it hits. Of course, it could be Thomas's job on the line and that's why nothing is getting out. I wanted to ask your opinion as Ian, as per the norm, thinks I should stay. There are no guarantees when you step into a new position and I am happy at *Upscale Dining*.'

My brain is still trying to process what this might mean. It was obvious before I left that Thomas was still getting pressure from above over what he referred to as *stagnant* sales figures. I got the distinct impression it wasn't his choice of word, which made me feel uncomfortable at the time. 'Thomas is good at what he does, one of the best in fact. He's trying everything he can to change things up and it's obvious he is fighting his corner for us all. But I can tell by your voice that you're really tempted by the offer you've received.'

'I am, to be honest with you, Lainey. It would be a new challenge, which is scary but exciting, although I already know a few of the people I'd be working with.'

'So, what's holding you back? Is it Ian, or is it fear of the unknown?'

'Both, I suppose. I've become comfortable and I know I'm not being stretched in what I do.'

'Well, that might be the case now, but, as you said, change might be coming anyway. Only you can make the final decision, Dario. It doesn't matter what anyone else thinks.'

He groans. 'Don't you just hate this adult stuff?'

'Sorry, lovely man. It's time to stand tall and make a decision. If I hear anything, I'll be in touch, but I doubt I'll be among the first to be in the know, anyway.'

'Helpful-ish,' he replies, sounding dejected. 'Anyway, how's our celebrity chef doing? It's all quiet on the social media front. Cathy's tour is going well, I hear. Well, apart from the one obvious little blip, of course.'

'Rick is fine. I'm glad there's no gossip though, at least that's comforting. Look, I must go as I'm meeting up with him shortly.'

'Purely business, of course,' Dario throws back at me, sceptically. 'Only joking. Have fun while you can. Hopefully, things will be a bit better here by the time you get back.'

'Sorry, I'm a bit late, but I had to take a work call.'

Rick's head jerks back and I realise he was nodding off. He stretches his arms, arching his back before standing. 'Well, that's a first for me,' he replies. 'Maybe I really am getting into the Spanish way of life. I've always laughed at the thought of power-napping, but in this heat it's common sense. Right, let's go exploring.' Rick pulls a leaflet from his back pocket.

'Have you recovered from all the excitement of this morning's session?' I ask as we walk through the reception area and Rick holds open the heavy wooden door for me.

'My heart literally skipped a beat for a second there, when I saw the size of those flames. How Louis managed to pull it all together after that, well, I have nothing but admiration for the guy. And then I couldn't believe it when that dish hit the floor,' Rick exclaims, and I can see that he's still reeling from today's dramatic turn of events.

'It was every chef's worst nightmare all wrapped up into one,' I agree.

'The crying shame was that the apple chutney that ended up on the floor was, without a doubt, a winning flavour. Ah, well, these things happen, I suppose. We're crossing here. Do you remember we walked past a place called Paseo Alfonso XIII on our way to the palacio?'

'Was it that long promenade with the sandy yellow floor and little bars and restaurants either side?'

'Yes. Big, sweeping, curved wall and that massive

bougainvillea hedging. According to this leaflet Felipe gave me, the Reina Victoria gardens are next to it.'

'Oh, so it's not a park,' I muse as I glance at Rick.

'Something tells me it doesn't float your boat. How about we grab a drink first, then? I'm sure we'll find somewhere pleasant to sit and while away an hour or two before it's time to think about heading back for dinner. You are eating at the monastery tonight, aren't you? I hear there are plans afoot for another trip into town this evening.'

'They all have more stamina than me. But they do need to blow off a little steam, as the pressure builds. They'd all love to win.'

Rick sighs. 'I know, but it's a competition and there can only be one winner. They should all be very proud of themselves performing so well. It's a big ask of anyone, isn't it?'

It would be wrong to discuss the individual chefs until the competition is over, but talking to Rick has given me an idea. 'The winner will feature in the second article, of course, but what if the magazine did a follow-up piece? You know, what happens to the winner after they return home. It might be possible to interview them wherever they are working and see what impact it has had on their career moving forward. What do you think?'

'That's a great idea,' Rick enthuses, glancing at me cagily. 'Would I get to come along?'

I'm not sure if he's teasing me, but it would be an amazing photo opportunity. 'When my boss is in a better mood, I'll run it past him. Who knows, if the budget can take another hit, we might get lucky. I imagine it wouldn't be that easy for you to slope off again for a while, but maybe in a few months' time,' I reply hopefully.

We cross a second road, then skirt around the beautifully

curved stone wall, above which a towering hedge of bright pink blossoms look almost too perfect to be real.

'Life feels very different here and it's because everything looks so vibrant, it lifts the spirits,' I remark, finding the riotous colour all around a real boost. 'If only I had a garden and not a window box,' I bemoan.

'I don't even have a window box,' Rick points out. 'Before I sold the house to cash in the equity, I had a vegetable patch and a greenhouse. I grew my own peppers and, even in the UK, with the weather we get, I've harvested some successful crops. Now I have to order a box of organic veggies online if I'm cooking something special at home. Sad, isn't it?'

The tone of his voice is sobering and for a second I find myself wondering whether Rick's dream is beginning to turn into a bit of a nightmare.

As we round the corner and step beyond the tall pillars which mark the entrance to the promenade, my shoe catches and it flicks some of the soft, sandy-yellow grit up into the air. I'm left hopping around as I ease off my shoe to tip out the sharp bits of grit and Rick catches my hand, steadying me.

'Thank you.' I slip my shoe back on and reluctantly let go of Rick's hand. His grip was firm, his skin warm. He's a gentleman in an age when many men aren't. Some women don't appreciate being helped, but my dad is old-school and that's stayed with me.

'Are you in the mood for a soft drink, wine, sherry?'

I shake my head, pointing.

'Beer?' he enquires, tilting his head to one side.

'Why not?'

We saunter down to a little bar on the right-hand side of the open promenade. There are only a couple of other people sitting at the small bistro tables and it looks wonderfully tempting.

The barman gives us a beaming smile as we walk up to him.

He speaks no English at all, but Rick is great, and he ends up ordering two bottles of Rosita Negra.

'This will be a first,' he informs me as we choose a table set back under the shade of the arched canopy.

'Well, I was impressed. You ordered as if you were a pro.'

Rick pulls out a chair for me and I take a seat, thanking him.

'The guy behind the bar wasn't fooled,' he grins back at me. 'Anyway, going back to the idea about a follow-up, I mean it when I say I'd be up for it if you can convince Thomas. You could do the interviews on your own, though, and I'm sure it would still make for a fine article.'

'Yes, but your input would make it far more appealing to our readers. I'm just a food writer, not a chef, or even a food critic and I'm not exactly famous.'

'But you just happen to have a way with words as well as a discerning palate.'

A waiter appears with a small tray and places two glasses of a honey-coloured ale on the table in front of us.

'English, yes?' he enquires and we nod. 'Enjoy!'

We raise our glasses and chink. The first sip is fruity and rather pleasant.

'Are you getting banana and red apple?' I ask, as Rick looks at me, frowning. The aftertaste, though, is now making me wrinkle up my nose.

'Hmm. Yes. But there's something else... molasses! Is it too heavy for you?'

I shake my head, not wanting to make a fuss, but Rick is already waving to our waiter, and when he hurries over, he orders a Rosita d'Ivori.

'It's a light blonde beer. You might like that a bit more,' he explains.

This one when it arrives is fresh and light. It has a refined, elegant sparkle in the glass, but isn't too gassy.

'Is that better?' Rick asks anxiously, which makes me smile.

'Hmm. I like this. There's a bouquet of citrus fruits, with orange peel most prominent. It's wonderful,' I reply.

'You'll get the aroma of cereals, especially wheat, and white flowers, too. That's what gives this beer a wonderful freshness.'

'I wouldn't have guessed that you were a connoisseur of beers.'

'It's a food pairing thing. I do, on occasion, cook with it, but sometimes a dish requires something a little more gutsy than a glass of wine. Personally, I think a blonde beer like this suits the typical Spanish tapas dishes.'

'Do you know, I think I agree with you. Wine is the go-to option, but if I'm eating a hearty pasta, or a pizza, for example, a light beer is far more satisfying.'

'And one tends to drink a lot less of it,' he points out.

'If you mean that beer bloats your stomach, I'm so with you on that one,' I retort and we both burst out laughing.

We sit back, content to sip our drinks and people-watch. It's that time of the evening when it's a little cooler and people begin to head out for a stroll.

'This is very pleasant,' I remark.

'And the Reina Victoria gardens are a mere stone's throw away, so we have plenty of time to enjoy our drink.'

We sit in silence for a while, happy to take in our surroundings.

'I feel like I'm on holiday,' Rick laughs, turning to face me.

'Me, too! Time isn't quite so meaningful here, is it?'

'It seems not, and people appear to be less stressed in general. The pace of life in the UK can be draining at times. It's easy to see why people decide to up sticks and move. It must have been a big upheaval for your mum, though, being on her own. Does she sell the produce she grows?'

'No, when she first started up, she was only offering bed and breakfast. The main building is a big, old farmhouse and there are outbuildings that have been converted into accommodation, too. It's a lot of work and her heart wasn't really in it, so she started advertising cookery courses. And she's now advertising week-long workshops for people who are new to the grow-your-own ethos and interested in starting up a small allotment. They get hands-on experience working in the garden and everyone is involved in preparing the meals, so it's quite informal. And easier for her to run. In between, she runs her Country Cook courses. They're more intensive, so she has an assistant to make sure her guests are able to keep up while she's demonstrating.'

Rick fiddles with his glass, sliding it along the table, as if he's deep in thought. When he looks up, I can see a moment of hesitation before he begins speaking.

'Am I right in thinking that when it all kicked off between your parents you stayed behind to keep an eye on your father?'

I nod.

'And you're worried that your mother thinks you took his side. But you didn't. You felt he needed your help more than she did.'

I feel winded, like someone has just punched me in the chest, because Rick has just said out loud what I haven't had the courage to explain to Mum.

He reaches out to touch my hand as it lingers on the table. 'You're strong, Lainey, and so I bet she is, too. Not only will she understand why you did what you did, but she is probably grateful to you. You gave her the space to escape at a time when she may well have been at her wits' end.'

I close my eyes, but his hand doesn't move and the warmth of it is reassuring. 'I was torn at the time and I had no one to talk to.

Warren was angry that it was over between us. He didn't care what happened after he walked away. Mum was heart-broken at what was unfolding. The way people turned their backs on my dad when they knew he was a lone voice standing up for the truth was horrifying. A truth they all acknowledged by the way, but no one had the guts to side with him. I would have loved to turn my back on everything and head off to France. It was the worst day of my life choosing between my parents, but Dad needed me the most.'

Rick slowly withdraws his hand, but I can see that it is with reluctance. He understands what no one else has, but I can't allow myself to get close to him. He has a fiancée and I have to keep reminding myself of that fact. Otherwise, this could be a disaster in the making.

'I remember reading about it in the papers. Something to do with a new miracle dieting pill, wasn't it? The company managed to get a few well-known names to promote it and it all turned very nasty.'

'Yes. It was quite a scandal at the time as there was a campaign to discredit Dad's reputation to try to limit the damage when the pills were withdrawn. But a lot of people lost their money and they weren't cheap.'

Sitting back in my chair, I straighten my spine in an attempt to regain control of my emotions. 'Sorry, it's not like me to wallow. That silly book is making me doubt myself. Anyway, what were we talking about? Ah yes, the next trip to a sunnier climate! I doubt Pierre will approve if you try springing another jolly on him, though.'

Rick takes a slow sip of his beer, his eyebrows knitted together in pure concentration as if he isn't listening to me. A second or two later, he turns his head.

'From what I hear, he's enjoying his stint of being in charge. I knew he'd step up and I need to allow him to do that more often. He reminds me of myself a couple of years ago.'

Rick is doing his best to sound blasé, but I can see that something is still troubling him.

'You sound concerned.'

'Sometimes the rumour mill gets to me. I'm sure it's nothing. Cathy can be charming when it suits her, but that doesn't necessarily mean anything other than she's determined to have her own way.'

I have to stop myself from sucking in a huge breath. Is something going on between Cathy and Pierre behind his back? I find it rather hard to believe as I remember Neil saying that Pierre can't stand her. But I wonder whether Rick is aware of that fact?

16

After a pleasant stroll around the Reina Victoria gardens, our moods gradually lifted and before long we were chatting and laughing again. Now, as I stand in the shower washing my hair, I find myself humming away as if I don't have a care in the world.

Rick's genuinely sympathetic words hit home and, for the first time, I begin to see what happened from a slightly different point of view. At the time, Mum begged Dad to rethink his actions, warning him that he was making a big mistake. The people who had alerted him to the scam in the first place were already beginning to withdraw their accusations. My parents rowed constantly, but what if it wasn't a difference of opinion that made him file for divorce? What if that was the only way to protect her from the unpleasantness to come. She packed her bags and went to stay with her best friend because they could no longer live under the same roof. He wanted her to start over again and he knew she'd head to France because for a while that had been his dream for the future, too. It's a lightbulb moment but one that is only clear in hindsight.

And now I need to pick up the pace as I'm already running

late. Rick has booked us a table for 8.30 p.m. which gives me fifteen minutes to get ready. As I glance in the mirror, not only is there a rosy glow on my cheeks even before I apply a little make-up, but I look as happy as I feel. There's something about Andalucía that resonates with me. Rick too is a totally different person to the one I first met in London. We're both less tense, despite the fact that there is still pressure on a daily basis, but it makes me wonder if Rick has noticed too. Is it the almost constant sunshine that makes everything feel so much lighter, brighter and less stressful? Why can't life be like this all the time, I wonder to myself, and then immediately push that thought to the back of my mind. Mum always says, 'enjoy the now and let tomorrow take care of itself' and that's precisely what I'm going to do.

Slipping into an ankle-length, silky floral dress that is cool to wear, I decide to scoop my hair up in a twist. There's no breeze at all tonight and it's stiflingly hot. A light touch of mascara and a slick of lipstick is the best bet, unless I want to risk my make-up sliding down my face while we're eating.

I arrive before Rick, and the waitress leads me over to a table, but I hesitate before sitting down and she looks at me, quizzically. Mabel doesn't speak any English and I wave out to Rosalia, as she's passing.

'Can I help?' she asks.

'Rick booked a table, but is it possible to eat outside tonight?'

Rosalia turns to Mabel and as soon as she explains, she nods her head.

'Of course. No problem,' Rosalia confirms.

'Thank you so much.'

Mabel escorts me outside and it doesn't take her long to lay the table with linen napkins, glasses and cutlery. She places two menus down and hands me the wine list. I scan it and point, going for the safe option as I know Rick has chosen it before.

'*Gracias*,' I add appreciatively.

It's lovely to be out in the fresh air and I let out an involuntary groan when my phone starts ringing. Then I wonder if it's Rick and he isn't coming after all, which makes my heart miss a beat. Snatching it up, though, I see that it's Thomas and it's a relief.

'Good evening, Thomas. This is a surprise.'

'Hi, Lainey. Sorry it's a bit on the late side, but I've been meaning to ring you to say congratulations on an excellent article and some great photos. It's been the week from hell over here and there aren't enough hours in the day, I'm afraid.'

It's nice of Thomas to apologise for not saying thanks, but why is he still working this late in the evening? I begin to feel a little uneasy. 'It's fine. I just assumed you were busy but I am sorry to hear that you've been rushed off your feet, Thomas.' It does make me feel a little guilty, not being there to help out.

The sound that echoes back down the line is a disparaging one.

'Sales are down slightly, but targets are up. Same old, same old. It makes no sense at all, but that's the business we're in. Website hits are up, though, which is something. I'm just checking in to see if you've any more ideas percolating away in that head of yours. This week's meeting was as flat as a proverbial pancake. Morale is down and I know I'm not helping matters. I'm good, but I'm no magician.'

Is Thomas slurring his words?

'Are you feeling all right?' I ask without thinking and then inwardly groan to myself.

'I've had a whisky, or two. Maybe, three, who's counting? I'm trying to conjure up a few new ideas, but instead I'm sitting in front of a blank page again. Have you got any off-the-wall ideas up your sleeve to cheer me up?'

'It depends on how much money you want to spend to get the story. I was thinking of a follow-up to this series for example. The winner will get lots of publicity, naturally, and I'm sure we'll be allocating a full-page to him, or her, in the second article. But what about we interview the winning chef on their own turf, a couple of months down the line, following their next steps?'

There's a hesitant, 'Hmm,' and Thomas lapses into silence.

'I mean, the contestants come from the UK, Spain, Germany, France, Italy, Greece and Portugal, so at worst it's the cost of three return flights and an overnight stay.'

'Three?' Thomas repeats.

'Ant, me and Rick, if we want to make a really big splash.'

'He'd be up for that?'

'Well, I've kind of run it past him, but I'd have to check that he was serious about it. What do you think?'

'Why just go for the winner, why not visit them all in a series of interviews? Every single one of them is a working chef, am I right?' Thomas throws the idea out there, his enthusiasm growing by the second.

'According to their bios they are.' This is so unlike Thomas as he seems to be totally ignoring the costs involved. On the other hand, this will be yet another first for our readers, following Rick as he catches up with the contestants. Rick is so photogenic, then we have all those wonderful locations and a whole variety of different cuisines... this could be huge.

'Okay. I like it. I really like it. Thank goodness someone can think outside the box and bring me something a little different.'

'You'll like my photo of a grill going up in flames, then,' I reply.

He starts belly laughing. 'Only you would throw in something like that, Lainey. There's a lot of your dad in you, girl.'

Now I know he is seriously drunk because Thomas would never say that to me when he's sober. No one in the business ever talks about my dad to me.

'Right, I must go as the wine has arrived.'

'I hope it's a cheap bottle if we're paying for it,' he mutters before the line goes dead.

Mabel is back and holds out the bottle of wine to me so that I can inspect the label. I nod, and she puts one hand up as if to query whether or not to break the seal as Rick still isn't here. I slide my glass towards her across the table, and she duly dispenses a little taster. It's fine and as she's topping up my glass, Rick hurries across the courtyard.

'I'm really sorry I'm so late. I bet you're starving.'

'It's not a problem. I just got off the phone with Thomas. But could we order straight away as Mabel looks keen to get us sorted!' She's hovering and as I glance down at the menu in front of me, I realise she's handed me one in Spanish and not in English. 'Why don't you choose for us both, Rick?' I suggest and he rattles off a string of words that obviously mean something to him but will be potluck for me.

As soon as Mabel is out of earshot, he leans in. 'The dish is Loin of Sea Bass with Lobster Cream.'

'Ooh, sounds lovely. Great choice.'

'It's a little late for a business call,' Rick comments as he pours himself some wine. 'I hope Thomas is pleased with what you turned in.'

'Yes, he seems to be.'

'That's worthy of a toast, then,' he says, lifting his glass. 'Here's to obliging managing editors and financial partners.'

As we gently tap our glasses together, I look at him curiously. 'You've spoken to Cathy?'

'I have. That's why I was late. I video called her, as it's easier to deliver bad news when you can at least see how the person you're talking to is reacting. And, I guess it was the right way to handle it, because she eventually agreed with me.'

I stare at him, hoping he's going to continue.

'Her initial reaction, admittedly, was... vocal.'

In my mind, I can see her face and the way it contorts when she isn't happy.

'But when I explained that spreading myself too thinly now might be detrimental to Aleatory, she saw my point. Everyone is assuming we'll get a star in this year's awards, but I'm aiming higher than that and I can't take the pressure off. I asked her to put her plans for a second restaurant on hold for another year.'

'And she agreed?'

'She didn't disagree,' he replies.

I take a large sip of wine. This is *the* Cathy Clarkson we're talking about here. She lives her life at a dizzying pace, and I would want it in writing if she were my business partner. But they're more than that, and I have to keep reminding myself of that because it changes everything.

'Anyway, enough about me. Thomas feels he's getting his money's worth, then?'

I almost choke on my wine. 'I doubt he'd ever say that, but he liked the idea of following up with the winner and maybe some of the other contestants in a series of articles.'

'Well, that's a good sign. He must be missing you, ringing this late.'

'I think he is, which is a blessing and a curse. At least if I am indispensable I'm proving my worth.'

Rosalia walk towards us and I sit back in eager anticipation as she places the plates down in front of us.

'*Maravilloso*,' I say and Rosalia gives me a little nod of her head. 'Now that presentation is worthy of a Rick Oliver dish.'

She walks away wearing the biggest smile, so maybe my compliment wasn't lost in translation this time.

'Would you have done anything differently?' I ask Rick absentmindedly as I gaze down at the food. 'And what is the sauce on the edge of the plate?' The fish sits in the centre of a large plate with a wide brim and on it is a flower, comprising a piped outline of a long stem, several tiny leaves and a thin slice of carrot which has been cut into a flower head.

Rick takes his fork, scooping up a little on the prongs to taste it. 'I think the decoration on the side of the plate is a little much, but it's a lemon and lime reduction. It's good, but unnecessary. The fish is perfectly cooked, slightly translucent still, and the lobster sauce has been applied very carefully. Some restaurants would drown the fish in the sauce, but I like the way it's been drizzled over and the remainder presented in a little jug. The timbale of rice with wild herbs is a perfect choice and the addition of a herbed potato is a nice surprise. Either/or, or both. The idea works for me. Anyway, the proof is in the eating. Let's tuck in.'

All Rick gets from me is 'ooh', 'yum', and 'umm' at various points while I'm eating.

'I'm so glad you aren't judging the competition,' he comments. 'You could get locked up for making noises like that in public.'

I know he's only joking and it makes me laugh. He's clearly feeling playful after talking to Cathy and now that a big worry seems to have been lifted from his shoulders, he's like a different man. I realise that I'm also feeling less anxious. I haven't heard anything further from Le Crotoy and I'm taking that as a good sign. If only this evening could go on forever, I reflect, how wonderful life would be. As I surreptitiously glance across at Rick, I hope Cathy appreciates how lucky she is, because men like Rick don't come along very often.

Looking down at my almost empty plate, I turn my thoughts to dessert. A fun evening like this one should end on a sugar high, at the very least. Food is the ultimate comfort when something is missing from one's life, isn't it?

* * *

At the end of the evening, I have to admit that my legs are the teeniest bit wobbly, and Rick insists on seeing me to my room.

'I really shouldn't have had that last glass of wine. I haven't felt like this since I was nineteen and someone gave me a couple of shots of tequila. Awful stuff. It knocked me out and gave me a thumping headache the next day. Anyway, I blame you,' I level at Rick, as he takes the key from my hand and undoes the lock.

'Why me?' He retorts light-heartedly.

'I was caught up talking and you kept refilling my glass. I lost count.'

'Oh, so it's my fault. I had no idea you were a lightweight. Foodies normally focus on the wines as well as the dishes they're tasting. Where's the light switch?' he asks, as I hug the door jamb.

'Go inside, it's further along on the right. Bit further. A bit further. There!' Watching him fumbling around makes me start to giggle.

He stands there, hands on his hips, looking at me.

'What? Is my hair sticking up or something?' I ask.

'It's not that,' he laughs. 'It's just odd seeing you like this.'

'Like what?'

'Using the wall to keep yourself upright and a little... err, giddy.'

'I am not giddy,' I reply firmly, as I step away from the wall and begin swaying.

Rick leaps forwards to steady me and walks me over to the bed, lowering me down gently. 'Goodness, now I have a dilemma. Do I stay and make sure you're okay, or do I leave you and worry?'

I look at him, puzzled. The words aren't sinking in as I flop back against the cool, crisp bedcover.

'I'm fine...' I yawn and close my eyes, unwilling to move as my limbs feel so heavy.

'Well, it wouldn't be the first time we slept under the same roof, I suppose,' I hear him groaning, as he tilts me onto my side.

My head is buzzing and all I want to do is sleep.

'Don't worry,' Rick whispers into my ear. 'I've got you... You had my back and tonight I have yours.'

I heave a sigh as I tune out and he very kindly assists me in easing off my shoes. The feel of his hands touching my bare skin is comforting. A sense of happiness envelopes me and suddenly I don't have a care in the world.

* * *

I'm swimming in the pool and the water washes over me so gently, it's soothing. Until my arm begins to itch, and I lift my left hand up to scratch it, but when I put it back down into the water, it all seems to have evaporated.

Levering myself up in the half-light, I realise I'm fully dressed and lying on the bed. Shaking my head and trying to clear my thoughts as I look around, I gasp when I see Rick lying on the far side of the bed. He's in serious danger of falling off if he rolls the wrong way. The movement wakes him and he turns over onto his back, rubbing his eyes.

'How are you feeling?' he asks, as if this situation is the most natural thing ever.

'Fine, I think. I just need some water and to wash my face. There was no need to stay, I wasn't that bad. The wine made me drowsy, that's all.' I'd remember if I embarrassed myself in any way, wouldn't I? I was merry and a little unsteady on my feet, but I wasn't drunk.

'After putting the blame firmly on me it was my responsibility to check you didn't do something silly like fall out of bed.'

That makes me smile and Rick, too, as I glimpse the white of his teeth when he looks back at me.

Reaching over to the bedside table, I grab a bottle of water. 'If you're thirsty there's another one on the console table,' I say, twisting the cap and taking a long slug.

'I'm fine, thanks. I don't know what the time is, but I should slink back to my room.'

'The birds are awake, so another hour at most before the staff begin moving around. I seriously can't believe you were worried, but thank you for looking after me.'

Rick eases himself up the bed, stacking the pillows against the headboard as he watches me drinking. 'Under the circumstances, this probably isn't the best time and place to say this, Lainey, but I want to be upfront with you. It would be so easy for me to take our friendship further. Being here – um, not in your room, I mean Andalucía, of course, well...' He stops to clear his throat and I'm glad it's not light enough for him to see my face clearly. My cheeks are growing hotter by the moment. 'Argh. It's hard to put into words. If nothing else in my world existed, this would be perfect. Being here, spending time with you and feeling... care-free is confusing. As each day passes, I'm growing closer and closer to you, and more disconnected from my real life, but I guess we have to remember that this isn't permanent, is it? For either of us.' He pauses, waiting for a response. 'Please say something, even if it's only to tell me to leave.'

I put the water bottle back down, scoot up the bed and tilt my pillow, lying back and turning my head to look at him. The empty space between us is like a yawning chasm. He's so close and yet so far away.

'We're sharing experiences and moments that are bound to—' I struggle to find the right words to express what's happening between us.

'Establish a more personal kind of friendship?'

Closing my eyes, I take in a slow, deep breath before answering him. 'I suppose that's one way to put it. But I agree that our lives are completely different outside of this little bubble we're in right now and we both know that's unlikely to change.'

'My instincts were telling me the same thing, but I wanted to let you know how I was feeling, just in case you didn't think it was a two-way thing. I so enjoyed being able to have fun and relax last night at dinner, and sometimes we all need to let down our guard a little.'

'Yes, well, I got a little too relaxed, didn't I! It was a lovely evening Rick, an evening to remember, but it can't be any more than that.' It's tough to acknowledge that fact because a part of me is filled with a sense of regret.

'Right place, wrong time, eh?' He sounds reflective but accepting. 'So, where do we go from here?'

'Well, I think we know where we stand, don't you? Friends we can do, anything else steps over the line. I don't do holiday romances and you aren't a cheat.'

'You're right, but I'm glad I said something. It's not who I am and it's not who you are. But that doesn't change the fact that—'

I jump in, cutting him off because if he keeps looking at me that way, or says much more, my resolve may crumble. 'That we can handle getting these feelings and still come out the other side as friends? The alternative is spending the next two weeks avoiding each other whenever possible and turning this into a miserable experience. That would be a shame, don't you think?'

Rick heaves a sigh, but it's one of relief – I hope. 'I blame that little bit of Andalucían magic. It's a dangerous formula to combine good food, good wines and blazing sunshine with amazingly blue skies. But you're right, I'm sure we're more than capable of having fun without messing up.' He sounds a lot more confident than I'm feeling. 'And now I really must go, as I'd hate for anyone to spot me leaving your room.'

We swing around at the same time, sitting with our backs to each other, and I don't know about Rick, but my heart is pounding. By the time I make my way to the door, unlocking it as quietly as I can to avoid disturbing the heavy silence, I'm back in control of my emotions.

Rick steps forward, placing his hand on the edge of the door and easing it open to glance out. 'It's all clear,' he whispers.

I take a half-step forward so I can close it quickly after he leaves, when, to my surprise, he leans in and his lips graze my cheek.

'You are a wonderful person, Lainey Summers. And some lucky man is going to have a truly amazing life by your side.'

With that, he's gone, leaving me wondering if I can hold up my side of the bargain. How can I be his friend, when being with him is all I can think about?

* * *

It's funny how things work out, as life seems to deliver Rick and I some space from each other just when we need it. After leaving my room on Thursday morning, there's no opportunity at all for us to talk privately throughout the remainder of the day. On Friday morning he texts me to say he's had a call from Pierre and he's flying back to London to sort out an urgent problem. I'm not around when he arrives back on Saturday afternoon, but Louis mentions, in passing, that he's seen him. I'm surprised when Rick doesn't call, or text me, and there's no sign of him at dinner, either. As I walk back to my room, though, Miguel calls out, hurrying across to me.

'Ah, Lainey, I've been looking for you.' I wasn't even aware he was around. 'Rick has asked me to arrange an informal workshop for the contestants tomorrow. Am I to assume you are a part of that? I'm just about to confirm numbers for the working lunch.'

It's the first I'd heard of it and I hesitate for a moment. 'If it's informal, then I'm sure Rick would have said if my presence was required.'

'Ah, I see. I think it's something Javier suggested just to...' Miguel stops to look behind him, checking no one is within earshot, '...boost morale.'

It makes sense, but I am disappointed Rick didn't have the courtesy to at least let me know what was happening. However, I suppose it is a good idea to get the chefs together to talk about the business in general. I'm sure they will welcome some time to get whatever pointers they can from Rick to help them going forward. I chide myself for being a little paranoid about being left out, because this has nothing at all to do with me.

But, as the days roll by in the third week of filming, it begins to feel as if Rick is avoiding me. My excuse is that I've been working flat out, because Thomas asked if I could come up with few general ideas to throw out at next week's staff meeting. He really is missing my input and I wanted to give him something worthwhile, but it's not easy to switch off from what I'm doing and think about the back end of the year. It's a task I could have done without, but Thomas wouldn't have troubled me unless he was really struggling to motivate the team.

Every day after filming, Rick heads off to the studio with Javier and I assume they have dinner together afterwards. My evenings are lonely, and I end up heading back to my room as soon as I've eaten, to work.

On the odd occasion when I do bump into Rick and no-one else is around, we're always heading in opposite directions. The few words we exchange aren't enough for me to gauge how he's coping, but it's clear that he's under pressure and I don't want to add to that.

Finally, Friday is here and after a hard day slaving over the keyboard, I'm ready to relax and enjoy a little company. Felipe arranges for a large table to be set up out on the patio so the group can all eat together. To my delight, Rick unexpectedly appears shortly after we take our seats. He wasn't expected, as there isn't a seat for him and I'm pleased when he carries a chair over, heading in my direction. Everyone moves up a little so he can sit next to me and the mood around the table is jolly.

'Is Javier pleased with the footage they have so far?' I ask Rick, breaking the ice.

'He's delighted,' he replies, sounding content. 'Sorry I haven't been around much. It's been rather stressful, but things are now moving along quite nicely. How are things with you?'

'It's all good. Lots to do, as usual, but I had to break off and pull together a few things for Thomas.'

'Sorry to hear that, Lainey. I hope you managed to grab a little time to relax in between, and I'm really sorry I haven't been here for you.' As our eyes meet, he leans in even closer. 'I promise I will make it up to you,' Rick says, lowering his voice.

Studying his face in earnest, I can see that he means it and he hasn't been avoiding me, as I feared. I wish I could say I haven't missed his company because I'm here to work, and that's just what I've been doing, but it would be a lie. It's been the loneliest week of my life.

17

LIFE IS EASIER WITH RULES, ISN'T IT?

Tomorrow marks the start of the final week. The competition is hotting up now and it looks like there are three contestants vying for the top place. I've decided to have a lazy Sunday, as I'm in no mood to work. After talking to Rick over dinner on Friday night, I was gutted when he texted first thing yesterday morning to say that Javier had been in touch and they were spending yet another day in the studio. He was apologetic and I could tell he, too, was equally as disappointed.

Ironically, about an hour later, Emilio rang offering to drive me around for a couple of hours to get some shots of the surrounding area. Whether there will be an opportunity to use them in the future, who knows, but he was very persuasive and I didn't have the heart to refuse him.

Emilio took lots of photos of me standing in a lemon grove, just outside of Palma del Río and he asked if he could put one of them on his website. I wondered if that was the real reason for our little trip, but I was happy to get out and about. The neat rows of trees seemed to go on forever and the peace was perfect, with only the odd car whizzing past disturbing the sounds of nature. I had never seen lemons that size before and it made me wonder why the ones we get in the UK are so small and hard. These were soft and the size of my hand. As I held one up close to my nose and inhaled, there was a sweetness alongside that acidity and I was oblivious to Emilio snapping away. When he dropped me back at the monastery, his parting words were telling.

'I'm delighted this opportunity came up today, allowing us to venture out into the countryside. It has been an absolute pleasure.'

I thanked him profusely, but as I headed back to my room, I had the distinct feeling that Rick had put him up to it, as how else would Emilio have known that I had nothing else planned?

Looking down at my watch, it's just after 9 a.m. and Mum texts to suggest a quick video call. When the screen lights up and she comes into view, there is a huge smile on her face.

'Hi, lovely,' she beams at me. 'You look sun-kissed. It suits you.'

'Well, it's not from lying out in it, you know me. It's been much too hot for that.'

'You were way too pale and pasty. But now you have a healthy little glow about you and a sparkle in your eye, even if you do look a little tired. I hope you aren't working too hard.'

It's true that I keep waking up and staring at the ceiling, thinking about my future and where I'm heading. My thoughts are crowded as I've had more worrying news from Dario. He handed in his notice and he says they aren't going to replace him. At a time when the magazine should be increasing its presence on social media to help boost sales, it makes no sense at all.

I shake off my concerns, conscious Mum is watching my every expression. 'There's just a lot going on as there's only one week to go. And the pressure is building for the contestants. Anyway, come on then, share your news. What was the verdict from your trainees? Did everything go smoothly?'

'Oh, my goodness, Lainey, it was amazing. The second group left yesterday afternoon and half of them have already rebooked for next year. And the activity on the website has suddenly surged by a whopping ten per cent this month already. People really are waking up to the need to go back to basics and steer away from mass-produced meals. If this continues and the bed and breakfast trade ticks over, I'll be able to afford to take on some permanent help next year.'

'That's wonderful, Mum, and so well deserved. It takes a while to build up a business from nothing and it's tough at the start. But now you really are flying. I'm proud of you, Mum.'

'Ah, Lainey, it means a lot to hear you say that. I know it was hard when I left, and I have you to thank for supporting your father.'

Oh no. How did we get onto this topic?

'When opportunities come up, you need to grab them, Mum,' I reply, trying to sound upbeat. 'Just keep doing what you're doing, because it's obviously working.'

'And do you know what, your dad really stepped up these last two weeks. His humour was much appreciated by everyone, and he joined in with everything, even social gatherings. We had a barbecue, and he did the dessert. Poached pears drizzled with local honey and finished off in foil over the coals. It went down a treat.'

Humour? Dad barbecuing again?

'He's been handy, then? I thought he had a deadline he was working on.'

'Oh, he has, but he's managed to get an extension. I have another course running in two weeks' time, and he's going to stay to help out with that before heading back.'

I'm momentarily stunned to hear this and I'm not quite sure how to respond. I mean, it's good news indeed, but Mum is definitely at pains to make it sound like it's no big deal. 'Is he around?' I enquire, hoping I can have a quick chat with him and find out what's going on.

'No. He's staying in one of the gîtes; it's a former pigsty would you believe it, and he's writing today. I'll take him in some lunch around noon, as he said he's unlikely to surface until early evening.'

'I didn't even know there was a pigsty.' My head is full of questions. Why is Mum waiting on Dad? Is she spoiling him for a reason, or is she simply enjoying having someone to look after?

'Which is why you need to come and visit. Anyway, everything is good. The bills are getting paid and I'm finally able to set some money aside, so I'm delighted.'

My phone pings. 'Hang on a second, Mum, I've just had a text. It might be work-related.'

Mum leans to one side of the screen, reaching out for something as I glance down at the phone in my hands. It's Rick.

I'm back, but I had a couple of things I needed to sort out first thing. Are you doing anything today? Felipe has arranged for a hire car and it will be here at ten. Interested?

I pause for a moment, torn between the reply I should give and the one I want to give. It pings again.

It's our last chance for that day out I promised you. No strings attached.

'Problems?' Mum asks, a frown creasing her brow as she stares back at me.

'No. Just a colleague wanting some company on a little day trip.'

My fingers tap lightly on the screen.

Sounds good to me. See you soon.

'Sorted. So, what's that?' I enquire as Mum holds up a spiral-bound notebook.

'Your dad thinks I should put together a recipe book, so I've made a start. He says it's easy to self-publish these days and I'm not doing it for the money, so what have I got to lose?'

I can tell, for the first time in a long while that they're talking, really talking and Mum couldn't look any happier. 'Nothing at all. I think that's a great idea, Mum. And I will work on sorting out a date to come and spend a little time with you.'

'I'd appreciate that, lovely. Just when it suits you, though. Anyway, I'm off to pick a few things from the garden ready for lunch. And you're off sightseeing, it seems?'

'I guess I am. Speak soon and give Dad a hug from me. Love you!'

* * *

'I'm glad you said yes. I had a feeling that if I didn't spring it on you, you wouldn't come,' Rick admits.

We both know he's right, but I say nothing and, instead, stare out the window as we speed along the sweeping curve of the road.

'There's been a lot to do and you've been busy, too,' I remark, a few minutes later.

'It's been crazy. Cathy turned up at the restaurant out of the blue and upset Neil, one of our waiting staff. He ended up walking out. Pierre contacted me and I spoke to Neil. He's had enough, but we'll really miss him as he's a hard worker and popular with the clients. Pierre interviewed some potential candidates, and I flew back to make the final decision.'

'Oh, I'm sorry to hear that, Rick,' I reply, unable to hide my surprise.

'You thought I was avoiding you?'

'No, of course not,' I lie.

'I put as much effort into selecting the waiting staff as I do the chefs in the kitchen. The service has to be on a par with the excellence of the food. But it's more than that, it's about the right personalities and the waiters work as a team within a team. Neil was priceless and Cathy was out of order. Apparently one of her friends turned up and expected everyone to jump to attention for him. It's time I explained that there can't be one rule for friends and another for customers. To be honest I've been ducking the conversation, but I have to face it when I get back. I just feel bad to let Neil go on a low point, when he did nothing wrong.'

I can hear the regret in his voice.

'It's not your fault, Rick. Neil understands and you knew he wasn't going to be around forever.' Argh. The minute I finish speaking I realise that I need to tread carefully here.

'You know him personally?'

'Not really, but we've chatted in passing a few times, and he mentioned going into business with his brother. He's very friendly and personable.' *Please don't pick up on this, Rick, please let it go*, my head is screaming inside. 'You never did tell me where you were planning on taking us,' I reply, desperate to change the subject.

'I'm guessing you're a *Game of Thrones* fanatic?'

I look at him, puzzled. 'How did you know that?'

'When we were at the palacio, you mentioned Daenerys. I knew then you were a fellow fan.'

'You bet. I was glued to every series but blindsided by the ending. It wasn't quite what I was expecting.'

'Well, we're going to the Castillo de Almodóvar del Río, where they shot some of the scenes.'

'You're joking,' I reply, slightly breathlessly.

'No, I'm not.' He's amused at my obvious excitement.

'How far is it? How long will it take to get there?' Suddenly, I'm full of questions.

'The town of Almodóvar del Río is about thirty kilometres, so half an hour away.'

I've always loved visiting castles. When I was a child my parents' idea of a Sunday drive out was to head to Wales and explore some of the old ruins and they always captured my imagination. I was a queen, wielding a sword, as my velvet cloak skimmed the floor and I defended my stronghold and my people. In my head, defeat was never an option and watching *Game of Thrones*, I was hooked.

'Anyway, how's the writing going?' he enquires.

'Good, but I won't know which of the weekly highlights will make my final cut for the second article until filming has been completed. I have so much content already, and who knows what will happen next week?'

I glance at Rick's side profile and it's obvious he's looking for a little feedback. 'Is the flaming grill likely to make the cut?' he continues.

I laugh out loud. 'Of course. Everyone enjoys a little drama and the action shot is going to literally jump off the page! Emilio also captured a great photo of Louis gazing down at the dish he'd just plated up, his expression is one of both relief and pride. He turned it around because he kept going and remained calm.

That's the sign of a true professional. How could I not feature that?'

'Can I tell you something in strictest confidence?'

I nod. 'Of course. What happens in Andalucía stays in Andalucía.'

Rick chuckles. 'Except for what makes the pages of *Upscale Dining*,' he points out.

'You know what I mean.'

'I'm going to offer Louis a job. If Cathy really pushes this idea of setting up a second restaurant, then Pierre will need a sous chef while I'm otherwise occupied.'

'Won't that upset the team?'

He grimaces. 'Well maybe, but at the end of the day, it's business. I have to deliver and people like Louis are rare.'

'But Louis might not win the competition.'

He shrugs. 'He hasn't played safe and that impresses me. Okay, he was having a bad day and things didn't go smoothly, but he brought it back from the brink of disaster. That takes skill, determination and guts. There's little difference between the pressure of a competition and a professional kitchen. Failure is never an option.'

Rick glances at me and I flick my hand across my lips as if I'm zipping them shut.

'Of course, Louis might not be interested in coming to London and, in truth, I'm still not happy about the financial backing Cathy wants to put in place. I'm looking at that to see if there are any other options to get her to have a rethink. She agreed to postpone the final decision until I get back, but in reality I don't know how much longer I can hold her off.'

Cathy is still determined to get things moving then. It does appear that he is no longer making excuses for her, but it sounds to me like he's gearing up for a battle. Good for him, standing his ground for a change. I just hope no one else is around when it all kicks off.

'Do you ever sit back and look at the world and wonder why things are going wrong? Happiness seems to be just a fleeting thing for most people,' I reflect.

'Life isn't easy. Maybe that's just the way things are.'

'Hard work should be rewarded, and it is, by piling on even more work. I only have to look at Thomas to see that, but it's a pattern that's repeated everywhere, isn't it?' I reply, venting my exasperation at the way Rick seems to accept how he's being manipulated. And I think of Neil and the unfair way that he's been treated.

'It's obvious something has upset you. It wasn't me, was it?' Rick asks, his brows knitting together in an unflattering frown.

'No, there are just a few things going around and around inside my head and it's getting to me a little,' I reply, grimly.

'I didn't mean to say anything to touch a raw nerve. You're the last person I'd ever want to upset, Lainey.'

'I know that, Rick. But we're all under pressure and some-times we forget to stand back and see what's really important. Maybe I need to rethink my priorities.'

'Why? I thought you had a plan all worked out.'

I sigh. 'My boss is great at what he does, but the pressure never lets up and it's taking a huge toll on him. And my aspira-tions are to follow in his footsteps. Does that make me crazy?'

We both know the answer, but he remains quiet, his eyes firmly on the road ahead.

'Nothing is ever going to be enough for some people, is it?' I continue. 'Where does it end? Your situation isn't too dissimilar,' I point out.

'Is this a criticism?' Rick asks, warily.

'No, I'm sorry, I wasn't getting at you. I was just thinking out loud. There's nothing wrong with empire building, but you're being pushed into something that doesn't feel right. It will double the pressure that you're already under. The point is, is it worth the risk? But this is about me, not you. I'm beginning to see why getting the job I dreamt of having isn't making me happy.'

My whole body sags.

'What do you want to do, then?' Rick asks gently.

'I have absolutely no idea.'

'Having recently gone through a bit of a roller-coaster time myself, it might help to know that some wild ideas went through my head before Cathy came along. I had a relatively short period – thankfully – during which it looked like I had nowhere to turn. It wasn't easy, that's for sure.'

'I'm sorry to hear that, Rick. It can feel like the ground is shifting beneath your feet and suddenly you start questioning everything,' I reply truthfully.

'Martine's game plan was to spread rumours and make sure no one else employed me. When you find yourself in a situation where telling the truth is as bad as saying nothing at all, it's tough to handle. Once people are talking about you and wondering what happened, they make assumptions. I thought about selling up and moving abroad. Opening a little tapas bar seemed appealing: somewhere hot and preferably near the beach.'

'The beach? Well, that's a surprise.'

'I spent a lot of time surfing down in Cornwall when I was a teenager.'

'Really?' I can't imagine Rick hanging out just for the fun of it. He's always so focused on what he does.

'I was young and taking each day as it came. The point is that when Cathy unexpectedly stepped in, Martine was in danger of making herself look foolish. No one was paying any attention to her any more because something bigger and more interesting was unfolding. All I'm trying to say is that – oh, what's that saying? It's always darkest before the dawn? My grandma used to say that all the time. But Cathy saved my career.' Maybe I was hasty in my judgement of Cathy and it's obvious Rick feels that he owes her.

'You think I'm just in a dark phase of my life, then?' I ask.

'Putting it like that makes it sound sinister. I think it's more a case of taking a brave step forward and maybe there are a few more steps to figure out before you find what you're looking for. What's right for you, that is.'

Rick has a point and perhaps I do just need to be patient and see where life takes me next. As I feel myself relaxing more and more being away from the treadmill, I'm wondering if I really do want a future career where I'm forced to live under a constant, unforgiving pressure. There has to be more to life than that, surely?

'I suppose one option is to freelance. I can write about a wide variety of things, not just food. And I love researching in general, and history.'

'There you go.'

'Thank you, Rick. You are the voice of reason.'

He bursts out laughing. 'Please never say that within earshot of Cathy because it would fire her up. Her take on it is that I'm overly cautious.' He turns his head for a brief second and winks at me, and just like that my spirits lift and I'm laughing.

Staring out at the fields of wheat as they flash by, then groves of olives and citrus fruits, it's time to enjoy the scenery. I stare out at the heavily laden lemon trees and then vivid pops of orange in between masses of dark green leaves.

A little further on, Rick pulls over to put an address into the satnav and I get out to stretch my legs. There's a light breeze today and the cornflower-blue sky is decorated with a swathe of fast-moving, wispy clouds that look more like a sprinkling of feathers.

The air carries the subtle hints of citrus trees and the tang of the olives. A small convoy of cars speeding past us scatters the dusty covering on this stretch of road and the dry grit as it's kicked up by the wheels of the cars, smells earthy.

'Is it much further?' I ask, as I manoeuvre myself back into the car and secure my seat belt.

'The road splits into two a little further along and we peel off to the right, according to this map. I'm putting my trust in the satnav after that as it looks like we come to a sort of square, where seven roads converge. We're looking for a road named Calle las Palvas, and then once we're on that we take the first right. There's a narrow, winding road up to the castle.'

'It's just a hill, though, isn't it?' I check.

'There are a number of hairpin bends according to the map, but it must be fully accessible as the leaflet says it's possible to park at the very top. It would be a long walk by the look of it and hard on the leg muscles.'

'I hope it isn't too steep. I don't do heights with sheer drops.'

Rick looks at me, shaking his head. 'Castles are usually up high. That's the whole point.'

'As long as the walls are thick, and the steps are sturdy, I should be good.'

'Now you're worrying me. It's too hot to get you somewhere and have to end up giving you a fireman's lift back down the hill,' he laughs. 'Right, remember those directions just in case.'

As it turns out, it's not hard to find, and as Rick turns off the main road, I crouch down a little in my seat to stare up at the castle high above us. The climb begins as we set off on the access road, which is really a wide track barely able to allow two cars to pass comfortably. My stomach begins to feel uneasy.

We climb higher and higher and the track gets narrower and narrower. It's now the width of a single vehicle with only a couple of feet clearance, as we have the hill rising up on the right-hand side of the car and the increasing drop on the left-hand side. We're so high up, I can't even look out the window on Rick's side any longer. From where I'm sitting, there's nothing but the sheer drop. It's a view that sweeps down over a town where everything appears in miniature, amidst a vast landscape of fields. And then ahead of us is one of those bends where the road appears to end with only a hellish drop in front of it and Rick has to negotiate the car around an impossibly sharp, right-hand turn. Even forgetting the fact that something could be heading down the track towards us, he can't see the ground beneath the car because of the steep uphill angle. How will he know if all four wheels have contact?

'I can't do it, Rick. I'm sorry. I just can't do it! My stomach is in knots,' I exclaim.

Rick steers the car as close to the bank on my side as he can, yanking on the handbrake and turning to look at me. 'You're not joking, are you? But it's still quite a way to go and there's nowhere I can pull off to the side, Lainey. If something comes around that bend it won't be at speed, but we're blocking the way down.'

'Sorry, but I'm walking. I'll meet you up there.'

He reaches into the back seat to grab me a bottle of water. 'Well, if you really mean it, then take this and don't forget your hat. Leave your backpack here, it'll be too hot to carry it. But it's almost noon, so I hope you know this is crazy, Lainey. Can't you just sit tight, close your eyes and trust my driving?'

I have already opened the passenger door as far as I can, and I swing my legs out, twisting around to look at him. 'I know, I'm a wimp and I'm sorry, but I trust my feet more than I trust four wheels. I just can't do it.'

The car is no more than eighteen inches away from the stony bank looming up in front of me. I slam the door shut and edge along to the front of the car, the verge at the bottom of the hill no deeper than my size four shoes.

Rick is reluctant to pull away, but I give him a reassuring smile and a little wave. I can't bear to watch as the car crawls forward and instead I take a moment to stare up at the hillside and the castle at its pinnacle. Rick drives slowly towards the tight turn in the road and I close my eyes briefly, re-opening them seconds later and he's out of sight. It is searingly hot and the heat is even seeping up through the soles of my flat leather slip-ons. But at least they have a little grip against the gritty surface of the road and my stomach approves of the feel of the solid ground beneath my feet. I studiously ignore looking to my left and stick as close to the bank as I can.

The grass is yellow, like straw, and interspersed with what looks like low-level gorse and the occasional gnarled olive tree, whose branches give a little shade. After walking for about ten minutes, I stop to lean against one of them and take a sip of water. Some birds forage among the leaves overhead and I'm surprised that I still haven't seen any other vehicles. There's no one else around and when I finally turn my gaze to the vista, even though I'm a good nine feet away from the edge of the track, my stomach turns over. But it has to be said that the view is incredible. It's like a carpet that extends way into the distance, meeting the horizon. The town laid out in front of me is a vision of white and terracotta, but too far below me to pick out the detail. I spot a line of cars travelling along a street, but they are tiny. Beyond that, and as far as the eye can see, are fields delineated by a ridge of mountains far, far away.

I walk on for a few minutes but my calf muscles are complaining, so I stand back in the part-shade of some branches extending out from a eucalyptus tree. The drop on this level is sheer and I find myself staring down at the track as it bends back on itself.

Below that is yet another level as the turns are now much closer together. The constant rattly buzzing of the cicadas is becoming increasingly annoying in this heat and I wonder how they find the energy to keep going.

'Have you given up?' Rick calls out, as I turn to see him walking towards me. I hurry to catch up with him, feeling silly, but I have no idea how he could see where the wheels of the car would land on each of these tight turns and I feel physically sick at the mere thought of it.

'I was distracted for a moment. This incline is hard on the legs. Is it as bad as I think it is?'

'Let's just say that it will be a lot easier driving back down as long as we don't meet anyone on the way. There are a handful of cars parked up, but they might belong to staff. The gates are open, but I can't see anyone inside. We may be the only tourists mad enough to come out in the hottest part of the day.'

I swipe a hand across my forehead, tempted to take off my hat as perspiration gathers on my forehead.

'Come on, it's not that far. The views are stunning, aren't they?'

I nod in agreement as we trudge along, side by side. 'It's beautiful. And, aside from the cicadas and the occasional raucous squabbles of a small group of birds chasing each other from tree to tree, I can't hear any signs of life going on around us. It's a little eerie isn't it?'

'It's because we're too high up to catch any sounds from down below and there's hardly any movement in the air right now.'

We round yet another sharp turn in the road, which I notice is even narrower here, if that is at all possible. Mercifully, it soon begins to widen out again, as thirty metres ahead of us is a car park. I stop for a moment to gaze up at the imposing façade of the stone walls of the castle which towers above us menacingly, and I almost topple backwards as my gaze continues to travel upwards. It's a little scary and my stomach is jittery. But it's solid, powerful, impenetrable and unbelievable really, given the location. How they managed to haul the stone up here is unimaginable.

Thankfully, there's a low wall with railings sitting on top bordering the left-hand side of the car park, to ensure no one drives too close to the edge when they are turning around. I notice that Rick has parked on the other side next to the gates.

Three ancient olive trees, with gnarled almost blackened trunks, stand in the shadow of the walls. Obviously, the castle was built on bedrock and huge chunks of it are exposed at foundation level, presumably too difficult to level, or move.

The entrance is an open, horseshoe-shaped stone archway into a tower and, high overhead from the battlements, two flags hang limply from the flagpoles. Rick and I walk through, stopping for a moment in front of the smaller, inner archway a couple of strides away that houses the oversized, heavy wooden gates. Either side are ironwork sconces, and it doesn't take much of an imagination to visualise flaming torches welcoming home a triumphant army.

'Are we doing this?' Rick asks, checking I'm not about to change my mind.

'You bet! I mean, the safest place to be is inside a fortress that was built to last forever. Solid I can handle, and as long as there's something for me to hold onto, I'll be fine. I'm excited,' I declare, hurrying inside. The worst bit is over and now the fun begins.

18

STORMING THE CASTLE

The ticket booth looks empty at first sight, but as we approach, a woman steps forward. She doesn't speak any English, but it's easy enough to buy the tickets, and I insist on paying. She points to some piles of printed leaflets in various languages and Rick thanks her.

What surprises me now we're inside is that there are trees growing within the boundary of the castle walls itself. It's a welcome contrast to the weathered stonework. Exposed to the elements, much of it is greyish in colour, weathered and pitted in places, but there are sheltered areas where you can see the natural colour of the buff stonework coming through.

We're standing in the shade of a massive tree, its branches extending out over a wide area. The sun beating down on us is reduced to little pools of sunlight, broken only by the natural movement of the clusters of leaves. It's enchanting and already I feel as if I've entered another dimension and am heading back in time. Despite the heat, it gives me goosebumps.

'Where shall we start?' Rick prompts me, flicking through the leaflet, but I'm already striding away from him. I am queen for the afternoon, as I step into the Middle Ages. 'Oh,' Rick mutters and I stop to glance back at him. 'There's a car park at the bottom, although I think if we'd walked up the whole way it would have been too much in this heat. I guess I was too busy looking at the satnav. Are you heading for the battlements? That's brave.'

'My neck is already aching from constantly looking up and we'll get a fabulous view of the entrance from up here. It's not that high, and some of these walls have been reconstructed so I'm not worried. Does it give any information in there?'

'I'm a tour guide as well as a driver now, am I?' Rick throws back at me, rolling his eyes. 'The hill this is built on is named La Floresta. It was built by the Moors in 760 on the site of an old Roman fort. It has undergone various reconstructions and renovations since then.'

'That's good enough for me,' I reply nonchalantly, over my shoulder. 'I don't think they had cowboy builders back then.'

I'm already stepping off the grey composite pathway that runs in a straight line from the main gates. Square, grey cobbles have been inlaid in a diamond pattern but alongside it, to our left, there's a ramp running parallel to the incredibly high inner walls. A fortress within a fortress. The castle covers the entire plateau on top of the hill and it looks like a huge site, but we're only on the edge of the outer perimeter. Although I can't wait to see the heart of this place, I climb up onto the narrow, raised stone wall to my right, where the battlements begin.

Rick suddenly catches up with me. 'I feel like I should be carrying a bow and a handful of arrows,' he enthuses. 'I bet the film company couldn't believe their luck when they discovered this place.'

We're at the lowest point, but it's still high up. However, staunch pillars topped with sizeable stone pyramid caps stand only two hand-widths apart. Enough room for soldiers to scan the area below and launch their arrows, but difficult for invaders to get a clean shot from such an incredible distance below.

'How awful to live in constant fear of being overrun,' I reflect, trying to imagine what it must have been like preparing for an invasion. 'This castle is especially hard to penetrate given its location. I wonder how many soldiers fell to their death, though, amidst the noise and the chaos of being under attack.' I'm talking as I walk, eager to mount yet another set of steps.

'Hey, wait for me,' Rick calls out, but I keep going until I reach the highest level accessible from this side of the castle.

Stepping up onto the metre-wide, fortified rampart, both sides have sturdy, metalwork railings. Rick joins me as I stand, my hands grabbing onto the rail while I stare out at the bird's-eye view.

'I see what you mean about holding on,' he laughs as he glances at my white-knuckled hands.

'It makes a difference and means I can enjoy the view. This is the other side of the castle, isn't it? We can't see the access road at all, so the track only hairpins around one side of the hill. That's why the turns are so tight.'

'Yes. The main route we came in via is over there,' he points his arm.

The wide, tarmacked road lies like a black ribbon on a flat landscape dotted with farms and clusters of buildings. The groves of trees seem to stretch out endlessly. Viewed from up here, in the distance are huge straw-coloured fields and dotted around are what are obviously farms, with clusters of out-buildings.

Rick leans over the handrail to stare down at the ground as it drops away in front of us. 'It's so dry and steep. Access from this side would be nigh on impossible.'

I tentatively ease forward. There are clusters of shrubs, olive trees and succulents which obviously thrive in these conditions.

But the slope of the hill looks like it has a dry, crumbly surface, with patches of scorched grasses and stubble.

We're standing in the shade of a tall olive tree and Rick and I turn to look down into the internal courtyard below.

'I could cheerfully hug you for this experience,' I admit, turning to look at Rick with gratitude. 'If ever I needed whisking away, it's today. I have no idea why I'm suddenly rethinking my entire life, but being here is magical. Thank you, it means a lot.'

We face each other and, for one heart-stopping moment, I instinctively lean into Rick and suddenly we're mere inches apart and I can feel his breath on my face. I draw back, and he clears his throat, nervously. Were we about to succumb to a kiss?

'Time to head inside and discover the real treasures,' I murmur as our eyes meet.

This is very probably our last few hours of real alone-time together, with no one watching. I think we're both aware of that fact and trying to push it aside. Is it wrong to enjoy every second of it, given that our paths will be going off in different directions so soon?

A movement overhead as a bird noisily flaps its wings disturbs a branch and sends a shower of dappled sunlight dancing over us. I start laughing.

'What so funny?' Rick asks, blankly.

'You don't look real, as if you're materialising before my eyes.'

Rick shakes his head, giving me a look that implies I'm a lost cause. 'You'll be seeing knights wielding swords next. If you do, I don't want to know. History needs to stay firmly in the past, I don't do the seeing spirits thing, but it's atmospheric, I'll give you that, and strangely peaceful.'

'It is. I thought it would be swarming with visitors, but I've only seen one couple since we arrived.'

We retrace our steps and head for the ramp taking us up into the main part of the castle. I'm trying so hard to keep my emotions in check and my heart is telling me that if I don't stay strong, then Rick won't be able to handle it. For all I know this might be the last memory I have of spending time alone with a man who makes my heart constrict every time he looks at me. And Rick is clearly on edge, too. Every time he opens his mouth to speak a look of uncertainty flashes over his face, as if the words coming out aren't the ones running through his head.

Shake it off, Lainey, I tell myself. *Make this easy for him and for yourself.*

To my surprise, Rick reaches out to catch my hand. 'Sorry, Lainey.'

I stare at him as our fingers entwine for a few brief seconds, before we pull away from each other.

'Why are you sorry?' I ask, wondering what he's thinking.

'I don't know, I can't explain to you how I'm feeling right now, I guess I'm sad that our time here is coming to an end. It's been quite... an experience, hasn't it?'

My heart is pounding and I have no words to answer him because if I say anything it will be the wrong thing.

'We should get on because there's a lot more to see,' I reply, softly.

'Yes, of course.' This time, his voice is firm and the moment has passed. We are not going to cross that invisible line and the hope that has begun to rise up inside of me shatters into a million pieces.

It takes a huge effort to shake off my sadness, but it's time to face the inevitable. I turn away, unable to look at him and when it's obvious Rick isn't following on behind me, I stop to see what he's doing. His back is towards me and he's staring out at the panoramic view. Something in his stance makes my lower lip quiver and I gulp down a lump that has formed in my throat. It's the first time I've ever seen Rick look vulnerable.

* * *

The interior of the castle is an incredible maze of narrow walkways between tall, stone walls. The surprise is how pretty it is and colourful, too. Even the detail in the construction of the pathways is charming, with bricks set out in geometrical patterns. Bordering the path we are on is a run of neatly clipped hedges on one side, with several climbers adding little pops of pink against the sandy-coloured stonework. On the other side of us, the low shrubs have a bluey tinge to their leaves, which is fragrant but not a smell I recognise.

I glance at Rick and see that he, too, is making a huge effort to enjoy what's left of our visit.

'It is as if we are in a courtyard garden, not a fortress, isn't it?' I remark, breaking the awkward silence between us.

'Yes. I'm glad we came.' He smiles at me and his eyes light up as they study my face. Sometimes a look can say more than a whole torrent of words and we're back on track.

At the end of the path, we take a sharp right up to the next level and continue on until we find ourselves looking down onto an expansive, open area, perfect for holding court. There are no more than a dozen people traversing it. Gazing around, I notice there are various archways leading though to what looks like a series of smaller, inner courtyards. It's like a rabbit's warren of pathways, with options to climb higher or drop down to the lower levels, and I'm eager to explore.

Rick looks on amused as it's clear he isn't walking fast enough for my liking, so I end up leading the way once more. We descend into an arched tunnel and negotiate a steep set of stone steps. It takes us down and down, and we leave the heat of the day behind. The air begins to feel distinctly chilly. There's nothing but solid stone walls all around us and it's obvious we are heading into one of the dungeons. At the end of the steps, it is a little daunting walking into the room, which has a metal grille set into the middle of the flagstone floor. The chamber has been set up using dummies dressed like prisoners, with long hair and beards. One is chained against the wall and another lies on a makeshift, wooden cot covered in sackcloth.

'I don't like the feel in here,' I remark, shuddering from the chill in the air. It was refreshing at first, but it's now beginning to make my skin feel clammy.

'Me, neither. Let's see if we can find our way through to one of those patio areas, as I noticed some tables and chairs half-hidden under a cluster of trees.' Rick's smile is irresistible and I quickly turn away.

The ascent is much quicker than the descent because I can't wait to get back out into the sunlight again. This time, Rick takes the lead, and I can see he's enjoying himself as we try to find our way down into the inner sanctum.

I fall behind for a moment, stopping to run my fingers over the stonework of a pillar, pitted with age and covered in little circles of flat, grey lichen and patches of moss. How many hands have touched this same spot over time? I wonder.

'Here you go, I told you there would be somewhere to grab a drink. Water, coffee... something to eat?' Rick calls out to me and I hurry to catch up.

'I'll get these,' I call out.

'No, take a seat in a shady spot and let your imagination run riot. Did you spot the poster over there with a scene from *Game of Thrones*?' He points to an archway in the far corner and a sign standing in front of it.

'Oh, I'll check that out, thank you. Coffee and a water would be great, but I'm not hungry.' Any appetite I had has totally disappeared. Rick brought me here because he knew it would be meaningful and he was right. But there is a poignancy to that which is hard to shake off.

Again, he gives me an intense look, which unsettles me, so I give him a fleeting smile and turn away, eager to distract myself. To anyone seeing us, we could just be a young couple on holiday enjoying a little sightseeing, but we aren't. There are moments when I forget that, and worryingly, I get the impression that Rick does too.

A small group of people are gathered around an impressive poster standing on a metal base and I stand to one side to catch my first glimpse of it up close. It's Jaime Lannister, the fictional character played by actor Nikolaj Coster-Waldau, in a shot where he's walking around the battlements. In the scene, he was in Highgarden, which is the seat of the House Tyrell, and the people in the background walk off and disappear through an archway. This archway. I'm transfixed. Standing here it takes little imagination, indeed, to conjure up a whole host of scenes, because the castle has been so meticulously restored and maintained, it feels as if it's ready and awaiting the soldiers' return.

Reluctantly, I head back to the trees and settle myself down, although my feet are more than happy as I kick off my shoes and flex my toes.

'That was good timing,' Rick says, walking towards me with a tray in his hands. 'I was just talking to a British tourist inside and there's a trail of those posters with scenes from *Game of Thrones* scattered around. They're placed alongside where the scenes were actually filmed.'

'That's a good idea,' I reply, as I pull out a chair for him. 'The one over there is of the battlements overhead and the archway. I bet it was amazing watching them shooting it.'

Rick places the drinks on the table, standing the tray up next to his chair. We both pick up our bottles of water, gratefully.

'I did once get to see a film crew on location. It's not as interesting as you'd think,' he replies, screwing the cap back on the bottle.

'Really?'

'It was a film about surfers, and I wasn't in it, but a group of us were there that day to catch a few waves. You'd think that something as simple as running down the beach would be a one-take shot, wouldn't you? They did it over a dozen times. And then there was a short conversation with a group of actors around a small fire and that went on for ages too. An aeroplane flew over at one point, someone's dog started barking behind them and then the actors themselves messed up the dialogue on numerous occasions. We lost interest at that point anyway, because we were hungry. I was always in charge of the barbecue at the end of the day and I'm not bragging, but no one went hungry.'

'So, it was a real hobby for you, then, surfing? Not just an occasional thing?'

'Hmm, yep. I was on the school swimming team and when I was twelve, I asked for a wetsuit and surfboard for Christmas. After that, I'd nag my parents to head to Cornwall every couple of months and we'd go there in the school holidays. As a teenager, a group of us used to take off in a mate's camper van for weekends and we'd pitch our tents and have a whale of a time. I was always one of the first to be invited, because by then I was well into my fascination with food and a legend of the firepit.'

'A legend of the firepit?' I smile and he nods. 'Not a legendary surfer, then?'

'Sadly, no. But I was okay. I wasn't into football or the other team sports my mates did as I was already spending my free time in the kitchen. When they were hungry, I was the one they came running to. But I saw surfing as a challenge, something I wanted to master every bit as much as cooking a perfect steak.'

'There is a bit of the adventurer in you, then?'

Rick cocks an eyebrow. 'Naturally. I mean, who wouldn't want to ride the perfect curl, or wield a sword, or climb a mountain? The tough bit is finding the time, and so it has been a couple of years since I've been able to hit the beach.'

'That's sad. How is it that we end up accepting that there isn't time for the things we once enjoyed doing? It's the same for me. I keep telling myself *one day*, *soon*. But that day never comes.' I pick up the coffee cup, frowning as thoughts crowd my head. I'm lucky enough to have a job I enjoy doing, so I know I shouldn't be complaining. But I'm beginning to wonder if I can do better. I just need to have the resolve to see some changes through.

'I guess that most of us start off with constraints that slow us down, but hopefully, it's possible to get to a stage where money is less of a problem. Well, that's the general idea, isn't it?' Rick responds enthusiastically.

I can't answer him because in my head I'm imagining a life here, in the Andalucían sunshine, with Rick by my... a man that I love by my side, embarking on a whole new adventure. No more ties, just a fresh start. I realise that Rick is talking to me while I've been wistfully daydreaming.

'—end up working through the problems and when it's time to reap those rewards, that's what sets us free. My parents are at a stage where they were able to retire a little early and are now enjoying working down their bucket list.'

Rick sounds totally accepting of that idea, and yet, hearing him say it like that makes me wonder if we haven't got it all wrong. You live to work so that eventually you can find time to experience all those things you've always longed to do? And then you end up cramming them into whatever time you have left?

Easing my shoulders back, I finish my coffee and tell my brain to stop it. Nothing is going to spoil the remainder of this afternoon with Rick. We have towers and battlements and turrets to explore, and I'm grateful to be sharing this experience with him. 'Thank you for being so thoughtful, Rick. I'll remember this trip here forever.' My comment comes from the heart and I say it without thinking. 'I keep doing that, don't I? Just blurting out my thoughts to you.' I feel embarrassed.

Rick takes a moment to study me, his eyes sweeping my face before he responds. 'No, I like that. It's refreshing to be able to be honest and real. It'll be hard to return to normality and this will all seem like a dream once we're back in our old routines.' He sounds sad and I nod in agreement. 'I hate to point this out,' he adds, 'but judging by that noise I think a coach party has just arrived.'

We glance up to see a whole mass of people crossing the first part of the walkway around the inner walls.

'Let's make sure we stay ahead of them. I figure another hour and we should head back, anyway, but I don't want you to miss a thing.'

Deep in my heart, I know this one brief moment in time will be forever etched in my mind. As Rick looks at me, I can tell we're both feeling the same – an *if only* moment of joy and sadness, and my heart pounds deep within my chest.

Breaking the spell, Rick's phone starts ringing and it's Cathy. He gives me an apologetic shrug as he walks off to find a shady spot to stand and talk. I try not to watch him, as I wander aimlessly just out of earshot, but he's animated, laughing at whatever she's telling him. They do say that absence makes the heart grow fonder and that seems to be the case. I guess that both Rick and I might be heading home with a fresh perspective on a few things and that, at least, is positive. But what happened between us earlier on put a little doubt back into my mind and it also unsettled him. That can't be right, can it? Sadly, even though I can't pretend I won't treasure these memories forever, the timing of Cathy's call drags me back to the harsh reality. I'm not famous, rich, or talented, and all I have to offer is my heart.

19

THE TENSION IS TANGIBLE

'Hi, Lainey, I just wanted to say that I hope the last day of filming goes well tomorrow.' Mum's voice is a welcome diversion from my thoughts, but I can't believe that even at my age she can't resist checking up on me.

'Thanks, Mum. Things were a bit tense this evening. There are three main contenders and I'm guessing that there are only a couple of points in it, so now it all hinges on the last cook-off of the competition. Then I have one day to write up the last part of the article, before I fly home on Saturday. On Monday I'll be in the office selecting the final photos and then it will be onto the next assignment.'

'Ah, that's a lot of pressure on you, lovely.'

I lie back on the bed, the room pleasantly cool with the air-conditioning unit turned up high. 'It has been full-on in one respect, and a big learning curve bonding with such a large group of people I had never met before. But I've managed to get out to do a little sightseeing. And just staying in the monastery itself is something I will never forget.'

'How was your trip out on Sunday? Did you go somewhere nice?'

'We went to see a castle. Some of the scenes featured in *Game of Thrones* were filmed there, so I found it fascinating.'

'That's not everyone's cup of tea, though, so I suspect some of your group weren't quite as enthused as you were,' Mum laughs.

'It, um... wasn't a group thing.'

'Oh. Who did you go with?'

'Rick. He's an avid fan of the show, too.' I keep my voice low-key, hoping she'll change the subject.

'I expect that was a welcome break for him. You must be getting on quite well with him to venture out together on a day trip,' Mum reflects, in a matter-of-fact tone.

'He's easy to talk to and obviously missing his fiancée, so I'm sure he appreciated the company. And, yes, we had a great day out. Anyway, how's Dad doing? I texted him at the start of the week, but we haven't spoken, so I assume he's still head down working.'

'I see him at breakfast and dinner, around seven each evening, and I creep in with a sandwich at lunchtime. You know what he's like,' she laughs, 'well, you're the same when you're working. He's totally focused on the job in hand and by the time we've eaten he's tired and not in the mood for conversation.'

'Oh dear, that's not much fun for you.' I sincerely hope Dad wasn't only making an effort to be sociable when Mum's guests were around and now he's ignoring her. It's a bit mean-spirited of him if that's the case.

'It's fine, I understand. It's not as if I don't have plenty of things to do in preparation for the next lot of arrivals. And I can lose an entire day in the garden and hardly notice the hours flying by.' Mum sounds perfectly happy for them to each have a little space.

'Anyway, back to you. I can tell something is up. Do you want to talk about it?'

A sigh escapes my lips before I have time to rein it in. Mum has cleverly caught me off guard. There's a low 'hmm' from the other end of the line as she waits for my answer.

'Well, getting away has allowed me a little time to think about the future. My masterplan might need a little... err, adjusting.'

'I thought you were happy and doing well. Didn't you say that things were beginning to come together nicely? What's happened to change that?'

Now Mum sounds anxious and I didn't mean to unsettle her.

'Nothing has gone wrong, exactly, but do I really want a job that is so full-on that I never really switch off? My boss is under constant pressure and that filters down. Coming here it's been different, like a wake-up call. The pace of life is gentler and even the stressful moments have been easier to handle.' I'm conscious it all sounds a little vague.

'So, what's the answer?' Mum asks and it's obvious she's struggling to understand something I'm not even sure I can explain, anyway.

'It's a great job, don't get me wrong, and I'm learning so much. And I feel so lucky to be able to cover something as big as this competition. The thing is, what if climbing further up the ladder isn't quite right for me? I'm wondering if I'd be better keeping my head down for a year or two, so that my CV is more attractive, and then I'd be in a good position to go back to freelancing and being my own boss again.'

Mum lets out a slow breath. 'My goodness, I didn't see that coming. Personally, I think that's a marvellous idea. You cut yourself off for a while and I wasn't sure whether it was because our... relationship was a bit awkward or work was your coping mechanism now you're on your own. There's nothing wrong with that if it makes you happy.'

'Oh Mum, I wasn't running away. I was in a relationship that had run its course and I have no regrets about it ending at all. What's troubling me now is that I have no idea why I'm suddenly looking at everything and seeing it all in a different light. This was supposed to be my dream job and a stepping stone on the journey to my career ambitions. What if I haven't got it in me to take on more responsibility and the pressure that comes with that?'

Mum gives a little chuckle. 'My lovely daughter, you have what it takes to do whatever you want if you put your mind to it. Settle back in after this trip and if you still feel the same way, then you'll know it's for a reason. That's the time to reassess things and tweak the plan.' I can hear the empathy in her voice. She simply wants me to be happy.

'Thanks, Mum. I'm probably just feeling unsettled at the thought of heading back and what I'm walking into at work. Dario has handed in his notice and that threw me a bit.'

'Ah, no wonder you're a little on edge, then. That's only natural. Once you're back, things will probably settle down again quite quickly. Your time in Spain will seem like a distant dream before you know it!' Her tone is reassuring.

'I bet you're right. Thanks for listening and give Dad a hug from me. Love you, and I'll ring you both on Sunday morning.'

As I was talking to Mum, what I kept coming back to was that Andalucía has captured my heart in a way I didn't expect. It's given me the time to trust that when something doesn't feel right it's okay to have a rethink. I'm free to steer my future wherever I want it to go, I just have to stop being scared of the responsibility that freedom brings with it.

* * *

My palms are sweating, and I can't believe how many things are going wrong as we head into the final twenty minutes of cooking time. Today's hero ingredient is the not-so-humble almond. Rick's masterclass dish was phenomenal, but the problems started when each of the top contenders decided to risk everything, rather than taking a safer option, and things quickly started to unravel.

Rick's masterclass dish on Monday was faultless and the dessert was stunning. A bitter dark chocolate torte layered with sponge, stood proud like a little tower of gooey deliciousness. It was offset on a small, rectangular white plate, with shards of richly toasted almonds, piled on top like peaks on a mountain. At the other end of the plate, Rick placed a single expresso coffee in a matching white china cup. In the middle was a tear drop-shaped, white ceramic amuse-bouche spoon filled to the brim with a pouring almond crème anglaise.

It was simple and yet the sight of it made our mouths begin to water. Setting aside a dish for the official still shots, Rick plated up a dessert for each of us. Drizzling the sauce over the top and letting it drip decadently down the sides of the torte, we were all enthralled. And, after that first mouthful, when I took a sip of the bitter coffee, the flavours just kept on coming. It had everything. The bitter dark chocolate with thin layers of almond-soaked sponge, the silky rich smoothness of the sauce and a gentler hint of that nutty flavour to give a sweetness that wasn't sugary. And finally, the satisfying crunch of almond pieces, toasted to perfection. The room was only silent for a few seconds before it was filled with the inevitably appreciative sounds, as people's taste buds reacted with pleasure and pure satisfaction.

And now we're here and it's neck-and-neck right up to the

wire. Things go wrong in the kitchen all the time, but chefs are used to thinking on their feet. In my opinion the leader board has changed and it's between Alexis Di Angelis, the Greek contestant, Louis Reno, from France and India Serrano, from Spain. In weeks one and two, India was lagging behind, and then suddenly last week she seemed to blossom and now I believe she has a real shot at winning.

Alexis has had a major problem with his almond ice cream, and he was holding his head in his hands at one point. He had no choice but to start again and because he has several elements to his dish, he's now running behind. But it's not inconceivable that he can still pull it off.

Joana Barradas, from Portugal, burnt her first batch of almond tuiles and had to start over again.

Javier is sitting next to me on the right, Emilio on my left, and we keep exchanging worried glances. How Rick is coping with the pressure, I don't know, but he's walking up and down with Miguel at his side, as the cameraman follows him, chatting to the contestants as they talk him through their dishes.

When the final countdown begins, I almost want to shut my eyes as I can't bear to see the ensuing panic. It takes at least a couple of minutes to plate up a dish to the standard required and three of the contestants are still cooking. One person will walk away with a trophy and a cheque for thirty thousand euros. But it's the job offers that will come flooding in afterwards, that are the real prize. Everything is now on the line and you can see Rick's feeling every second of their anxiety.

Two of the chefs stand back from their workstations, the look of relief on their faces clear. Louis is next, but he isn't smiling, just mopping his brow. Then it's the turn of the English chef, Ben Andrews, who I've only talked to in passing a couple of times, but he always has a smile on his face. Even if he achieves a score of ten today, it's unlikely that he has enough points to get in the top three, but he told me that he'd learnt so much that he was simply grateful to have made the cut and to be taking part. Everyone here is giving it their all because a good chef is always up for a challenge.

We're all on the edges of our seats. Three, two and as Rick calls, 'Your time is up,' Joana stands back, looking defeated. Her dish is not complete and while her second batch of almond tuiles are finally out of the oven, she didn't have time to tease one off the baking tray and get it onto the plate. She looks crestfallen.

'Well done, everyone. That was a tough one,' Rick says, sounding emotional. 'Cooking is not exactly a precise science, as I'm sure you all know. There is a whole host of factors that affect the timing of individual elements of the dishes, and we've all had occasions when something that we've prepared without a hitch innumerable times in the past suddenly goes pear-shaped. But I'd like to congratulate you all, because no one gave up. You kept going and that's the sign of a true professional. We choose to be chefs because it's our passion. We are at the forefront of show-casing quality produce in celebration of the best of the best. We strive to keep raising the bar and I hope you are all truly proud of your efforts today. Thank you.'

Javier is talking to Miguel, who steps forward to inform everyone there will be a ten-minute break before the judging begins. I feel like I've just run a marathon, so I can't imagine how these guys are feeling right now.

Rick walks towards us and beckons Emilio and me forward. 'Feel free if you want to take a few quick shots while we're on a break. I'll get everyone to plate up a second dish for you to photo-graph later, but this tasting could take a while today.'

'I don't envy you making the final decision,' I reply and Rick stares back at me, raising his eyebrows to show the seriousness with which he takes his role. The fact that we've had virtually no time to talk privately since our trip to the castle makes me feel distant from him today. If we were alone I'd give him a few words of encouragement, but I can't do that in front of Emilio.

'We'll make sure that for the final shots we get every little detail right. I'm not a fan of rushing things and the chefs deserve to show off their dishes to the best of their abilities.'

Rick knows that at least three of them ran out of time and while he can't allow anyone to add anything to the finished plate for judging purposes, he can at least give them the time to present it properly for the record.

Emilio and I head straight over to the workstations and seconds later he's happily snapping away. The dishes all smell delicious, but two of them really do look as if they've been plated up in a Michelin-starred restaurant. Unfortunately, Ben's has too much sauce on the plate and it looks heavy-handed. And Louis' plate is missing something, a little colour maybe.

Rick comes up behind me. 'A tiny sprig of mint would have done it. I know what he was trying to do and that was to separate the flavours so they could be tasted either individually or assembled on the spoon. It's a deconstructed almond layer cake with a lemon drizzle. It just lacks a little bit of an impact, which is a real shame if the taste is as good as I think it's going to be.'

His voice is low, not that Emilio can hear us, as he's already down at the far end of the table.

'Would you do something like this again?' I ask Rick, looking up at him. He rewards me with that disarming smile of his and it instantly makes my pulse quicken.

'We don't always get to choose what we want to do, so who knows? And are you looking forward to getting back to normality next week?'

'What I'd actually like is to take a few days off, but that isn't going to happen. Well, not just yet, but I'll be working on it.'

The sound of voices indicates that everyone is filtering back into the room already and it's show time once more.

Watching Rick perform in front of the cameras, he is a natural. He doesn't seem to be aware of anything other than the food he's tasting. He takes his time, making notes as he goes while sharing with the audience the highlights of each dish. Rick waits patiently while Miguel translates his words, and he does a brilliant job of mirroring a sense of genuine enthusiasm. And then it's time to select the dish of the day.

'The winning dishes in reverse order are: Louis Reno, Mirra Cegani and, taking the first place for our final dessert challenge is India Serrano. Congratulations, India, your dish today is a dessert masterclass in its own right.'

There's a spontaneous round of applause and filming stops. It's time for everyone to construct their final plate for the official photographs. But first there's a lot of hugging and shaking of hands going on, as everyone rushes up to India. It's her first win and she's delighted.

When things start to settle back down, it doesn't take long for Emilio to capture some shots of the final dishes together, and then it's crazy time as everyone crowds around to sample each other's desserts.

I walk over to join Rick, who is leaning up against one of the stone pillars watching the reaction and listening to the comments.

'I'm assuming that the final result will be a close call?' I whisper, leaning into him.

'Yes. It's obviously either Louis, or India, as Alexis didn't get into the top three today. But until the final tally is done, I think it could go either way. The beauty of the points system is that even I don't know the exact score so far. We're all going by the number of times a candidate has been in the top three. India deserved her ten out of ten today. She turned a humble dessert into an experience and that's where India is going to make her mark in her future career, I'm sure of it.'

Humble is most definitely not a word I'd associate with any of the dishes here today. However, I can't wait to taste India's dessert, as it really does stands out from the rest. She presented a tasting plate comprising five individual elements. Displayed in an arc on a circular plate is a bite-sized shortbread almond biscuit, a chocolate and almond madeleine, a shot glass with a frosted almond cream, a miniature almond and coconut macaroon, and a cinnamon-roasted almond truffle. She has created two little teardrop swathes, one was a crystallised ginger coulis and the other a pear purée.

'It's true that none of the elements are complex in terms of culinary skills,' Rick adds, 'but it's the vision and the flavours that make it an outstanding ten. Sometimes the cleverest and most inspiring ideas come back to basics.'

Miguel puts his hand in the air to attract our attention. 'Congratulations, everyone. Javier has confirmed that the overall winner will be announced at 2 p.m. if everyone can head back here for the presentation and the group photographs.'

It's like waiting for the final count to come in for an election, as everyone tries to work out in their heads which of the two main candidates will win. And it's agonisingly close.

* * *

Standing next to the bar in the courtyard outside of the restaurant, everyone is gathered together, and the atmosphere is electric. India was announced as the deserving winner, but with

Louis being only one point behind her in the final count, he was also given a massive round of applause.

I lost sight of Rick for a while and he reappears in view, heading straight towards me.

'Ooh, I could do with one of those, what is it?' he asks, pointing to the drink in my hand.

'It's a Fino Martini. I'm on apple juice after this one, though,' I reply and as our eyes meet, he grins at me.

'Ah, no chance of a repeat then.'

I give him my best attempt at a withering look, and he laughs it off.

'Only joking,' he says as he turns to the bartender and points to my drink. It's a relief to have slipped back into comfortable mode again with each other.

'Cathy rang and so I popped up to my room for a quick video call. She wants me to change my flight so we can meet up tomorrow, as she won't be back in the UK for another week at least. I guess that's going to mean a couple of hours online tonight trying to sort it all out.'

As an outsider, it looks to me as if Rick is constantly at Cathy's beck and call, but I suppose that when you truly love someone, you would do anything for them. Including walking away. My stomach does an unexpected somersault as Rick turns around, glass in hand to look at me. He freezes for a second or two, sensing a change in my demeanour, but I instantly plaster on a fake smile, unwilling to let the mask slip now.

'Let's toast to what has been an amazing time here in Andalucía!' I propose light-heartedly.

He raises his glass and we chink. Then his eyes search mine for a moment. 'I will be very sorry to leave, and to say goodbye,' he replies sadly.

I assume Rick is referring to Andalucía, but how I wish he

was sorry to be walking away from me.

He begins talking about the contestants and how impressed he's been, but I tune out. Glancing around in the semi-darkness, lit by the glow of the overhead lights strung beneath the trees and the uplighters bordering the courtyard, a warm feeling rises up within me. It's nearly over and we are both trying to remain light-hearted. But the way Rick keeps glancing at me, the sparkle in his eyes and the animated tone in his voice, I'm grateful for every single moment we've shared. This has been a time I will always treasure, no matter where life takes me.

It hurts to feel as strongly as I do about a man who can never be mine. I've let my longing, maybe even my jealousy, colour the way I've stood in judgement over his relationship with Cathy. It was wrong of me and that's why I'm glad it's almost time to head home.

20

BACK TO REALITY

I've never been one to wallow when life doesn't go smoothly, but the moment I'm on the plane, a huge sense of loss begins to wash over me. And back home, as I unlock my front door and drag the suitcases over the threshold, it isn't long before the tears begin to spill out over my cheeks. I'm surprised to realise they are angry tears. *Why fall in love with a man you know you can't have, Lainey?*

As darkness descends, so does a general gloominess and my emotions are all over the place. It's hard because I can't quite let go of the thought that Rick doesn't appear to be a man who is head over heels in love, but someone on the end of a tight leash. I keep telling myself that's probably wishful thinking. I'm hurting because I'm in love with someone who isn't in love with me. End of.

'Get over it, Lainey,' I say out loud as I look around, feeling the emptiness and missing the warmth and vibrancy of Andalucía. Although, in my heart, I know that I miss Rick even more. 'You have tomorrow to get it all out of your system and prepare yourself to face the world. It won't be the first time you've had to claw your way back from disappointment, and it probably won't be the last.'

Back in the office on Monday morning, Thomas greets me with a lukewarm smile, and I can see that something is wrong, very wrong.

'It's great to have you back, Lainey,' he says, indicating with his hand for me to shut the door and take a seat. 'First of all, hearty congratulations on the Andalucían project, you did an amazing job. That second article was spot on again and it was a great interview with the winner, too. When will I get to see the final photographs to whittle them down?'

Studying his face, he looks different. It's been five weeks since I've seen him, and he seems to have aged considerably.

'That's the first job on my list today and I'm glad you think the investment in time and money was worth it. So, are we talking about a huge advertising campaign to back it up?' I try my best to keep my voice upbeat and ignore the cold feeling that is beginning to settle in the pit of my stomach.

'Yes, we definitely need to do that,' he replies with no enthusiasm whatsoever. It's obvious to me that his mind is elsewhere.

'What have I missed?' I ask, fearful of what the answer is going to be.

'I've had to keep this close to my chest, Lainey, but recent developments mean that there are going to be a few changes. And one of them involves you, I'm sorry to say.'

Taking a deep breath, my heart is now pounding away inside my chest.

'I've been given an ultimatum with a deadline. I have six months to increase our sales by at least eight percent or we're pulling out of the print market altogether and going totally digital.'

My hands fly up to my face. 'You're joking!'

'I wish I was, Lainey. If the growth isn't there, it's a done deal, I'm afraid.'

I flop back in my seat. 'I'm trying to imagine a totally digital world. They tried it with books and yet a couple of years down the line there was a resurgence in paperback sales. The print industry isn't dead yet. If sales were plummeting, it would make sense but they're steady, right?'

'Yes. But our targets increase year on year and it's a constant battle. Recent changes at the top have given this a new sense of urgency and, in the interim, there's been a shake-up. There's no easy way to say this, so I'm just going to launch into it.'

Thomas shifts around uneasily in his chair, the look on his face stony.

'Our department is losing two posts following a recent review by head office. It's the first in a series of changes, apparently. All temporary promotions are suspended with immediate effect and as the cuts are being done on a last in, first-out basis... well, um—'

He falters and I jump in. 'I no longer have a position here.'

Thomas bows his head, staring down at his desk to avoid eye contact.

'There was no way I could break that news to you while you were away and doing such a sterling job.'

Looking back, I believe there were several phone conversations where I felt that Thomas was simply checking up on me and it did feel a little strange. Now it's clear that he was trying to get up the courage to warn me what was coming, but he didn't have the heart to drop the bombshell.

'When is the change effective?'

'You will be given one month's notice. HR will call you in later this morning, as you have options. There is a redundancy package, of course, but—'

I interject. 'But it's negligible because I've only been here what... coming up to eighteen months,' I reply, counting in my head.

'You really don't deserve this, Lainey, because you've more than proven yourself. That's why I'm gutted and angry on your behalf.'

'And the other post that was cut?'

'Dario's role, but he handed in his resignation before any of this was common knowledge. I think he could sense what was coming. His workload is being taken on by one of Ben Cameron's people on the digital team. In a way, that at least made some sort of sense. But I felt bad letting Dario go. I knew it wasn't in his interests for me to try to talk him out of it. It was still management-in-confidence information at that stage, of course, so my hands were tied.'

My stomach begins to churn as I struggle to accept what's happening. I flew back thinking that if I can't have the man of my dreams, I have a job I enjoy doing to keep me going until I can sort myself out, and now I have... nothing.

'Look, there is another option on the table. I've called in a favour to keep you here, but I fear it's not something that will fire you up. It's a position writing advertorials. I'm not naïve enough to think that your potential has gone unnoticed, so the fact they went with my idea is meaningful. They want you to stay, just not on my print team. But if it gives you a little breathing space before you decide what comes next, then at least that's something.'

Ben Cameron would be my potential new boss and he's the sort of man you pass in the corridor who wouldn't even acknowledge your presence. Unless, of course, you were someone he considered to be of use to him.

'I don't know what to say, Thomas. It isn't really sinking in right now.'

He looks directly at me, his eyes blazing.

'It's a travesty, Lainey. You're caught in the crossfire because it's me they want to oust. I'm standing in the way of the plans they're so eager to push through.'

I look at him aghast. 'I could feel the tension when I walked through the general office just now. Surely, they are all looking for new jobs as it's obvious where this is heading.'

Thomas shakes his head, sadly.

'People like you and Ant will get snapped up quickly if you start looking. Some of the others, well, they prefer to keep their heads down and hope for the best. Eventually everyone will wake up to the reality, but it's my job to keep it going as long as I can to at least give them a chance to get out before they're pushed.'

'Thanks for looking out for me, Thomas, that means a lot.'

'It's nothing, I only wish I could do more. When the time is right, I have plenty of contacts I can put you in touch with. I just feel bad that this is what you've walked back into, when it should be a day to celebrate a project that is going to be a resounding success.'

'Anything is better than nothing and even if it's short-term, financially it will give me a little leeway to consider where I go from here. Is there anything I can do to help you?'

'I'm being left out of the loop, Lainey, and my gut is telling me that this change might already be timetabled, no matter what happens. If I'm right, then before too long there will be a major revamp of the website in readiness. I've never walked away from a challenge before, but this is different. If I don't even have a chance to prove print is still a viable option for us, well then, I'm damned if I'm going to let my team work themselves into the ground over it. I'll hang on as long as I can. One by one, those with any get-up-and-go will begin to look elsewhere. The problem is that I have no idea what the timescale is, but I feel that things are speeding up.'

'This is so wrong, Thomas. They are threatening people's livelihoods at a time when the job market is tough. Loyal employees who have given their all to their jobs. Where is the recognition of that? If we were making a loss then it would be perfectly understandable, but this is simply about making an even bigger profit and satisfying the shareholders, isn't it?' I point out angrily.

'That's the truth of it, but it's not your fight, Lainey, so just do what's right for you.'

I can't pretend that I'm thrilled at the thought of joining the group of writers on Ben's team producing feature articles for kitchen gadgets and any product even remotely connected to the industry. *Upscale Dining* is respected for its rigorous testing and honest reviews, but for me it's a backwards step. But off the back of that, the companies whose products do well tend to follow up with a programme of advertising. Which means more revenue for the magazine. It's definitely not where my heart lies, but it will do for now, I suppose.

'Ben's team will be in the forefront of the changes, won't they?'

Thomas looks at me, furrowing his brow. 'Yes, why?'

'If I do take the job it might help you to have a friend in the other camp,' I smile.

Thomas shakes his head at me, but his face immediately brightens. 'What's that saying... ah, yes, hell hath no fury like a woman scorned.'

'I guess I'm more like my Dad than I thought,' I declare. 'The worst they can do is sack me, isn't it?' And with that, I burst out laughing. Thomas, however, is sitting there looking at me as if I've totally lost my mind.

* * *

The one good thing about seeing your life falling apart around you is that it's a sharp reminder not to take anything for granted. The truth is that while life was taking Rick away from me, it was also giving something back. Well, at least it was pushing me in a direction I was supposed to follow.

As I lie in bed going over today's events, I realise that the little epiphany I had while I was in Andalucía about my future career, had already been forgotten as soon as my feet were back on UK soil. After talking to Thomas, it's beginning to feel like an omen. My old job is gone, and my new job isn't going to make me happy. I will end up leaving at some point in the not-too-distant future, with absolutely no regrets. If I can help Thomas in the interim, then I will for as long as I can. But the end of this chapter of my life is coming and who knows what might happen next?

AUGUST

21

I'M DONE

'I'm sorry, Thomas, but I've had enough and I'm about to hand in my notice to Ben. I think between us we've sussed out the master-plan and the timescale, and if I stay any longer, I'll end up blurting out exactly how I feel. It's impossible not to be angry and I'm sick of the spin they are putting on everything to justify their actions.'

The main agenda was clear from the start, but Thomas felt he owed it to us all to at least put up a fight. I admire him for that, because it has taken a huge toll on him.

'You hung in there, Lainey, so I just want to thank you for what you've done. The only comfort during this whole mess is that I've seen you blossom, and I know that won't go to waste.'

It's sad to see him sitting here, his shoulders slumped, as he, too, is ready to admit defeat.

'Will there be a place for you in the new set-up, Thomas?'

'Apparently, yes, but it's not a role I've a mind to accept, and they know that. When news gets out that you're leaving, I think a few others will follow suit very quickly too, and that's the point at which I will consider bowing out gracefully. I don't care about the people at the top, but I care about the remaining members of our team.'

Thomas has been in the magazine business too long not to have other options and I'm glad about that, because the pressure here is getting more and more unbearable by the day.

'Have you decided what you're going to do next?' he asks, and I see a look of concern flash over his face.

'Truthfully, no. I want to make that decision with a clear head and while I'm still working here, the anger and frustration is beginning to cloud my thinking. It's turning me into the sort of person I don't want to be. I have some savings though, so I can survive for a while without having to worry. I'm thinking of setting up a website.'

Thomas does a double-take. 'That's a surprise.'

'I know. I've been pottering away at it as a way of filling my evenings and getting my mind off work. It's not ready to go live yet, but I'm going to blog about food, travel... whatever interests me, and if I decide to try freelancing, I'll use it as a showcase for my work. I was going to ask if you'd be willing to write a testimonial for me.'

Thomas purses his lips, as it begins to sink in that our working relationship will soon be drawing to a close. 'Of course. Whatever you want. And once you're all set up, let me know and I'll spread the word. We gave it our best, Lainey. That's not a bad way to close the door on something, is it? Onwards and upwards.'

I'm too emotional to repeat his mantra, so I plaster on the best smile I can muster and try to reassure him that I'm not defeated, I'm simply tired of fighting.

* * *

'Any news from your landlord?' Mum enquires brightly.

'Nothing concrete. The feedback from the guy I showed around was that it's a little more than he's prepared to pay.'

Mum tuts. 'That's frustrating, Lainey. He knew what the rent was and if he couldn't afford it, then he shouldn't have bothered you.'

I shift in my seat, uncomfortably. 'Well, it's probably a ploy. I can only get out of my contract if I can find someone to take it over and even that is a concession. This guy is looking for a *contribution*,' I reply, trying my best not to sound as annoyed as I feel.

'Ah, lovely, that's infuriating. Look, Dad and I have talked about it and just for your mental well-being alone, we think you need to get away. You're stuck inside, working hard online and you could just as easily do that from here for a while. What do you think, Lainey? A change of scenery might do you the world of good.'

Mum's right and I know it. Ant and Dario keep phoning to check up on me as if they fear that one day I won't answer. I'm not depressed, I'm just disappointed in life, but I know I can't carry on wallowing like this.

'It's tempting,' I concede.

'We're not trying to tell you what to do, but Dad and I are going to transfer some money into your account. Do with it as you want. If it was me, I'd come to an arrangement so you can put your belongings in storage and continue to focus on launching your new business. If you'd like to come here and make use of one of the gîtes, it's nothing for me to cook for one extra person and it's peaceful. The walks are rejuvenating at this time of the year and nature is a great healer when we're feeling a little jaded.'

'Is that why Dad's still there?'

Mum's laughter filters down the line and I imagine her face, cheeks glowing as she realises nothing is lost on me. I am a journalist, after all. 'He has his privacy, and he says that he finds the environment conducive to the writing process. I have one final, week-long course booked for the second week in October, and he's offered to stay until then to help. The least I can do to repay him is to give him the space he needs and make sure he's well fed while he's in his writing cave.'

I try hard to suppress a chuckle. 'That's very obliging of you, Mum.'

'Not really, lovely. When your dad wants company, I'm here for him. And when he doesn't, that's fine too. Mrs Mullins is keeping an eye on the house and when he's ready to return, I'm sure it will all be sparkly clean.'

If only we could all be like my mum. She doesn't place her expectations on other people's shoulders. What will be, will be.

'Listen, please don't send me any money. I have savings and you're right, I'm not thinking clearly, and I am letting anger influence my decisions. That's counterproductive. I'll strike a deal with this guy and get myself sorted as soon as possible, so that I can come visit.'

My ear is filled with the sound of Mum sucking in a deep breath. 'Oh my! To have you both here, even for a short while, would be amazing. No pressure, Lainey, but I know you won't regret it. It's time to recharge those batteries and kick-start your motivation. I love you, Lainey, and you are always in my thoughts and prayers.'

A lump rises in my throat and I clear it, feeling a rush of positivity I haven't felt in a while. 'France, here I come!'

We end up giggling like we used to when I was a child and Mum encouraged me to do something adventurous. Like the time she insisted we go to the park and take off our shoes, walking barefoot on the grass around a tree she said was over a hundred years old. I remember her words, clearly. '*Do you feel it, Lainey? Do you feel it? The energy?*'

I'd wrinkled up my nose, not sure what exactly I was feeling at the time. But I'm finally feeling it, Mum, and you were right all along. I'm not going to let negative people drain my positive energy and I'm going to get through this and come out the other side a happier person.

* * *

I stare back at the faces of my two closest friends who have been my main support system for the last couple of years, and I can see their concern.

'I know how much you want your parents to be there for each other, even if they can't mend their marriage, but it's down to them, Lainey,' Dario replies as soon as I share my news.

'That's not the reason I'm going, really it isn't. Yes, a little time with us all together is appealing, but Dad has a book to write and I'm going to be spending my days doing some podcasts and uploading them to YouTube ready to build my brand.'

'You sound like you read a book called Marketing 101,' Ant jumps in, sounding dubious.

'Guys, please listen to me. This isn't about my parents, I promise. It is about having a break away to finish off the last bits before I can launch the website. It might take a few months and at least heading to France my overheads will be low. Then I can eke out my savings as long as possible, because I don't know when my next payday will be.'

'It's ridiculous that it's come to this, Lainey, 'Ant mutters, dejectedly. 'I'm all but done with them, myself. It's a huge step for me to walk away from a salaried position, but I'm convinced that I'll earn more going freelance, anyway. Hayley says I should give it a shot.'

'Good photographers are always in demand, Ant.' I look at Dario. 'How's the new job going?'

'The money's good,' he replies, sounding totally unenthusiastic, which makes me feel sad.

'And how is Ian?'

'He's keeping me positive. The right job will come along, but in the meantime at least the bills get paid, and we're planning on jetting off on a little jaunt to Italy next month.'

I'm glad Ian is doing his best to distract Dario and together they'll get through this phase. But I can't help wish I had someone as solidly reliable as Ian, or Hayley, in my life to make this uncertain time bearable. There are moments in the middle of the night when I wake up in a cold sweat, wondering if everything I've done so far in my life has been for nothing. I haven't heard anything at all from Rick and after watching the first two episodes of the competition I was tempted to reach out and offer my congratulations. A bit of soul-searching made me decide it was best not to make contact. The competition is only being televised in Spain, of course, but I gave my old friend, Hugh, at *Upscale Dining* a call. He talked me through how to change my IP address to a Spanish one, using a VPN service.

Rick's name is certainly out there right now and it's not just in the UK any more. Thomas also confirmed that the August edition of the magazine flew off the shelves, so they increased the print run for the September issue. It's another achievement to add to my own CV, of course, but the memories are still bittersweet for me.

Pulling myself together, I turn my frown into a smile. 'If I end up staying in France for a while, would you be up for coming over in early spring, before the first rush of visitors are due to arrive? Mum is planning on running courses regularly from May to October, in future. Outside of that, there's plenty of room for everyone, as she has space in the main house, as well as the gîtes and converted outbuildings.'

'Sounds like fun. In the meantime, you're gonna become a social media queen in your own right, Lainey,' Dario laughs. 'I've taught you all I know and now it's time to sit back and see you fly!'

'And you're going to be taking your own photos for that swish new website of yours. I hope you listened to all those pointers I threw your way, because I'll be checking up on you,' Ant levels at me.

'I'm so grateful to you both, and I'm going to miss you like crazy. And when you come over to France, we'll be fighting over taking turns to spend time with baby Ellie, Ant. You and Hayley can go off for some romantic walks in the countryside, as you'll have more than enough babysitters willing to take over.'

He laughs. 'Never mind the walks, we'd just be happy to have a few lie-ins. Ellie wakes up every day at 5 a.m. without fail!'

We say our goodbyes and I wonder how long it will be before we see each other again. I just hope that when we do catch up, we've turned the corner and are feeling excited about the journey ahead. Right now, autumn and winter are looming and spring feels like an eternity away.

SEPTEMBER

22

THE AUTUMN CHILL IS IN THE AIR

'I'll just put the kettle on. Can someone please stoke up the fire?' Mum turns, disappearing into the kitchen with the last of the plates.

'I'll sort it. We need some logs and I could do with a little fresh air,' I inform Dad brightly.

'You never did like doing the dishes. Suits me. It's not like we have a log shortage,' he laughs.

He's right there. My first few days here were spent working together cutting up an old tree on the border of Mum's property that blew down last winter. With two handsaws and a petrol chainsaw, the three of us made a pretty good job of getting it back here. Dad has already split some of the logs ready for the fire, but there is still a whole stack in the barn waiting for a day when we're all feeling energetic enough to tackle it. It's hot, sweaty work.

Pulling on my padded coat, I gulp in the chilly night air. It makes me cough a little as it hits my lungs, but it's refreshing and energising. I can feel my entire body coming alive and it's been that way since the first day I arrived. I've been savouring the whiff of bitter earthiness from the soil and the dampness from the piles of fallen leaves, contrasted with the sweetness of the grass beneath my feet.

I head over to the barn and as I swing open the wide door, the musty odour from the wood as it begins to dry out hits me. It reminds me of spending time at my granddad's house and helping him carry kindling from his shed to feed his old wood-burning stove. The smell used to make my nose wrinkle up and he always laughed at me and ruffled my hair.

I feel like I'm continuing a change that began while I was in Andalucía. I'm noticing things that normally wouldn't make it onto my radar. Tiny little details that not only trigger memories but are making me realise how switched off I'd become to what was going on around me. There's so much I've been taking for granted because my focus was on a particular set of goals. Now the goals have changed, my world hasn't imploded, as I feared it might, and I'm moving forward with renewed determination. Even so, there's a sadness that sometimes settles over me and I thought at first it was because I missed the familiarity of my old life. It's true that I miss my friends, but there's someone else I miss even more. This intense sense of loss I feel deep-down inside of me refuses to go away, but I can now accept that there's no point in daydreaming about what might have been.

I perch on what Dad laughingly refers to as my stool. It's a massive chunk from the widest part of the tree that we spent hours cutting up. We were too tired at that point to continue and I told him I thought it was beautiful. I found myself running my fingers over the roughly cut surface, fascinated by the growth rings which were the tree's map of life, until gale-force winds toppled it. We decided to rescue the stump the next day, although it took the three of us to roll it across the garden and into the barn.

As I reach out to begin stacking a pile of the smaller pieces of wood into a basket, it occurs to me that it's been a long time since I stopped to count my blessings. Finally, I'm free in a way I never thought possible and I'm heading in the right direction. All those hours I wasted letting my noisy neighbour wind me up and dreaming of moving to a nicer place with more space. Was I happier after the move? No, as it turns out. One problem was simply replaced by another. Leaving the magazine is the best thing that's happened to me in a long time.

And now, both Dad and I are temporarily living with Mum. We are all taking each day as it comes, but the more time they spend together, the closer they are becoming. I turn to look out the open door and gaze back at the farmhouse. Even in the gloom, I can see the trail of wispy grey smoke from the chimney. Lights from the kitchen and the sitting room glow like a warm, welcoming beacon. No wonder people enjoy their stay here and, as Mum is discovering, many are eager to come back. Mum stayed true to her dream and we're all reaping the benefits.

* * *

'Perfect timing! I'm off to do some proofing, so I'll say goodnight, Lainey,' Dad says, as he holds the back door open for me. He leans in to plant a kiss on my cheek.

'Night, Dad. Where's Mum?'

'She's on the phone. Are you two getting your heads together for a bit, or calling it a night, too? Do you need a hand with that?' He steps back as I manoeuvre myself around the scrubbed pine kitchen table, arms firmly hugging the basket to my body.

'No, I'm stronger than I look. If Mum's not too tired, I thought we could do an hour or two on her website. It depends on how long she's going to be on the phone. Is it a client or a friend?' There's no point in stoking up the sitting-room fire if I end up going back to the gîte and working from the comfort of my bed.

'I'm not sure. Anyway, work's calling. Sleep well, Lainey.'

As I walk into the sitting room and make my way over to the open fireplace, I can hear Mum's voice like a low mumble in the background. Pulling off my hat and slipping out of my coat, as I walk towards the door to hang them up in the hallway I'm brought to an abrupt halt.

'Well, if you are convinced it's the right thing, then of course it's doable.' Something in the tone of Mum's voice makes me pause to strain my ears. She doesn't sound quite as positive as the words coming out of her mouth. There's another pause and then she begins talking again. 'Oh, I see. Ah, I understand. I will add you to the list, then. It was nice talking to you.'

I hope it isn't a cancellation for the next course at this late stage as the numbers are even, which means Dad and I can be general helpers, rather than one of us having to pair up with a guest.

I dump everything on the chair and collapse down onto the sofa, grabbing my laptop.

By the time Mum returns to the room, I have the website up and I'm doing a final proofread of a page we're about to make live.

'Sorry to keep you waiting, lovely,' she says as she comes to join me.

'Is everything okay?'

Mum gives me a beaming smile. 'Yes, everything's fine. Is that article ready to go?'

'Yep, almost there.' It's taken a while to get to this point, as Mum wanted to include photos taken during one of her previous cooking sessions. To do that, she had to contact the attendees to get their permission. I wondered for one moment there if someone wasn't happy about it, but there's no hint of disappoint-ment in her demeanour.

'I can't believe the difference you've made. My website looks so professional now. And having an online booking facility is going to make things so much easier for me. I really appreciate the long hours of work you've put into it, Lainey.' Mum reaches out to place her hand on my arm and give it a squeeze. The look in her eyes is full of gratitude and yet I owe her so much.

'It's my pleasure, Mum. It's all a learning process for me, but every new thing I learn is something that might come in handy in the future.'

She looks at me in earnest. 'Once you show me how to load the photos for myself, you can get back to your own work. I know how busy you are and you've done more than enough already. I'm conscious that you won't get much free time next week, either.'

'Don't worry about it. I only take on what I know I can manage. Besides, I'm looking forward to helping on the course, it'll be fun.'

I notice Mum interlacing her fingers, as her hands lie in her lap. It's clear there is something on her mind.

'Dad's work seems to be going well,' I remark, watching for her reaction.

'Hmm,' she replies absent-mindedly. 'I believe so.' She's looking in my direction, but her gaze isn't on me, a sure sign she's thinking about something else entirely.

Perhaps she's just tired. The fire is on its last legs and she's made no attempt to throw on any more wood. 'We can finish this off tomorrow if you like?'

Unlacing her fingers, she eases back her shoulders. 'That's a great idea, if you don't mind. I'm still tinkering around with the programme for next week.'

'I thought it was all done?' I ask, surprised, as Mum is the most organised person I know. She doesn't do last-minute panics.

'Oh.' She pauses, turning to look at me. 'Um, well, it is but I, um, thought that maybe it would be nice to tie in some of the things we'll be cooking with the evening meals. Our guests might get a thrill out of sampling the apple chutney they've made with a nice roast pork dinner. It's just a case of switching a few things around.'

'Oh Mum, you think of everything,' I reply affectionately. 'I'll let you get on then. If there's anything I can do to help, just let me know. I'll grab my things and leave you in peace.'

'I didn't mean to turf you out, but it has been a long day,' Mum says as we stand. Then she steps closer, wrapping her arms around me and we hug for a second or two. 'It is lovely having you here, Lainey, but I know you miss the company of your friends. I hope that having a group of new faces around next week will be a tonic for you. It's a mixed age group this time, which tends to work particularly well.'

'Well, don't stay up too late. I'm sure it will all work out just fine. Love you, Mum.'

* * *

I know I should be working on my website, but I have another idea. Dad suggested that Mum write a cookery book. When she mentioned it to me, she seemed keen but hasn't said a word about it since. I think there might be a way of getting her to consider it if I take on the admin. Okay, so I have no experience whatsoever of self-publishing, but hey – if I can teach myself how to set up a website from scratch, then I'm sure I can get my head around publishing a recipe book.

I'm surprised when my phone rings, as it's getting late. Then I see that it's only 9 p.m. – my version of late these days is most definitely getting earlier and earlier.

'Hey, Lainey. I thought I'd give you a call as I've just had a text from one of our old colleagues. I was going to ring you tomorrow, anyway, about something else, but this is breaking news.'

'It's good to hear your voice, Ant. I was thinking about you today, actually.'

'Yeah, missing my scintillating conversation which is in short supply these days as I spend a lot of my time handling toddler tantrums,' he laughs. 'Seriously, though, I'm ringing about Thomas. I've just heard that he's tendered his resignation.'

My stomach begins to churn as his words sink in. 'It's over, then.'

'It's the end of an era, for sure.'

That world is now so far away from my current reality and yet instantly anger leaps up inside of me. 'Poor Thomas. Do you think I should call him?'

'Hmm... maybe wait a day or two. This has literally just been leaked so it will still be very raw for him.' Ant sounds really cut up about the news.

'Thomas knows the score and he has a lot of contacts, Ant. I'm sure he'll be fine, but it will still hit him hard and I know how sad he'll be feeling to walk away. But you said you have something else to tell me? I hope it's happier news,' I remark, trying to push away the negative feelings that creep back so easily if I let them.

'Ellie is going to have a little brother, or sister.'

'No way! Congratulations to you all!'

'Thanks. It... was a nice surprise for both Hayley and me, and I'm still getting my head around it, but it has put the biggest smile on my face. It's just the thought of those sleepless nights again when Ellie is now sleeping right through,' he bemoans, but I can tell he's thrilled about it.

'It's funny, but Mum only said to me the other day that whenever bad news arrives, you don't have to look far to see something good happening. People just forget to look.'

'I guess we do. That's a cool way of seeing it,' Ant replies. 'I'll be more mindful of that in future.'

'Goodness, my mum will love that attitude of yours when the two of you finally meet up. We must get you all here. New baby included, at some point.'

'You're staying for good?' He sounds surprised.

'No. I'm missing everyone. I'll probably sort my work schedule – when I have one, that is – around coming back to help Mum out when she needs it. There's a course running next week and the final one for the year begins two weeks after that. Then I'm heading back to the UK until spring, most likely. When's the baby due?'

'The eleventh of March. Hayley wouldn't let me tell anyone until she passed her first trimester. I'm excited, but I still get moments when I break out in a cold sweat. Managing two can't be that bad, can it?' There is a definite hint of terror in his voice.

'No. I hear the first is the worst,' I say, trying hard not to laugh. How on earth would I know?

'I hope you're right. How's it going over there, then?' he asks, in all seriousness.

'Better than I thought. I needed this time away to get my head straight. My website is still a work in progress, and there's another project I want to set up before I leave Mum to it, but it's all good and the freelance work is rolling in.'

'And your dad is still there?'

'Yes. By day they tend to do their own thing, although we do a few family activities like chopping up a fallen tree and digging over one of the veggie plots. But it's perfect, as Dad and I have our own gîtes and Mum is in the farmhouse. When I return to the

UK, I'm not sure where I'll end up settling down. It depends on what I can afford to rent, so I'll probably find a quiet little backwater somewhere. I can work from anywhere and I've already written half a dozen advertorials for a copy writing agency just to get some funds in.'

'I'm glad to hear you have a plan, Lainey. We miss you and can't wait to catch up in person. Ellie has grown so much, you won't even recognise her. In the meantime, I'll send you some more photos. Anyway, wait a bit before contacting Thomas. But if there's anyone he'll want to talk to about it, it will be you. Oh, and Aleatory got their first Michelin star, I hear, but you may already know that. Take care of yourself, lovely lady, and speak soon!'

Why would Ant think I'd know about what was going on with Rick? I haven't heard from him since I left *Upscale Dining*. Circumstances forged a temporary friendship, but it seems that I was the only one left reeling when it finally hit home that was all it was destined to be. He's a rising star going from success to success, I'm sure, but I'm no longer a part of that world. While I wish him well, whether he realises it or not, Rick broke my heart without so much as a backwards glance.

OCTOBER

23

OUT OF THE BLUE

Mum and I spent the last couple of days before the final course of what has been her most successful year to date, cleaning and making up beds. Dad has been busy chopping firewood and raking up leaves to tidy the garden. They both insisted I take today off and assured me they could handle getting everyone checked in and settled. Dad has moved into one of the attic rooms in the farmhouse, as his gîte is one of the bigger ones. Mum said there was little point in disrupting me too, as everyone else was accommodated. She has three single rooms and two doubles in the farmhouse and the annexe, and two of the couples have booked the larger gîtes.

With an entire day at my disposal, it's a chance for me to get some work done. At lunchtime, there's a knock on the door and when I open it, Mum is standing there with a tray in her hands.

'Ah, you didn't have to do that,' I say, ushering her in.

'I'm feeding people as they arrive, but there are still five more to come. As there was a lull, I thought I'd sort you out next. It's certainly toasty in here,' she remarks, placing the tray down next to my computer.

Straightening, she glances at me nervously.

'What's wrong?' I ask, wondering why she's standing there awkwardly.

'Nothing. It's just... well, this is the nerve-wracking bit until everyone's here. I'm planning on serving dinner at seven-thirty. Will we be seeing you before then?'

I chew my lip, thinking that it would be nice to finish what I'm doing, which is adding a gallery of photos to an article I've written about trends in food presentation.

'I'll probably skip the welcome drink, if you don't mind, and slip in just before you dish up, unless you need any help? I want to finish this off and then have a leisurely bath before I think about making myself look presentable.'

Mum's eyes flash over my jogging bottoms and sloppy, woollen jumper. She shakes her head at me, smiling. 'You look amazing, you always do. There's nothing wrong with comfy and warm, lovely, that's all that matters. I'm glad it's going well today, so I won't disturb you. If you need anything, just give your dad a call and he'll pop it down to you.'

'I feel spoilt. Room service on call.'

'You've more than earnt a restful day catching up. And it's going to be quite a week,' she says, expelling her breath in a way that makes me worry a little. Does Mum always get nervous before a course gets started? I wonder. That never occurred to me before. After all, she's the one who will be standing at the front of the room demonstrating, and the attention will be firmly on her.

'It's going to be great,' I enthuse warmly. 'Who wouldn't want to be making jams and chutneys and winter puddings at this time of the year? It's a reminder that Christmas is coming.'

I know Mum is planning on getting everyone to make a gingerbread house as a bit of fun next Friday, the last day of cooking. As the guests can't take them home, any that will survive a car journey will be transported to the local school, to be sold off at a Christmas fair in aid of charity. I'm looking forward to joining in with that.

'It'll be easier once everyone is here and the introductions are over. There are always one or two quieter ones who take longer to feel at ease so if you can keep an eye out, I'd be grateful. I want everyone to feel at home and relaxed as it's supposed to be a fun course, not stressful.'

'You can count on me, Mum.'

'Thanks, Lainey. Well, I'd best get back, although your dad loves this bit. He's been on his own for far too long and now he's back on form, it's lovely to see. Anyway, I'll see you later, lovely.'

* * *

'Hi, Ian, how are you?'

'I'm good, Lainey. And you? Are you still in France?'

'Yes. Only for another couple of weeks, though. It's beautiful here in the forest in autumn and it's hard to keep my head down working and not to keep going out for a bracing walk to enjoy the scenery.'

'Heh, heh! I can imagine. It's time Dario and I got out our hiking boots and communed with nature. Talking of the main man, he's here somewhere. Let me find him for you.' Sounds crackle in my ear as Ian walks and talks. 'We're off to Italy next week, though, and I can't wait. He told you about the new job, did he?'

'Yes, it's brilliant news. Writing a weekly column about the hottest topics trending on social media will allow him to raise some of the weightier issues. I know Dario has a wide range of interests, including politics, and I'll certainly be following him.'

'Here he is... what *are* you doing?' The last few words fade a little as he hands over the phone. I hear Dario respond, but can't hear what he's saying. Then Ian calls out loud, 'Bye, Lainey. Take care!'

'Hi. Give me a sec,' Dario says, and it all goes quiet. Then there's a loud bang and a bit of cursing as he scrabbles with the phone. 'Sorry about that. I decided to put up another bookshelf and these plasterboard walls are a nightmare. It's one of those Saturday jobs I keep putting off. What're you up to?'

'Are you near your computer?'

'No, but I'm heading over to it.'

'Type in laineysummersfoodlifeandstyle.com.'

It's an agonising wait as the seconds slip by.

'Wow! You have been busy.' The line goes quiet and, as I wait, my anxiety is building.

'It's not finished, obviously. I'll gradually add more content, but it went live an hour ago and I—'

'And you did a great job, Lainey! Love the title and it keeps your options open for the future.'

Dario has no idea what a boost his response has given me.

'I didn't know if it worked. It wasn't an option to have more than one website to maintain and it just seemed logical to have separate tabs for articles about food, general life and style products, and then the *hire me* tab with my CV. And the website URL, I took ages thinking that through and felt it needed something more than just my name.'

'It helps and if anyone searches for you solely by name it will come up alongside the various articles you've written in the past. So, great call. You'll need to work on your SEO, but I can help you with that.'

I can't help feeling a little proud of myself. 'That's on the list of things to look at next,' I confirm, having heard of it but with no idea what it entails. 'But I'm delighted to have the website up and running. I've also updated Mum's site and shown her a few things that I've learnt in the process.'

'It sounds like you're really getting into it,' he muses.

There's another loud crash and some more expletives.

'I am, but I'll leave you to it as it sounds like the shelf has just fallen off the wall,' I reply, trying not to laugh.

'It has and Ian isn't going to be happy as it's chipped the skirting board. Anyway, when we get back from Italy, let's do a video call and if you need any pointers you can pick my brains.'

'Yes, sir,' I reply laughing. 'Now go and fix that shelf before you get into any more trouble. Enjoy your holiday, bye for now.'

As I place the phone down next to the computer, my name is staring back at me in large letters. I reach over to turn on the side light as it's getting rather gloomy and I notice that the fire needs attention, when there's a loud tap on the door.

'Coming,' I call out as I quickly throw on the last piece of wood. I hope the flames don't die down before the log can begin burning through because I'm in no state to wander over to the barn for some kindling. I knew I should have topped up the basket first thing this morning. Swinging open the door, I can't believe what I'm seeing.

'Surprise!'

'Rick. What are you doing here?'

We stare at each other for a moment and I realise he's waiting for me to invite him inside. I open the door fully and he walks past me, ignoring the look of bewilderment on my face. He looks so different to the last time I saw him when he was sporting a flattering tan and wearing a white chef's jacket, tailored navy trousers and a navy and white, pinstriped apron tied around his waist. Today he's dressed in a pair of comfy-looking jeans, a pale blue roll-neck sweater and a warm-looking, wool, navy blue jacket with the collar pulled up. I hate to dwell on it, but he looks good. Really good.

'I'm here for the course,' he confirms, glancing at me with a look that I can only describe as sheepish. I'm wearing pale grey jogging bottoms, and an oversized, cream-coloured cable-knit jumper with pulls in it.

'You're here for the cookery course? Why?'

'It's research and, well, to be honest, a bit of a break for me. Having looked at your mum's website, I'm sure I'll go away with a few inspiring ideas to add to my list. And after three weeks on the road, I thought it would be a great opportunity to look you up on my way back to Calais. Especially given the success of the two features you wrote about our time in Andalucía. I wanted to express my sincere thanks and offer my congratulations.'

The question in my head is who told him this was where he could find me.

'I managed to watch all four episodes of the competition and I'm glad things are going so well for you,' I acknowledge, thinking a text, or an email, would have sufficed. And why seek me out now?

I indicate for him to take a seat on the sofa, as I sink down onto the chair in front of the computer desk. Instinctively my hand goes up to my hair, as I'm not even sure I looked in the mirror after getting out of the shower first thing. 'Sorry, I've been working and wasn't expecting visitors,' I reply awkwardly, feeling more than a little put out. 'Does my mum know who you are?'

He looks at me, frowning. 'Of course, I didn't use a fake name. I wanted to surprise you, though, and I thought you'd be pleased.'

Now I understand why Mum looked so nervous this morning. I'm just shocked that she went along with it. 'You asked her specifically not to tell me you were coming?'

'I didn't think it would be a big deal. I assured her you'd be fine with it,' he says, looking slightly offended. 'I thought it would be nice to catch up. To be honest, when I rang your work number and was told that you'd left, I was shocked. They put me through to Thomas and he said you'd moved on and were going freelance. I was kind of disappointed that you hadn't let me know what was going on. I... um, was a little worried about you, to be honest. Then I remembered what you said about re-thinking your future and realised you probably needed a little space. But clearly you've figured it all out, now.' Rick raises his eyebrows, acknowledging my reaction isn't quite what he was expecting.

Now the teeniest spark of guilt begins to fester in my stomach. Rick deserved to hear the news direct from me, given that in the last conversation I had with him we'd been talking about a series of follow-up interviews with a few of the contestants. 'It all happened quite quickly once I decided I'd had enough and I had to focus on the future and not the past,' I reply truthfully.

'Ah, right. And I'm a part of the past. So, what's the plan, then?'

I shift uncomfortably in my seat.

'Sorry,' he adds. 'We can chat later. You're not too upset by my presence, though, are you?'

My arms are folded across my body and my left hand is pressed against my mouth. He's caught me unawares and I don't know how I feel about that. 'I just need to finish up what I'm doing and make myself presentable,' I say, firmly. If Rick thinks he can breeze back into my life as if we're old friends, then he's wrong. And to turn up with no warning whatsoever isn't fair on me and I can't understand why he would do that after all this time. It's taken me too long to get over him and I won't let him unsettle me a second time. 'Of course, you're very welcome to be here, but, just so you know for the future, I'm not big on surprises.'

His face pales a little as I stare at him pointedly. 'Ah! Um... understood. But now at least I'm finally on holiday, so I'm going with the flow. I'm trying to get my rustic vibe on.'

'What does that even mean?' I ask, laughing at him. 'Instead of fussing with tiny dots on the plate you'll be spooning on a generous helping in future? Or handing out ramekins heaped with spiced winter apple chutney in place of a slick of apple sauce?'

'Don't knock it. I believe there's a middle ground and that's why I'm here. There's always something new to learn.' He eases himself up off the sofa. 'Now I'll leave you in peace and, hopefully, see you later if you decide to forgive me for the faux pas.'

Rick disappears out the door, pulling it shut behind him and I'm left sitting and wondering what on earth is going on.

When I do move, I'm like a whirlwind, tidying up and grabbing my phone as I head into the tiny bathroom to run a bath. 'Mum, can you talk?'

'Yes, I'm alone in the kitchen making teas and coffees. I think I can guess what this is about. I had my doubts... I even rang Thomas and he said that you and Rick were good friends. You seemed to get on well when you were in Andalucía.'

This isn't Mum's fault. She can't turn someone away if they make a booking. 'It was unexpected, that's all. Just out of interest, what did he say to convince you to go along with the surprise?'

'Oh, oh, only... um, I can't really remember. It was all about being interested in living off the land and a...' I have never heard Mum sounding so flustered before and it's clear she feels she's made a big mistake.

'Please don't fret. It's really not a problem at all. I just didn't want you to feel uncomfortable, given that he's a professional chef. But you're a wonderful cook, Mum, and Rick said he's looking forward to joining in.'

'Do you think any of the other guests will recognise him? He seems to want to blend in, as he put it, when I introduced him to Dad.' Mum has lowered her voice to a whisper now.

'What did Dad say?'

'He was polite, but afterwards he said I was wrong not to tell you about it in advance. It was a last-minute thing and now we have an odd number of guests. Oh dear!'

Inwardly, I groan. 'I'm sure it will be fine, Mum. I'll jump in the bath to unwind for a bit, then I'll make my way up to the farmhouse to help with dinner.'

'Oh, I wasn't sure what to do for the best,' Mum mutters, as if to herself. 'I didn't mean to cause you any trouble, Lainey. See you in a bit, lovely.'

I wanted a clean break with the past, but it seems the past isn't ready for a clean break from me.

24

CAT AND MOUSE

The new course is made up of a jolly, if eclectic, bunch of people. Rick has the second attic room, next to Dad's, and I get the feeling Dad is happy about that as he's keeping a firm eye on him. He already knew quite a bit about Rick from our chats and I get the distinct impression that Dad is worried it will remind me of my life in London. He's wrong on that score, but he knows something is bothering me. Something I can't voice.

The first two days have been fun and I'm not even sure anyone has twigged who Rick is, which suits us all. Pairing up with him for each session hasn't been as awkward as I feared it might be, given the fact that I've been avoiding him. And I notice he's making copious notes, so he appears to be taking it seriously.

In this morning's session, Mum is talking a little about nutrition and the importance of planning a balanced meal, teaching us all that ounce for ounce, fresh herbs like rosemary, parsley and basil are among the most nutritious greens you can find.

'Herbs are a very concentrated source of both flavour and nutrition. In both respects, a little goes a long way,' she explains.

Rick leans in to whisper into my ear, his breath warm against my cheek. 'She knows her stuff, your mum.' He grins at me, before making yet another note in that little book of his. Is he really expecting us to fall back into the easy friendship we had before? It might not have hurt him, but it broke my heart and the wounds are still very raw.

Mum moves on to talk about the benefits of using onions and garlic in cooking, not just for the flavours they bring to the dish, but the fact that they can help protect and heal the body.

After a light lunch of a croque monsieur, accompanied by a small dish of what Mum calls her mushroom casserole, we spend the entire afternoon making classic French lamb sausages. Mum explains that it's a spicy lamb sausage recipe that originates from Morocco but is well-loved in France and popular as street food.

'I've had these Merguez sausages a couple of times,' Rick says. 'I've never made them before, though.'

The list of herbs and spices is impressive. As we're supposed to be working as a team, Rick insists that I toast the cumin, fennel and coriander seeds in the dry skillet.

'Remember, folks, two minutes on a medium heat and constantly stirring until the fragrance hits your nose. Longer than that and they will burn, then you'll have to start all over again.'

Dad, I notice, is already rushing across to one of the benches as a distinctly acrid smell begins to fill the air. He opens a couple of the windows while the contents are thrown in the bin and the couple start again.

'I think you're about done there,' Rick prods my arm with his elbow, and I immediately drag the pan off the heat. 'Quick, tip them out into the dish so they don't go on cooking,' he points out.

Then we move onto the next step of adding paprika, cayenne pepper and cinnamon and he takes over to pop them into the spice grinder. I stand back for a while, watching Rick as he glances at the recipe, but instinctively seems to know what to do.

He doesn't use the scales once, as he mixes the ground lamb, drizzling in a glug of olive oil and adding some of the spice mixture, crushed garlic and a little salt.

'Are you going to give me a hand?' he asks cheekily.

'You seem to be enjoying yourself. What do you need?'

'Can you chop up the herbs and throw a handful in here?' he asks, withdrawing his messy hands and waving his fingers at me.

'Be patient, I'm on it,' I reply.

We're a little ahead of everyone else and he laughs at me as the coriander leaves decide they don't want to be chopped up and big pieces keep flying off the board.

'It's easier if you stack and roll them, then slice your way along. Use the stems, too, they are full of flavour.'

Mum's voice pipes up in the background. 'I thought instead of making them into sausages, we'd form them into patties and cook them on the barbecue tonight. So, make sure you get the seasoning right, as you will be eating what you make.'

There's some muttering going on and she holds up her hands.

'I will have a batch in reserve if anyone ends up being a little heavy-handed,' she assures the class.

A woman's voice down at the front pipes up, 'Just as well, as my eyes are watering and I think I've added too much cayenne pepper.'

Her partner bursts out laughing. 'I told you that, but you didn't listen to me.'

It's funny seeing how couples are when they are cooking together. Some are in tune, others have a lead and a skivvy. I'm definitely the skivvy in our team of two. However, it's becoming increasingly clear to me that at least two of the people in this room have just twigged who Rick is, and we are now being watched with increasing interest.

'I'm impressed, Lainey, and I can see where your interest in food comes from,' Rick says.

'Mum's all about a healthy and natural world, and a big part of that is governed by what we eat. Don't get her started on processed foods, though, as she's like a woman fighting a personal battle on that front.'

I can see that Rick is finding Mum's informative little talks interesting, as they link into the sessions quite nicely. But I can't help thinking it's ridiculous him being here as none of this will be new to him. He's clearly enjoying himself and here I am, having to grit my teeth and get through it as best I can.

As soon as our patties are chilling in the fridge ready for this evening, I make a quick exit yet again, as I've been doing my best to avoid being alone with Rick. Do I really want to hear what problems Cathy is causing him and how hard it is being pressured into setting up a second restaurant? No more than he wants to hear all about my little problems, like where on earth I'm going to stay when I go back to the UK.

* * *

'I thought I'd come and give you a hand.' Rick's voice startles me, as my back is to the door and I didn't hear him enter. I'm busy filling the log baskets. With a packed course and the temperatures dropping, it needs doing twice a day.

'Oh, that's not necessary. I thought everyone was up at the farmhouse having a pre-dinner drink. You should join in. This won't take me long.'

'If I help out, we can head up there together,' he replies genially.

'Rick, why are you here?' I blurt out, feeling at the end of my tether.

He looks at me warily. 'You mentioned your mum ran courses and I asked Thomas about them. He referred me to the website. I'm interested to see what she does with the local produce.'

I straighten, placing my hands on my hips as I stand looking at him accusingly. 'Really? And you expect me to believe that? Mum doesn't do dainty. She focuses on hearty food to feed a family and educating people who want to know more about growing their own and eating more healthily. Sorry, but I can't see why you are so interested, or what you can possibly learn that you don't already know,' I challenge him.

I can see Rick is surprised at my forthright comment. He inhales sharply, as if I've put him on the spot. 'I... err... had this idea about a French-inspired theme for the new restaurant and going back to basics.'

'In a top restaurant? You really mean *basics* as opposed to organic, quality ingredients, which is exactly why diners pay more to eat at the best places, anyway.'

'Hear me out. I'm talking about the traditional French prix-fixe menu with an appetiser, entrée, dessert and a half-bottle of house wine. I've been over here for three weeks discovering small, family-run establishments, where, often, one room of the house has been turned into a bijou restaurant. They're off the beaten track, although lorry drivers seem to know them all. Those little places you stumble across when you're doing a road trip and so hungry you stop at the next sign advertising food. It's often where the locals eat, too. Nothing fancy, just hearty food, with recipes passed down from generation to generation. And I'm gathering ideas.'

'But Mum isn't French, she just happens to live over here now. Admittedly, she is working with some of the French influences, but they will all have her spin on it and she doesn't claim to be using age-old recipes.'

He lets out a quiet groan. 'You're taking this too literally. I'm also here to have a little fun after a tiring road trip. Can't we leave it at that?' His voice has softened, as if he's appealing to me to let it go.

I shake my head at him, sadly. 'No Rick, we can't, because it isn't fair on me.'

I turn to walk away from him, but he reaches out to catch my arm.

'Don't go. Please don't turn your back on me.'

I indicate for Rick to take the basket I've just filled with kindling and logs, and bend to pick up the one alongside it. 'You can explain as we walk. Didn't it occur to you that there's a reason why I didn't keep in touch, Rick? This is my fresh start and whatever happened in the past is now just that.'

Rick doesn't answer me, just trudges alongside as we head over to the two, semi-detached stone gîtes at the far end of the garden.

'This was Dad's temporary home before he was moved into the attic room. Let me just get the key out of my pocket for the log store,' I say, as I lean my knee up against the stone wall and balance the log basket on it. 'These two gîtes were formerly pigsties,' I witter on, sending him a clear message that I don't want this to get any more personal than it has already. 'Wait a second while I pop this inside.' I change over the baskets, ignoring the fact that he's watching me intently. I'm conscious that Rick is a paying guest, and I don't wish to be rude, but I do intend to be firm with him. This is merely a distraction for him, and honestly? I deserve better. If he's here to *have a little fun*, as he so eloquently phrased it, then there are plenty of guests with whom he can mingle.

'The gîte next door has a log store at the side. It's around here.' He follows me, the atmosphere between us subdued. 'I'll just pull out the empty basket,' I inform him as I swing open the door to the wooden lean-to and then stand back so he can place the full one inside.

When he straightens to look at me, his gaze makes me hold my breath for a second, but I refuse to let him unnerve me.

Trudging back in silence together takes awkward to a whole new level. Eventually he finds something to say. 'Was this a going concern when your mum bought it?' Rick asks and at last we're back on a safe subject.

'Yes, the farmhouse and gîtes were used for bed and breakfast, but originally the adjoining three fields were pitches for tents and caravans. What is now the large kitchen block was used as a shower and toilet facility. The fields had already been sold off by the time Mum looked at the property. She had the disused block gutted and the kitchens installed. It couldn't be more perfect. My grandma would have approved of the way Mum has used her legacy.'

Rick turns to look at me as we amble back to the barn. 'Do all the gîtes have log burners?'

'Yes, although they all have oil-fired central heating too, as does the farmhouse itself. But people like a real fire. And Mum likes to keep both of the open fires going in the farmhouse during the coldest months as it's a draughty old place. If she ever makes her fortune, her dream is to install an eco-friendly, biomass heating system.'

'It really was a lifestyle change for her, wasn't it? I'm beginning to understand now.' There's an empathy in his voice that throws me for a moment.

'Right, two more baskets for the stables and then two left for the farmhouse and we're done.'

Rick chuckles. 'So, you're living in a stable then, sounds rather biblical to me.'

'I sure am. A living room for my study, a small kitchen, a bedroom, and a cosy little bathroom is all I need right now,' I reply, contentedly.

'While you get things all set up, that is?'

'Yes.' My future plans are my business and I'd rather he didn't know that I'm heading back to the UK very shortly.

He swings open the door to the barn and we walk over to grab two more baskets.

'You're happy here, aren't you, Lainey?' he reflects, turning to look at me. Why does he keep making this personal?

Instead of answering, I raise my arm to look at my wrist. 'We need to step up the pace, or we're going to be late for dinner.'

I cannot, and will not, let Rick into my world. My heart hurts whenever I'm around him. He's chosen his path in life and his future is mapped out. And yet it seems that a part of him can't let go. But if he isn't strong enough to fathom out what he really wants out of life, he isn't the man for me.

* * *

Tomorrow everyone heads for home and so this evening it's party time. A marquee has been erected down in the orchard and the big firepit will be lit. Mum and I are in the farmhouse kitchen loading up some crates with plates, cutlery and glasses, as Dad ferries them down to the party area.

'It's been a great week,' she says with a sense of satisfaction. 'And what a delight that I could arrange for everyone to spend the day checking out Le Crotoy's Semaine du Goût. I wish you'd gone with them, Lainey. Next year I might have a stall at the festival and run the autumn course a week later. I could do samples of some of the recipes I use. It's a celebration of the local produce and it would be nice to contribute. Anyway, your dad and I could have coped, you know. We didn't want to rob you of a little extra time with... our guests.'

I'm on a small stepladder, reaching way back into Mum's storage cupboard, looking for large serving dishes. Turning my head, I peer around the door jamb. 'No, I wanted to help out. One for all, and all for one – remember?'

Mum chuckles. 'I remember. When you were little, you had this thing about swords, and I blame your dad for his obsession with watching *The Three Musketeers*.'

'I loved that film, Mum! Paris, romance, villains and adventure. It had it all.' That makes us both giggle.

'We had some great times, didn't we?' Mum asks whimsically. Her voice is full of nostalgia and I know she's preparing herself for things to go back to normal once Dad and I leave. Curiously, the man who used to help Mum out when she first started running the courses hasn't reappeared, but it's not something I feel I can mention. I can't help but wonder whether she asked him to stay away until Dad leaves. Dad covered for me, but why he then stayed on is a bit of a puzzle. He was at a low point, even I could see that, and I bet Mum wanted to make sure he didn't return home until he was in a better place mentally and physically. He's certainly gained a few pounds and is looking a lot less gaunt and tired. 'Lainey.' Mum stops sorting cutlery to glance across as me, as I snap the steps shut and close the cupboard door. 'You do know that Rick is in love with you, don't you? It's plain to see, lovely, and yet you've been doing your best to avoid him all week.'

Reluctantly, I look in her direction, shrugging my shoulders and then letting them droop. 'We want different things, Mum, so it would never work. Besides, he's engaged to Cathy Clarkson. Their lives are inextricably linked, not least because they're in business together, too.'

She stares off into the distance for a few moments, a deep frown puckering her forehead and I hate the fact that she's worried about me. 'It's not that you don't care for him, then?' she asks pointedly.

'It doesn't matter how I feel, Mum, because it won't change anything. He shouldn't have come here. It was wrong of him and now I think he realises that.'

As I watch Mum, her chin sinks down onto her chest and I feel an overwhelming sense of sadness fill the space between us. 'You're right, lovely. You can't make someone wake up to the reality of what they are doing if they're too caught up to see the bigger picture. It was the same with your dad. It still breaks my heart, thinking about what he went though, even after all this time.'

A tear forms in the corner of my eye and I know she's right. Both Mum and I understand all about the pain of moving on.

2020

February

Rick's parting words when I waved him off from Mum's were cryptic: 'It's not over, Lainey, I promise you.' Then he kissed my cheek, before he jumped into his car and drove off. That was almost four months ago. Four months ago!

What did I do? A week later, I went back to the UK and I moved in with Dario and Ian, much to Ian's delight, as neither of them enjoy cooking. And it's been wonderful being able to repay their kindness in giving me a temporary home. I might not be as good a cook as my mum but having two friends giving me their thumbs-up and thanks, night after night, has been a real boost to my confidence.

I rush to grab my phone off the console table as it lights up and I see that it's Ant. I've been on edge for the last hour awaiting his call.

'Hey, Lainey. Hayley is fine. As the doctor thought, the contractions stopped after a couple of hours, so it's just her body practising for the real event. We're still on target for the eleventh of March. When do you leave?'

'I'm just packing up the last of my things, now. There isn't an inch of space left.'

Ant begins to laugh. 'I can't imagine you driving a people carrier. You are going to miss your beloved Mini.'

'I know, but this is more practical. I can take a few more things with me to France and it will come in useful for when we take the guests out for little day trips. With both cars, we'll be able to fit in twelve people comfortably.'

'That would be day trips for wine-tasting events, I presume?' Ant jokes.

'Maybe,' I muse, 'and local food markets, of course. Anyway, you'll get to experience it for yourself once the baby is here and you're able to travel.'

The line goes silent. This is tough.

'We will make it happen,' Ant says, firmly. 'And your other job is gathering speed?'

'Yes. It was worth coming back to the UK just to have a few face-to-face meetings. Thomas and I have been talking, too. He wants me to write a column in diary format, for his new magazine, *Living the Country Life*. It would be free advertising for Mum's business, so it's a win-win situation.'

'I'm glad Thomas is settled now. I suppose we all are in different ways, although I do miss everyone.'

'I know. But the future is looking exciting and you have the new baby to look forward to. I'm my own boss now and, to be honest, since I returned to the UK, I've really missed Le Crotoy. I think Dad felt the same, too, the moment he arrived home. I will admit that I never thought I'd see a "For Sale" sign outside of our former family home, but Mum is beyond thrilled that we're all going to be living and working together.'

'Well, travel safely and once you're settled let me know how things are going.'

'I will, Ant, and give Hayley and little Ellie a huge hug from me! Keep me up to date with the baby news as everything happens. And wish me luck driving The Bat.'

'The Bat?'

'It's black and I'm hoping it has radar capability in case I misjudge any tight spaces.'

That sends us both into laughter.

'Love it! I bet it feels like a tank to you, but you'll soon get used to it. True to form, you've never backed away from a challenge and I'm happy for you, Lainey.'

I hope Ant is right, as the last few days of February herald in some heavy frosts and there are moments when life feels, and looks, very grey. Everyone is talking about this new virus that doesn't sound like a simple variation of the normal winter flu, and it's such a worry.

* * *

I turn my phone back on and slip it into my handbag. Kicking the engine into life, I wait in the queue to exit the Eurotunnel train. Minutes later I'm on French soil again. In the back, there are a series of muted pings. Once, twice and then a third time.

'Sorry, you'll have to wait until I get to my destination,' I say out loud, as if my phone can hear me. 'The Bat won't drive itself and I don't need any distractions right now.' Then I turn up the volume on the CD Mum sent, letting the gentle sound of a piano, cello and guitar calm me. I have one goal and that is to get The Bat to Le Crotoy without a dent, or a ding, despite the fact that I'm a nervous driver and it's the biggest vehicle I've ever driven. 'New beginning, here I come,' I shout out at the top of my voice, narrowly missing the crucial lane-change as the tunnel exit disappears in my rear-view mirror.

An hour later, hunger makes me pull over when I drive

through a small village and spot a boulangerie. Walking out with a bag of two croissants in my hand, I savour the aroma. I guess that from here on in this will be a daily treat and I wonder if the time will come when I won't groan with ecstasy at the first taste. France is now my home and it feels good. I find myself smiling as I walk back to the car, until my phone rings, interrupting my happy moment.

Dipping into my bag, I yank it out and hold it to my ear. 'Hello?'

'Lainey, it's Rick. I've been texting you, but I'm not sure they've been getting through. How are you?'

I'm already taking the first bite of the pastry, having eased a croissant to the edge of the top of the greaseproof bag with my free hand. 'Good. Sorry, I'm eating and walking at the same time.' He sounds happy and I wonder why he's calling.

'Are you free for dinner tonight?'

I almost choke on a few flaky crumbs. 'I am, actually, but as I'm on the other side of the Channel, it's not doable, I'm afraid.' *Tough luck, Rick. You've had more than enough time to get in touch, but you left it too late.*

'Why are you in France?'

'Because I'm moving here.'

'Just like that? You woke up this morning and decided to take off?'

'Err, no... It involved a fair bit of planning. Le Cuisinier de Campagne is going to be expanding. We'll be running more courses and, with the blessing of the local mayor, expanding the accommodation we can offer. So it's all go.' The excitement must be very evident in my voice.

'So you're just giving up your career in journalism?' His voice is full of disbelief.

'Not exactly. I'll be working freelance in my spare time,

certainly in the short term, anyway. And I'm writing a regular column for *Living the Country Life* magazine. Was that why you were calling?' Is he looking for another favour? I wonder. If he is, I don't quite see how I can be of help.

Arriving back at the car, I slide into the driver's seat to continue munching on what's left of my croissant. Checking in the rear-view mirror, I brush away a few crumbs from my chin as Rick begins talking, stumbling over his words.

'I was, um, hoping... I wanted to meet up with you and... so much has happened, it, um... well, I don't know quite where to start, as I didn't intend to do this over the phone, so you've thrown me. Why didn't you tell me what was going on?'

'Hmm,' I murmur, as I finish chewing and clear my mouth. 'You didn't ask. And, quite frankly, Rick, I don't see what it has to do with you. I think you were the one who told me when we were at the monastery that people's paths cross and then they move on.' I can't even bring myself to say the word Andalucía, because that doesn't feel real to me any more. One thing I do thank Rick for, is making sure we didn't cross the line from friendship to anything else, because it would have haunted me forever.

'Only because there were so many complications and I wouldn't take advantage of our situation, any more than you would. But I thought I made it clear that I felt a strong connection between us.'

My laugh is more like a guffaw. 'Yes, well, chemistry happens, doesn't it? But I'm respectful of other people's relationships. Look, Rick, I have to go as I'm running late now.'

'No, please don't put the phone down on me, Lainey. I've messed up even when I was trying to do the right thing, in the right way. Your dad warned me that I had one chance to get it right.'

'Oh, did he? And why have you been talking to my dad behind my back?'

'No, it wasn't like that, it—'

'Rick, why are you doing this? If you're not happy with your life, then can I kindly suggest that you decide what you really want and do something about it. I just don't think we can be friends, because you are right, there *was* a connection between us. I've already had one disastrous relationship and so although I wish you well, it's Cathy you should be sharing your thoughts and feelings with, not me.'

I press end call, throw the phone onto the seat next to me and turn the key in the ignition as I let out a big sigh. But it's a sigh of relief and letting go of any last, lingering doubts. Mum may have been right when she said Rick loved me, but clearly he loves his business and his success more. If it was true he'd be by my side now, wouldn't he?

* * *

Honking the horn as I ease the car through the gate alongside the farmhouse, I take the sharp right-turn into the main parking area. There's a builder's van next to what I assume is my parents' new, second-hand Renault Scenic.

As I swing open the driver's door to stand and stretch my legs, both Mum and Dad appear, hurrying across to me.

'We were getting worried. You didn't answer your phone and we thought you might have broken down. Still, you're here now!' Mum exclaims, throwing her arms around me and squeezing tightly. I can tell she's ecstatic that we're all together again, and even I didn't see that coming until quite recently.

'Car looks okay,' Dad mumbles, as he walks around

inspecting it. 'It's tightly packed, though. I hope we can find some space for all this stuff.' He looks over at Mum and winks.

'Ignore him, Lainey. He's teasing. You look well. Are you hungry? Thirsty?'

'No. But I'm curious. Whose van is that?'

Dad throws his hands up in the air, staring straight at Mum. 'It was your idea,' he informs her, avoiding my gaze.

'It belongs to the builders. I guess it's time to reveal your surprise,' Mum replies, linking arms with me. 'This way, lovely. Oh, it's so good to have you here. All these rumours about this awful COVID virus, I've been worried sick. Now I can relax.' She presses my arm into her side and while it's not in Mum's nature to voice her worries, I can see that the timing is perfect. If something bad is coming, at least we're all together.

'There's no point stressing over it. I'm sure we'll be fine,' I reassure her. 'I can't wait to see what work you've had done in my absence.'

'Well, I think this is going to be a rather nice surprise,' Mum replies, as we walk through the gate at the side of the farmhouse and follow the path around to the rear. There are two guys in front of the stables, struggling to pick up what looks like a piece sawn from a wooden ceiling beam.

'What on earth is going on?' I exclaim. 'I thought the plan was to get permission to erect two log cabins. Are you extending the stables?'

'That part of the plan has now been rubber-stamped. But this was your mum's special little project. The stables have been turned back into one building again.'

'But isn't the idea to have more units, not less? The individual gîtes were a good size. I was certainly very happy to live in one of them for a few months.'

'This isn't for the guests, Lainey, it's for you. Come and take a look. It won't be ready for another two weeks, as you have to make a few decisions about flooring and tiles, et cetera, but the bare bones are almost complete.'

The first obvious change is that what was previously two separate front doors standing side by side is now a pair of impressive, double-opening oak doors. The grain in the wood is beautiful.

'You're doing a grand job, guys,' Dad offers, as we head inside. We watch as the two builders manoeuvre the solid wooden lintel into the newly created fireplace.

'Oh Mum, an open fireplace. It's amazing! I can't believe the changes in here. You've knocked through into the other sitting room. This space is huge.' I step forward into the middle of the room, where a plasterboard wall used to separate the two units and glance up at the now exposed beams above us. 'I can't even believe it's the same building,' I gasp. 'This is incredible. I'm overwhelmed. Truly overwhelmed.'

'Julien thinks the original conversion was done in the late eighties and it wasn't done very sympathetically in our opinion,' Mum replies, beaming at me. 'Dad and I wanted you to have something special. It wasn't that much work really. Just pulling out sheets of plasterboard and the worst bit was getting those original beams sandblasted once they took the old ceiling down. Messy, wasn't it, Julien?'

'Yes, but it was worth it, no?' he replies, turning to look at me for confirmation as he wipes his free hand on the leg of his paint-splattered overalls.

'You've both done a wonderful job, thank you so much.'

'Is time we talked about the floor. And the bathroom. Will you have time tomorrow to take a trip to look at some options?' Julien asks and I'm sure he can see from the look on my face how excited I am.

'Just let me know when and I'm there.'

'Good,' he grins back at me and gives his mate a thumbs-up. They exchange a few words in French and Dad smiles.

'What?' I ask.

'Paul said, "Thank goodness! It's easier to pull things down, than put them back up again," and we had our fingers crossed you'd approve. Glad it was the right thing to do, Lainey. After all, this is your new home.'

I turn around in a full circle taking it all in. Home. And something inside of me clicks into place. London never was home to me even after the move because I wasn't really that go-getting, career-driven person at all. I was simply going through the motions because I couldn't see any other option. Coming here isn't running away, quite the reverse. I'm running towards the future and the people I love. Life doesn't get any better than this.

MARCH

26

THE PIECES BEGIN TO COME TOGETHER

I've worked non-stop since the first day I arrived and the time has flown by. As tempted as I am to keep popping out to what has now been officially renamed The Old Stables and carries a hand-carved name above the front door, I hardly move from my temporary office set-up in the farmhouse kitchen. With the panic over the COVID-19 situation, every day further updates are released and it's not looking good.

'The website hits are increasing day on day,' I inform Mum and Dad as we sit around the table drinking coffee. 'All the courses on offer are fully booked from the beginning of April until the end of September, the pressure is on to come up with an emergency plan. If people can't travel, then dates will have to be moved back.'

'Well, it's official now. It's just been announced that France is in a mandatory lockdown from noon tomorrow, for fifteen days,' Dad confirms grimly.

I shake my head sadly. 'I don't think it's sinking in with people that we don't really know how long this situation is going to last. What if things get even worse?'

'We need to contact the guests on the first two courses in April and give them a refund on their deposits,' Dad replies. 'All we can do is wait and see what happens next.'

'It is worrying, the thought of having no income at all,' Mum says, voicing what we are all feeling.

'I have a cash buyer for the house and unless he pulls out unexpectedly, that's money in the kitty, Jess.'

'That's your money, Mike. You don't owe me anything,' Mum reminds him. 'What if you change your mind at some point in the future?' The fact that Dad is here demonstrates his commitment, but to heal such a big rift takes time and they aren't quite there yet.

'Have you ever known me to go back on a decision? Or make one rashly, in the first place? No, we're all in this together. After what we've been through there is no way we're going to sit around worrying about paying the general running costs. I have money in the bank doing nothing and a sizeable chunk of equity when I hand over the keys to the house. Maybe we could offer self-catering breaks over the Christmas period to help make up for what we lose at the start of the season.'

'It's an option. Once the new log cabins are in situ, we'll have four family-sized self-contained units to offer. We could trim one of them up to make it look festive and start advertising them on the home page,' I suggest.

'I really want us to have a family Christmas this year, rather than having to cater for guests, but if we go with that idea, it might be nice to include a cooked turkey delivered to the door on Christmas Day. It's nothing for me to use the ovens over in the cooking centre and then guests can then sort out their own trimmings. What do you think?' Mum joins in.

'Brilliant idea. How about a free turkey *and* a Christmas

hamper of goodies from the pantry? People love home-made chutneys and jams,' Dad adds.

I shake my head. 'Stop there or we'll end up talking ourselves into hosting a big Christmas lunch.'

Mum's tempted, I can see that, but this year it should be just us.

'That's agreed then? Show of hands everyone.'

We all raise our arms.

'Great minds think alike,' Dad comments as there's a double tap on the front door.

'That'll be the postman. It might be the new bedding you ordered, Lainey,' Mum says, jumping up eagerly.

I scribble down a few notes and when Mum returns, she holds out a small box to Dad. 'It's for you, Mike.'

'Me? I haven't ordered anything.' Dad takes it from her, giving it a shake.

Mum passes him some scissors and he cuts through the packing tape. It's stuffed full of crumpled tissue paper and after ferreting around Dad withdraws a small box and an envelope.

'This is strange,' he says, staring at the two items as he places them on the table in front of him.

'Well, open them,' Mum encourages.

I'm still making notes, but I look up when Dad says, 'It's from my publishers. It says *congratulations*.'

'For what?'

'I don't know. Perhaps they think it's my birthday,' he says, 'which is embarrassing. Should I tell them they have the wrong date?' He proceeds to lift the lid off the small, rectangular box, pulling out what looks like a smart case for a pair of glasses, but as he flips the lid back his eyes open wide. 'It's a silver pen,' he remarks, his eyebrows knitting together. He passes it to Mum.

'That's nice,' she squints, before handing it back to him. 'It's engraved on the side, but I don't have my reading glasses.'

'Good grief! It says *The Day the World Woke Up*. That book was released last summer.' He scratches his head as he gazes down at it.

I'm online looking him up on Amazon and I spin the laptop around for him to see. 'Well, it's number one in the UK charts right now, Dad.'

His jaw drops and Mum looks stunned. 'Really?' he says, as if he can't believe what he's seeing with his own eyes.

'Do you ever look at the charts?' I ask him and he shakes his head.

Grabbing his phone, he heads out of the kitchen, leaving Mum and I staring at each other, not sure what to do.

'This is big, isn't it?' she whispers across the table to me.

'I think so. I mean, how many people get to number one?'

There's another double tap on the front door and Mum and I exchange a glance. 'Don't say they've sent him something else,' she says, easing herself up out of the chair and hurrying off.

I take a screenshot because I can't help myself. My dad's book is number one and he didn't even know!

'Lainey, you have a visitor,' Mum says sheepishly, stepping aside and ushering Rick into the kitchen. 'I'll just go and see what your dad's up to. I think he's in shock.'

Rick stands there, looking at me awkwardly as I stare up at him in total disbelief.

'I clearly remember telling you the last time you were here that I don't like surprises,' I blurt out. 'Seriously, Rick, France goes into lockdown in less than twenty-four hours, what are you doing here?'

Rick looks dejected. 'Can I at least warm up a little before I begin? And a cup of coffee would be really appreciated, as I only stopped twice on the drive down.'

'Oh Rick, that was rude of me. Sorry, I'm just shocked to see you. I assume you're not here for a holiday, so why don't you take a seat and tell me why you've come all this way. Couldn't you have just picked up the phone?'

As he slumps down onto a chair, I take the seat next to him and he can't even look me in the eye. If he's bringing his problems to me to sort out, then he's wasted a journey. 'I'm just going to let it all out before I lose my nerve. I've been trying to work out what to say on the drive here, but now it's all just a jumble of words. The truth is that I fell in love you when we were in Andalucía, Lainey. It wasn't planned and I wasn't playing games. In fact, I was very honest with you, because what else could I do at the time? Tethered financially, and in a so-called relationship with Cathy, it wasn't possible to simply walk away. It's taken me months to negotiate an exit strategy and jump through every hoop Cathy laid before me. There was a real chance this decision could have ended up bankrupting me if I had made one wrong move. Does that mean anything at all to you?'

I sigh. 'It's only money, Rick. It's what's in your heart that counts and everything else is simply a problem to get around. I would have given up everything I had to be with you without question, if only you'd asked me. But the point is, you didn't.'

He bows his head. 'I call it pride, you'd probably call it vanity, but I've worked hard for the last ten years and to walk away with nothing at all would mean I was a failure. The deal I took isn't great, but at least I'm not penniless and Cathy is no longer threatening to sue me for breach of contract.'

I am surprised that he found the courage to stand up to her at last, but why didn't he tell me how he felt at the time? I want to believe him, but what if this isn't coming from his heart, but his head? He's free at last and that's a scary situation to suddenly find himself in, I should imagine. It's hard to trust someone who has already broken your heart once, because trust has to be earnt. What I've seen so far is a man who doesn't really know what he wants and I'm wondering whether he's one of those people who is afraid of making a commitment.

'I also have a message from my mum. She sends her love and says she knew the truth that day, whatever that means. But I'm all out of things to say, because the words floating around inside my head all sound like a feeble excuse. Cutting the ties wasn't easy and it wasn't quick. A price had to be paid and I was more than willing to pay it, so now I truly am free. The question is, do you want me in your life, or was I just a passing distraction?'

His words hit me like an arrow strike to the heart and, to my horror, I burst into tears. Rick looks broken and desolate, nothing at all like the happy, vibrant man I still picture in my head whenever I inadvertently let my thoughts wander to Andalucía. Maybe he didn't fully understand the depth of my feelings for him. Were we both guilty of holding back for fear of getting hurt? I think of that day when we were sitting in the orchard at the Palacio de Portocarrero. I remember looking at Rick and knowing if circumstances were different, I could give my heart to this man. But he didn't give me any reason at all to hope my feelings could be returned. And now, here he is, speaking up for the first time and the decision is in my hands. It's not easy to fall in love and then find yourself having to lock up your heart, or risk getting it broken for a second time. Am I brave enough to unlock it again and dare to trust that we could make a life together?

'Please don't cry, Lainey,' Rick whispers, his voice hoarse. He throws his arm around my shoulders, trying to comfort me. It's going to be a long night, because it isn't over... yet.

* * *

'Are you sure you want to come and chop wood? You could just settle in and put your feet up for a bit. You've had a long drive,' I point out to Rick, but he's already pulling on his coat.

'You might struggle in those,' Dad says, looking down at Rick's immaculately shiny, brown leather shoes. 'Let's see if we can find you something a bit more practical. I have a couple of pairs of steel toe-capped boots if you're interested.'

I leave the two of them to sort it out and go in search of Mum. She's in the utility room, folding laundry. 'Are you hiding in here, Mum?' I ask, outright.

She reaches over to place a hand on my right shoulder, giving it a comforting squeeze. 'It's hard looking on and seeing two people who... well, there are things you both need to talk through in private, I'm sure. I can tell you didn't see this coming and yet it's obvious that Rick has thought of nothing else, probably since he returned home. And I don't mean from Le Crotoy.'

'But he never came out and said how he felt, not really. Not in any way I could understand.' If he had, I wouldn't have walked away from him.

I can see Mum is troubled. 'I'm old enough to know that it's best not to meddle and I try really hard not to take sides, interfere, or judge people. But I will make one observation, Lainey. You closed your heart when you flew back from Andalucía. Rick, on the other hand, started to open his. You have this one chance now to rethink your decision. Just take your time to make sure it's the right one, for you and for him, that's all I'm saying.'

'Thanks, Mum. I'll sleep on it and hope that when I wake up, I'll have all the answers I need.'

She laughs. 'Oh, if only life was that simple, Lainey. Now, go and chop wood while I make a celebratory dinner. It's not every day we find ourselves sitting around the table with a number one, best-selling author, is it?'

That has me chuckling as I walk off to grab my coat from the hallway. Dad deserves a little fussing over tonight. Mum and I are so proud of him because he never gave up. Even in his darkest hour, he just changed tack and kept on being productive. And that deserves a toast.

* * *

Mum cooks a hearty chicken in red wine casserole, with crispy roast potatoes cooked in goose fat, accompanied by honey-roasted root vegetables. I had to hide a little smirk as she spent ages in the huge cupboard where she stores all the crockery, digging out some rustic hand-made bowls. I know it was supposed to impress Rick. They did look great, but there wasn't much room for anything other than the stew and I noticed Rick kept adding potatoes, one at a time. He might like fine dining and dainty portions, but he too appreciates a hearty meal when he's starving hungry.

As soon as the plates are cleared and Mum reappears, I get her to take a seat.

'It's time for a toast. To Dad, a fighter, a writer and a sharer of truths. May that never change and now you can add the title of best-selling author to your list of credits. Well done, you!'

We all chink glasses and both Mum and Rick say, 'Hear, hear! A great achievement!'

Dad looks embarrassed. 'Thank you. It's a rather nice surprise that I certainly wasn't expecting. And I'd like to raise a glass to my lovely ex-wife – that was a wonderful meal, Jess, and much appreciated,' Dad gazes across at Mum and she begins to colour up as we all take another sip. 'It's a favourite dish of mine from way back,' he explains.

Mum is about to move and begin thinking about dessert, when Rick pipes up.

'Am I allowed to propose a toast too?'

'Of course,' Dad says, amiably. His attitude has changed towards Ross, I notice. I'm not sure if that's because Mum has taken him to one side and had a word, or whether Dad is beginning to feel more comfortable around him. Either way, it's a good omen as he is a good judge of character.

'Here's to the continuing success of Le Cuisinier de Campagne. When I first came here, I had no idea the impression it would leave on me and I'm sure many of the other guests on the course felt the same way that I did. I can see exactly why Lainey is back here to stay. Here's to you all and to a bright and happy future the other side of the lockdown!'

We all say cheers and then there are a few moments of silence before Dad busies himself topping up glasses, and Mum and I head off to the kitchen. I organise the dessert bowls, while Mum lifts the warm pie dish onto a wooden board. It looks and smells heavenly.

'Can I ask you a personal question, Mum?'

'You may.'

'What attracted you to Dad, in the first place?'

She stops for a moment, staring off into the distance. 'Well, he wasn't like the other young men of his age. They all had slick chat-up lines in those days. Your dad didn't have that approach and he was oh so very nervous, but natural. And he never, ever told me a lie. Even if it didn't do him any favours. We were on maybe our third date, and I was wearing some new earrings that were very fashionable at the time. I asked him if he liked them and he said he wasn't a fan. Imagine that.' She chuckles. 'Honest.

Real. And he didn't change, even when things got really difficult between us. That means everything to me because I know I can trust him, always.'

'It wasn't love at first sight, then?'

'Of course it was. I knew before we shared our first kiss that he was going to be mine. And even when things went wrong, I had faith that he'd eventually come back to me, but it had to be on his own terms and when he was ready. That's life, lovely.'

A single tear tracks down my cheek and Mum comes over to give me a hug.

'So that's why you didn't fight him over the divorce? I thought you'd hardened your heart to him, Mum.'

'A piece of paper doesn't make a marriage, Lainey. It's wanting to be together that matters. And a piece of paper can't end one either. The divorce didn't change how I feel about the man I love.'

'That's good to hear,' I croak, my voice breaking up. And the fact that Dad wants to be here now, tells me everything I need to know. Life has gone full-circle, and this was meant to be.

'We always know deep down inside, don't we,' she whispers.

I find myself nodding my head in agreement.

27

AS DARKNESS DESCENDS A NEW DAWN IS COMING

After giving Rick a tour of The Old Stables, we decide to build a fire out the back and sit chatting for a while.

'So, this is your new life now, Lainey. You couldn't have chosen a better setting. It's beautiful even on a cold night, surrounded by the shadows,' Rick remarks. Placing another log in the brazier, it quells some of the flames that were shooting up like red-hot arrows.

'Yes, it's perfect, isn't it? I like the peace and quiet.'

'You seem content and you must be so delighted with the work that's been done to restore some of the original character.'

'I am and it's almost ready for me to move in, but I haven't had time to think about furnishing it yet. It still hasn't really sunk in that this is going to be *my* home. What was there originally was fine for a rental, but not what I'd choose and so it's all in storage ready to reuse once the log cabins are erected.'

'Look, we both know why we're sitting out here, alone together. I'm well aware that I've only skated over the details of the mess I've left behind. There are loose ends still to tie up, but all of that is irrelevant, isn't it? The thing is, Lainey, you do love me, don't you? It's not just one-sided and I'm grasping at straws?' Rick immediately laughs, almost to himself and puts up his hand to stop me from responding. 'I think I already know the answer to that question. If I didn't believe you could love me, I wouldn't be here now, would I?'

I stare at him and the beaming smile on his face that he simply can't hide melts my heart.

'The point is,' he continues, 'can you forgive me for not sorting it out sooner? And how do you feel about me now, I mean, this minute, as we're sitting here? When I leave, it could be the last time we see each other, and I'll be honest, that thought terrifies me. I can't help thinking that without you by my side I'm lost.'

Tears begin to fill my eyes and it takes a moment to compose myself. 'What I discovered when I found myself falling in love with you,' I half-whisper, 'is that it's scary. And I realised that for the first time I knew what true love meant. Spending time with you in Andalucía was magical, Rick, and flying home, my heart was aching for something that wasn't meant to be. If it had been, then I felt you would have opened up to me and we'd have made a plan. But you didn't.'

Rick turns to look me in the eyes, a pained expression on his face. 'But neither did you, Lainey. That night we spent together in your bedroom you told me it was a lovely evening, but that was all it was. Those were your very words.'

'I know,' I admit, as sadness washes over me. 'It's called self-preservation. How could I compete with someone like Cathy Clarkson? Together you two were a tour de force. I had to be realistic, recognising that little bubble of unbelievable happiness I was feeling being around you would burst once I returned to my normal life. Why would you choose me?'

Rick reaches out to grab my hand, cupping it in his and rubbing my fingertips, which are now turning white with cold. I swipe away my tears with my free hand. 'Oh, Lainey. What fools we've been, you and me. Please don't cry. I'm here now and I'm not going anywhere unless you throw me out.'

That makes me chuckle. 'Really? Who knows how long you could be stuck here though? There will be no escape once France goes into lockdown at noon tomorrow.'

'I jumped in the car because I was desperate to see you and... finally tell you how I feel. Anyway, where else would I want to be other than with you, if life is about to change? If you're willing to have me, that is.'

Rick slides along the bench, throwing his arm around my shoulder as he draws me closer to him. The flames begin to lap up around the new log, the gentle hiss as the wood dries and the crackle as it begins to burn more fiercely is as comforting as the heat which begins to radiate out.

'I'm scared of what we're facing, Rick, but do you know something? Everything that has happened has made me realise how important it is to hold onto what really matters in life, and that turns out to be the people you love. It feels like a bit of a miracle to me that you're here. That night we spent together felt so special and my gut instincts were screaming at me that we both felt the same way about each other. But I couldn't allow myself to believe that as it all seemed like an impossible dream that could never come true.'

Rick's arm pulls me even closer. 'And I said right place, wrong time,' he murmurs. 'What else could I say at that moment? *Trust me and I'll figure out a way to sort out my life?* I don't do empty promises and I wasn't even sure whether I could sort it out.'

'I was gutted, wanting something I thought I couldn't have. And now this feels like the right place and the right time, even amongst the chaos and uncertainty. That can't be a coincidence, can it? I chose you and now you've chosen me. I love you, Rick, and I can say that with all my heart.'

'That's all I needed to hear you say, Lainey,' Rick replies, as he leans in to place a gentle kiss on my lips.

We sit for a while, holding hands and staring into the flames of the fire, letting it sink in that nothing will ever be the same again. Now that we are finally together, the future is ours to make.

* * *

'Morning, guys, how did you sleep?' I ask, as I walk into the kitchen.

'It took me a while to go off,' Mum replies and she does look tired. 'Breakfast is almost ready.'

'Same here. My brain just wouldn't switch off,' Dad says, frowning.

Moments later, Rick appears, looking a little hesitant, but then he strides over to me, planting a kiss firmly on my cheek. The look we exchange makes the blood rush to my head and my heart begins to hammer in my chest.

'Is there anything I can do to help, Jess?' he enquires, looking across at Mum.

'It's good of you to offer, Rick, but I'm just about to plate up. I thought we could all do with a hearty English breakfast this morning.' She gives him a brief smile and indicates for him to join Dad and me at the table.

Rick takes the seat next to me, placing his hand over mine. He coughs, clearing his throat and I can see he's not sure quite what to say to kick things off. He turns to look directly at me, expectantly, and I know what I'm going to say. Rick and I talked into the early hours, heading into the sitting room when it became too cold to sit outside enjoying the starry sky overhead. And suddenly everything fell into place.

'If Rick leaves today, we don't know when he'll be able to come back,' I spell out.

Dad looks at Mum as she begins to carry the plates across to the table and Rick immediately jumps up to help.

'This is a great-looking breakfast, Jess, thank you,' Rick says as he takes the plates from her.

As Rick places them on the table, Dad gives an appreciative nod in Mum's direction, but he makes no attempt to begin eating. 'You and Rick talked for a long time, last night. Is there an actual plan?' he enquires, always one to get straight to the point.

I glance at Mum as she takes a seat and then back at Dad.

'It's rather up to the two of you,' I acknowledge.

'We're happy with whatever works for you both, Lainey,' Mum jumps in. 'The main thing is that you two seem to be on the same page now, am I right?'

I turn to look at Rick. 'You're right, Jess. The problem is that if I don't head back soon, then you could all be stuck with me for a while. And who knows what's going to happen, or how long this situation is going to last.'

He's nervous and my parents can obviously see that.

'The thought of being apart now is unbearable, for us both,' I add.

Mum claps her hands to her mouth and Dad sits there with a smug look on his face.

'The thing is, Rick doesn't have to head back,' I explain.

'Of course. The restaurant will be shut, anyway,' Mum replies, shaking her head sadly.

I stare at Rick encouragingly. 'I'm no longer head chef at Aleatory,' he declares and both Mum and Dad look shocked. 'Officially, I'm a silent partner until such time as I'm bought out.

There was an interested party, but with all the rumours over the last couple of days about everything being shut down, he withdrew his offer yesterday. Sadly, I can't see anyone else coming forward until life returns to normal. As things stand, I'm jobless, and homeless, as my lease is about to run out and I can't afford to renew it. I'm not quite penniless, but it feels like it's back to square one for me, I'm afraid.'

'Oh, Rick, that's tough. We are so sorry. None of us really saw this coming, did we?' I notice that Dad reaches out to hold Mum's hand. 'You are very welcome to stay here, Rick, for as long as you want,' Mum adds.

'That's very generous of you, but I need to hand over to Lainey as she has something to say before we go any further.' Rick gives me an encouraging nod.

'Moving to France, was the best decision I ever made,' I begin, 'but now Rick and I realise our future is together. It changes it all at a time when everything around us is changing, too.'

Mum's grip tightens on Dad's hand, her knuckles are white. 'You two must, of course, do whatever is right for you both as a couple.' Mum's voice wavers and I can see she's on edge.

'Oh, I don't intend going anywhere, but if Rick stays, then we really are all in this together. I'm not sure how that works for you, though.'

'Well, your dad and I have decided that we're going to use the time productively. There are lots of jobs that need doing and now we have the chance to tackle them.'

'There are other options to consider, too.' I can see they are intrigued as I hand over to Rick.

'If people can't come here, what about setting up a video channel?' Rick throws the idea out there, quite casually.

'Video?' Dad asks, puckering up his brow in the most unflattering manner.

'We start recording a whole catalogue of *cook while you watch*, real-time videos. Dad and I can work as a team on the filming side,' I explain, 'and Mum and Rick, you'll do the demonstrations. It will be an add-on to the website.'

Dad goes very quiet while stroking his chin and Mum looks aghast.

'Me, on video?' she queries.

'Yes, why not? You stand in front of people talking them through the recipes as you show them how to do it. Most things only take about half an hour. We'll put out a few to start building subscribers and do some paid advertising. Then put out mini clips of upcoming videos and invite people to subscribe and pay a small monthly fee to access the videos for free. We build an audience and when this crisis we're about to go through is over, I'm sure the people watching will want to come and experience it all first-hand. What do you think?'

The silence is deafening. I visualise the second hand on a clock filling my ears as each tick booms out ominously.

'Welcome to Le Cuisinier de Campagne, Rick. And to the family,' Mum says, making eye contact with Dad.

We all jump up for a group hug. What is touching is that this all feels so right and so natural. Facing the unknown is a worry, but pulling together we are going to try our level best to build something meaningful.

'Think of all those people, stuck at home and desperate for inspiring ideas. Let's get families invested in cooking together,' I add, as we all pull back.

'And we could encourage people to start thinking about growing things indoors ready to plant out. I'm sure kids will love getting involved in that. What do you think?' Mum enthuses, her eyes sparkling.

'That's a brilliant idea, Jess,' Rick replies and the look Mum gives him tells me everything I need to know. She knew as soon as she clapped eyes on him that day he arrived for the course that Rick was genuine. There is no way she would have let him stay if she felt her daughter wasn't going to be in safe hands. What she didn't know for sure was how I felt.

'It seems we have a new business plan in the making, then,' Dad smiles.

Rick slides his arm around my waist, half-turning to look at Mum and Dad. 'That suits me fine and I'm very grateful to you both. Everything I want is here and I couldn't be happier than I'm feeling right now.'

* * *

'Was your mum okay when you explained why you didn't make it back in time?' I ask Rick as I roll into him.

'She was relieved, actually, and she sends her love. Well, what she said was, "Give Lainey my love and my thanks," but that sounds a little like she's glad to get rid of me, doesn't it?'

I lay my hand on Rick's chest, feeling the reassuring beat of his heart. He's real. This is real. And it feels strange because I know that right now so many people are feeling scared, panicky, and fearful of what's to come. And here we are, wrapped in each other's arms in the darkness, feeling blessed. 'No. Mums worry about their offspring no matter how old they are. It isn't until they know you are truly happy with your life that they can relax and you only have to look at my parents to see the change in them.'

'Are you sad that your fresh start here, in The Old Stables, has turned out to be a compromise?' he asks.

'What do you mean? Moving in this odd collection of furniture, or moving in with a strange man and trying to make it feel like our new home?' I scoff.

Rick's hand moves against my cheek, softly brushing away a strand of hair. 'I might be strange, but we're no strangers. And we can do something with what's here. I know it's probably not what you'd pictured, but upcycling is fun. We can do it together. There are enough tins of paint in the barn to cover every available surface and some. And I'm good with a drill, so tomorrow I can start putting up the curtains. Whatever you need doing, I'm at your disposal.'

I laugh. 'Well, it's not like you're going anywhere soon, is it? But it's going to take a lot of work and a big learning curve making the first few videos, getting them up online and growing a little community.'

Rick gives out a satisfied sigh. 'It's going to be fun, though, isn't it? We're so lucky. Heck, I'm just grateful you didn't send me away. If only I had pressed harder, moved things forward with more urgency, then I wouldn't be in a position where I could potentially lose everything. Imagine how much pressure that would have taken off the next few weeks and months if I'd already sold up.'

He sounds regretful, as if he has failed me.

'Don't you see that it's made it easier, not harder? We're starting over together. This is our chance to build the life we want. My parents, ironically, are doing the exact same thing. We each have a different skillset, but we're also people who will give anything a shot. And that's why this is going to work. We might not have had this chance if things had happened any differently. I don't think any other start would have worked for us as a couple, Rick.'

He raises himself up on one elbow, to lean over me and, seconds later, his lips are on mine. Softly at first, and then more insistent, until he suddenly pulls back a little. 'When life does get back to normal, whenever that is, I promise you one thing. We'll go shopping for an engagement ring and I will get down on one knee and ask the question in time-honoured fashion. But, for now, let's focus on making this place our sanctuary. At the end of each day, no matter what happens, this is where we'll end up. And for better or for worse, for richer, for poorer, in sickness and in health, I promise you that you will never, ever be alone.'

For one moment my heart skips a beat as if it's about to stop, but I know that it's simply signalling a new beginning. When you find your soulmate, every fibre of your body, every single cell, recognises that and I realise that what we're about to go through together will make us stronger. I feel blessed and if I had not trodden the path that brought me here, I would not have discovered the true magic that happened in Andalucía. It's the place where Rick and I fell in love and when two people are meant to be together, nothing can keep them apart.

ACKNOWLEDGMENTS

A heart-felt *thank you* to Sarah Ritherdon, my awesome editor and publishing director, for her patience, ideas and amazing support. Sarah's wealth of experience shines through in the final manuscript. And not forgetting the wonderful line editors and diligent proofreaders who polish the story in a way only they can.

My wonderful agent, Sara Keane, is also very instrumental in the process and only a phone call away whenever I need advice. My career has blossomed under your guidance, Sara, and no words can quite express how blessed I feel.

And to the wider Boldwood team – a truly awesome group of inspiring women I can't thank enough for their amazing support and encouragement. The sheer enthusiasm of everyone involved is wonderful.

I'd also like to thank my family and friends who understand my erratic lifestyle as a compulsive writer. The person I am now is rather different to the person I was before I gave up the day job to write novels. It is hard to switch off when a story simply wants to be written and the characters fill one's head with constant chatter. I tend to disappear for long periods, coming up for a breather in between to catch up on what's been going on around me. Fortunately, my husband Lawrence is always there to help with fact-checking and research, and for that I'm enormously grateful.

As usual, no book is ever launched without there being an even longer list of people to thank for publicising it. The amazing kindness of my lovely author friends, readers and reviewers is truly humbling. You continue to delight, amaze and astound me with your generosity and support.

Without your kindness in spreading the word about my latest release and your wonderful reviews to entice people to click and download, I wouldn't be able to indulge myself in my guilty pleasure – writing.

Feeling blessed and sending much love to you all for your treasured support and friendship.

Lucy xx

MORE FROM LUCY COLEMAN

We hope you enjoyed reading *Summer In Andalucía*. If you did, please leave a review.

If you'd like to gift a copy, this book is also available as an ebook, digital audio download and audiobook CD.

Sign up to Lucy Coleman's mailing list for news, competitions and updates on future books:

http://bit.ly/LucyColemanNewsletter

Explore more glorious escapist reads from Lucy Coleman.

ABOUT THE AUTHOR

Lucy Coleman is a #1 bestselling romance writer, whose recent novels include *Summer in Provence* and *A Springtime to Remember*. She also writes under the name Linn B. Halton. She won the 2013 UK Festival of Romance: Innovation in Romantic Fiction award and lives in the Welsh Valleys.

Visit Lucy's website: www.lucycolemanromance.com

Follow Lucy on social media:

facebook.com/LucyColemanAuthor

twitter.com/LucyColemanAuth

instagram.com/lucycolemanauthor

bookbub.com/authors/lucy-coleman

ABOUT BOLDWOOD BOOKS

Boldwood Books is a fiction publishing company seeking out the best stories from around the world.

Find out more at www.boldwoodbooks.com

Sign up to the Book and Tonic newsletter for news, offers and competitions from Boldwood Books!

http://www.bit.ly/bookandtonic

We'd love to hear from you, follow us on social media:

facebook.com/BookandTonic
twitter.com/BoldwoodBooks
instagram.com/BookandTonic

Printed in Great Britain
by Amazon

64558931R00200